SECOND CHANCE BRIDES

VICKIE McDONOUGH

BARBOUR
PUBLISHING

OTHER BOOKS BY VICKIE MCDONOUGH:

TEXAS BOARDINGHOUSE BRIDES
The Anonymous Bride

© 2010 by Vickie McDonough

ISBN 978-1-60260-648-7

All scripture quotations are taken from the King James Version of the Bible.

For more information about Vickie McDonough, please access the author's Web site at the following Internet address: www.vickiemcdonough.com

Cover design: Faceout Studio, www.faceoutstudio.com
Cover photo: Pixelworks Studios, www.shootpw.com

Published by Barbour Publishing, Inc., P.O. Box 719, Uhrichsville, OH 44683, www.barbourbooks.com.

Our mission is to publish and distribute inspirational products offering exceptional value and biblical encouragement to the masses.

 Member of the
Evangelical Christian
Publishers Association

Printed in the United States of America.

Dedication/Acknowledgments

This book is dedicated to my good friend, Margaret Daley, award-winning author of over 70 books. The first time I met Margaret was at a local RWA chapter meeting. I'd read a number of her books—and loved them—but had no idea she lived in the same town as me. I literally stood there awestruck, shaking and thinking, "Oh my goodness! Margaret Daley lives in Tulsa?!"

I never could have dreamed back then that we'd become such good friends and travel across the U.S. together, promoting our books, attending writers conferences, and serving together as ACFW officers. Thanks so much, Margaret, for the encouragement you've been to me and for your patience when I vented and didn't believe in myself. We've laughed together and cried together and shared our joys and frustrations over many a meal and mile. I couldn't ask for a better friend, and I thank God for bringing you into my life.

CHAPTER 1

Any moment, the wedding would commence and signal an end to her dreams. Shannon O'Neil cast a longing glance back toward the safety of the boardinghouse. Whoever heard of a mail-order bride attending the wedding of the man she was to marry—especially when he was marrying someone else? "We should not be here." Her voice trembled almost as much as her legs.

Her gaze flitted over the huge crowd gathered in the open field next door to the church. Only because her friend Rachel had requested her presence had she agreed to come. "People are staring at us."

Leah Bennett sidled up beside her, mouth twisted to one side. "They've gawked at us ever since we came to town. Besides, we've got just as much right to be at this wedding as anyone else. Even more if you ask me. All things considered."

Shannon shored up her apprehension and forced her steps forward. She squeezed through the group of men clustered around an array of makeshift benches and hurried toward one of the few remaining spots on the back bench.

Several men gaped at them and whispered among themselves.

5

That was nothing new, since she and Leah were mail-order brides without a groom. She'd been in Lookout more than a month but still hadn't gotten used to being the focus of attention. Shannon dropped her gaze to the ground, but that did nothing to silence the loud murmurs. Leah sat next on her left, her nose pointed in the air, not in the snooty way it sometimes was, but in a way that dared anybody to challenge her right to attend the wedding.

"I can't believe they had the nerve to show up," a man to their right slurred, his tone dripping sour like unsweetened lemonade.

"They'll ruin everything," another said.

"Of all the nerve. This is Luke and Rachel's special day, not theirs."

Crushing the handkerchief in her hand, Shannon willed her trembling to cease. But her efforts were futile. She leaned toward Leah. "Perhaps 'twould be better if we left."

"We're staying put. Rachel wants us here, and that's what matters. If those folks don't like it, *they* can leave." The sternness in Leah's voice made Shannon feel like a scolded child. If only she had Leah's boldness, perhaps her future wouldn't look so bleak.

Shannon peered up at the ash gray clouds—clouds that mirrored her future. Clouds that swirled in waves, taunting and threatening like a schoolyard bully.

Never had she seen clouds such as these, not in all of Ireland nor during the seven months she'd lived in America.

The oppressive heat sent streams of sweat trickling down her temples, back, and chest. A canvas canopy erected to protect the bride and groom in the event of rain lifted on the breeze and deflated as if it were a living, breathing being.

Let it rain. At least if showers fell, no one would notice her tears.

Men stood in a rough half-circle around the benches their womenfolk and children filled—benches they had constructed over the past few days. The pounding of their hammers had resembled a death knell to Shannon, with each whack bringing her closer to the end of another dream.

She looked around at the growing crowd. Nearly the whole town had turned out to see Lookout's marshal, Luke Davis, marry Rachel Hamilton, the owner of the boardinghouse—the very same boardinghouse where Shannon resided. The very same marshal she had expected to marry. Shannon's chin wobbled.

"Don't you dare cry, you hear me?"

Shannon blinked her moist eyes, stiffened her chin, and glanced at Leah. She, too, had come to town, expecting to marry the marshal, although she seemed less distraught than Shannon felt over losing him. She clenched her hands. What was she going to do now? Would she never have a home of her own?

Leah leaned closer, her lips puckered as if she'd eaten a persimmon. "If I can make it through this wedding without weeping, so can you. We're Texans now, and you're gonna have to find a backbone if you plan to survive here."

Leah was right. Crimping the handkerchief tighter, Shannon turned to face the front where the parson had taken his place. A fiddler off to the right zipped his bow across the strings, playing a lively tune she'd never heard before. The trees shimmied and swayed, dancing in the brisk breeze, cooling Shannon's damp neck.

Leah might be in the same boat as she, but the pretty blond had a family to return to—she just chose not to do so. Shannon would give anything to have her parents back, but no sooner had they stepped onto the shores of America than they'd come down with influenza and died. With her three siblings already dead and buried back in Ireland, she was completely alone in a foreign country.

Why hadn't God healed her parents when she'd begged Him to? Her throat stung as if she'd run a race in winter's chill. But the only thing cold in Texas was her future.

Sympathetic glances swept her way, along with the others. How was it possible to be so alone in such a large crowd?

Leah leaned toward her. "Here he comes."

The murmurs silenced as Luke Davis strode past the front row of townsfolk and took his place next to the parson. His two conniving, hooligan cousins, Garrett and Mark Corbett, followed, along with the old yellow dog that rarely let Luke out of his sight. The dog sniffed Luke's shoes, sending chuckles rippling through the crowd. Jacqueline, Rachel's ten-year-old daughter from her first marriage, sat on the front row. She smacked her lips, and Max lumbered over to her and laid down at her feet. Jack, as the mischievous child preferred to be called, would benefit from having a kind man like the marshal for a father.

A sigh of longing slipped from Shannon's mouth as she pulled her gaze back to Luke. He looked so handsome in his new suit and hat. He was a comely man, in a rugged way. But her marriage to him had been doomed before she ever set foot in Lookout. Just imagine—three women coming to town to marry him when his heart already belonged to a woman who'd stolen it more than a decade before. Now, two of the marshal's mail-order brides were stuck in Lookout while the third was locked up in a jail in Dallas for bank robbery. Shannon shook her head and clutched her handkerchief to her chest. What a kettle of nettles.

And now that the marshal was marrying, she was stranded in one of the smallest towns she'd ever been in outside of Ireland. But this wasn't the first time, and if she had managed before, she could do it again. She dabbed at her eyes and stiffened her back. The music grew louder, and heads turned toward the rear of the crowd. Shannon stood along with the others, but her gaze didn't search out the bride. How could one feel happiness and sorrow at the same time?

Rachel passed Shannon's row and walked toward her groom, looking beautiful in the cream-colored dress her aunt had brought from Kansas City. The bride held her Bible in front of her, and on top lay a bouquet of daisies tied together with flowing rose and lavender ribbons that fluttered on the gusty breeze. Shannon sighed at the joyful smile on Rachel's face.

If Shannon ever doubted the marshal's love for his bride, she did so no more. His face all but glowed, as if he'd battled a hard-fought race, come out the victor, and won a coveted prize. Would a man ever look at her with such love in his eyes?

"I now pronounce you man and wife." A cheer rang throughout the crowd, and Shannon jumped. She blinked, realizing she'd been lost in thought and had missed the whole wedding.

"Well, that's the end of that." Leah stood and looked around. "There are plenty more unmarried men we can set our bonnets for."

Leah might be snippy and bossy at times, but Shannon admired her determination. They'd once been competitors, but being the losers of the bride contest had put them in the same wagon, and they were becoming friends.

Shannon studied the townsfolk swarming the newly married couple, offering their congratulations. Men outnumbered women ten to one. "Aye, there's truth in what you say. There surely are many men in Texas."

"I suppose we should make our way over to the refreshment table and help serve. I know Rachel was hesitant to ask for our help, given the situation and all, but it seems the least we can do."

Shannon nodded and followed Leah over to the west side of the church, where a makeshift table had been erected with sawhorses and wooden planks. A lacy white tablecloth hid the ugliness and boasted the biggest cake Shannon had ever seen. "Miss Dykstra surely outdid herself makin' that lovely cake."

Leah nodded. "Don't know as I've seen one so big before. Why, it must measure three feet across."

"Aye, and 'tis so colorful." Lavender and yellow flowers dotted a green ivy vine that encircled the cake. Large letters saying, *Congratulations to Luke and Rachel*, along with the date, filled the center of the cake, which she hoped would serve the whole crowd. A haphazard collection of plates in various colors and designs were stacked on one end, as well as a collection of mismatched forks. It looked as if every family in town had donated their plates and forks to be used for the wedding.

A trio of ladies Shannon recognized from the church stood behind the table, awaiting the guests. All three cast apologetic glances at her and Leah. Shannon doubted a soul in attendance didn't know her odd circumstances. She glanced down at the ground and felt a warm heat on her cheeks. She despised being the center of attention and hoped that with the marshal now married, chatter about the boardinghouse brides—as she and Leah had been dubbed—would die down.

"You ladies need any help?" Leah offered.

Sylvia Taylor, the pastor's wife, smiled. "We just might at that. There's quite a crowd here today, and we need to hurry before the storm lets loose."

"Yes, that's true. I suppose everyone wanted to see for themselves that the marshal was truly marrying Rachel Hamilton and not one of you two," Margie Mann said.

Mrs. Taylor's brow dipped, while Agatha Linus's brow dashed upward.

"Now, Margie, I don't think that's a proper topic of conversation today. These young ladies are well aware of the importance of this event." Sylvia, always the peacemaker, Shannon had learned, tried to calm the turbulent waters Mrs. Mann had stirred up.

"Well"—Leah looked around the crowd—"I don't think we'll have much trouble finding another man to marry."

"It's true that there are many unmarried men in these parts," Mrs. Taylor said, "but don't jump into anything. Marriage is a lifetime commitment, and you want to be sure you marry the man God has set aside for you. You're both still young and have plenty of time to find a good man to marry."

Shannon pursed her lips. Plenty of time, aye, but an empty purse and no way to survive had driven many a woman into the arms of a less-than-acceptable man. That was why she had agreed to marry the marshal before meeting him. A man who enforced the law must be honorable and upright. Only she found out later that it wasn't Luke Davis who'd penned the letters asking her to come to Lookout to marry him but rather one of the Corbett brothers pretending to be Luke. Her gaze sought them out and found them plowing their way through the crowd, making a path so the bride and groom could get to the cake table.

The Corbett men were quite handsome, similar but different. They both had those sky blue eyes that made a woman's heart stumble just looking into them. Blond hair topped each brother's head, but Mark's was curly while Garrett's was straight. Mark's face was more finely etched than Garrett's squarer jaw. But they were pranksters, full of blarney, the both of them. Jokers who'd turned her life upside down. She clutched her hands together at the memory of that humiliating bride contest. Four women competing for one man's hand. Who'd ever heard of such shenanigans?

Mrs. Mann cleared her throat, pulling Shannon's gaze back. "I don't mean to be rude, but it's probably best that you not help serve." She glanced at the bride and groom, halfway to the table, with Rachel's daughter holding on to the groom's right arm and grinning wide. "It might be distressing to the Davis family, what with all that's happened."

Leah scowled but nodded and turned away. Shannon realized what the woman meant. What bride wanted the women who'd competed for her husband's affection to help with her wedding? She slunk away and found a vacant spot under a tall oak tree, whose branches swung back and forth in the stiff breeze. Holding her skirts down, she searched for Leah and found her talking to a stranger.

A man cleared his throat beside Shannon, pulling her gaze away from Leah. A heavy beard covered the short man's smallish face, and dark beady eyes glimmered at her. "I was wonderin'." He scratched his chin and looked away for a moment. Shannon couldn't remember seeing him before. He captured her gaze again. "I ain't got a lot, but I do have a small farm west of town and a soddy. Since you ain't marryin' up with the marshal, I was hopin' we could get hitched."

Shannon sucked in a gasp. Was the man full of blarney? Why, he had to be twice her age. His worn overalls had ragged patches covering every inch of his pants' legs. He scratched under his arm and rubbed his beard again. She hated hurting people's feelings, but she could not marry this man, no matter how much she longed for a home. "Um. . .thank you for your generous offer, sir, but I don't plan to stay in Lookout. I'll be leaving by the end of the week."

His mouth twisted to one side. "I didn't figger you'd wanna marry up with me, but I had to ask. Guess I'll try that blond, though she's a might uppity for my taste."

With a mixture of relief for herself and pity for Leah, Shannon watched him approach her friend. Leah's eyes went wide, and then she shook her head. The poor farmer shuffled away and disappeared into the crowd.

As the last of the people wandered toward the refreshment table, a mixture of glances were tossed her way. She felt odd being at the marshal's wedding, and yet she'd wanted to support Rachel, who'd been so kind to allow the brides to stay at her boardinghouse. How difficult that must have been for Rachel when she was still in love with Luke.

Pushing her way through the people, Shannon drifted to the edge of the churchyard. She'd done what she felt was needed, and all she wanted to do now was to get away from the gawking townsfolk. She walked toward the street, feeling relieved to have made her getaway.

Mark shoveled cake into his mouth and watched Shannon O'Neil wander through the crowd, looking lost and alone. His gut tightened. With her auburn hair and pine green eyes, she reminded him too much of another pretty woman—of a time he'd just as soon forget. But he couldn't forget Annabelle any more than he could ignore his brother.

He tore his gaze away and handed his dirty plate and fork to the preacher's wife, knowing it would be quickly washed, dried, and returned to the cake table for someone else to use.

"Some wedding, huh? And pert near the best cake I've ever eaten," Garrett said. "Think maybe I'll get Polly to bake one up for your birthday."

Mark shot a glance sideways at his brother. "Just so you don't go orderin' me a bride like you did Luke."

Garrett grinned wide. "You ordered one, too, if I remember correctly."

Mark's lips twisted up on one side, and he ignored Garrett's comment. "It's good to see Luke and Rachel finally wed."

"I wondered if he'd ever get around to marrying. You suppose our ordering those brides had anything to do with it?"

Mark shrugged, wishing he'd never allowed himself to get caught up in his brother's scheme to marry off their cousin. If he hadn't, he never would have written to Miss O'Neil on his cousin's behalf, and she wouldn't be stranded in Lookout right now, stirring up rotten memories. "I reckon the Lord wanted Luke and Rachel together. Our messing with things just made them worse. Kind of like when Sarah in the Bible gave Abraham her maidservant."

"Oh, I don't know about that." Garrett rubbed his chin with his forefinger and thumb. "We've got two more pretty women of marrying age in Lookout than we had before. That can't be a bad thing."

Mark shook his head. From the tone of his voice, Garrett was scheming again, and this time Mark wanted nothing to do with it. They'd be out plenty of money before Miss O'Neil and Miss Bennett found a way to support themselves or got husbands, since the marshal had ordered him and Garrett to pay the ladies' room and board. Never again would he let his brother sway him into one of his schemes. Pranks were meant to be fun, but people

13

kept getting upset at them.

The fiddler tuned up again. Men separated from their groups, seeking out their wives. Mark's gaze sought out Miss O'Neil again, and he found her standing at the edge of the crowd. She put him in mind of a frightened bird that desperately wanted to join the flock but was afraid of being pecked by the bigger birds. She looked as if she might flit away without a soul noticing.

But he noticed—and the fact irritated him.

"You gonna ask her to dance?"

"What?" Mark frowned at his brother. Had Garrett seen him watching the Irish girl and misinterpreted his stare?

Downing the last of his punch, Garrett seemed to be studying Miss O'Neil himself. "She's a fetching thing and free to marry now. Reckon we'll have to find her and that blond a husband soon, or we could be paying their room and board for a long while."

"Guess you should have thought of that before dreaming up that confounded plan to find Luke a bride. You'll remember that I warned you this could come back to bite you."

Garrett grinned. "Yeah, and I also remember you writing to one pretty Irish gal, pretending to be the marshal. If you were so opposed to my idea, why did you join in?"

Mark kicked a rock that skittered across the dirt. "Guess I just got caught up in your excitement. I wanted to see Luke settled and happy, too. He'd been through so much."

"Well, if you're not going to ask a certain redhead to dance, I reckon I will." Garrett set his punch glass on the church sign.

Mark grabbed for his brother's arm as he strode off, but he clutched air instead. Why couldn't Garrett let things be? He always had to meddle. But he had no way of knowing how Miss O'Neil set off all kinds of warning clangs in Mark's mind. He was wrong to compare the two women, but Shannon reminded him so much of Annabelle.

He clamped down his jaw. He wouldn't let another woman close like he had Annabelle. Not that Miss O'Neil was any threat.

He just had to stay away from her. Not let his guard down around her. He'd fallen for a woman once, and it had been the worst mistake he'd ever made. If anyone found out, his reputation would be ruined.

The Irish girl shook her head at Garrett, and Mark smirked. So she was immune to his brother's charms. Good for her. A stiff breeze nearly stole his hat away, but he grabbed hold and pressed it down tighter. His gaze lifted to the sky. Shivers of alarm skittered down his spine. He didn't like the looks of those yellow-green clouds. Could be just a bad thunderstorm brewing, but they had an ominous look about them.

He searched for his brother and straightened when he found him waltzing with Miss O'Neil. His hand tightened into a ball. Why should he care? But knowing Garrett was just trying to raise his hackles—and doing a decent job of it—irritated Mark. He had half a mind to march over there and cut in, but that was probably exactly what his brother expected him to do.

The song ended. Garrett leaned toward Miss O'Neil and said something. She shook her head, then tilted it to the side. Mark read her lips. "Thank you."

She drifted through the crowd, looked over her shoulder, and then headed across the churchyard. She was trying to run away; he knew that. Things must be terribly awkward for her here. He watched her stop and talk with Leah Bennett for a moment until Homer Jones asked Miss Bennett to dance. Shannon watched the two walk toward the group of waltzing townsfolk.

If not for him and his brother, neither woman would be stuck in Lookout. He felt bad about that, but when he and Garrett had offered to pay their passage back home or somewhere else, both had refused. Maybe they liked it here.

He gazed at the town, trying to see it from their viewpoint. Lookout was small as towns went. The layout resembled a capital E, with Bluebonnet Lane the spine and Apple, Main, and Oak Streets the arms. Most of the buildings were well kept, but a few of them were weathered and unpainted and had seen better days. Yeah, they had a small bank, a store, marshal's office, livery, café, a church, and even a newspaper office, but that was about all. Why would a woman with no means of support want to stay here if she had family to return to?

Screams rose from the crowd, yanking Mark's attention toward the ruckus behind him.

"Tornado!" Frantic voices lifted in a chaotic chorus, joining with frightened wails.

Men grabbed their women and children and raced to find shelter. Mark shoved away from the tree he'd been leaning on. He looked back at Miss O'Neil. She stood on Bluebonnet Lane, her wide eyes captivated. Mouth open. Didn't she know the danger she was in?

Foolish woman. He quickened his steps. People scattered in all directions, yet she didn't move. He might not want to dance with her, but he sure didn't want her to come to any harm.

A flying tree branch snatched his hat off like a thief, almost knocking him in the head. He galloped faster, dodging men. Dodging women dragging their stunned children. "Run," he yelled.

But she couldn't hear him.

The menacing winds stirred up dust, flinging dishes and cups and forks like a naughty child throwing rocks at someone who'd angered him. Mark reached Miss O'Neil, but she stood immobile, her face as white as the wedding cake. He jerked on her hand, hoping she'd follow him.

Explosions, one after another, rent the air. Miss O'Neil squealed and flew toward him, clutching his arms. Mark's gaze swerved past her. The church bell clanged as if screaming with pain. His heart stampeded.

Fierce black clouds devoured the road at the far end of town. He scooped up Miss O'Neil and raced away from the encroaching whirlwind. She clung to his neck and buried her face in his shoulder.

The boardinghouse had a root cellar. If they could make it there, they should be safe. He didn't stop to look over his shoulder again, but he could feel the monster breathing down his neck.

Where was Garrett? Had he taken shelter? What had happened to Luke? To Rachel and Jacqueline? They were the only family he had.

Mark ran past the Dykstra and Castleby houses, knowing they could well be destroyed by the storm. The safest place for him and Miss O'Neil was underground. Flying debris pelted them. A frantic horse pulling a buggy with no driver raced ahead of him. The storm bellowed like a locomotive barreling down on him.

Miss O'Neil continued clinging to his neck, and her tears dampened his shirt. She was light as a child, but carrying her this far was stealing his breath. He dashed around the side of the Castleby house, glad to have a barrier between them and the storm.

Garrett galloped around the back of the house with Rachel's daughter under his arm. He reached the root cellar first, flung open the doors, and the girl ran down the stairs. "Hurry!" Garrett yelled.

Mark set Miss O'Neil on the ground and pulled her through the narrow opening onto the stairs, relief making his limbs weak.

Jacqueline lit the lantern, chasing most of the darkness from the small room. She glanced at them, then up at the door, her face pale.

"Did you see Luke and Rachel?" Garrett yelled.

Mark shook his head, his gaze dashing toward Jacqueline. "They were near the church. I'm sure they made it inside."

Jack huddled in the shadows against the corn crib, her eyes wide and her normal spunkiness subdued. She shrugged. "I—I couldn't find them once everybody started running around. And what about Max?"

Garrett stopped partway down the steps and wrestled the doors shut. He held tight to the handles. With the drop-down bar on the outside, there was no way to lock them from the inside. The storm screamed in rage and fought to yank the doors off their hinges.

Still on the stairs, Mark looked past the Irishwoman and watched Garrett's struggle. He needed to get Miss O'Neil situated and then help his brother. Suddenly, she gasped and stumbled on the stairs. She fell into his arms, her momentum pushing him back. He flailed one arm, grasping for the handrail—for anything solid. His feet fumbled down the final half-dozen steps, and he fell, yanking Miss O'Neil down beside him on top of his arm. Something popped. His back and head collided with the packed dirt floor. Pain radiated through him.

Miss O'Neil cried out.

Mark squinted up at his brother. Garrett's form blurred, then darkened, and everything went black.

CHAPTER 2

Shannon lay on the hard, dirt floor, Mark's arm caught awkwardly under her back. Stabbing pain radiated through her foot and up her leg. She sat and grasped her leg, trying to catch her breath. Her ankle throbbed in unison with her pounding heart.

Jack crawled to her side. "Are you hurt?"

"Aye, my ankle." She scooted back against the dirt wall and huddled against the potato bin, trying to get comfortable and to catch her breath. She glanced up at Garrett, who still wrestled with the doors. The wind moaned and screeched, as if angered that it couldn't get in to devour them.

Garrett held tight to the handles, leaning back, using the full weight of his body to keep the doors shut. What had happened to all the other people? Surely there weren't enough cellars in town for everyone.

Why had she just stood there staring at the monstrous black cloud like some befuddled ninny? If that Mark Corbett hadn't grabbed her and hauled her off like she was a burlap bag of potatoes, surely she would have gotten hurt—or worse.

Had she thought if she allowed the storm to sweep her away

her problems would finally end? That she would be reunited with Mum in heaven?

"Mark. Mark!" Jack's frantic cries drew her attention. She shook the man's shoulders. "Wake up!"

Shannon scooted over beside him and put her arm around the lass. Had she killed the very man who'd come to her rescue? *Please, Father, no. Let him be all right.*

Mark moaned and lifted his arm. Suddenly, he cried out, and his eyes shot open. He blinked and looked around, then reached for the arm Shannon had fallen on. "Oh, my arm. Feels like it's busted."

"You all right, brother?" Garrett held tight to the doors while gazing down over his shoulder at Mark.

"Do I look all right?"

Shannon's gaze leaped to Mark's right arm. Sure enough, his wrist had started swelling. At least the bone hadn't broken through the skin. Could be it was just a bad sprain. She prayed it was.

Mark attempted to sit up, and Shannon reached to help even though the effort made her ankle scream. "I don't need your help. You've done enough." She let go as if he'd been a rattlesnake, and he fell back to the ground with a sharp grunt.

Jack hurried to Mark's other side. "I'll help you."

"Take it slow, Jack. Besides my hand hurting like a horse kicked it, my head is buzzing." The girl pulled while Mark pushed off from the ground, and he managed to sit. He scowled at Shannon as if she were to blame.

She carefully moved away and leaned back against the potato bin. She hadn't meant to hurt him and felt awful that she had. Closing her eyes, she tried to remember being back in Ireland. The memories were fading, and it was getting harder to remember her mum's face.

She'd never wanted to come to this country, but she and Mum had followed along as Da chased his dreams. Would her parents still be alive if they'd stayed in Ireland? If her da hadn't been so insistent that they come to America?

At least she would be in a place where she had friends, friends who cared about her. But in America—in Texas—she had no one.

Her high-top shoe felt tighter than it had earlier. If her ankle swelled too much, her boot might have to be cut off, and these were the only shoes she owned. On top of everything else, she'd have to put her plans to leave Lookout on hold.

She scowled across the small cellar to the other side where Mark sat, rubbing the back of his head. His brother still clung to the doors, but they no longer rattled as if a bear were on the other side trying to get in.

Mark cradled his right arm with his other hand and winced when he shifted positions. His gaze shot fiery arrows at her. "Why did you just stand there gawking at the storm? Don't you know how dangerous a tornado is?"

A tornado. So the monster had a name.

She'd heard of them before, even in Ireland, but she'd never seen such a vengeful storm. Fear had melted her in the road like a spent candle stuck to a plate. Shivering, she clutched her arms around her. Had Mark just saved her life?

"Can you hear me, Miss O'Neil?" Mark leaned forward and grimaced from the movement. "Why didn't you run?"

Jack jumped to her feet. "I need to find my ma and Luke." She headed for the stairs, but Mark grabbed hold of her arm and pulled her back.

"You're not going anywhere until that twister passes."

"But they might be dead. And I gotta find Max."

Mark moved around, as if trying to get comfortable. "Your parents are safe; I'm sure."

Jack crossed her arms and leaned against a wooden bin. "How do you know?"

Mark grinned. "It took your ma eleven years to get Luke to the altar. She's not about to let a tornado steal him away on her wedding day."

Shannon watched the interplay between man and girl, amazed at how gentle Mark's voice was. She was also thankful that he seemed to be all right, except for his wrist.

"But what about Max? I saw him under the cake table just before that storm blew in." Jack flipped her long, auburn hair, almost the same color as Shannon's, over her shoulder, and she nibbled her lower lip. The pristine yellow dress she'd donned this morning was now covered in dirt and grime.

"Aw, you know that ol' yellow dog," Garrett said. "He's scared of his shadow. He's probably back hiding out in one of the jail cells, and not even a tornado could uproot one of those heavy iron cages."

"I guess so."

Shannon leaned her head back, glad that Mark had been diverted with the lass's questions and forgotten about interrogating her. She truly hoped nothing had happened to the newly married couple. Although not marrying Luke Davis had created a multitude of problems for her, she knew Luke was the love of Rachel's life, and Shannon couldn't begrudge them their happiness.

She glanced down, staring at her dirty hands. She brushed off the dust from her fall, but only soap and water would remove the rest. She allowed her injured foot to relax, but just the slight movement made her nearly scream out. Her boot felt unusually tight, and she was certain her foot was still swelling.

Mark glanced at Shannon. "You never answered my question."

She ducked her head again. "I don't know why I didn't run."

She hoped he would be satisfied and leave her alone. All her life, she had tried to make herself small. Tried to remain unseen. Tried to stay out of her da's way when he returned home from the pub. It had mostly worked—until she'd grown up and was too large to hide.

The chill of the cellar seeped into her bones, and no amount of rubbing her arms could drive it away. What was she going to do? How could she survive on her own?

A scrape and thud sounded on the stairs; then a shaft of sunlight illuminated the dimly lit room. Fresh air streamed in. Dust motes floated on the shaft of sunlight that fell through the open door. A mouse scurried under a set of shelves that held jars of green beans and jellies.

Shannon jumped up, instantly regretting her sudden movement. She held onto the potato bin, keeping her sore foot off the ground, and gazed up the stairs. How was she going to manage them?

Mark stood also, then fell back against a wooden bin that held onions. He hung his head, rubbing his brows with his thumb and forefingers.

"You all right?" Jack asked.

"Yeah, just stood up too fast. Got a tornado of my own swirling in my head."

Garrett clambered down the steps. "Most likely, it's from that blow you took to your head when you fell. We'd best have the doc take a look at it."

"I'll be fine." Mark swatted his hand in the air. "We need to get up there and see if any of the town is left. See if anyone is injured."

Shannon's pulse soared. Here she'd been worrying about herself when others may have lost their homes, livelihood, and even family members. She had to find out if Leah was all right. They may have been opponents at one time, but their similar loss had drawn them closer.

"What's wrong with your hand?" Garrett glanced at Mark's cradled arm. "Looks like it's swellin' up."

Mark wiggled his forefinger and grimaced. "Yeah. Broken wrist, I think."

Shannon lifted her hand to her mouth and sucked back a gasp. Mr. Corbett had been trying to help her, and she'd caused him injury. She longed to creep around the bin and hide in the shadows, but her wounded foot and shame held her immobile.

"You won't be able to help much until the doc sets your hand, so we might as well head over to his office first." Garrett hurried to Mark's side.

"I don't need any help, but I reckon Miss O'Neil does. Looks like she hurt her foot in the fall."

"Well, I'm goin' looking for my ma and my new pa." Jack dashed past Garrett.

He grabbed for her arm, but she slipped past. "No, wait!"

"You're too slow, brother." Mark grinned.

Garrett shook his head. "I wanted to keep her close—just in case." He swallowed hard.

Mark patted his brother's shoulder. "Yeah, I know. But Luke finally married the only woman he's ever loved. He's not gonna let a twister steal her away from him."

"I don't reckon he would, but that was one fierce storm."

"Yep, you're right there. Let's see what's left of the town." Mark undid the middle button of his shirt and stuck his injured hand inside, using it as a sling. He winced as he relaxed his arm; then he nodded at Shannon and walked up the stairs.

"What part of you is hurt, ma'am?" Garrett ambled closer to her.

She fought the urge to hide, knowing that Garrett Corbett was a prankster, but he was still a gentleman. What part of her hurt? *All of me. My heart. My dignity.* "Just my ankle."

"Might be easiest if I simply carried you up."

Shannon shook her head. "I can walk."

She lowered her foot and tried putting her weight on it. Pain ratcheted through it and up into her lower leg. She bit the inside of her cheek, and sucked in a breath. Had she broken her ankle?

Without so much as a warning, Garrett scooped her into his arms and carried her up the stairs. He was just like his brother, forcing a woman to do things she didn't want to do. If not for the Corbett brothers, she wouldn't even be in Texas. But she had to be honest, even if she didn't like it in this case. Without Garrett's help, she'd have had a difficult time climbing those stairs.

"Blessit be! The store is gone." Shannon's gaze roved around the town. Thank goodness, the boardinghouse was still standing, though it had sustained some damage. Shingles were missing, some windows broken, and debris littered the yard and porch, but the house itself had withstood the storm, as had the neighboring homes. The store was a different story.

Letting out a slow whistle, Garrett set her down. "I've never seen anything like this."

" 'Tis amazing so many buildings are still standin'." She held on to Garrett's arm, keeping her foot off the ground. People slowly crept out of every nook and cranny she could see, all looking first at the sky, where the sun had broken through the clouds, and then at their town. They crawled out from under wagons, out of buildings, and one man even crawled soaking wet out of the horse trough.

Mark was bent over a man lying in the street. He straightened and looked around. "Anyone seen the doc?"

People near him shook their heads, but several men turned in different directions as if looking for the doctor.

"Let's get you off that foot." Garrett picked Shannon up again and hurried toward the boardinghouse. "Get that boot off right away, raise up your leg, and stay off of it. That can help with the swelling, so I've heard."

"Garrett!"

Shannon locked her arms around Garrett's shoulders as he spun around. A wide grin lit his face. "Luke. Rachel."

"I found them in the church." Jack had an arm wrapped around both Luke's and Rachel's waists. She grinned like a kid at Christmas. "All the windows was blown out, but the church is still there."

"Glad to see you made it," Garrett responded.

Shannon knew his relief must be as huge as the ocean. Luke was his and Mark's cousin and their only living relative as far as she knew.

Rachel hurried toward Shannon, looking worried, her wedding dress damp and dirty, as was Shannon's garment. "What's wrong? Are you injured badly?"

"Not so much. 'Tis just my ankle that hurts."

Relief softened the worry lines on Rachel's face, and she smiled. "Well, thank the good Lord for that. Do you know where Leah is?"

Shannon shook her head. She was concerned for her new friend, but Leah was tough—Texas tough—and would surely be all right.

"That was some storm. We're fortunate that most of the buildings in town are still standing. Looks like the store's gone, though." Luke ran his fingers through his hair. "That's a shame. This town needs the mercantile."

Rachel nodded. "God was certainly watching over us. So far, there have only been minor injuries. Let's get Miss O'Neil into the house and then send for the doctor."

"I imagine the doc will have his hands full," Luke said.

"You're right," Rachel said. "I'll tend to Shannon, and you men see if you can help the others who might be trapped or injured."

Garrett followed Rachel back to the boardinghouse, shaking his head. "Not even married an hour, and she's already bossing you around."

Luke grinned wide. "Ain't it great! She's bossing you, too, in case you didn't notice."

Shannon felt Garrett's chuckle as it rumbled in his chest. She longed to have family—to feel the closeness these cousins felt for one another. But she was alone in this world—and she wasn't even sure if God was still on her side.

Using his left hand, Mark fumbled with his shirt button. "Ahh!" He flung his hand in the air. With this stiff cast keeping his right hand and wrist immobile, the pain was less, but even the simplest of jobs was nigh on impossible. The turkey egg bump on the back of his head ached, and his vision blurred if he turned his head too fast, but the wound had stopped bleeding. He looked down at his shirt and tried to fasten it again. He'd have thought someone had greased that little booger. He blew out a breath and flipped the irritating button with his finger. Who would notice his shirt partially undone with everything else that had happened?

He slapped on his hat, then realized it didn't fit right, what with his head bandaged and all. He adjusted the sling around his neck and marched out of the doctor's office, ready to help with the cleanup. The line at the doc's office had been long, but fortunately, most injuries were minor. In fact, his was one of the worst. And it wasn't the storm that had taken him down, but a bumbling Irish gal. Thank goodness nobody knew that except those who'd been in the cellar. He doubted Garrett or Jack would have reason to mention it to anyone.

Mark bent down and picked up a board lying in the street. When his vision cleared, he examined the plank but was unable to tell which building it had come from. At the end of the street sat a growing stack of debris, and he walked over and dropped the board on it.

Dan Howard dumped an armload of fragmented timbers, broken dishes, and unrecognizable things. "You oughta be takin' it easy, Mark. No one expects you to work with your injuries."

Mark shrugged. What had he done? Dumped one lousy board on the pile.

The mayor lumbered up beside them and tossed a broken chair on the growing stack. He patted Mark on the shoulder. "Yes sir, Mark Corbett's as good as they come. You won't find a finer citizen than him. Most men would go home and take it easy after being knocked out, but not Mark."

Shifting his feet, Mark winced from the compliment. He, least of all, deserved any praise. He was nothing but a scoundrel in sheep's wool. The problem was, nobody knew it but him. He longed to be a good citizen, a man people looked up to, and they did. But he was a phony, and there was nothing he could do about it. He craved the respect of the good, upstanding citizens of Lookout, but he didn't deserve it. One deed done years ago had been all it had taken to ruin his life.

The pastor had said confession was good for the soul, but Mark had never told a single person about what had happened in the small town of Abilene. He'd been a young man away from home for the first time, seeking adventure—and he'd certainly found it. The trouble was that adventure had almost destroyed him. He kicked at a piece of wood lying in the street. Maybe he should tell Garrett what happened.

His brother could be bossy and a tease, but he was a good man. Mark couldn't stand the thought of Garrett looking down on him because of what had happened. Or lowering his opinion of him.

Mark stuck part of the mercantile sign under his arm. *Sorry, Lord. I know You must be disappointed in what I did down in Abilene.* He shook his head and looked for something else to do. Hard work would pull him out of this foul mood.

He glanced around and felt his heart warm. The Lookout townsfolk might have their differences on occasion, but when disaster struck, they joined in and worked together to set things right.

"Mark!"

He swung around and found Rachel on the boardinghouse porch, waving at him.

Dodging the remaining debris—two shiny new coffeepots from the store, several articles of clothing, tree branches, and other items—he strode toward the porch. He slowed his steps as he reached his destination. "How's your building?"

Rachel shrugged. "Not so bad. Some broken windows. A tree limb went through one window upstairs, and the storm must have gotten the others. It's the weirdest thing, but there's a fork stuck in the wood just outside one of the upstairs bedroom windows."

Mark shook his head. "I've heard of strange things happening during tornados."

"Me, too." She lifted her chin. "How's your head?"

"Not bad. Better than my wrist, I reckon."

"So it was broken?"

Mark nodded.

"That will make it hard for you to do your bookwork and load freight."

He hadn't even had time to consider that yet. Garrett was the muscle man, did most of the loading of the freight, but he left the ledger and recording of information to Mark. It would be weeks before he'd be able to write again. What in the world would he do about that?

"Since Garrett's not so good with numbers and paperwork, I suppose you might need to hire some help." Rachel must have read his thoughts. Her eyes sparkled. "What about seeing if Miss Bennett or Miss O'Neil could assist you? That way you'd be getting some help back for the money you're out on their room and board."

Mark held up his hand, palm out. "Just hold your horses. The last thing we need is one of those women coming in and changing things all around."

Rachel shoved her hands to her hips and swung one side of her mouth up. "Nobody said anything about making changes, Mark."

"Well, isn't that what women do?"

She shook her head and crossed her arms. "You and your brother have been alone too long. It wouldn't hurt either one of you to marry."

Mark backed up several steps. "No thanks. I'm happy for you and Luke, but don't go playing matchmaker."

Rachel chuckled. "You're a fine one to be making that statement after you and Garrett ordered all those brides for Luke."

Mark backed up some more, taking care to avoid the debris. Time to get back to work. All this talk of matchmaking was making him antsy. "That was mostly Garrett's doing."

He tipped his hat and turned, but not before he heard Rachel's comment that he was as much responsible as Garrett. And she was right. He never should have allowed himself to get caught up in Garrett's scheme to find Luke a bride. But where his brother was concerned, good intentions never got him anywhere. Somehow, Garrett always managed to make Mark see his side of things. But no more. At twenty-seven years of age, he should be man enough to stand up to his brother.

He was tired of living in Garrett's shadow. Tired of working in the freight office, tired of hauling goods back and forth from Dallas to the ranches and smaller towns in the area. He had his own plans. His own dreams. And it was time he started reaching for them.

CHAPTER 3

Leah Bennett hoisted her skirts and attempted to climb out of the ditch again. Just like the previous four times, her foot slipped on the rain-soaked mud, but this time, she slid back and stumbled, falling to the bottom of the gully filled with cold runoff from the storm. Water dampened her backside and drenched the last dry spot on her dress. Having lost half of her pins, her hair threatened to fall in a pile around her shoulders. She shoved a handful out of her face and stared at the hill again. Somehow, she had to make it to the top.

The child who had wailed all during the storm, making Leah's eardrums ache, kicked his scream up another notch. Though frustrated to the core with his tantrum, part of her wanted to say, "I know just how you feel."

"Hurry up. The rest of us want out of here, too." The boy's father, one of the farmers who lived outside of town, wrinkled his brow and glared at Leah, as if all their problems were her fault.

A branch half the size of Texas had broken off a giant oak tree and blocked their exit from the far side of the culvert—a much easier climb, she noted. The section of the ditch where the man, his wife, and son had hidden sported moss-covered sides too steep to climb.

"Get a move on, lady. We need to get our boy into some dry clothes afore he catches his death."

His wife gasped. "Don't say such a thing, Herman."

Leah looked up at the steep incline again. She hadn't wanted to hide out from the storm in the grimy ditch, but when she'd tried to get into the church, it had been crammed full of people. A stranger had grabbed her arm and dragged her to this ditch, but he'd crawled out as soon as the tornado passed, saying he had family to search for. Now, she was stuck in the muck and mire of the ditch and couldn't get out. Could things get any worse?

A rope landed with a loud thud right beside Leah, and she jumped.

"Give me your hand, and I'll help you up, ma'am."

Leah looked past the thick hand that reached for her and found its owner. A huge, broad-shouldered man, probably six foot four at least, waited for her response. Past him, she could see the sky had brightened, and patches of blue peeked through the thinning cloud cover. None of the storm's ferociousness that had sent the whole town scurrying for cover remained. They had tornados in Missouri, but she'd never had one breathing down her neck, trying to devour her before.

"If you prefer, you can tie the rope around your waist, and I can haul you up."

Leah winced. That made her sound like a piece of freight. Standing, she shook out her skirt. She'd never get all the mud and stains from this garment, and she couldn't afford to lose one of her few dresses. Thin as they were, they were all she had.

Gathering her strength and fortitude for another attempt up the slippery slope, she stepped forward. The man above her looked well capable of lifting her weight. Wasn't he the town's blacksmith or something like that?

She wiped her muddy hand on her dress and held it up. He

grabbed her around the wrist and pulled. Her body flew upward, but her feet felt as if they were anchored in quicksand, and for a second, she thought she'd be torn in two. But a sucking smack sounded, and her feet followed her body. Even her boots were still attached. Good thing, since they were her only pair.

She landed hard on solid ground and wavered, trying to regain her balance. The man kept a hand on her shoulder until she quit wobbling. She glanced up—way up into a pair of eyes so dark she couldn't distinguish the pupils from the irises. He nodded and released her, moving past her to help the family still in the ditch.

Watching him so effortlessly help the woman up and then gently reach down to receive the squalling baby quickened something deep inside of Leah. The man's wide shoulders had to be at least three feet across the back. If her father had matched her up with a man like this instead of that ancient curmudgeon, she'd have never run away.

The father of the baby shinnied up the slope, using the rope. He shook the big man's hand and smiled for the first time since the storm. "Thanks for coming to our rescue, Dan."

The big man—Dan—nodded and turned back to Leah as the family walked away. "You all right, ma'am?"

Leah snorted a laugh and looked down at her filthy dress. "Do I look all right to you?"

His gaze traveled down the length of her body, and a crooked smile tugged at one side of his mouth. "A little mud don't change a thing. You're mighty fine in my eyes."

Leah's heart skipped a beat, and she glanced up to see if he was serious. His eyes held no humor, no jesting. "Well. . .uh. . . thank you, Mr. . . . ."

He yanked off his stained hat. "Howard, ma'am. I'm Dan Howard."

"Leah Bennett."

That quirky smile returned. "I know who you are, ma'am. I reckon the whole town does."

Leah's smile melted, and she pursed her lips. "I suppose you're right. Thank you for helping me out of that ditch."

"Happy to help, ma'am." He tipped his hat again and looked past her as if he wanted to be on his way. "Reckon I'll go help out at the store. Looks like it caught the worst of the storm."

Leah gasped as she noticed its remains. All that was left of Fosters' Mercantile were the floorboards, and debris of all kinds littered the boardwalk and street nearby. Even worse, the Foster home, which sat right behind the store, was lying in a crumpled mess across Bluebonnet Lane. Two dozen or more of the townsfolk were helping with the cleanup. How would the town get by without its only store? She allowed her gaze to roam over the small town. Thankfully, most buildings were still standing, though a number of them had minor damage and broken windows.

But what about the boardinghouse? Everything she owned in the world was in her room on the second floor. She stepped past Polly and Dolly Dykstra's garish pink house and gazed down Bluebonnet Lane. Relief flooded her to see the lovely Victorian home still standing. Painted a soft green with white trim, the house was always inviting.

At least it had been until the owner had agreed to marry the town marshal—the same man Leah had come to town to marry. Now things at the boardinghouse were uncomfortable, even though Rachel tried hard to make Leah and Shannon feel welcome.

Leah had hoped to find employment of some kind and to save enough money so she could find a small place to rent. If only she was a man and could do carpentry or window repair, she'd have it made. Instead, she could sew and clean, but who would pay her to do that? Most men would marry rather than hire a woman to do such menial chores.

Leah sighed and walked toward the boardinghouse. She needed to get changed and see what she could do to help with the cleanup, and she needed to get this dress soaking if she was to have any hopes of salvaging it.

Her life felt like that dress: muddy, torn, a mess. How was she going to get by?

Something shiny on the ground snagged her attention, and she bent and picked it up. How odd. How could a hand mirror get thrown so far from the store or the home it came from and not get broken?

It was like a message from God. Yes, she was wet and mangy as a stray dog after a thunderstorm, but God had brought her through the storm without a scratch. Yes, she was stuck in Lookout, but God had provided room and board for her through the Corbetts. But she couldn't live off of them forever and maintain her dignity.

What she needed was a husband. Her thoughts turned back to Dan Howard. Yes, he was strong and fairly comely, but was he a man she could spend the rest of her life with?

She shook her head, knowing the truth. She wanted a man with more standing in town than the livery owner. A man who didn't smell like horses when he came home each night. No, Dan Howard wasn't her idea of the perfect husband.

∽

Rachel Davis added the final batch of potatoes to the stew and stirred it with the long, wooden spoon Luke had carved for her. She'd used her largest kettle and hoped it would be enough to feed the hungry mob cleaning up the town. Of course, once Jacqueline spread the word for folks to come and eat at the boardinghouse, other women would probably bring food here as well. Feeding folks at the boardinghouse just made sense with her having the biggest table in town, but even then, they'd have to eat in shifts or over at the café.

Footsteps sounded behind her, and she smiled. Luke ran his arms around her waist and tugged her back against his solid chest. He leaned down and nibbled on her earlobe and ran kisses down her neck. Finally, he sighed and rested his chin on her head. "Some wedding day, huh?"

Rachel turned in his arms and laid her head on his chest. "Certainly not the way I'd imagined our special day, but at least nobody will ever forget it."

Luke chuckled. "You're right about that. I'm just thankful nobody was hurt too bad."

"It amazing that there weren't any deaths, considering how fast that twister pulled together and attacked the town."

Luke brushed his knuckles along her cheek. "I'm sorry, Rachel. I wanted this to be the happiest day of your life."

"It is. Don't you know that? I married the man I've loved all my life. Nothing can ruin that." She smiled up at her handsome husband. "I still can't believe we're actually married."

"Oh, believe it." He leaned down and melded his lips to hers. At first, he was gentle, exploring, but then he became more urgent, staking his claim on her. And she didn't mind one bit. The back door slammed shut, and she and Luke jumped apart like a courting couple caught spooning instead of newlyweds.

Jacqueline's eyes widened, and she grinned. "Caught you smooching, didn't I?"

Rachel snickered as Luke's ears turned red. "You might as well get used to kissing in front of our daughter. You are her pa now."

Luke's mouth tilted up on one side, doing funny things to Rachel's insides. Oh, how she loved this man. A man she had thought would never be her husband. But God had worked a miracle and moved mountains of persistent regret and refusal to forgive.

"I like the sound of that—Pa."

"Me, too!" Jacqueline hurried over and wrapped her arms around both of them. "I wanted you for my pa almost since the first time I met you."

Luke pulled back from their embrace and cocked one eyebrow at Jacqueline. "From the first time? I seem to remember nearly getting drowned in the river the first time we met."

Jacqueline giggled. "Well, maybe it was when you adopted Max."

"Where is that ol' mutt, anyway?" Luke asked.

"Where do you think? Hiding in the jail. All that tornado ruckus scared him half to death."

Reluctantly, Rachel pulled away and stirred the stew again. The aroma of beef, onions, and other vegetables filled the air, blending with the scent of biscuits baking in the oven. "You two scoot on in to the dining room and set the table. I want things ready when folks start coming in to eat."

Luke shook his head, but his eyes glimmered. "Not even married three hours, and she's already bossing me around."

"Might as well get used to it," Jacqueline said. "She bosses me around all the time."

Rachel laughed with her daughter and husband. For far too long, this house had lacked joy and laughter. In spite of all that had happened today, she felt giddy. Tonight her dreams would come true, and she would be Luke's wife in all ways.

She walked to the back door and stared up at the clearing sky. The cool temperatures that followed on the coattails of the storm were giving way to the normal August heat. A bead of sweat trickled down from her right temple, and she swiped it away.

So many forces had worked to keep her and Luke apart, but the storm had come too late. She was Mrs. Luke Davis, and nothing could change that now. Rachel grinned up at the sky. "Thank You, Lord."

❧

Leah stood in the hallway, wishing she could shrivel up and blow away like a piece of dust. She hadn't meant to eavesdrop—to see the marshal kissing Rachel or to overhear their private moments with Jacqueline. She'd only come to see if Rachel needed any help before venturing back outside to aid in the town's cleanup.

Though truly happy for Luke and Rachel, Leah couldn't help feeling disappointed that she wasn't the one married. She longed for a home of her own and a husband coming home each night, but after helping Ma tend ten younger brothers and sisters, she could well do without the child. She never wanted children. They were so much work, and a woman never had a moment to herself when she had a brood of young'uns. But what man would marry a woman who didn't want to bear him children?

Luke and Jack were in the dining room, rattling silverware and plates as they set the table. Leah backed up a few steps, hoping the floorboards didn't creak, then walked to the kitchen door, making her footsteps sound louder than normal. She cleared her throat. "Um. . .I was wondering if you needed some help."

Rachel spun around from the pot she was stirring and smiled. "That would be nice, Leah. I wouldn't normally accept your help, since you're a guest here, but with the wedding and then the storm. . .well, I hadn't planned to cook today, but it seemed the thing I could best do to help. People will need to eat after all their hard work cleaning up the aftermath." She blushed, as if she hadn't planned to make a speech.

"I don't mind helping. I thought I'd go back outside and work some more after changing clothes, but I'd prefer not to get all muddy again."

Rachel, still in her wedding dress, glanced around the near-spotless kitchen. "Hmm. . .the stew isn't ready, so we can't dish it up yet." She snapped her fingers. "Why don't you check on Shannon and see if she needs anything. She badly twisted her ankle running during the storm and is resting in the parlor. Then you can slice the pies. I made extra so I wouldn't have to bake for the next few days since. . .um, well, since I was getting married."

Leah smiled. "Congratulations. It was a very nice wedding."

Rachel chuckled. "Thanks, and wasn't that party afterward something?"

"I'm sorry your reception was ruined by the storm."

Rachel shrugged. "At least most everybody had eaten their cake."

Leah studied the ground a moment, curious about something

but reluctant to ask. A table covered with a lacy cloth had been used to hold gifts from the townsfolk. The table had been piled high with handmade towels, table coverings, jars of food, baskets of fresh produce, and even a ham or two. She hated the thought of all those things being destroyed in the storm. "What happened to all your gifts?"

"Most things were spared. Folks grabbed an armful as they raced into the church. Only a few jars of beans were broken. It was awfully kind of folks to think of those gifts at a time like that."

Leah nodded. "People in Texas seem friendlier than where I'm from."

Rachel moved over to a bowl that held dough and started rolling it out. "Texas is a rough land, even in this modern time. People here stick together and help their neighbors. It's how we survive against the odds."

"Well, I'll just check on Shannon now." Leah slipped back into the dim hallway. Rachel hadn't said anything about her or Shannon moving out of the boardinghouse, but it must be uncomfortable for a newlywed to live with the two women who had been vying to marry her husband.

Glancing in the door to the dining room, she saw Jack race around the far side of the table and stop, grinning back at Luke, eyes gleaming. "I've got the last fork, and you can't have it." The girl's singsong voice sounded playful and teasing. One would never know she'd taken cover from a nasty storm less than an hour before.

Luke growled and lunged for the child. She squealed and ran back into the kitchen. "Save me, Ma!"

Leah shook her head. Such playful nonsense would never have been tolerated in her parents' home. With so many mouths to feed and her father a poor farmer, everyone was expected to work. Hard. There was little time for fun.

She stopped in the doorway to the parlor. Shannon lay on the sofa with one arm over her eyes. Her boot had been removed from her injured foot, which looked swollen even from across the room. How would she manage to get up stairs this evening when it was time to retire?

Leah tiptoed into the room, not wanting to wake her friend if she was sleeping. They'd been opponents, both competing for Luke Davis's affection. She hadn't treated Shannon very nicely in the past, mainly because she'd been so desperate to win the bride contest, but now they were in the same wagon.

A floorboard creaked, and Leah froze. Shannon lifted her arm and looked out from under it. She smiled, though pain creased the young woman's forehead and dulled her normally bright eyes.

"Rachel asked me to check on you. Do you need anything?"

"That's kind of you, but I'm fine."

Leah glanced at Shannon's ankle. It looked twice the size it should be. "Does your ankle hurt much?"

"Oh, 'tisn't too terrible."

Shannon attempted to sit up. She grimaced and stared at her ankle. " 'Tis a fine kettle of fish I'm in."

Leah rushed forward to help her. "I imagine in a couple of days your ankle will be almost back to normal."

"Aye, you're probably right, but I had decided to accept the Corbetts' offer for a ticket out of town."

Leah felt her own eyes widen at the woman's unexpected declaration. She dropped in a side chair. "But where would you go? I thought you had no relatives in America."

Shannon pressed her lips together until they turned white. "I don't, but 'tis so awkward here now that Rachel has married. Don't you think?"

Leah nodded. "Yes, but Luke and Rachel are good people, and she runs this boardinghouse. They will have others staying with them and sharing their table most of the time."

"Aye, 'tis true. But not the women who competed to marry her husband."

Leah wrung her hands together. Shannon was voicing the very

same thoughts that she'd had ever since the day Luke announced that Rachel was the woman he loved. "What else can we do besides bide our time until we find someone else to marry or some kind of employment?"

Shannon shook her head. "You could return home to your family."

Leah stiffened her back. "That's not an alternative."

The pretty, auburn-haired woman's gaze flickered from Leah to across the room and back. "If I'm not stickin' my nose where it doesn't belong, might I ask why you can't?"

"It doesn't matter. I just can't." Leah stood. "If there's nothing you need, I'll go help Rachel." She spun around and scurried from the room like a rat caught raiding the pantry. She should have just told Shannon the truth—that her father had for all intents and purposes sold her to a creepy old man. If she returned home, she'd be expected to marry Mr. Abernathy. She shuddered, just thinking of his leering gaze and the white hair that grew from his ears and nostrils. No, she'd rather marry an Apache than that old curmudgeon.

CHAPTER 4

Mark snapped the pencil in half and tossed it across the room. The pieces clinked against the window, drawing a curious glance from a passerby. He exhaled a frustrated sigh. "How am I supposed to tally the ledgers and do bookwork if I can't write? Seems like the doc could have left more than just my fingertips free of this wretched cast."

"Patience, patience." Garrett propped his feet on his desk and sipped his coffee. "I've been saying it for a while: We need to hire some help."

"I thought you wanted to hire someone to lend a hand with deliveries, not the bookkeeping."

"Well...that changed when you busted your wrist. We could get someone to work in the office, and you can keep going with me on deliveries."

Mark harrumphed. "Fat lot of help I'd be. I can't lift freight until this heals." He held up his hand with the cast on it.

"You can drive the wagon while I sleep." Garrett grinned.

Mark tossed a paperweight at him. Garrett dodged it, flailing his arms like a young bird trying to fly, and fell out of his chair.

Mark chuckled for the first time since the storm.

Garrett sat on the floor, his arms on his knees, and shook his head. "You're sure in a foul mood, brother."

"You would be, too, if you only had one hand to work with." Mark knew he was being a cantankerous grump, but he could use a little sympathy. The problem was, Garrett wasn't offering any. His brother had no idea how hard it was simply to do feats like getting dressed, shaving, or tending to his daily needs. Mark had just about decided to grow a beard. He'd nicked himself four times shaving today. Too bad Lookout didn't have a barber.

Garrett righted himself in his chair and sipped his coffee again. Mark strode over to the coffeepot, carrying his cup. He stood staring at the pot for a second before he realized he couldn't lift it and hold the cup at the same time. He smacked his cup on Garrett's desk, drawing a raised brow from his brother, and then poured his coffee. The fragrant aroma wafted up, calming him.

"I could have done that if you'd asked me to."

Mark scowled. "I'm not totally helpless."

Garrett grinned. "I noticed you managed to eat just fine with your left hand. Learning to write shouldn't be all that hard."

Mark ignored him and studied the map on the wall behind Garrett's messy desk. A pin was stuck in each of the surrounding towns where they delivered the freight they picked up in Dallas once a week. They'd been two kids from a poor family—two kids who'd pulled plenty of pranks and practical jokes—but they had realized Garrett's dream of starting a freight company and had built it into a successful business. In the beginning, the townsfolk had bets going on how quickly the Corbett Freight Company would fold up, but by the time he and Garrett had grown up and the business started taking off, the brothers had gained the respect of the town.

Respect was something Mark cherished. He'd had none growing up. Their father had drunk away what little money he made, and their mother took in laundry and cleaned the saloon just to get by. Mark liked having people look at him with respect in their eyes, but he knew he didn't deserve it.

And he was soon going to have to face facts. He no longer wanted to be in the freight business. He had dreams of his own. Dreams that had been squelched but refused to go away. He just had to figure out how—and when—to tell his brother.

〜

Shannon closed her book and stared out the parlor window. The morning sun shone bright, and few traces of the storm still remained other than the damage to the buildings and trees. Boards covered most of the window openings she could see, and piles of broken wood and debris still littered the lot where the mercantile had been. Sweat trickled down her chest and back. Though only midmorning, the temperature was sweltering enough to sear bacon on an anvil.

After two days, her ankle was better, but she still had to stay off her feet a while longer per the doctor's orders. Walking was difficult, but she far preferred the pain to having Luke Davis carry her up and down the stairs, not that he wasn't capable of doing so.

"Silly lass." She heaved a sigh, reminding herself that he was no longer a free man. All her hopes and dreams had been placed on marrying him, but it wasn't to be.

She flipped open her book, and the wrinkled page of a letter stared up at her. Shaking her head, she knew it was foolish to write such a missive, but doing so had helped her in a small way. She glanced around the room, even though no one was there other than her. The wooden furniture gleamed with the fresh waxing it had received yesterday, and dust had not yet had a chance to settle and dull the shine. Two matching settees sat on opposite walls with a quartet of side chairs sitting at angles to the settees, and several small tables helped fill the room. A piano, not used since she arrived, sat looking as lonely as she along the far wall.

Smoothing open the letter, she stared at the words. What kind of person wrote a letter to a dead woman?

Dear Mum,

I miss you so much and wish you were here. I miss your smiles, your hugs, and kisses on my cheek.

You won't believe this, but I'm in Texas now. 'Tis such a grand, wild state, Texas is. Cowboys fill the streets, sometimes hooting like banshees and firing guns, but the marshal quickly confiscates their weapons and gives them some cooling-down time in his jail.

Shannon twisted her mouth up, disgusted with herself. The marshal, again. Shaking her head, she continued reading.

Lookout—'tis such an odd name for a town—is small compared to some of the Texas towns I traveled through on my way here from Louisiana. Things are so much drier than in our homeland. I miss the green of Ireland.

There's a high ridge across the river where outlaws and later soldiers used to watch for their enemies, so I've been told. That place is called Lookout Ridge and is where the town's name comes from. There's a river west of town that flows to the south. Then it makes a sharp turn at the ridge before traveling eastward. A pool formed there, and the townsfolk use it as a swimming hole when the water is deep enough. I have not been, though 'twould feel grand on a hot day like this one. Thankful for fall, I'll be.

I participated in a bride contest—have you ever heard of such a thing? Only in America. 'Twas quite an event. People for miles around came to town to see the competition and judging. Three women, me being one, traveled here to marry the same man, but one bride turned out to be an outlaw and is now in prison or jail somewhere. I've never been so close to

an outlaw, unless one counted Da as one—forgive me, Mum.
But Carly didn't seem like an outlaw. Lonely like me, she
was, and I think she wanted to live a normal life. But 'twas
not to be for her—nor for me.

Shannon's eyes stung, and she attempted to smooth out a place on the letter where several tears had dropped and crinkled the paper. Footsteps drew near, and she stuffed the missive into the book, slammed it closed, and held the novel against her chest.

Rachel stepped into the room and smiled. "How are you doin'? Anything you want?" Her gaze traveled around the room, as if searching for anything out of place.

Shannon shook her head. What she wanted was to live somewhere else, even though she loved her room upstairs. 'Twas the nicest place she'd ever stayed, yet she wanted to be free of the awkwardness that existed now that Rachel had married Luke. But the town had nowhere else a decent woman could stay. If only she hadn't injured her ankle, she would have been gone by now, on yesterday's stage. But to be fair, Rachel had been only kind and had tried hard to make the best of the situation. To act as if nothing had happened.

"It's a bit warm in here. Mind if I open a few windows?" Rachel smiled, the glow of being in love, of being a newlywed lingered about her. She pushed up a window, allowing in a gentle breeze that fluttered the curtains. She opened another, and a stronger gust cooled the room a small measure.

"You sure you don't need anything? Some tea or lemonade, maybe?"

"Nay, but I thank you. I would just like to be up and about, helpin' somehow."

"I'm sure you must be bored half to death." Rachel tapped her forefinger against her lips. "Perhaps there's some way you could help with the meals. I'll think about it and let you know."

Shannon nodded her thanks as Rachel started to leave.

The boardinghouse owner suddenly stopped and then came back into the room. She twisted her hands together, then lifted her pale blue eyes to gaze into Shannon's. "I know things seem difficult for you now. I can't imagine what you're going through, not knowing what the future holds, but I believe that God brought you to Lookout for a purpose."

She glanced toward the window, and when she looked back, her cheeks had a red tinge. "Though marrying Luke is no longer an option, there are a number of fine men in Lookout and others who live on surrounding ranches who would love to find a good woman to marry."

Shannon's cheeks warmed, and she turned to look out the window. A wagon drove by with a big man driving the team. Probably one of the town's fine specimen of a man.

"Don't give up, Shannon. Trust that God has a purpose for bringing you here. He doesn't make mistakes. It took me a long time to learn that lesson." She flashed a smile and hurried from the room, as if she'd just uttered a speech she'd been building up to give.

Shannon laid her head back and stared up at the ornamental plaster design in the ceiling. Could Rachel be right? Had God merely used her supposed marriage to Luke to bring her to town for another purpose? It had been so long since she'd believed that God cared for her. Nothing but bad had happened since she came to America, and she'd spent the past few days since the storm dwelling on those things. Believing God had guided her steps and brought her to Lookout for some grand purpose was too mind-boggling to consider. Why would He care about her?

She shook her head and tried moving her foot. Her ankle didn't hurt as much as it had. Sitting up, she rearranged her skirts and tried putting some weight on her foot. A sharp stab made her suck in a breath. She grabbed the side pillow and smacked it against the settee. She'd do about anything to feel useful and to get her mind off her troubles. Leaning back down, she lifted her foot onto the pillows that had kept it elevated.

What she needed to do was figure out where she'd go when she left Lookout. There were a myriad of tiny towns like Lookout in Texas, but did she want to stay in the state? At least it was somewhat familiar now.

One thing she knew was that she had no desire to return to Louisiana. Only bad things had happened to her there. Maybe she'd go to Dallas. She'd heard it was a big city and would surely have opportunities for employment for a woman.

Her hand ran over the edge of the letter. It wasn't finished and probably never would be, for she'd lost the desire to complete it. Hasty footsteps sounded on the front porch, but where she lay, she couldn't see the visitor. A quick knock sounded, and the door opened.

"Rachel? Luke?"

'Twas one of the Corbett brothers, but she couldn't tell which from the sound of his voice. She scowled, not wanting to see Mark. What could she say to him? She felt a clod for being the cause of his broken wrist. If he hadn't come to her aid, he'd still be fine and not suffering, but she might well be dead.

"Hello?" Garrett stopped in the parlor doorway, and Shannon held her breath, hoping he wouldn't notice her. He looked down the hall, up the stairs, and turned his head. His eyes sparked when he saw her. He tipped his hat and grinned like a rogue. "Just the person I wanted to see."

Shannon sat up straighter, combed a loose strand of hair behind her ear, and peeked at her skirt to make sure it covered her ankles. Why would he be wantin' her? Would he expect her to pay the doctor's fee for setting Mark's arm? He'd be sorely disappointed, for she had not a penny in her handbag.

"Morning, Miss O'Neil." He approached, still grinning and his sky blue eyes twinkling.

"'Tis a fine day, Mr. Corbett." She nodded, fearing the man was up to no good. Having been on the short end of his interfering with other people's lives, she was wary of him. 'Twouldn't happen again.

"Indeed, it is."

Rachel entered the room, wiping her hands on the bottom of her apron. "Garrett, what brings you here today? Luke's out somewhere doing his rounds."

"I don't need him anyhow. Came to talk to Miss O'Neil, here."

Rachel's brows lifted, and she made no effort to hide her surprise. "All right. Can I fetch something for you to drink?"

"No, thanks. I'm fine. Just had my last cup of coffee for the morning." He shifted from foot to foot and fiddled with the hat in his hand.

Rachel's gaze darted to Shannon. "Would you. . .uh. . .like me to stay?"

Garrett chuckled aloud. "No need. You know I'm a perfect gentleman."

Rachel's brows dashed clear up under the edge of the scarf that held her long, brown hair away from her face before they dropped back down. "I'm not so sure about that, Garrett. You're a rascal and a prankster."

Garrett's smile grew even wider, as if she'd offered him the greatest of compliments. "True, but I'm always nice to the ladies."

Shaking her head, a bemused smile wrinkled her lips. She looked at Shannon. "Would you like me to stay?"

Part of her wanted to say aye, but she didn't fear this man, in spite of all the trouble he'd caused her. "Nay, I'll be fine. If he bothers me, I'll conk him on the head with your lamp."

Rachel splayed her hand across her chest, her eyes dancing with mirth. "Oh, not my new lamp. Please. Use that footstool down there beside the settee. It's made of walnut and sturdy enough not to break against Garrett's hard head."

A wounded look crossed Garrett's face. "Ladies, please. I've simply come to do business with Miss O'Neil. I promise her virtue—and everything else—is safe."

"All right then. I suppose I'll go back to my kitchen. But if you need me, Shannon, just holler." Rachel left the room, casting a curious glance back over her shoulder at Garrett.

He grabbed a side chair and pulled it closer to Shannon. Even though she'd told Rachel not to stay, not knowing what Mr. Corbett wanted made her apprehensive. What business could he possibly have with her?

He placed his arms on his legs and leaned forward until his face was just three feet from hers. His startling blue eyes were the exact same shade as his brother's. His straight hair was a wee bit darker than Mark's curly blond hair, and though they looked similar, there was something about Mark that appealed to her. Something that wasn't affected by Garrett's presence.

"How's your leg? Better? Can you walk yet?" He fired questions like a shooter fired bullets.

" 'Tis somewhat better, but I cannot put much weight on it yet."

"Hmm. . .we can work around that." He stared into her eyes. "The reason I'm here is that I want to offer you a position of employment at Corbetts' Freight Office."

CHAPTER 5

Leah trotted downstairs to the lower floor of the boardinghouse. She simply had to find something to do or she'd go batty. As she reached the final step, she heard voices coming from the parlor. Slowing her steps, she glanced in as she reached the doorway. Shannon sat on one of the settees with her feet lying across the cushion. Her shoes were off, and one ankle had been wrapped in a bandage.

Garrett Corbett had moved one of the side chairs closer to the settee so that he could sit facing Shannon. What could he want with her? Maybe he was just checking up on her since his brother had been partially to blame for her injury. She longed to listen, but Garrett was speaking in such a low tone, and she knew eavesdropping was rude, so Leah forced her feet to keep moving.

She found Rachel in the kitchen, where the woman spent a large portion of her day. Leah knew what slaving over a hot stove for hours at a time felt like. Hadn't she cooked hundreds of meals for her family? At times she missed her parents and brothers and sisters, but she wouldn't return home for all the pecan pie in Missouri—and there was plenty, to be sure. She'd worked from before sunup to well after dark and never seemed to catch up. Her mother's health was poor from bearing so many children, and Leah felt guilty at times for abandoning her, but her twin sisters were old enough to help out, and it would cause the girls to grow up.

Leah leaned on the door frame. Besides, if she'd stayed at home, by now she'd probably be married to old Mr. Abernathy and wouldn't be helping her ma anyway.

"Oh, Leah. I didn't see you standing there." Rachel rested her floured hand over her chest. "Do you need something?"

Leah straightened. "Sorry, I just got caught up thinking about home."

Rachel returned to braiding the lattice top of her apple pie. "Do you miss it?"

Leah pressed her lips together for a moment, fighting a smile. Rachel had an almost perfect handprint on her chest from the flour. Once she regained her composure, she nodded. "Sometimes I do."

"But not enough to return home?"

She shook her head. "No."

"Might I ask why?" Rachel paused, holding a strip of dough in the air.

What could she say that didn't make her sound selfish? That she didn't want to care for her siblings all the time but rather wanted a life of her own? That she couldn't marry the man who all but purchased her from her father? That she'd wanted an adventure before settling down to marry?

Leah fought back a snort. Well, she'd certainly gotten that, hadn't she?

She looked at Rachel, who still watched her. "I suppose it mostly comes down to the fact that I couldn't marry the man my father wanted me to."

Rachel's eyes widened. "You were betrothed?"

"No, not betrothed." She pressed her lips together and cocked her mouth up on one side. What did it matter if Rachel knew? She wasn't the kind of person to tell everyone. "There was an older man in town, one with a goodly amount of money, I'm told. He offered my father a sum of money to marry me, and my pa accepted."

Rachel's mouth opened and closed, reminding Leah of a fish. "Your father sold you? I can't imagine how awful that must have felt."

Leah shrugged, not wanting to reveal the depth of her pain and betrayal. After working herself half to death, not socializing as young girls her age did because of her responsibilities, nearly raising her siblings because her ma had taken to her bed so often, her pa showed his gratitude by selling her. It sounded so much worse when someone said it out loud. "I might have gone along with it if the man hadn't been nearly as old as my pa and rather creepy. He gave me the shivers."

"I'm sure." Rachel wiped her hand on a towel and crossed the room. She laid her hand on Leah's shoulder. "I know it must be uncomfortable at times for you and Shannon to live here with Luke and me, but you're welcome for as long as you need to stay."

Leah offered a weak smile, grateful for Rachel's hospitality and compassion. "I'm much obliged for that. I'm not sure what I'll do. I just know I don't want to go back home."

Rachel nodded. "Would you like to sit down and have some tea?"

Leah glanced past her to scan the kitchen. Rachel tended to keep things tidy as she worked, so it didn't look as if there was much to do here to help her. Other than the area where she was making pies, the only thing out of place that Leah saw was a jar of what looked liked last night's stew. "I was actually hoping you might have some work I could help you with. I'm sick to death of doing nothing."

Rachel turned and looked around the room. "Um. . .well. . .I feel odd asking a guest to help me."

"You didn't ask; I volunteered."

Smiling, Rachel nodded. "I suppose that's true. Well, I was going to take a basket to Mrs. Howard, but you could do that if you wouldn't mind."

"Sure, I'd be happy to. It would give me a reason to go outside and take a walk."

"Clara's been ailing for a while. Her son takes good care of her, but he works hard, and I like to help them out with a meal now and then." Rachel opened her pantry door, rummaged around for a minute, and pulled out a basket and a bowl covered with a towel. "She's Dan Howard's mother. Do you know Dan? He runs the livery."

Leah felt her cheeks flush at the name of the man who'd rescued her from the ditch after the storm. She was grateful that Rachel didn't look up and was busy packing the basket.

"You'll like Clara. She's a real sweetheart, but she doesn't get out much anymore. I know caring for her is a weight on Dan's shoulders, but he's a good son and does what he can. Don't know that he's much of a cook, though." Rachel tossed a grin over her shoulder. "Clara is always so thankful when I bring food."

A few minutes later, with directions to the Howard home, Leah walked out the kitchen door and around the side of the boardinghouse. On her right was a house known around town as the Sunday house. It was a small structure with a roof that slanted down in the back like a lean-to. She'd gone there once to deliver a meal to the marshal and had seen the inside. One big room was used as a parlor, except it also had a table and chairs. In the back of the room where the roof slanted down was the bed. What would happen to the house now that the marshal was living at the boardinghouse with his new wife?

It would be the perfect place for her to set up a home, if only it had a kitchen and stove. But she had no means of making money to pay rent. She shook her head. No sense dreaming such foolish dreams as living on her own.

She crossed Bluebonnet Lane and stared at the pile of rubbish that had been the mercantile. People had been working to clean up the mess since the storm, but there was still a ways to go. How would the town survive without it? What a shame.

Two men she didn't recognize, who were working on the edge of the property closest to her, straightened and then tipped their hats. She nodded and smiled but continued walking. As she walked down Oak Street, she noticed that the Foster home, which had sat right behind the destroyed mercantile, was also severely damaged. A tent had been set up behind in the back yard behind where the house had sat. Were the Fosters living there? Or maybe they were keeping the stock they'd salvaged in it. Those poor people. How would they ever manage to rebuild after this devastating loss?

She shifted the basket to her other arm and counted houses until she found the Howards' home. The house looked well maintained, with a fresh coat of pale yellow paint and white trim on the woodwork. The lace curtains were closed, though. Could Mrs. Howard be resting, even though it was midmorning? What if she was asleep?

Leah hated bothering the woman if that was the case. She looked past the house to the livery and nibbled her lower lip. Perhaps she should ask Mr. Howard if it was all right to visit his mother. Besides, it would give her a chance to see him in his workplace.

She continued walking and stopped at the side entrance of the livery. Her eyes took a moment to adjust to the dim interior. The placed smelled of hay and horses and reminded her of her pa's barn. Six stalls ran down one side of the gray, weathered building, three of which contained horses.

She found Dan at the front of the building unloading a wagon filled with large burlap bags with another man's help. Dust motes drifted lazily on fingers of sunlight that stretched into the livery, attempting to drive back the shadows. Dan hoisted a heavy-looking bag over one shoulder and toted it to an empty stall, where he dropped it. The other man did the same but seemed to have a harder time lifting and carrying the large sacks. As Dan reached for another bag, the back of his shirt pulled tight across his shoulders, making Leah's mouth dry. Muscles flexed in his tanned forearms, made visible by his rolled-up sleeves. Dan was the tallest man in town, so far as she knew, and though he was wide-shouldered, he didn't look to have an ounce of fat on him. Perhaps she shouldn't be too hasty in ruling out Dan Howard as husband material. He had come to her rescue, after all.

She stepped farther into the livery, and when Dan's gaze landed on her, he stopped suddenly without acknowledging her. He stared for a moment, then turned and dropped the bag he'd been carrying. He strode across the livery to a bucket and tossed water on his face, arms, and hands, then dried off on a towel. He ran his hand through his brown hair and turned to face her as he rolled down one sleeve.

"What can I help you with, ma'am?" His gaze ran down her length, then back up, not in a leering way like Mr. Abernathy's but as if she was someone he cherished. She swallowed hard.

"I. . .uh. . .Mrs. Hamil—I mean Mrs. Davis sent over some soup and other things for you and your ma's dinner. I noticed her curtains were closed and wondered if I should knock on the door or just leave the food out on the porch. Of course, I'd hate for a stray dog to get into it, so I came over here to see if you thought your ma would be awake." Leah clamped her mouth shut. She was rambling more than the ivy running up the side of the town's only bank.

"It's near lunchtime. Give me a few minutes to tally up with Stephen, and I can walk over to the house with you."

Leah nodded. She wasn't sure if she wanted his company, but she'd best get used to the idea. At least she'd have a chance to get to know him better. But was that what she really wanted?

Yes, he'd been kind to her, but, no, he didn't fit her idea of the perfect husband. At least Dan should be a good protector, built like he was. She waited several minutes until he paid the man who'd brought the sacks, and then Dan Howard walked toward her, his near-black eyes capturing hers as he moved lithe and steady in her direction. "I'll carry that for you, ma'am."

She handed over the basket and tried to swallow, but it felt as if she had a biscuit stuck in her throat. Goodness.

She peeked at him as they fell into step together, walking toward his house. She liked how it felt to walk next to a man and could almost pretend he belonged to her. He stood a solid eight inches taller that she, and with his hat back on, even more. His long, brown hair was pulled back and tied with a leather strand. Though only near noontime, his beard had already started growing back in. She guessed his age to be somewhere around the midtwenties.

She stumbled on a rock, taking several quick steps to keep from falling, and his hand shot out, gently clutching her arm and stabilizing her. Heat stormed to her face. If she hadn't been gawking at him, she wouldn't have missed a step. "I, uh, thank you for assisting me."

His lips turned up on one side. "My pleasure."

At the porch steps, he handed her up, then followed. With him on the covered entryway with her, the area seemed to shrink in size. Dan opened the door, and stood back, allowing her to enter first. His steady gaze made her squirm, and she broke eye contact and stepped into the dim parlor. Heat slapped her in the face, and she wondered if a fire was burning in the stove.

Dan entered behind her leaving the door open. He went straight to the front window and lifted it open. The lacy curtains fluttered on the light breeze. "Sorry about it being so hot in here. When Ma has one of her spells, she keeps things closed up." He shook his head, walked through the dining room and into the kitchen, and opened the back door.

Dan set the basket on the kitchen worktable. "I'll check on Ma and be right back. Have a seat if you'd like."

"Don't make her get up on my account," Leah called as he

disappeared around a corner. She looked around the Howard home. In the parlor, a sofa and two wingback chairs faced the fireplace. Though the furniture looked old, the room was tidy. Against one wall was a table covered in harnesses, bridles, and tools she didn't recognize. A dining table and hutch resided in the next room, which sported faded floral wallpaper. The house smelled musty, with the lingering scent of leather polish. Leah tugged at her collar as sweat trickled down her chest. How could Mrs. Howard stand this heat? And if she was so ill, how did she manage to keep her house clean?

A rustling sounded just before Mrs. Howard shuffled into the room with Dan close on her heels. A wide smile graced the woman's wrinkled cheeks. "Welcome, my dear. I'm so glad you could visit."

Leah pulled out a chair at the table, and Dan helped his mother to sit. "I'm happy to make your acquaintance, Mrs. Howard."

"Sit down, dear. Dan doesn't mind fixing the food, do you, sweetie."

Leah glanced up at Dan. She hadn't planned on staying to eat and preferred to leave the food and go, but she didn't want to disappoint this kind woman. Dan shook his head and turned to go in the kitchen. She leaned toward Mrs. Howard. "Excuse me for a moment, if you would."

Leah followed Dan into the large kitchen, and he turned around, surprised to see her. "Let me do this, and you go sit down."

His thick brows lifted. "That wouldn't be proper. You're our guest."

Leah shook her head. "Nonsense. I came to help. Show me where the bowls are and then go visit with your ma."

He opened a cabinet and pointed at the bowls, as if she hadn't seen them. He rubbed the back of his neck, obviously uncomfortable with her serving him. She strode past him and reached for the bowls at the same time he did. His hand landed over hers. She lifted her gaze to his, and her heart stampeded.

For a moment neither moved. His calloused hand warmed hers, and ever so slowly, he drew back, trailing his fingers over hers. All breath left her lungs until he stepped back. Her hand trembled as she took the bowls off the shelf.

Dan leaned back against the cabinet, his gaze watching her every move. What had just happened? She'd only ever been attracted to one other man—and Sam Braddock had been just a boy compared to Dan. Sam. How long had it been since she'd thought of her first love?

She busied herself so she could forget both Sam and Dan. "Do you have a ladle?"

Leah removed the jar of stew from the basket and unscrewed the lid, sending a savory fragrance into the air. Footsteps sounded behind her, and a ladle appeared over her shoulder. All she had to do was turn around, and she'd be in Dan's arms. She kept her feet from moving a speck and snared the ladle. "Thank you."

"Smells good," Dan's voice rumbled behind her, and her hand shook a little more.

"Do you. . .uh. . .have something to drink? For dinner, I mean?"

He stepped up next to her and grabbed a pitcher from the corner. "I'll fetch some water."

Leah finally caught a decent breath once he left the room. What was wrong with her? She was acting like a lovesick schoolgirl. She was acting like her twin sisters did over a cute boy.

Forcing her mind back on business, she ladled the stew into two bowls and carried them into the dining room. Mrs. Howard smiled again, and her faded eyes twinkled.

"Dan's a good son. He takes better care of me than most men would for their old mother."

Leah set a bowl in front of the woman and placed the second bowl on her right. "It's good that you have him then."

Mrs. Howard nodded. "Don't know what I'd do without him."

Leah returned to the kitchen and rummaged around until she

found the silverware and some napkins. She folded the fabric and laid the silverware on top.

"But there's only two place settings. Where's yours, dear?" Mrs. Howard looked up with such a hopeful gaze that Leah hated hurting her feelings.

"Mrs. Davis is expecting me for dinner at the boardinghouse, but thank you for asking." She hurried back into the kitchen and placed the biscuits on a plate and then sliced some of the cheese that Rachel had sent.

Dan stepped back through the open door, his face and hair dripping wet, just like the tin pitcher. He held it up. "Got the water, and it's fairly cool."

Leah smiled at his exuberance. She couldn't imagine her own pa doing something so menial as fetching water. "That should taste good on a warm day like today."

He nodded and placed his fingertips in the top of three glasses and carried them into the dining room. In a half second, he stormed back to the kitchen. "Where's your bowl?"

Leah opened her mouth, prepared to explain again, but stopped. Rachel would probably figure out that she'd stayed and eaten with the Howards if she didn't return for the noon meal. Why not stay and learn more about the Howards and maybe even brighten an old woman's day? "I didn't get one, but I will now. Thank you for inviting me."

A few minutes later, they all settled down to eat. Mrs. Howard's eyes watched Leah and continued to sparkle as she nibbled her stew. Was the woman always so friendly?

"Tell us about yourself, dear."

Leah winced. She dreaded talking of her family. She dabbed her lips with the napkin and sipped some water before answering. "I lived on a farm in Missouri with my parents and brothers and sisters before coming here."

"We lived on a farm—before my Owen died. I'd always hoped for a big family, but Dan is my only child to survive. Do you have many siblings?" Mrs. Howard broke off a piece of biscuit and stuck it in her mouth.

Leah peeked at Dan. He shoveled his food in as if he hadn't eaten in weeks. He caught her watching and winked. Leah yanked her gaze back to Mrs. Howard and realized the woman had seen their exchange. "I come from a big family—eleven children at last count."

Dan dropped his spoon, but his mother's smile widened. "How wonderful. And where do you fit in that lineage?"

"I'm the oldest."

"Ahh. . .no wonder you came here."

Leah hastened eating her stew and stuffed the last bite into her mouth. She needed to leave before this woman had her married off to her son. Leah stood, and Dan hopped up. "Please, keep your seat. I'll just refill your bowl and then wash the dishes."

"Nonsense, Dan can do those."

Leah waved her hand at Mrs. Howard. "I don't mind. In fact, I'd like to help you, and that's the best thing I know to do."

Mrs. Howard leaned toward her son and mumbled something that Leah was certain sounded like, "She's a keeper, son."

Grabbing the bucket sitting by the back door, Leah charged outside. She pumped water as fast as she could. She couldn't help thinking about Dan. She liked him—a lot. He had a nice home, a healthy business—or so it seemed—and he was fine to look at. Yes, sir, she definitely needed to reconsider him as husband material.

CHAPTER 6

Mark slammed his book shut and muttered a frustrated sigh. Reading while riding in the wagon on a good day was difficult, but trying to hold the book steady with one hand just didn't work. His shoulder banged into his brother's as the creaking wagon dipped into a deep rut and then careened back out.

"Is that another one of those law books you're always reading?" Garrett glanced sideways. "Sure sounds like boring stuff to me."

"Yes, it's a law book, and no, I'm not reading. Can't hold it steady enough."

"What do you find in there that's so fascinating? I picked up one of those fat books and read a few paragraphs and found it more boring than looking at a wood wall all day." Garrett shook his head.

"It's just interesting to me. I can't explain it." Mark studied the rolling hills dotted with wildflowers. The tornado may have torn up the town some, but the heavy rains it brought had caused the grass to green up and wildflowers to bloom again. The sky was a brilliant blue with a few white, puffy clouds drifting by.

What would Garrett say if Mark told him that he was thinking about quitting the freight business and hanging out his shingle as a lawyer? He'd probably starve to death in Lookout. No, if he were to become a lawyer, he'd need to move to a bigger town like Dallas.

Mark rubbed his jaw. He'd left Lookout once before, and the situation couldn't have ended any worse.

"I've got a surprise for you."

Mark's gaze shot back toward his brother. The hair on his nape stood up. A surprise from Garrett could mean anything from sand burrs in your underwear to oiled front-porch steps. He nearly broke his neck the day he stepped on those and his foot flew out from under him. Then there was the time when they were still boys and Garrett hitched the wagon and handed the reins to Mark. When he slapped the reins on the horses' backs, instead of the wagon moving forward, Mark was yanked to the ground and dragged halfway across the county because Garrett hadn't hitched the harnesses up right. Narrowing his eyes, he glanced sideways at his brother. "What kind of surprise?"

Garrett grinned wide. "Guess you'll just have to wait till we get back home to find out."

His curiosity rising, he nudged his brother's arm with his elbow. "Go on, tell me what it is."

"Nope. Not gonna do it."

Great. Mark scowled. Now his imagination would run faster than a stampeding herd of cattle in a thunderstorm. What if his brother ordered *him* a bride, but no, he wouldn't do that again. Mark peeked sideways. Would he?

He adjusted the brim of his hat to keep the sun's glare from reaching his eyes. No, Garrett wouldn't order more brides when they were already supporting two. "You know, it's costing us a pretty penny to pay room and board for those two brides."

Garrett nodded. "Don't I know it. I guess we should be grateful things turned out like they did, and that third bride ended up going to jail."

He remembered how Carly Payton, a member of an outlaw gang, had pretended to be Ellie Blackstone, the third bride who came to Lookout to marry Luke. Carly was a pretty thing with her black hair and deep blue eyes, but she had a roughness to her. She was in prison now, and the real Ellie Blackstone had returned home with her brother. "I heard Rachel say she was writing to that outlaw bride."

"Yeah, that's what Luke said. If anyone can help her change her ways, it's Rachel."

"Yeah." Mark swatted at a mosquito on his hand. "Luke sure seems happy these days."

"Marriage agrees with him."

"You ever think of marrying up?"

Garrett grimaced but kept his gaze on the road ahead. "Yeah, sure. But I've never met a gal that interested me enough that I wanted to make a lifetime commitment to her. What about you?"

Mark thoughts raced straight to Annabelle. At one time he thought he'd die if she didn't become his wife. But he wasn't the one who had died. He gritted his teeth. What a disaster that whole situation had been. Since then, he hadn't trusted himself around women and had kept his distance. "No, I don't reckon I'll ever marry."

Garrett fired a surprised look in his direction. "Why not? Don't you want kids of your own? We've got a solid business, and you could support a family now—at least if we don't have to pay for those brides much longer."

Mark didn't answer. He couldn't tell his brother what had happened back in Abilene. All his life he'd wanted Garrett's approval, just like he'd want his father's, before their pa lost his business and became a drunk. But Mark never seemed to measure up to his pa's expectations. He liked to read, and his ma had encouraged it while she was alive, but Pa wanted him to work more, like a man, rather than spend his time with book learning. His pa couldn't read and didn't understand how a book could take you to a time and place you could never travel to yourself. In a book, Mark had explored the Alaskan wilderness, traveled on a ship to Europe, and fought pirates and rescued royalty and—damsels in distress. His thoughts returned to Miss Bennett and Miss O'Neil. Both were more or less stranded in Texas thanks to him and his brother. Who would rescue them?

"We've got to do something about those brides." Garrett successfully yanked Mark right out of his musings.

"Such as?" Mark asked.

"We need to find them work or else someone to marry."

Mark held up his good hand. "Just hold on. You aren't concocting another one of your schemes, are you?"

Garrett held a hand to his chest. "You wound me."

"No, I just know you."

"I've been thinking on the situation, and what would it hurt to talk to some of our customers and see if any of them are looking to marry?"

"It could hurt a lot. We might lose all our customers."

"Stop being so cynical. We'll just ask around, and if we find someone wanting to marry, we can tell them about Miss Bennett and Miss O'Neil."

Mark leaned back in his seat and tugged his hat down farther. "No thanks. I'm not stepping in that pile of manure."

"You're making a mountain out of a molehill. I'll do the asking if you're not at ease doing it."

"Fine. You do that." Mark tried to get comfortable. He wasn't even sure why he'd come along since he couldn't load or unload anything unless it was something small. It wasn't likely they would get robbed since they were just hauling wood and building supplies for the new store and a few smaller crates for local ranchers, but you never knew when someone with a gun would show up. Even if he couldn't shoot, having two men together might steer away some thieves.

Mark listened to the jingle of the harnesses and the peaceful plodding of the horses' hooves. A light breeze stirred the hot air, cooling him a bit. He thought about the book he'd been reading. For years, he'd consumed law books. He felt ready to set up shop as an attorney, but somehow he had to find a way to tell his brother. And he had to consider leaving Lookout again. He could only hope and pray this time would turn out far better than the last.

A buzzing intruded into Mark's dreams, and he jumped, swatting a fly away from his ear. His blurry gaze sharpened, and he saw Garrett standing on Flip Anderson's porch.

"It's like I said, both those women thought they'd marry the marshal, but we all know that didn't happen."

Flip yanked off his hat and rolled the brim. The tall, thin rancher sported a moustache nearly as wide as his face. "Yeah, I kinda felt sorry for them gals. So ya think they're willing to marry someone else?"

Mark narrowed his eyes and glared at his brother. What was Garrett doing? He climbed off the wagon and stretched the kinks from his body, then ambled toward the porch. A dipper of cool water would taste good about now.

Flip nodded. "Mark, good to see ya."

"You, too. Mind if I grab a drink from your well?" Mark smiled at Flip, then cast a warning glance at Garrett.

"Help yerself. I just hauled up a fresh bucketful." He pointed across the yard to the well, as if Mark hadn't already spotted it.

The screen door creaked, and Flip's mother, Lucy Anderson, walked out carrying a tray covered in cookies, cups, and a coffeepot. Mark swung around and headed back to the porch.

"Mornin', boys. Come have a sit-down and take some refreshment." Mrs. Anderson set the tray on the porch table and started pouring coffee. After serving the men, she poured herself a cup and sat down. "I heard you talkin' about them gals. I sure wish that my Flip could marry one of 'em."

Flip turned beet red and seemed to be studying the porch floor as if something was wrong with it.

Garrett chuckled. "Well, maybe we need to figure out a way to get him together with them so they can meet face-to-face."

Lucy stared out toward the pasture, where several dozen head of short horn cattle grazed. "Hmm...I could invite them leftover brides out here for dinner. Maybe one of 'em would take a shinin' to my Flip."

"Ma, that don't hardly seem proper, inviting two unmarried women clear out here."

"And one of them has a twisted ankle. She hurt it during the storm." Mark wasn't sure why he'd come to the boardinghouse brides' defense, but it didn't seem right that everyone was talking about them.

"Yeah, it'd be better if you went to town, Flip. Maybe what you boys need is to have a shindig of some kind so's the local bachelors could meet them gals." Lucy helped herself to another sugar cookie. The older woman's faded blue eyes twinkled. "I'd sure like to see my Flip married before my foot's in the grave."

Flip's head jerked toward his mother. "Don't talk like that, Ma."

"I'd just like to know someone was taking care of you after I'm gone, that's all. And I'd sure like to see my grandkids."

Flip jumped up so fast the coffee cups rattled. "I reckon I ought to head back to the barn. Got a horse with the colic. Need to keep my eye on her."

Mark held back a chuckle. Seems like he wasn't the only man who didn't want folks matchmaking him.

They said their good-byes and returned to the wagon. Mark climbed up beside his brother, well aware that the wheels were churning in Garrett's mind. "What are you thinking?"

Garrett slapped the reins down on the horses' backs and yelled, "Heeyup!"

The wagon lurched forward, groaning and creaking. Once back on the main road, Garrett leaned his elbows on his knees, allowing the reins to dangle in his fingers. "I've been ruminating on some ideas."

Mark's stomach clenched. What was Garrett up to now? Whatever it was, he wanted no part of it.

"What do you think about starting up a social on Saturdays? Have some ladies fix food, have some music and dancing?"

"Why?" Mark's voice rose higher than intended.

Garrett's gaze darted in his direction. "So we can get those gals married off. That's why."

Mark leaned back and crossed his arms, shaking his head. It might sound like a half-decent plan, but something was sure to go wrong. "That's a bad idea, brother. You best leave well enough alone."

"Nope, I think it's a great idea. We'll get unmarried men to come, and sooner or later, someone's bound to catch the eyes of them gals."

"Have you considered that it will cost money to hire musicians? And you can't expect the women to come and bring food for free all the time. If you did something like that, you'd need to hire Polly to cook, most likely. Besides, there are dozens of unmarried men, and just those two gals. Doesn't sound like much fun for either side."

"Hmm. . ." Garrett rubbed his chin with his thumb and forefinger. "You're probably right about the food. But the single men around here are desperate. They won't care if they only get one dance with a pretty gal, but maybe we could invite folks from other nearby towns and ranches. Maybe some of the ranchers will bring their older daughters. You're right. We'll need more than the two boardinghouse brides for the men to dance with."

"I'm warning you. This is a bad idea."

"Aw, stop your fretting." Garrett glanced at him and grinned wickedly. "Don't forget about your surprise."

Mark heaved a sigh, and his mind raced. He had forgotten, and from the look in his brother's eyes, he had a feeling he wouldn't like this surprise much.

Shannon practiced walking around the parlor using a crutch the marshal had borrowed from the doctor's office. The long branch had a nub halfway down where her hand rested, and though the V under her armpit had been wrapped with fabric, she still found it uncomfortable. But if she was going to work at the freight office, she had to get mobile.

Her skirt snagged against the long stick, making forward progress difficult and throwing her off balance. A chuckle sounded behind her, and she took several small steps in a half circle until she was facing the other direction.

Rachel smacked her husband on the arm. "Don't you dare laugh at her."

The marshal pressed his lips together for a moment. "Sorry, but I think that crutch is too long."

"Well, cut it down to fit her." Rachel glared at Luke playfully with her hands on her hips.

He shook his head. "I can't. It belongs to Doc Phillips."

"Well, I don't see how Shannon will manage that bumpy street when she can barely get around the parlor."

Shannon stared at the newlywed couple. Rachel looked pretty clothed in her brown work dress with tiny yellow sunflowers on it. A fresh apron covered the garment, and her long brown braid fell down over her shoulder, hanging clear past her waist. Dressed in black pants and a medium blue shirt, Luke stood next to her, staring down at the stick that held Shannon upright.

Truth be told, she didn't like the crutch, but the marshal had been so nice to fetch it for her that she hated to say so. She tried again and managed three steps before she lost her balance. She reached for a nearby table and missed.

"Oh!" Rachel squealed.

Shannon's hand brushed the arm of the settee, but she missed it, too, and landed on the floor. Pain clutched her ankle and hand, but it was nothing compared to when she first injured her leg. She tried to push up from the floor, but her long skirts had wrapped around her legs, and she was stuck between the settee and coffee table legs.

How humiliating!

Hurried footsteps sounded behind her, and she closed her eyes. Could things get any worse?

"Are you all right?" Rachel leaned toward Shannon's face.

"Aye, but I do feel quite foolish."

"Do you mind if Luke helps you up?"

Shannon shook her head. "I'm tangled in my skirts."

A quick knock sounded, and Shannon peeked through the table legs. Garrett Corbett strode in. "Mornin', folks."

Heat raced up Shannon's cheeks. What would her new boss think?

His eyes widened, and he hurried forward to help Luke assist her up. Back on the settee, she rearranged her skirts and avoided looking at anyone. Would they all think her a clumsy fool?

Rachel picked up the crutch. "Shannon was trying this out to see if she could walk with it."

Garrett grinned. "Uh, let me guess. It didn't work."

Luke stood beside him chuckling, and Rachel glared at her husband.

Garrett forced a straight face. "Have no fear, I brought the wagon."

Warmth flooded Shannon's cheeks again. He didn't even think she could walk a few hundred feet. She thought about the crutch again. Well, perhaps he was right. But if she couldn't walk that far and rode the wagon to work, she'd be stuck at the freight office, dependent on the Corbett brothers—and that was the last place she wanted to be. Wasn't that why she'd accepted the position of employment in the first place? So that she could support herself instead of relying on them?

"Maybe she should wait a few more days before starting work," Rachel said.

Three sets of eyes fell on Shannon, and she resisted the urge to squirm. She'd already lost almost two nights' sleep worrying over working with Mark Corbett. If she didn't start today, she'd only worry more. "Nay, I'll ride in the wagon."

"Are you sure?" The concerned look in Rachel's eyes warmed her. Made her feel as if someone cared about her.

"Aye."

"Great. Then let's go." Garrett strode toward her and swooped her up without asking permission.

Shannon wrapped her arm around his neck and sat up stiffly. These Americans were uncouth and did as they pleased without so much as a by-your-leave. She thought back to being in Mark's arms when they were running from the storm. She'd actually liked him carrying her. Liked being close to him. Then why was she so nervous about working in the same office?

Garrett helped her up to the wagon seat, and she climbed aboard and sat down. Rachel reached up her hand and laid it on Shannon's arm while Garrett walked around the front of the wagon. "I'll come down in an hour or so and make sure things are all right."

"That's not necessary, but I thank you. I'm sure I will be fine."

"It's no trouble at all." Rachel smiled, winked, and stepped back. "Don't let those yahoos boss you around too much."

Shannon finally smiled. "I won't."

"Hold on." Garrett lifted the reins and smacked them down on the horses' backs. "Heeyah!"

The wagon lurched forward and then settled. Shannon held tight to the side and gazed at the remains of the store. Boards that were long enough to be reused had been stacked along the property line. A half-dozen men and women were sorting through the last of the rubble. " 'Tis a sad sight."

Garrett looked to his left and nodded. "Mark and I brought in a load of lumber from Dallas yesterday. Got another couple of trips to make, and then there will be a store raisin'."

"I've never heard of such a thing."

"It's just like a barn raisin' except we're building a store. Since it's the only one in town, we need it to survive, so everyone's chipping in to help."

They passed the remains of the Fosters' home, and Shannon wished there was something she could do to help the older couple. A man tossed a bucket of water into the dirt road, and one of Garrett's horses jerked his head up and snorted. The wagon creaked down Bluebonnet Lane, then veered left onto Oak Street. They passed a number of houses before reaching the end of the road, where they made two quick left turns and ended up on Main Street. The boardinghouse rose up in front of her at the far end of the street. It surely was a lovely building with its soft green color and white trim. The porch practically begged people to stop and sit in the matching white rockers. Perhaps later she could do that very thing, but now she had to concentrate on learning her new job.

"Whoaaa." Garrett pulled the wagon to a stop and set the brake. He hopped down, patted each horse on the forehead, and muttered something before coming around to help her down.

Shannon's stomach swirled. She'd never worked in an office before. Aye, she could keep it clean and tidy once her ankle healed, but Garrett had said something about helping Mark with the recordkeeping. How would she know what to do? Was Mark even agreeable to teaching her or letting her work with him?

Surely if he'd not been, Garrett wouldn't have hired her. Yet she had a hard time believing Mark would assent. Even though he'd come to her rescue during the storm, he didn't seem to favor her for some reason.

Garrett lifted her down and held her steady. "Guess I should haul you on inside."

Balancing her weight mostly on her good leg, she broke from his gaze and looked around. The marshal had left the boardinghouse and now stood outside his office, talking to several men. Two ladies exited Dolly's Dress Shop and walked toward them, talking and laughing.

"Perhaps you could walk on my weak side and offer support." She eyed the women, who'd suddenly taken note of her and Garrett.

"Mornin', Mrs. Mann. Mrs. Jenkins." Garrett tipped his hat to them. "Nice day, isn't it?"

Both women smiled at the handsome rogue, then turned suspicious glances in Shannon's direction. Fortunately, they continued on past the newspaper office and turned in to the bank.

"Curious ol' biddies. You know they're just fit to be tied wondering why you're here with me."

Shannon's mouth turned up in a grin. Aye, she could imagine. She knew the two ladies were quite the busybodies, from their visits with Rachel at the boardinghouse.

"Shall we?" Garrett's brow lifted.

Shannon gently put weight on her twisted ankle and grimaced, not so much from the pain but from the fear that it would hurt. Garrett wasted no time, and hauled her up in his arms. He grunted as he carried her up the stairs from the street to the boardwalk, and Shannon was sure she'd never regain her dignity.

Garrett fumbled with the door handle, then shoved it open, and stepped into the freight office. She glanced around and noticed right off that one desk was immaculate while the other was quite the mess. The tidy one had to be Mark's. He always took time to dress nicely and combed his hair, whereas Garrett seemed like a ragamuffin, with his mussed hair and his clothing often wrinkled.

Mark entered from a side room. His eyes went wide, and his mouth dropped open. Shannon realized Garrett still held her.

Mark's gaze narrowed as he took in his brother holding her. "Please tell me you didn't run off and marry *her*."

CHAPTER 7

Jack baited her hook, tossed it into the water, then sat back against a tree and waited for a bite. She plucked a strand of grass and leaned to her left, where her good friend Jonesy had fallen asleep in the warmth of the August sun. Holding back a laugh, she stuck the stem under Jonesy's nose and tickled him. His loud snores shifted to a series of grunts and gurgles, and he reached up and rubbed his nose without even opening his eyes.

Jack giggled and sat back.

"Why do you continue to pester him? His pa probably worked him like a plow mule since sunup." Ricky, her other best friend, picked up a rock and tossed it to the far side of the river.

"How come he got to come fishin'?"

" 'Cause his pa had a hankering for fish for dinner."

"Well, his loud snores are scaring them all away." Jack stared out at her fishing line, wishing for a bite.

"Nah, it's probably just too hot for them to care about eating." Ricky yawned and stretched. The summer sun had darkened his skin and turned his blond hair white. "So how do you like having the marshal for a pa, *Jacqueline*?"

Jack shoved Ricky in the arm. "Don't you call me that."

"Your ma told me to."

She leaned back, keeping a hold on her pole. "I don't care. I hate that name."

"Why? I think it's kind of pretty, for a girl."

Jack swung her gaze back to meet Ricky's dark blue stare. Was he teasing her? His thick hair hung over his eyebrows and almost into his eyes. He was nice-looking, for a boy. "You really think so?"

He shrugged one shoulder. "Yeah, I guess."

Jack gazed up at the sky and considered that. She'd never once thought her given name was pretty, and she still preferred Jack, but it was nice to know someone liked her name.

The arms of the sun reached through the canopy of trees overhead, touching the river with its light. The quiet water rippled on the gentle breeze, but the heat still made her hot. She swiped at a river of sweat tickling her cheek. They ought to be swimming instead of fishing, but her ma would have a conniption fit if she swam with the boys.

A proper lady never swims with gentlemen, she'd said. But then, Jack knew she was far from a lady—or being proper for that matter. It seemed that women had so many rules they had to abide by while men got to do whatever they wanted. Why couldn't she have been born a boy?

Jonesy's snores grew louder, and she gave him a shove. "Hush up! I cain't hear myself think."

He murmured something in his sleep and rolled over with his back to her. Maybe now he'd be quieter.

She thought about her new pa and smiled. Things sure had changed since he'd married her ma.

"What's so funny?" Ricky asked.

"Aw, nothing. I was just thinking about all that has changed since my ma married Luke."

"Like what?"

She sat up straight and wrapped her arms around her knees.

"I got my own room now. It's the yellow one upstairs, where that outlaw stayed."

"That must be nice. I share a room with my two little sisters. At least I got my own bed. Jonesy shares one with his two little brothers."

She leaned toward her friend. "I've got a double bed."

"All your own?"

"Uh-huh. I like it. Ma don't put her cold feet on my legs no more."

"That's no problem these days, as hot as its been. I get all sweaty at night, even with the window open. Half the time, I take my quilt and lay it on the porch or in the hay loft 'cause it's cooler to sleep there."

Jack nodded. "That's a good idea. I'd try it, but Ma wouldn't let me if she knew about it. She's such a worrywart."

Ricky stretched and rubbed his belly. "Maybe she won't feel so much that way once her and the marshal have some kids."

Jack bolted up. Thoughts of little brothers and sisters bounced around in her mind. "You think they will?"

He shrugged. "Couldn't say, but that's usually what happens not too long after a wedding."

Hugging her knees, she considered what it would be like to have a younger brother or sister. It would be fun while they were a baby, but she didn't think she'd like sharing her bed. "How long you reckon it would take?"

"For what?" Ricky yawned and rubbed the back of his neck.

"For them to. . .you know." She felt her cheeks grow warm. "To have a baby."

"At least nine months."

She leaned back and relaxed. That was a long while. Why, her whole life had changed in less than half that time, starting when Luke returned to Lookout after being away eleven years. And she'd met a real live outlaw, and her ma had even been kidnapped by one. Jack frowned, remembering how scared she'd been then.

If her ma hadn't returned home, she'd have been an orphan. But now she not only had her ma, but a new pa, too. And maybe soon a new brother or sister. Yep, school was out, and life was about as good as it could get.

"You smell somethin'?" Ricky lifted his nose in the air and sniffed.

"Smells like a pigpen." Jack's gaze collided with Ricky's.

"Oh no." He looked past her just as she heard footsteps.

Jack turned and saw Butch Laird coming toward them, a fishing pole on his shoulder. As long as she could remember, he'd been their enemy. His pa was a hog farmer, and Butch always stank, just like he'd wallowed in the muck.

Jack stood. "Guess I'll head back home. We ain't catching nothin' anyhow."

"You don't have to go just 'cause of him."

"Ma don't want me around him. You know, since I got that black eye at the end of school."

Butch slowed his steps when he saw them. "Nice day for fishin', ain't it?"

"It was," Ricky said.

Jonesy sat up, rubbed his eyes, and sniffed the air, then looked up at Butch. "Thought I was dreamin' that I smelled hogs, but I really was."

"Go find your own place to fish, Laird." Ricky tossed a rock at Butch's bare feet, but the boy didn't move.

Jack reeled in her line, picked off the worm, and tossed it in the water.

"Hey, I coulda used that." Ricky shot her a glare.

"You can have the rest in my jar," Jack said. She wished she could go past Ricky to leave, but a downed tree blocked the way. She'd have to pass Butch. Holding her pole in one hand, she held her other hand over her nose.

Butch stared at her with his dark, solemn eyes. His skin had tanned even darker than Ricky's, reminding her of the rumor circulating that he was part Indian. His black hair hung thick and shaggy, where most mothers had sheared their boys' hair off for the summer. But Butch didn't have a ma and not much of a pa, so Luke had said. His clothes were torn and dirty. Though just thirteen or so, he was almost six foot tall, and half that wide. If he didn't smell so bad, she might feel halfway sorry for him.

He stood in the opening between the shrubs, so she had to squeeze close to him to get by. She held her breath and hoped she didn't retch from the stench.

Butch took a step, either to block her way or to get out of the way, she wasn't sure, but his foot flew out in front of him, shooting pebbles like bullets. His fishing pole flew one way, and he flailed his right arm, catching her right across the chest. Jack fell back onto the hard ground, hurting her hand on the rocks.

"Hey!" Ricky yelled and jumped up.

Before she could even check her sore hand, Ricky and Jonesy were on Butch. Though taller than both boys, Butch ducked his head and turned his back on them. When he wouldn't throw any punches, both Jonesy and Ricky stopped their assault.

"What's wrong?" Ricky's chest heaved. "You can hit girls but are a coward to face men?"

Jack's chest ached from the hard blow, and a few scratches marred her hand, but she didn't think Butch had hit her on purpose. He might be a bully, but she'd never seen him hit a girl. "Stop, y'all."

Ricky glanced down at her, anger filling his gaze. "A man don't hurt no woman."

"She ain't no woman. She ain't even hardly a girl." Butch mumbled as he straightened and cast a furtive glance her way. "Leastwise, she don't dress like one."

"But she's our friend." Jonesy ducked his head, growled loud, and struck Butch right in the belly. Butch backpedaled his arms, eyes wide, and fell backward into the river. He splashed and sputtered and then managed to stand.

Ricky hooted with laughter.

"At least he finally got a bath." Jonesy bent over, slapping his leg, and snorted. Jack just sat there watching them. She was grateful to her friends for their quick defense, but she kind of felt bad for Butch. She was sure he'd just slipped on the loose rocks.

Suddenly, Butch's face scrunched up, and he growled like a bear. Ricky and Jonesy both stood up straight and stared for a moment. Butch jolted into action, taking long-legged strides up the bank. Jack's two friends spun around and pedaled their legs but didn't hardly seem to be moving.

Jack jumped up, a scream ripping from her chest. She took off running toward town, not bothering to look behind her. Someone once said a person didn't have to outrun a bear—just outrun the slowest person in the group. She knew she couldn't beat Ricky in a race, but Jonesy was a cinch.

By the time she reached the edge of town, Jack's lungs were burning. She ran all the way to the marshal's office before stopping. Bending over, she sucked in air and tried to catch a breath.

Luke must have seen her, because his chair squeaked and he strode out of the office. "What's wrong, half bit?"

She gazed back in the direction she'd been running and saw Butch close on Ricky's tail. Jonesy was nowhere to be seen. She hoped her friend wasn't beat up or dead.

Luke pursed his mouth. "I'll take care of this. It's time that boy learned he can't pick on the good kids of this town. Maybe a few days in jail will make him think twice."

"But…" Jack didn't know what to say. If she told the truth, her friends might get in trouble, and she knew Jonesy's pa would take a tree branch to his backside. Ricky would be made to do extra work, and she wouldn't see either of them until school was back in session.

Luke glanced at her, then made fast strides to intercept Butch. Both boys stopped when they saw the marshal. She couldn't hear Luke's words but saw Butch talking with his hands up, as if defending himself. Luke took him by the arm and hauled him toward the jail.

Jack couldn't watch. Maybe Butch hadn't been the cause of this fight, but he'd started plenty of other brawls he'd never been punished for. Still, she didn't want to be there if Luke locked him up. She turned and started walking home.

"Hold up there, half bit."

Jack's heart jolted. She wanted to pretend that she hadn't heard Luke, but she knew he'd just follow her home. She turned around but didn't walk back toward him until he motioned for her to.

"Butch says he didn't do anything to start that fight with your friends. Is that true?"

Luke's piercing brown eyes gazed down at her, imploring her to tell the truth, but how could she rat on her friends when they were just protecting her? And Butch did say she wasn't even a girl. Maybe she should take his words as a compliment since she tried so hard to be a boy, but they just didn't sit right with her. She'd just tell as little of the truth as she had to. "He knocked me down, and Ricky and Jonesy were just defending me."

"That ain't true. I slipped." Butch's pleading eyes looked almost black compared to Luke's brown ones.

"Did you knock down my daughter?"

Jack's gaze darted toward Luke. She'd never heard him refer to her as his daughter. A warm feeling wrapped around her.

"I guess." Butch hung his head as if all the fight had gone out of him.

Luke's gaze swerved to Ricky. "Is that true?"

Ricky nodded his head, his blond hair shaking. "Yup, I saw him do it. Jonesy, too, but he. . .uh. . .he went on home."

"Hmm. . .well, I've had enough of you causing trouble in this town, boy. Maybe staying a few days in my jail will make you behave better."

Butch tried to pull his arm from Luke's grasp, his eyes wide. Almost crazy-looking.

Jack covered her nose. Now he didn't just smell like a hog, but like a wet, moldy one. "I cain't stay in yer jail. My pa expects me to tend to the hogs. He'll bust my hide if'n I don't."

"Maybe you should have thought of that before picking on a girl half your size." Luke hauled him toward the jail door.

Butch sent another frantic glance her way, but then he narrowed his gaze at her, sending caterpillars crawling up and down her spine. She could say he slipped, but her friends would get in trouble and be mad at her. Butch deserved being in jail, didn't he? Her chest still stung from where he'd whacked her.

She turned and trudged toward home, unable to look at him any longer. If he did deserve being in jail, why did she feel so bad?

Garrett kicked the door shut with his boot and carried Miss O'Neil farther into the office. A whiff of a soft floral scent whispered around Mark as she passed by, teasing his senses. He clenched his fist as thoughts of Annabelle surfaced.

To Miss O'Neil's credit, she didn't seem to enjoy being in Garrett's arms, but rather sat stiff. Prim and proper—at least as proper as could be in such a situation. For some reason he couldn't pinpoint, that made him happy. But why should he care?

Garrett set her down in Mark's chair, not his own, he noted. What was she doing here? He checked her ring finger and relaxed a smidgeon. Surely if Garrett had married the woman, she'd be wearing a ring. He tried to imagine his joke-playing brother and the shy Irish gal together, but the puzzle didn't fit.

An ornery grin revealed Garrett's straight teeth, and his eyes gleamed. Something in the pit of Mark's stomach curdled.

"Here's your surprise, brother."

Miss O'Neil's gaze jerked up to Garrett's face and then to Mark's. She looked as stupefied as he. Mark cleared his throat. "What are you talking about?"

Garrett crossed the room in three long steps and plopped down in his desk chair. "Did you forget I told you I had a surprise?"

"I don't understand." Miss O'Neil raised her hand and pinched the bridge of her nose.

"That makes two of us. What are you talking about, Garrett?"

Mark leaned against his desk and crossed his arms, keeping his back to Miss O'Neil. It was best he didn't look at the pretty woman. His expression would only trouble her, anyway.

Garrett leaned back and put his feet on his desk, looking smug. "You were complaining about breaking your wrist and not being able to keep up with the bookwork. Miss O'Neil needed to find work, so I offered her a job. Solved two problems at once."

"Well, she can't stay. I'll figure out something else." Mark crossed his arms and clamped his teeth together. He didn't need daily reminders of how he'd messed up his life.

Miss O'Neil gasped.

Garrett dropped his feet and rested his arms on his desk, all teasing now gone. "We need her, brother, and she needs us."

Mark closed his eyes, knowing the Irish gal couldn't see his face. How was he going to get out of this situation without hurting her feelings? But then it was probably already too late for that.

He pushed up from the desk and paced to the door, spun around, and strode back to his desk. As much as he didn't like it, he could actually see the ingenuity of Garrett's plan. They were already paying Miss O'Neil's room and board, so if she worked for them, they might be out some additional money, but it wouldn't be nearly as much as if they hired someone else to keep the books and still had to support Miss O'Neil. And he didn't want just anybody knowing the state of their finances. The one favorable thing about Miss O'Neil was that she knew few people in town. He glanced at her, wincing at her troubled expression.

"There's been some mistake, I'm thinkin'. You'd best be helping me back to the boardinghouse, Mr. Corbett."

Garrett pursed his lips and stood. "Now see what you've done. You've ruffled her feathers."

Mark stopped right in front of his brother. "You could have at least discussed this with me first."

Garrett leaned closer. "There's nothing to discuss. We need her, and she needs a job. It's simple."

Mark didn't see anything simple about the situation. She reminded him of Annabelle, and that was the last person he wanted to think about. How could he work with her day in and day out? Maybe he could get her trained and then stay away from the office. Study his law books more. But they had a business to run. He shook his head and pressed his lips together.

"You don't have to look so disgusted, Mr. Corbett."

She stuck her cute little nose in the air and glared at him. Wisps of reddish-brown hair had escaped the net thing that held most of her luscious hair curled around her pretty face. Now that he'd taken time to look at her directly in the face, he realized she really didn't look all that much like Annabelle, other than her coloring. She was smaller, more petite, and younger—and dressed far more modestly.

Using the desk as support, Miss O'Neil pushed to her feet. "I shall leave."

She took a step, grimaced, and dropped back down in the chair. Mark had to admit that she looked pretty when she was riled. But could he work with her, day after day, when she reminded him so much of his past?

He ran his fingers through his hair and blew out a breath. His past wasn't her fault, and he wasn't being fair. "You can stay."

But he and his brother would be having a heated discussion tonight.

CHAPTER 8

Shannon sat stiff in the desk chair as Mark Corbett leaned over her shoulder, explaining the ledger books. With most of his right hand and half of his lower arm in a thick plaster casing, he couldn't write and keep the records.

Gathering her courage, she voiced a question. "Why does your brother not keep the books?"

Mark's lips pursed. "Garrett doesn't have an eye for figures and accounting."

She wasn't sure she did, either, but now that she was here, she would learn. She had to. Her independence and her very life depended on it. Having two unmarried men support her was humiliating and certainly not proper.

"So, does that make sense to you?"

Shannon's heart leapt. What had he just said? She'd been lost in her thoughts and not following along. "I. . .uh. . ."

Mark rubbed his hand across his cleanly shaven jaw and heaved a sigh. "Look, it's fairly simple when you've done it a while."

After his initial outburst, Mark seemed resolved to have her there, but she felt if he had his druthers, she wouldn't be. And if she could have walked out with dignity, she'd be gone. But Garrett hadn't taken her hint about leaving; in fact, *he* left without her, leaving her alone with his brother.

Shannon held her trembling hands in her lap. Every time the man came close, she shivered like she had in the frigid hull of that ship that had brought her family to America. To their deaths.

Mark opened a ledger book about two feet wide, sending up the scent of leather and old paper. He riffled through the large pages and stopped at the last page with entries. The date was two days before the tornado had hit.

"All right. In this book we keep track of each individual transaction, each thing someone orders. That's the file box over there where we file the order forms when we're done." He pointed to a rectangular metal holder sitting on a counter against the wall. The box had sheets of yellow paper standing upright in it, separated by metal dividers. "We record what each person has ordered on an ongoing basis."

She tried to wrap her mind around what he'd said, but she failed to see how the ledger and file box were different.

He moved around and sat on the edge of the desk, cradling his wounded hand with his other one. His cast looked awkward and uncomfortable. "Do you understand? If you don't, ask questions."

He stared at her. Oh, she had questions, but she hadn't learned enough to voice what they were yet. Maybe if he explained some more, she'd catch on.

He scratched his head and stared out the window. Shannon took a moment to study him. His jawline was more finely etched than his brother's, and his nose had a perfect slant. Both men had almost the same hair and the exact same eye color, though Mark's shorter dark blond hair had a curl that Garrett's didn't, tickling his collar in an enticing manner. He turned back to face her, and for a moment, she couldn't look away. Her breath caught at the intensity of his gaze. She loved the color of his eyes—a cross between the light blue Texas sky and a robin's egg—and they made her heart jump each time she looked into them. She might live a short life if that kept happening. Her heart could only take so much.

Breaking from his gaze, she looked down at the ledgers. How could she be thinking such thoughts about the man who didn't even want her here?

He cleared his throat. "Let's. . .uh, get back to work." He opened the middle desk drawer on the right side, pulled out a stack of papers, then shut it with his leg. "These are the orders for supplies. See how Mr. Foster's names is atop this one?"

Shannon nodded and noted the order for wood.

"This page shows Foster's order for a wagonload of lumber. This column shows the type of wood, this one the quantity, then the length, and the price. You record each of those in the appropriate columns on the ledger. Pretty simple."

Simple enough, if her mind wasn't befuddled by his nearness. His clean scent wafted around her every time he moved. She'd never known a man could smell so fresh. Even his clothing was spotless and wrinkle free.

"Miss O'Neil, do you need to take a break?"

"Nay, I'm. . .uh. . .beginning to understand. Perhaps if you'd permit me to record a few transactions, it would become clearer."

Mark nodded. He crossed the room, grabbed his brother's chair, and hauled it next to hers. Shannon's heart thudded like a dancer's feet pounding out a fast-paced jig. How could she concentrate when he was so near?

"All right. List Foster's name in the first column."

She dipped the pen in the ink bottle and did as asked, taking heed to make her printing neat.

"Now, see how he ordered different lengths and sizes of wood? Look across the top columns of the ledger and find the correct size of wood, then go across on Foster's line and record the amount ordered. There are columns for the other things people most often order, but if you can't find what you need, use the last column. There's room to write in the item description, if you write small. Try to be neat, because this is our permanent record."

She nodded, but his emphasis on neatness made her hand shake. She hadn't had call to write anything other than her name since coming to America. Pushing her fretful thoughts away, she recorded another entry. She dipped her pen into the bottle, and Mark heaved a boisterous sneeze. Shannon jumped. The bottle tipped sideways. Her hand shot toward it, but the ink spilled across the desk in a spreading pond.

Mark muttered something she couldn't make out and grabbed the ledger. "Bottom drawer. Ink blotters."

She tugged hard on the lowest drawer, pulled out a stack of blotting papers, and dabbed at the mess.

"Don't push on it." Mark snatched a stack of papers off the pile. "You have to dab it, or you'll press it into the wood."

Shannon sat back, feeling like the village *eejit*. She'd been here less than an hour and had already made a mess of things. Looking down to avoid Mark's glare, she sucked in a gasp. The ink on her hands had stained her dress. How would she ever get it out?

Mark threw the dirty blotters into the trash can. The pool of ink was gone, but a nasty stain marred his immaculate desk.

He shoved his hands to his hips and stared at it. Finally, he looked up at her. "I knew this wasn't a good idea."

He stormed out the back door, letting the screen slam. Shannon jumped. She wanted to flee back to her room at the boardinghouse, but she was stuck in Mark's chair. Tears blurred her eyes, but she forced them away. If she swiped at them, she'd probably end up with ink on her face. Oh, what a nightmare.

Leah had told her she needed to toughen up if she was going to survive living in Texas. But that possibility looked far slimmer now. Surely Mark would dismiss her, and if he didn't, how could she face him again?

A few minutes later, the bell over the door jangled. Shannon glanced up to see Rachel enter, carrying a teapot and two tin cups.

"How's it going so far?" Rachel's smile slipped from her face as she stared at Shannon. "What did those yahoos do?"

Shannon shook her head. " 'Twasn't them. 'Twas me." She waved her ink-stained hand over the large blotch. "Not here one whole hour, and I've ruined Mr. Corbett's desk."

Rachel hurried over and set the teapot down on a clean corner of the desk. "Oh, dear. Is that why the men are gone?"

"Garrett left Mark and me alone right after dropping me off." She glanced down at her hands. "He hadn't even mentioned me to his brother. Mark was not happy at all about me being here. And then this happened."

Rachel sat in Garrett's chair and took Shannon's hand. "Things aren't as bad as they might seem. I've got a spare apron you can wear over your dress to hide the stain, and I would imagine the men can sand out the stain on the desk."

Shannon's heart flip-flopped. "You truly think it can be removed? I feel like an *eejit* for making such a mess."

Rachel smiled. "I'm afraid I have no idea what that is, but I'm sure you aren't one."

"I believe you say idiot or imbecile."

"Well, I know for certain you're not one of those. Let's have our tea before it's cold. Then I'll find Luke, and he can help you back home."

Home. Shannon liked the sound of that, but the boardinghouse wasn't her home. It was only a place she was staying until she could make it on her own or find a husband. In truth, she had no home.

Rachel held the lid to the pretty teapot covered with violets and ivy and poured tea into both cups. "I apologize for bringing tin cups, but I was afraid I'd break the china ones if I tried to lug them down here along with the pot."

" 'Tis fine. Thank you for thinking of me. I'm very glad you came when you did."

Rachel set a steaming cup of tea in front of her. Shannon sipped it, allowing the warmth to soothe her. "I don't know if I should be leavin' or stayin'. I need this job, but I don't think Mark Corbett wants me here."

"Maybe I could talk to him. I've known the Corbett brothers since I was a girl, and they're practically my relatives now. It's not like Mark to be unkind or inhospitable. He's a good man with a big heart. Far more patient and tolerant than most."

Shannon tried to get Rachel's description to match what she'd seen of Mark Corbett, but it didn't. Yes, he'd rescued her during the storm but had done so begrudgingly. And he'd been angry at her ever since, casting stormy looks her way whenever he saw her. For some reason, she brought out the worst of him. "I don't believe he wants me working here, but I so need the employment."

"Mark will come around. He doesn't like it when Garrett pulls something over on him." Rachel sipped her tea and gazed toward the window. "I don't know if you can tell, but Garrett is the oldest. Mark is the solid one, though, and Garrett is. . .well, let's just say he hasn't fully grown up yet."

Shannon smiled at that. "He does behave more like a lad."

"Yes." Rachel nodded. "Mark has always felt he followed in Garrett's shadow. Their pa didn't like that Mark could read and was studious, especially when he couldn't read and thought book learning was for womenfolk."

Swallowing hard, Shannon remembered how she had tried to please her da, but nothing she ever did made him happy. He'd wanted a son, not a wee lass. She ducked her head as the unpleasant memories of him repeating that every time she angered him made her tears burn her eyes. They were not so much different, she and Mark. Perhaps she'd misjudged him. All she'd done was cause him trouble, albeit not intentionally. She needed to prove to him that she had value. That she could ease his burden and do the work he needed her to do.

"I don't want to paint Garrett as a bad person. He has a good heart, but he just gets too carried away with his teasing and prank-pulling."

"Like when he ordered all of us brides for your husband."

Rachel's cheeks flamed. "Yes, like that. He wanted to help Luke get over me, but God had other plans." Rachel reached across the desk and laid her hand over Shannon's wrist. "I believe God used Garrett's scheming to get you and Miss Bennett to come to Lookout because He has plans for you here."

"Truly, you believe that?" A flame of hope flickered within Shannon's heart. Did she dare believe that her very steps had been orchestrated by the hand of God? She believed in God but felt He'd turned his face from her.

Rachel nodded and smiled, her pale blue eyes shining. "I believe it with all of my heart. If God can work the miracle He did to reunite Luke and me, it's a small thing for Him to bring you here—maybe to give you a husband, too."

Shannon so wanted to believe, but God had not answered many of her prayers since she'd come to America. Her parents had died in spite of the many pleas she'd sent heavenward. She'd lost the man she'd hoped to marry, and at the same time her only hope of support. And now she may well have lost her job.

Maybe if she could prove her worth, Mark might let her stay.

Rachel stood and stretched. "I'd better get back home and start on dinner. Noon will be here before we know it. I'll find Luke and have him come and get you."

"Nay, I'll stay, but if I'm not back by dinner, could you please send the marshal for me?"

Rachel nodded but stared at her with concerned eyes. "Are you certain?"

Shannon nodded. "If you could just hand me that ledger on Garrett's desk, perhaps I can show the Corbett brothers that I'm an asset and not a liability."

❦

After having lunch at the café, Mark strode back into the office, and breathed a sigh of relief that Miss O'Neil was no longer there.

But instead of enjoying that fact, guilt needled him. How had she gotten back to the boardinghouse? Had she hobbled home on her injured foot? Had his uncouth actions caused her more pain? More humiliation?

He crossed the office and stared down at the large stain on his desk. His mouth twisted up on one side. He'd worked hard to keep his desk looking nice, but Miss O'Neil had certainly made a mess of it. Thank goodness she hadn't spilled the ink on the ledger.

Speaking of the ledger, he looked around the room and found it on the shelf beside the file box. He snatched it up, determined to try and record the orders in spite of his cast. He'd just have to work slow—if he could even hold the pen.

He dropped down into his chair and opened the drawer that held the orders. At least half the pile was gone. His heart skittered. Surely Miss O'Neil hadn't opened the wrong drawer and used the orders to wipe up the spill. He tried to remember, but things had happened too fast. Trying to remember the details of all those orders would be a nightmare.

He yanked open the other drawers and searched them, then he got up and rummaged around the stacks of catalogs and papers on Garrett's desk. He picked up the trash can and poked around the ink-stained papers but didn't see any of the completed order forms. He shoved his hands to his hips and looked around the office. Where could that frustrating woman have put them?

Seemed like every time he got near her, something unpleasant happened. She was like a bad luck charm. He lifted his nose and sniffed. Her flowery scent still lingered.

Heaving a sigh, he sat down and opened the ledger book. He found the page where the last entries had been recorded, and his hand halted. Several new pages of entries had been recorded in a slanted, feminine handwriting. He studied the entries, and each one looked accurate, based on his memory of those orders.

"Hmph! Would you look at that."

Maybe she was sharper than he'd given her credit for. But

where were the order forms?

He carried the ledger back to the shelf and set it down. Then he thumbed through the file box until he found Foster's account card. Each of the items from Foster's last order had been recorded in the proper place, and the order form had been filed behind the account card as if he'd filed it himself.

Mark stared out the window, a slow appreciation for Shannon O'Neil growing within him. She'd stuck to her guns and finished her task, even though she'd been upset and hadn't been completely taught how to do the job. She hadn't tucked tail and hobbled back to the boardinghouse like he'd expected.

Evidently, she was quite capable of tending the books. But every time she got near him, something bad happened. Could he survive having her work here?

He thought about the worry in those big green eyes when she'd spilled the ink. She'd looked scared to death, as if he might strike her. He scowled, wondering what she'd endured in her young life that would make her so fearful when she'd just had an accident.

Yeah, she'd ruined the top of an expensive piece of furniture, but it could be repaired. He was certain he could sand out the stain and refinish the top of the desk. She didn't know how well he took care of his things and how it bothered him when other people didn't. Had his fierce reaction to the accidental ink spill wounded her?

He hung his head, ashamed that he'd lashed out and made her feel worse. Her feelings were far more important than a desk, and he was certain that he'd thoroughly stomped on them. A flicker of warmth welled up within him. A desire to protect Shannon O'Neil from further pain. As far as he knew, she had no one to take care of her. To watch over her.

He had no idea why and might well die trying, but the desire to protect her heated his chest.

Mark hung his head as another thought charged into his mind. Hadn't the very same reaction—the desire to protect Annabelle—been what had caused all his trouble in Abilene?

CHAPTER 9

Leah sat on the front porch of the boardinghouse, rocking her chair and staring out at the small town. She simply had to find some kind of work or she would go batty. But what kind of work could an unmarried woman do in such a small town?

When the Corbett brothers had offered to pay her way back home, she'd said no. Definitely, no. But maybe she should have allowed them to send her to Dallas or some other big town where there would be more opportunities for a woman.

At least here in Lookout, she knew a few folks, but in a big town, she would be alone.

The screen door creaked, and Shannon strolled out.

"Off to work, I see." Leah smiled. Now that they were no longer competing for the same man and were bound together by their similar situation, she and the Irish girl had become friends.

"Aye." She fanned herself with her hand. "'Tis hot already. I will be happy when the weather cools some."

"Don't hold your breath. It may be awhile. I've heard it's sometimes November before cool weather decides to stick around."

"Blessit be, how will we ever make it that long?"

Leah shrugged. "We'll do what we have to do, just like we have been."

Shannon nodded. "Aye, you're right. We'll do as we must."

"Are things going better with the Corbett brothers, now that you've been there a few weeks?"

Shannon lifted one shoulder. "A wee bit. Garrett likes to play jokes on his brother and me, and Mark gets angry at him. I don't mind them so much, except that day he put a snake in Mark's desk drawer, and I was the one to find it. Ach! I nearly did an Irish jig. Good thing my ankle had healed."

"I'd like to have seen that." Leah chuckled and then shook her head, glad she didn't have to deal with the Corbett brothers on a daily basis. "That Garrett needs to grow up. Sounds like he's pulling schoolboy pranks."

"Aye, that's exactly what he's like. Maybe he just needs a good woman to settle him down." Shannon waggled her brows at Leah.

"Don't look at me. I've had my fill of those brothers. Mind yourself. You be careful around them."

"Well, I should be off. Have a grand mornin', and I shall see you at noontime."

Leah waved and watched Shannon walk away, her mulberry-colored skirt swaying. She'd purchased the new dress with the money she'd made working two weeks for the Corbetts, and well she needed one. Shannon had had only two old faded dresses when she came to Lookout, and one of them was stained with ink. Now the Irish girl wore an apron to work covering her new dress.

Leah leaned her head back and considered a new garment. Having one would be wonderful. Yeah, she had four, but like Shannon's, hers were old and faded.

She mentally calculated each item in her hope chest, wondering if there was something she could part with that might be worth some money. Sam—she smiled, remembering the man she'd hoped to marry—had made the small wooden trunk, which had served as her hope chest, for Christmas the year before they were to marry. But the trunk was all she had left, and her hopes and dreams had been buried more than two years ago, along with Sam.

She closed her eyes, trying hard to imagine his face. He always smiled, and his brown eyes had glimmered with orneriness and love for her. Tears moistened her eyes. Life would have been so much different if he had lived. Why, she'd probably be a mother with a child by now. At least she'd been spared that.

While most women longed to marry and have children, she was different. She wanted to marry—Dan Howard's tall form intruded into her thoughts—but she didn't want children. And what man would marry her, knowing that?

After changing hundreds, if not thousands, of diapers, wiping noses for her youngest siblings every winter, watching babies die...

No, she wouldn't put herself through that. If she couldn't find a man who didn't want children, she'd remain unmarried. She'd be a spinster.

But even a spinster needed a way to support herself. What could she do?

Teaching school was out of the question. Even if she had more than her sixth-grade education, there was still the issue of dealing with children day in and day out. She shuddered. No thank you.

She was an excellent cook, but she'd talked to Polly Dykstra, and the woman didn't need any help other than what she already had. Her sister was a seamstress and owned the dress shop across from Polly's Café, but with so few women in the town, she only worked part-time making dresses.

The screen screeched, and Rachel walked out. "My, it's cooler out here. The kitchen is always so hot. I halfway wish I had one that was separate from the house."

"That would help keep the rest of the house cooler, but you'd have to carry the food farther—and what would you do if we had rain?"

"True. I hadn't considered those issues." Rachel dropped into the rocker beside Leah's and fanned her face with her hand. "How are you doing today?"

"Bored. I wish you'd let me do more around the boardinghouse."

Rachel smiled and leaned her head back against the rocker. "I just can't let a boarder work. It doesn't seem proper."

"So? Who cares?"

"I suppose just me. I guess you've not had luck in finding employment since we last talked?"

Leah shook her head. "I was just sitting here, trying to think of something."

Rachel yawned and stretched her arms out in front of her. "Luke mentioned that his cousins are talking about having a get-together this Saturday and asked Polly to bake some cookies and pies. Maybe she could use help with that?"

She shrugged. "I asked her about working in the café, but she has all the help she needs." She glanced sideways at Rachel. "Just what kind of get-together are those conniving brothers planning?"

"A social, I think. It's a chance for unmarried men and women to meet."

Leah stiffened, and her hackles rose. "You mean they're trying to find husbands for Shannon and me?"

Rachel's brows darted up. She opened her mouth but then closed it. She stared down the street for a moment. "I hadn't thought about it that way."

"They are probably trying to marry us off so they can quit supporting us—or rather, me." Leah crossed her arms. "Well, it won't work, 'cause I'm not going. All those men can dance with each other."

Chuckling, Rachel shook her head. "It would serve those rascals right if only men showed up."

"I've had enough of the Corbett brothers matchmaking and interfering in my life."

A wagon drove by, and the driver lifted his hat to the two

women. He stared until his wagon turned down Main Street.

Leah faked a shiver. "I sometimes feel as if I'm on exhibit."

"Men around here admire pretty women. There are so few of them to be had in Texas."

"Men everywhere admire women. Pretty or not. It's their nature."

"True. But if they know of one who is available, that piques their interest even more."

Leah crossed her arms over her chest and jiggled her foot. "Just who told them I was available?"

"I'll give you one guess."

"I guess it's no secret how that bride contest turned out." Leah shot to her feet, sorry for making Rachel squirm but irritated to the core. "I'm about ready to march over to the freight office and give those two scalawags a piece of my mind."

Rachel stood. "Try to see that they mean well. They messed things up by bringing you and Shannon to town, and now they're trying to fix that mistake."

"I can't believe you're defending them after the trouble they caused for you."

Rachel walked down the steps and plucked several dead leaves off a rosebush. "You know, if those two men hadn't sent for you brides, Luke might never have forgiven me and gotten up his courage to ask me to marry him. So in a strange, roundabout way, I'm beholden to Mark and Garrett."

Leah opened her mouth to comment, but Rachel held up her hand. She flipped her long braid over her shoulder.

"That doesn't mean I condone what they did. It was wrong to pretend to be Luke and to write to you. But now that you're here and neither of you want to leave, I guess they feel they owe it to you to find you a husband."

Leah shoved her hands to her hips and paced the porch. "I don't need their help in finding a mate. I've already got my eye on someone."

"Oh yeah?" Rachel's eyes lit up, and she cocked her head. "Who?"

Leah realized her mistake too late. "I. . .uh. . .am not ready to say. I don't even know if he's interested in me."

Leaning her arms on the porch rail, Rachel stared up at her. "Well then, going to the social could be a good thing."

Leah narrowed her eyes. "How so?"

"It would give you a place to get to know this man better. Other than outright courting, there aren't many opportunities for a man and woman to spend time together."

"Hmm. . ." Leah tapped her index finger against her lips. "You may be right. But it would mean talking to other men, too."

"True, but you might meet someone more interesting than the man you've got your eye on. Or you will confirm that he's the one for you."

What Rachel said made sense. But was getting to know Dan Howard worth having to dance with and talk to all those other men? Leah shuddered at the thought of being near some of the uncouth men. Still, she *would* be able to talk with Dan there and somehow let him see her interest. "I think you may be right."

Too bad she didn't have a new dress to wear to the social.

Shannon stared at the man standing in front of Mark's desk. "You want what?"

The lanky cowboy wore a faded, red plaid shirt, dingy denim pants, and worn boots. He twisted the brim of his hat in his shaking hands, and his ears turned the color of his shirt. "I asked if you'd like to get hitched to me, ma'am. Got me a ranch over toward Dennison a ways, and an ailing ma. I need a woman to help care for her and cook for my men."

"So you need a cook, not a wife?"

The man scratched his head, his hazel eyes darting around the office. "Uh. . .what's the difference, ma'am?"

Shannon's mouth quirked. She knew little of married life, but there had to be more than just cooking. She felt sorry for his mother, but she wouldn't marry unless she was in love. Her own mum had married the man her parents wanted—a man she didn't love—and she'd never been happy. "I'm sorry, Mr. Harkins, but I have a job already."

His brows dipped again. "I didn't offer you a job, ma'am. I asked you to marry me."

She felt sorry for the clueless cowboy, but she shook her head. A noise sounded from the right, and she saw Mark standing in the doorway to the side room, scowling. How long had he been there?

"I believe the woman said no, Abbot."

The cowboy frowned. "What am I gonna do, Mark? I need someone to help care for ma and feed my men."

Mark's gaze gentled, and he crossed the room and laid his hand on Abbot's shoulder. "I'm sorry to hear about your mother. If Garrett and I can do anything, be sure to let me know." Mark rubbed the back of his neck. "Maybe what you need is to hire a cook rather than take a wife. Or maybe a neighbor could help out for a while."

Abbot nodded and seemed to be studying the floorboards. "Maybe so, but ma has her heart set on seeing me married before she—" The man swallowed hard, and his Adam's apple bobbed.

"Marrying isn't something done in haste. You need time to develop a relationship and to fall in love."

Shannon watched Mark, admiring the gentleness in his voice and how he treated the man with respect in spite of his misguided mission. In the two weeks that she'd been working at the freight office, she'd come to admire Mark—on most occasions. There had been a few times when he'd dropped his guard and horseplayed too roughly with his brother for her taste or even argued with Garrett. She'd never had siblings who lived long, but she couldn't help thinking she'd fight less and love them more.

Abbot nodded. "I reckon you're right. You think that other bride would be interested?"

"In what? Marriage or being a cook?" Mark asked.

Abbot shrugged; then his eyes glinted with an ornery gleam. "Could be I'll just attend that Saturday social you and your brother are planning and see if I cain't win her heart."

Mark's gaze darted to Shannon's, and she didn't miss the apprehension there. What was Mr. Harkins talking about?

He patted the man's shoulder again. "You do that, Abbot. You've got as good a chance as anyone else."

The rancher nodded and tipped his hat to Shannon. "G'day, ma'am. Mark." His spurs jingled as he crossed the room and walked out the open door, carrying with him the scent of dust and cattle.

Shannon stood and crossed her arms. "What exactly is this Saturday social thing?"

An odd look crossed Mark's face, and the tips of his ears turned red. "Uh. . .just a gathering of folks and a dance."

Shannon narrowed her eyes. "Sounds like more than that. Why would the two of you be hosting a social? Could you be looking for a wife now?"

"No, we're not looking to marry." Mark crossed to the open door and stared outside. He heaved a heavy sigh. "It was Garrett's idea."

"Why does that not surprise me?" Shannon mumbled.

Mark leaned against the doorjamb and turned to face her. His blue eyes looked troubled, and his short hair twisted in enticing curls, giving him a softer look than his brother. "For the record, I told him that it was a bad idea and that I wanted nothin' to do with it."

"Why is it he felt the need to organize such an event?"

Mark's mouth twisted to one side, and he broke from her gaze.

"Do you not feel you owe me the truth?"

He captured her gaze again, and it set her heart thumping. She shifted her feet, not wanting to admit how attracted she was to him. Her pa had been rough, dirty, and hairy, but Mark was always clean and smelled fresh. Garrett's desk was always a mess, with things tossed haphazardly, but Mark's was always tidy, even while he was working. After he'd gotten used to working with her, he'd been only kind and patient in showing her how to do everything. But how could he stir her senses after all he and his brother had done? It made no sense to her.

"Garrett has. . .uh. . .been talking to some of our customers and discovered there are a number of them who'd like to marry. We also have found women in other towns who are looking for husbands."

Shannon's ire simmered to a boil, and she bolted to her feet as she realized the truth. "You mean your brother is hosting a social so that you can marry off Leah and me? Isn't that correct?"

Mark's silence was all the answer she needed.

Shannon lifted her chin and straightened her back. These men had meddled enough in her life. "I believe that I've finished working for today."

She marched to the door, but Mark didn't move. His fresh scent wafted over her. Looking up, she hated to see the pain she'd inflicted. Mark was somewhat a victim of his brother's shenanigans, but he was a grown man—a man who needed to stand up for what he believed and not be swayed by his conniving sibling.

"Shannon. . .Miss O'Neil."

"Pardon me, Mr. Corbett."

His heavy sigh warmed her face, but he stepped back. Shannon strode out of the office, uncertain if she'd ever return.

CHAPTER 10

While Rachel was busy in the kitchen, fixing their noon meal, Leah tiptoed into the dining room and quietly set the table. Maybe Rachel wouldn't willingly ask for help, but Leah had decided to find small ways to help anyway. She completed her task without getting caught and left the room feeling good.

A shadow darkened the screen door, and Shannon strode in with a scowl on her face.

"What's wrong?"

"Oh, those. . .those. . ." She stomped her foot. "They fuel my ire like a match to lamp oil."

Leah's mouth twitched. She'd never seen Shannon so worked up before. Normally, the girl would turn quiet and withdraw when upset, but seeing her angry encouraged Leah that maybe Shannon had more of a backbone than she thought. "Those what? Or should I say who?"

Shannon's green eyes flickered with fury. "Do you know what those hooligans are plannin' now?"

"Ah, you've heard about the Saturday social."

"You know about it? Why didn't you say something?"

Leah held up her hand and leaned against the parlor doorjamb. "I just learned about it this morning."

"And are you goin'?"

Leah waved her hand toward the parlor. "Let's sit down."

Shannon followed her to the settee and turned to face Leah. Taking a moment to organize her thoughts, Leah straightened her skirt.

"Surely you are not actually considering goin'. 'Twould only encourage the Corbett brothers." Shannon eyed her with skepticism.

"Now hear me out. I've got my eye on a man."

"Aye?" Shannon leaned forward, brows lifted. "What man would that be?"

Leah pressed her lips together, not sure she was ready to share that information. "Uh. . .just someone I've met a time or two."

"How can you know a man when you've only just met him?"

Leah shifted on the seat. "That's the thing. I can't. Attending the social would give me the chance to talk with this man and learn more about him. He might even ask me to dance."

"If he attends it." Shannon seemed to be considering what Leah said as different expressions crossed her face. "Aye, I can see how 'twould be beneficial to you, but I won't be attending."

Leah gasped, suddenly not so sure of her plan. "Oh, but you have to. I don't want to go alone."

"Perhaps you can go with Luke and Rachel."

Leah shook her head. "They aren't invited. It's only for unmarried folks."

Shannon nibbled on the inside corner of her lip and stared across the room. "I don't know. 'Twould almost be as if I were advertising for a husband."

A warm breeze fluttered the curtains at the open window. A bird flitted on the bush just outside the window, chirping a lively tune. "I can see why you'd think that, but I'm pretty sure that it's just a social. Yes, men and women will meet, but what's wrong with that?"

Shannon shrugged and wrung her hands.

"I realize that you now have a job and are no longer dependent on the Corbett brothers for your support as I still am."

Shannon muttered something about quitting her job, then looked at Leah. "It's one and the same. I may be working and earning a wage, but I'm still dependent on those hooligan brothers since I work for them."

"I see your point, but it's different. You're earning your keep, I'm just a...dried-up old cow, no longer giving milk but too tough to eat."

Shannon sucked in a loud breath and whacked Leah on the arm. "Don't you say such a thing. You can't be much older than me."

Leah shrugged. "I know, but it just seems that way at times. I don't want those men supporting me, but what else can I do? There are no other jobs available."

"Perhaps I could help you. I have a wee bit of extra money."

Leah placed her hands over her friend's. "Thank you, but you know that isn't true. Maybe you have some money left after paying room and board, but it's precious little, I'd imagine. You need that to buy yourself some more dresses. You can't wear this one every day."

Shannon looked down and fingered her sleeve. "Aye, there's truth in what you say. Perhaps I could ask to work more hours."

Leah smiled, warmed by Shannon's desire to help, but she shook her head. "No, I very much appreciate your offer, but I need to make my own way. I need to find a man to marry or a job."

"So, you are serious, then, about attending the social?"

"Yes. It seems the thing to do. Hopefully, I'll be able to get to know the man I'm attracted to better, but at the same time, I can ask around about employment."

Shannon's grip tightened on Leah's. "Just be careful. Not all men are honorable. Don't be going off alone with any of them."

"Yes, Ma." Leah grinned, and Shannon chuckled. "Why are you back early from work, anyway?"

Shannon sighed. "I got irritated with Mark when I overheard him tell a cowboy about the social."

"Oh, it's Mark now, is it?" Leah couldn't resist teasing.

Shannon's face turned five shades of red, and she looked away. "I do work with two Corbett men, and 'twould be confusing to refer to them both as *Mr. Corbett*."

Leah couldn't help wondering if Shannon was attracted to Mark. She couldn't imagine having an infatuation with either man, but at least Mark seemed less ornery and more sensible than his brother. "Do you also call Garrett by his first name?"

Leah could hardly believe it possible, but Shannon's cheeks flamed more.

"I. . .uh, no. He isn't in the office very often, and it wouldn't seem proper."

Leah sat back, smiling. "I see the way of things."

"Nay!" Shannon held her palm toward Leah. "I. . .it just makes things easier since we work together so much."

"So, you're not attracted to him?"

Shannon ducked her head and fiddled with her apron, not answering at first. "It does seem hard to believe, but I am attracted to him, though he couldn't care less about me."

"Why would you say such a thing? You're a beautiful woman, and he has to be intrigued by your lovely accent."

Shannon lifted one shoulder and dropped it back down. "His brother hadn't told him that he'd hired me, and Mark was quite angry when he first found out. I was so embarrassed to witness their disagreement, especially with me being the topic of it. I wanted to run from their office, but I couldn't because of my ankle."

"Oh, Shannon, I never knew. What a horrible thing for him to do. I can understand why Mark would be upset."

"Aye, me, too, now that I've had time to step back and think about the situation. But Mark quickly adjusted and has been quite gracious and patient since then."

"Just give him some time. He's seems a levelheaded man, even if he does let his brother involve him in his high jinks." Leah squeezed Shannon's hand. "Let me tell you: That's often the case of a younger brother following his older one. I've lots of brothers, and it most always happens."

Shannon stood, as if uncomfortable with the topic of conversation. "I should go and clean up. I imagine dinner will be ready before too long."

Leah watched her scurry from the room. Had the girl already fallen for Mark Corbett? Leah shook her head, unable to envision such a union. She stood and walked out onto the front porch. The heat of the day made her sweat, even though the August sun wasn't yet fully overhead.

A worm of jealousy inched its way into Leah's heart. If Shannon were to marry Mark Corbett, she'd have a home and a family—of sorts. Yeah, she'd be permanently supported by a Corbett, but that would be different since she'd be married to one.

Leah blew out a breath. She was getting the cart before the horse. Shannon seemed only mildly attracted to Mark. Besides, even if they did happen to get married, she should be happy for her friend, not jealous of her.

Shoving those thoughts aside, she studied the town. Several horses were tied in front of the bank and also the café. Their heads hung low, as if they, too, were bothered by the heat. Leah longed for the cooler temperatures of fall, but the uncertainty of her future nagged at her. There must be something she could do to make some money.

After lunch and an afternoon rest, Leah ventured down to the café. An idea had percolated in her mind, and she hoped that Polly would still be there. She passed the lot where the store had been, and the marshal's office, but she didn't look inside. It no longer mattered to her what Luke Davis did. He might have once been the target of her sights, but no more. He was a happily married man.

She opened the door to the café and stepped inside. Aromatic scents lingered even though all the customers were gone. The front windows were wide open, but the room was still overly warm. A fly buzzed near her head, and she swatted at it. Pots clanged together in the back room, so she made a beeline in that direction.

Polly was standing over a large pot with her arm clear down inside it. Leah hated to disturb her, but they needed to talk. "Ahem."

Polly jumped and turned. "Goodness, you nearly scared what little life I've got remaining out of me."

Leah smiled at the older woman's joking. Polly's chubby cheeks were bright red, and wisps of grayish-brown hair had escaped her bun and curled around her face.

"I'm sorry to bother you, but I wondered if I could talk to you about something."

"Sure thing. Just let me finish up this pot. Help yourself to some coffee, if you've a mind to."

Leah skipped the coffee and surveyed the large kitchen. Something simmered on the stove, and several pies cooled near the open window. Beside her was a large shelf that held dozens of blue tin plates, bowls, and coffee cups. Almost everything was in its place, ready for the next round of serving to begin.

"You picked a good time to come. The lunch rush is over, and supper won't start for a few hours yet." Polly lugged the big pot to the back door and tossed out the soapy water; then she poured in fresh water from a bucket, swished it around, and threw it out the door, too. She set the pot upside down on a table that had spaces between the wooden slats, which served as her drying table. Polly wiped her hands on her apron and set them on her ample hips. "Now, how can I help you—Miss Bennett, isn't it?"

"Care to sit down?" Leah asked. "I'm sure you must be exhausted. And please, call me Leah."

Polly nodded and limped into the dining room. She picked up a mortuary advertisement that was attached to a flat stick and started fanning herself. "I'm getting too old for all this work, but I've got to have some income."

"Have you never married?"

Polly lifted her hand to her chest. "Of course, but my Wilbur died young. So sad."

"How is it you have the same last name as your sister?"

Polly smiled. "Dolly and me married brothers, we did. They weren't twins like us, though. Walter was Dolly's husband. He lived two years longer than Wilbur. Farming is hard on men and can be dangerous."

Leah wanted to ask what had happened, but it wouldn't be proper. She might as well get to the point. "Mrs. Davis told me that you'd be baking cookies and pies for the social the Corbetts are hosting."

Polly swatted her fan at a fly but missed it. "Mercy sakes, I told them boys I don't have the time or energy for any more baking, but they insisted. They begged me and offered good money. It's hard to resist their handsome smiles and those charming blue eyes of theirs—and trust me—they use them to their advantage as much as they can."

"Well, that's what I wanted to ask you about."

Polly's brows darted up. "You interested in one of them boys? I think of them like sons, I do."

Leah's heart jolted, and she lifted her hand up. "No, that's not it at all. I was wondering if I might be able to help you with the baking. I need to earn some income, and I'm sure you understand that."

Polly leaned back in her chair. "Well, phooey. I'd sure like to see those boys marry you and that purdy Irish gal."

Leah choked back a gag. She would never marry a Corbett, no matter how desperate she was. "Sorry, but I don't think that will happen. Those two rascals are responsible for our being stranded here in town, as I'm sure you know."

Polly shrugged. "Maybe, but could just be God's means of getting you here. Time will tell."

Leah stared dumbfounded. Polly was the second person today to insinuate such a thing. Yes, she believed that God could work in miraculous ways, but why would He bring her to such a town as Lookout? And then leave her dependent on the ornery coots who had brought her here under false pretenses?

"How about this: What if I let you use my kitchen and supplies, you do the baking, and we split the money? You can bake, can't you? I remember them pies you gals made in that bride contest didn't turn out so well."

Leah nodded, feeling a tad bit offended that her cooking abilities were in doubt. "Of course I can cook. Even won some ribbons at the county fair for my pies."

"That's good to know. I wouldn't want to disappoint them boys. They're two of my best customers."

Leah considered the offer. In truth, it made perfect sense. How would she buy the supplies, even if she'd talked Polly into letting her cook the desserts for the social? And where would she have done the baking if the woman hadn't offered her kitchen?

She looked at the middle-aged widow, smiled, and held out her hand. "Polly, you've got a deal."

Rachel looked around her tidy kitchen, then pulled out a chair at her worktable. Too bad this room couldn't stay clean for more than a few hours at a time. She tugged a letter out of her pocket and smoothed it out, remembering Carly Payton. The black-haired, blue-eyed young woman had lived in the boardinghouse, posing as Ellie Blackstone. Rachel shook her head, thinking of how Carly had fooled them all, even Luke, though he'd been a bit suspicious of her. Carly had thought the real Ellie was dead, but she was, in truth, recovering from being shot and accidentally stabbed by a

knitting needle during a stage robbery that took a bad turn.
She opened the letter and started reading:

Dear Rachel,

I'm still in Dallas, awaiting trial. There ain't much to do here. I'm locked up in a cell but kept apart from the men, thank the good Lord for that. When I was in a cell next to my brother, he pestered me the whole time, blaming me for his getting caught. How do you figure that? I wasn't even there when he robbed the Lookout bank.

Each day drags by so slowly. I'm bored half out of my mind, but I do have ample time to pray. I only wish I had a Bible and could read better. The marshal's kind wife, Iona, has taken me under her wing and is teaching me to read better. She's the one penning this letter for me. I can read some but hope to get better soon so I'll be able to read some books and God's Word to help the time go by faster.

They say my trial should happen by the end of the month. With all the trouble in this part of the state, the judge is backed up on holding trials. I don't know what's to become of me. Iona says most women who are jailed here are black women or Mexicans. They are often sent to the penitentiary. Sometimes the judge is lenient and will sentence a woman to work off her sentence for a local rancher. I'm praying for that but don't hold out much hope. I'm a Payton, and though I never shot no one, I did steal and pretend to be that other bride. I don't know what's to happen, and I'll admit I'm scared. Please keep me in your prayers. Have you married that marshal yet?

Truly your friend,
Carly Payton

Rachel bowed her head and spent the next few minutes thanking God that Carly had given her life to Him, just before her capture. How would the young woman have endured imprisonment without His help?

A noise sounded behind her, and she looked over her shoulder. "Leah, don't you look lovely?"

Leah's lightly tanned cheeks turned a rosy pink. "You really think so?"

She nodded. "I do. I'm glad you've decided to go to the social." She noted Leah's apron ties were hanging down her side. "Turn around, and I'll tie that for you."

Leah smiled. "Oh, would you? I appreciate your help. I've always had a hard time fixing my own bows."

Rachel motioned for her to turn around and then tied the bow to Leah's new apron and fluffed it up to make it look pretty. "I think this was a wonderful idea."

Leah spun around, glancing down and looking apprehensive. She smoothed the front of the apron. "You don't think it's too casual for a social?"

Rachel shook her head. "Not at all. If you'd made a white apron, then it wouldn't have looked as nice. The ruffles around the bib fancy it up, and the navy calico accents the lighter blue of your dress."

Leah chuckled. "Light blue—that's a such a nice way to say faded." She sighed. "I wish I had enough money to make a new dress."

"Stop worrying. You look beautiful, and those men will be stumbling over themselves to dance with you."

Leah's cheeks flamed. "I don't know about that."

"I do." Luke walked into the kitchen, staring at Leah. "There's more than a dozen cowpokes and other men down by the church already, and the social doesn't start for another hour yet."

"I certainly hope some other women attend. I don't think Shannon and I could dance with all the men who are likely to show up."

"I wouldn't worry about that. I've heard plenty of chatter all week. Everyone's excited about the social." Luke leaned back against the counter and shook his head. "I have to admit, though, I thought this was just another of my cousins' cockamamie ideas, but this one just might turn out well."

"From what Shannon said, it was mainly Garrett's idea," Leah said.

Luke nodded. "Most of them are. Mark's more levelheaded than his brother."

Rachel studied her husband, amazed again that God had given Luke to her. He caught her staring and winked. Butterflies danced in her stomach, and she felt her cheeks warm. How could he still move her as he had back when they were young?

Leah glanced from Luke to her and back. A playful smirk danced on her lips as if she'd understood Rachel's thoughts. "I suppose I should head on over to Polly's and start hauling the refreshments over to the social," Leah said.

"I'm available if you need help." Luke grabbed a coffee cup off Rachel's shelf and poured some coffee into it.

"That's probably not too warm, sweetheart. I let the stove burn down after fixing supper." Rachel touched the side of the pot. Lukewarm at its best.

"I'm obliged for the offer to help, but Shannon already said she would assist me, and Polly offered also. We'll be back before dark." Leah waved and turned down the hallway.

Luke set his cup down and growled. "Come here, wife. I'm hankerin' for some spoonin'."

Rachel glanced to the spot where Leah had been, then walked over and peeked down the hallway. She and Shannon were walking out the front door together, and Jacqueline was outside somewhere, which meant she and Luke were alone. She slowly turned back to face her husband. "If you want me"—she wiggled her brows—"come and get me."

Luke's brown eyes sparked, and a slow grin pulled at his lips. "You don't have to ask twice."

He pushed away from the cabinet, moving with unhurried but deliberate steps. When he got within three feet of her, Rachel squealed and spun down the hall. She darted into the dining room.

"Hey, darlin', you're not getting away." Luke chased after her, deep chuckles rattling in his chest.

Rachel gasped for a breath between laughs, and managed to keep the dining table between her and her husband. "You're getting slow in your old age. There was a time I'd have never gotten away."

"You're *not* getting away. Ever." His eyes gleamed with love and possession.

Suddenly, all teasing fled, and Rachel wanted nothing more than to be in his arms. She sauntered toward the end of the table, batting her eyelashes like she'd seen a saloon girl once do.

Luke held his position at the middle of the table as if he wasn't too sure that she wouldn't cut back the other way. But as she rounded his side of the table, a slow burn glimmered in his gaze, and he stepped forward. He lifted his hand and trailed it down her cheek; then he cupped her nape, tugging her up against him.

"You're so beautiful. You've no idea how many times I dreamed of holding you when I was gone." He crushed her against his chest. It was muscled. Solid. But his kiss was soft. Gentle.

Rachel stood on her tiptoes, kissing the only man she'd ever loved. Luke deepened the kiss, and their breath mingled together. Rachel felt lifted out of this world into a realm only a husband and wife madly in love could visit. Oh, if only they could go on like this forever.

The back door banged, and they jerked apart. Rachel grabbed the back of a chair for balance, and her chest heaved, and her pulse soared. Her lips felt puffy. Damp.

"Ma?"

Luke stepped back and acted as if he were straightening the chairs. Jacqueline's gaze swept back and forth between them. Her mouth swerved up to one side, and she crossed her arms. "Guess you two were kissing again. Is that all married folks do?"

Luke grinned wickedly, and his gaze sought Rachel's. "No, half bit, we do other things besides that."

Jacqueline scowled. "What kind of things?"

Rachel's heart stampeded. Surely Luke wouldn't mention things her daughter was too young to hear about.

Luke ambled toward Rachel, and her breathing picked up speed again. Just having the man near set her senses racing like a heard of mustangs. He put his arm around her shoulders.

"Oh, sometimes we hug, like this." He pulled her against his side.

Jacqueline's mouth curved up in disgust. "That's nothing. You hug me, too."

"Other times. . ." Luke gazed down at Rachel with an ornery glint to his eyes.

No, please don't tell her.

"Sometimes. . .we tickle!"

Luke's fingers dug into Rachel's side, and she jumped. "Don't! Stop!" Rachel giggled and tried to get free, but his other arm held her captive.

"Don't stop? Isn't that what your ma said, half bit?" Luke renewed his efforts.

Tears blurred Rachel's eyes. She wiggled and squirmed but couldn't get free. He held her tight, but not so much that it hurt. "Luke, please."

"Ah, now she's begging for more."

Jacqueline giggled and raced around the table. "I'll save you, Ma." She grabbed Luke's arm and tugged.

Luke released his hold as if the girl had overpowered him, but just that fast, he scooped her onto his shoulder. "Where do you want this sack of potatoes, Rach?"

Jacqueline screeched with delight. Rachel's heart warmed seeing her daughter and husband at play. This was what she'd longed for in a marriage.

114

"Help me, Ma."

Luke jogged around the table with Jacqueline hanging over his shoulder. Rachel smiled, knowing her interference was the last thing her daughter wanted just now.

CHAPTER 11

Butch Laird stood on the outskirts of the crowd, leaning against a tall oak, watching the dancing. Cowboys and ladies in pretty dresses sashayed around the circle, doing a complicated square dance he'd seen before. How did they remember what steps to do next?

His gaze drifted over to the table of food again. Several kinds of cookies sat in stacks next to a half-dozen pies. The two boardinghouse brides hustled about, setting out plates and forks. His mouth watered, and his stomach growled when the blond picked up a knife and began slicing one of the pies. Was the food just for the dancers? When was the last time he had pie?

He and his pa rarely ate anything except for pork, eggs, beans, and potatoes. Bacon, ham steaks, pork chops, ham, and beans. That was his lot in life as the son of a hog farmer. Some folks would envy him, but he was sick of pork—and sick of his own cooking.

Butch winced. The last time he'd had pie was when he'd stolen one off a windowsill. He closed his eyes at the memory of how good it had tasted. But he'd eaten the whole thing, and then gotten sick. Besides an upset belly, he'd been riddled with guilt. He'd found some work and earned a dollar, then returned the woman's clean pie plate to her windowsill with the dollar on it. He hadn't eaten pie since then.

He moseyed toward the food. At close to six foot tall, he had the look of a man—at least he would once he lost his pudge and muscled up more. People often thought he was older than just thirteen. But no matter how much he worked, he couldn't seem to lose his big belly. He was tired of the other kids making fun of him for being fat—for calling him Butch Lard instead of Laird. His stomach growled, reminding him that he'd skipped dinner. He just couldn't stand slicing another steak off the ham roast that sat on a plate in the kitchen. If he ever got away from Lookout, he'd never eat pork again.

A group of eight couples danced in and out to the lively music, and the women swirled around, their colorful skirts flying. Phil Muckley deftly swung his bow across his fiddle strings, while Nathan Spooner sawed his harmonica back and forth across his mouth. A man Butch didn't recognize played guitar and tapped his foot to the tune.

Butch's gaze swung back to the dancing ladies. He liked to watch them. Whenever they whipped past him, he got a whiff of their flowery scents. What would things have been like if his mother hadn't died when he was young? Would his pa have been different? Kinder? Not a drunk?

He shook his head to rid it of such glum thoughts. Movement on the other side of the dancers caught his attention. Jack—Jacqueline Hamilton—stood in the shadows of the church building, watching the dancing couples. She was probably too young to join in, as he was, but that didn't keep her from watching.

He scowled, thinking of how her lies had caused him to spend two days in jail for something he didn't do. And yet, he couldn't stay angry with her, even though his pa had beat him for not being home to care for the animals and to cook the meals. Even though he still hurt in places where his pa had taken a broken hay fork handle to him. He knew she had also endured a similar fate when her pa was alive, and for some odd reason, he wanted to protect her—if only she could tolerate him.

Jacqueline strolled over to the food table and started chatting with the two women. He couldn't hear what she was saying, but her lively facial expressions held him captive. He'd always wanted to be her friend. She reminded him of his little sister, Zoe, who'd had red hair and had been as feisty as a piglet. But Zoe had died before her first birthday, just before his ma gave in to the fever. He'd buried them together while his pa was away on a hunting trip. His pa returned without any meat and took out his grief and anger on him. But even a stiff beating didn't drive away the guilt. Somehow, he should have helped his ma and sister better.

One of the boardinghouse brides put a slice of pie on a plate and handed it to Jack, along with a fork. Butch shook his head. Why did such a cute girl want to wear overalls, go fishing with the boys, and be called by a boy's name?

He moved closer to the table, but lost his courage as he reached the back of the church. For some reason, Jack had it in for him. Yeah, sometimes he lost his temper when the kids ranted at him and blamed him for things he hadn't done, but he tried to get along. It just seemed that nobody wanted to get along with him.

He sniffed his shirt, hoping it didn't smell. The kids constantly berated him for carrying the hog stench, but he could never catch the odor on his own clothes. He hadn't taken a chance tonight, though. He'd scrubbed clean his nicest shirt and overalls, even though both were faded and frayed. The dance was for folks of marrying age—he knew that—but he had just hoped to be able to get a slice of the pies he'd heard they'd be serving. His mouth watered, and he forced his feet forward.

The bride whose hair was nearly the same color as Jack's saw him coming and smiled.

"Sure now, would you be caring for a slice of pie?" She smiled at him and held up the pie knife.

He sucked in a breath and nodded, unable to believe his good fortune. Jack eyed him suspiciously as she continued to finish her pie.

"Would you care for apple or peach?"

What a choice. "Um. . .apple, I guess." He was pretty sure he remembered his ma baking apple pies, but it had been so long that his memory had dulled.

The lady handed him a fork and a plate with a fat slice of pie. The dancers noticed the food being served and drifted toward the table while the music faded. Even the musicians were setting aside their instruments and heading for the feeding trough, as if they thought they'd miss out. Butch got out of the way and reverently carried his pie to where Jack stood eating hers.

She narrowed her eyes. "What are you doing here?"

Her spiteful tone grated on him. Why did she dislike him so much? "Same thing as you, I reckon."

"And what's that?"

"Eating pie."

She shook her head, tossing her long braid over her shoulder. "I can eat pie every day. I came to watch the shenanigans."

Her comment gored him to the core, but he doubted she meant to hurt him. Of course she ate pie every day; she had a ma to fix it and guests who probably expected dessert served with their meals. Even though he wanted to savor each bite, he shoved the pie into his mouth, and in seconds, it was gone. He licked his fork and then his plate, catching every little taste that was left.

"Eww. . .don't you got no manners?"

He halted mid-lick and glanced out the corner of his eye. His pa always licked his plate—said that was how he helped with the washing. Didn't other folks do the same?

Jack eyed him like he was a crude no-good. He lowered the plate and set it on the empty table behind the brides that held a bowl of soapy water. He shoved his hands into his pockets, not quite ready to leave. If there was any pie left after all the dancers got their share, maybe he could have another slice.

He moseyed back over by Jack. She took her last bite and frowned at him. She held up her nose and sniffed, then looked down at his boots. Butch ducked his head and gazed down. Rats, he'd forgotten to clean them, and he'd fed the hogs just before leaving. He sniffed, but didn't smell anything bad.

Jack walked around him and took her empty plate to the wash table. She cleaned her plate in the soapy water then dipped the plate into another bucket of fresh water, and dried it off. Then she did the same with his plate and their forks. Butch stood mesmerized by the action. Why would she wash his plate? Should he have done that?

He'd thought the brides would tend to the dirty dishes. He wandered around the churchyard, waiting for the folks to finish eating and start dancing again. Soon enough, the music filled the night air again, and the ladies were quickly claimed while the men without partners stood around the dancers, awaiting the next song.

Jack washed more of the dirty dishes, with the brides helping once all the serving was done. Butch kept his eye on the half pie that was leftover. He couldn't tell if it was peach or apple, but that hardly mattered. He just had to get another slice. Maybe if he offered to help. . .

He meandered back to the food table. "I. . .uh. . .could fetch some clean water, if'n y'all need some."

"Why, 'tis a kind offer you make, young man." The Irish gal dumped the rinse bucket and handed it to him. "If you'd be so kind as to refill this, I'll have another slice of pie waitin' for you when you return."

His heart jumped, and he grabbed the pail. "Yes'm, that sounds fair to me."

He hurried around to the back of the church where a well had been dug, and in a matter of minutes, he'd filled the pail and returned to the washing table.

Jack leaned against one side of it, eating a cookie. She scowled at him. Butch grinned. Knowing he'd get to eat another piece of pie made his whole world look better, for the moment, at least.

He slowly ate his second slice, closing his eyes and savoring each bite.

"You're gonna have a bellyache, eating all that."

Butch eyed Jack, who held another cookie in her hand. "What about you? How many cookies have you eaten?"

She made a face at him, shoved her treat into her mouth, and then helped herself to another one. The rate she was eating those, there wouldn't be any left by the end of the next dance.

Dan Howard wandered back to the table, looking a bit green himself. He fiddled with the brim of his hat and stirred up dust with the toe of his boot. Miss Bennett kept casting glances his way, her cheeks turning red. Finally, Mr. Howard closed the distance between him and the woman. "Would you. . .ah. . .care to. . .ah. . . dance with me?"

Miss Bennett nodded, looking shy, but her eyes glimmered. She looped her arm through the livery owner's, and they strode off together. Butch finished his pie and got a sudden idea.

It wouldn't work.

But then, maybe it would.

He'd never know if he didn't try.

He set the plate on the table and walked back to Jack. She tilted her head to look up at him.

"What do you want?"

This was a stupid idea. He knew it, but he had to ask. "Would you care to dance?"

Jack's blue eyes widened, and he thought she would gag. She fanned her hand in front of her face and looked as if she couldn't catch her breath. Finally, she said, "Eww. . .you've got to be kidding."

Butch shook his head, not quite ready to give up.

"I don't know how to dance, and besides, I'm wearing pants. How weird would that be? Anyway, I wouldn't dance with you if you were the last person on earth." She crossed her arms, hiked up her little chin, and marched off.

Butch's insides ached as bad as when his pa had beaten him. He knew she wouldn't dance with the likes of him—and anyway, he didn't even know how to dance. She'd probably just kept him from making a fool of himself. Still, her rejection ached as bad as a gunshot wound would. Someone touched his forearm, and he jumped.

"Don't let the lass bother you." The pretty Irish gal—Miss O'Neil, he thought—smiled up at him. "She's at an age where she's not yet attracted to males. Give her a few years, and all that will change."

He offered the woman a half-smile and then sauntered away, tired of hearing the festive music. Jack wouldn't change, no matter how many years passed. Why did she have to hate him? What had he ever done to her?

One thing was certain: He would never ask her to dance again. Ever.

❧

Jack stomped back home, her irritation burning, not so much from Butch's offer to dance as from her reaction to his surprising question. Imagine, her dancing with Butch Laird. Why, her friends would never let her live that down. She shivered and turned around, walking backward. Her steps slowed, and her gaze scanned the crowd. He was gone.

His rank pig stink made her nearly retch, although she had to admit he didn't smell nearly as bad tonight. In fact, he looked as if he had on clean clothes. Had he been planning all day to ask her to dance? Had he gotten cleaned up just to look nicer for the social?

Something in Jack's gut twisted as she remember the hurt in his black eyes when she so adamantly refused to dance with him. She didn't like disappointing people, but why should it bother her to upset him?

He was her enemy.

But hadn't the preacher said something about loving your enemies? She shuddered as a sick feeling twisted her belly at the thought of loving Butch Laird. She'd rather eat a grub worm.

She picked up a stick and dragged it along the picket fence in front of Polly and Dolly's house, making a clicking sound with each picket it hit. Why did she feel guilty for being mean to Butch? The fact that she'd told a falsehood that caused him to spend two days in jail still bothered her. She heaved a sigh and flung the stick into the street.

Too late, she noticed the cowboy riding there. His horse squealed and kicked up his hooves when the stick hit its flanks. "Hey, kid!"

Jack took off running and dashed between the Dykstra house and Mr. Castleby's. She ran past her house and down the side of the Sunday house where Luke had lived before he married her ma. The house sat empty now, so she opened the door and darted inside. Her side ached, and her chest heaved. She peeked out the window, relieved when she didn't see the cowboy looking for her.

"It was an accident." She dropped the curtain and looked around the dim room. "I didn't mean to hit that horse."

Butch claimed he hadn't meant to hit her at the river that day, and she kinda sorta believed him. But hadn't he done other things to her and her friends?

She sat in the rocking chair across from the cold fireplace and rocked. Why did she struggle so much with her feelings for Butch? Was she being unfair to him?

He had been nice tonight. Hadn't done anything to upset her besides asking her to dance. And he'd politely offered to fetch that water for Shannon.

Jack squeezed her head with her palms. All this thinking about Butch was making her head hurt. Maybe he wasn't as bad as he seemed, but the thing was, if she befriended him, every other kid in school would turn against her. And how could she stand that stench all the time?

Nope, they just had to stay enemies. There was no way around that.

CHAPTER 12

Leah swayed to the rhythm of the lively music. Dan Howard wasn't a half-bad dancer, especially compared to the other men she'd sashayed around the grass with tonight. Working at the food table had kept her busy, but now that most everything was gone, she had no excuse not to dance with the men.

"That was some good-tastin' pie, Miss Bennett. As good as my own ma used to make. You ought to open up a bakery."

Leah felt her cheeks warm at Dan's compliment, and being so near to him made her pulse race. "Thank you. But what do you mean by 'used to make'? I know your ma was doing poorly that day I visited, but does she not bake at all anymore?"

Dan pursed his lips and stared over her head. "She hasn't been doin' too good the past few weeks."

"Oh, I'm sorry to hear that. Does she need some help with the house or the cooking?"

Dan's dark gaze pierced hers, sending delicious tingles throughout her body. Not since Sam had a man had such an effect on her.

"That's right nice of you to offer, ma'am. I don't like asking for favors, but Ma could use some help, and it would do her good to have another woman's company."

Leah smiled. "Then I shall go visit her under one condition."

Dan's eyes narrowed, as if he suspected she was going to ask for the world. "What would that be?"

"That you quit calling me ma'am. It makes me feel like a spinster."

Dan leaned his head back and laughed, warming her face and delighting her whole being. For a big man, he was quite comely. His dark hair and eyes blended well with his tanned face, sun-kissed from hours of working outside.

He pulled her a tiny bit closer and leaned down. "You've got a deal. . .ma'am."

"Oh, you." Leah smacked him lightly on the chest and felt it rumble as he chuckled. "Do you think your mother would be offended if I offered to do some cleaning or baking?"

Dan twisted his lips to one side, and he gazed up at the sky. "I don't know, but she needs more help than I can give. Maybe I should just hire you to clean house."

Leah stopped dancing and held up her hand.

Dan glanced around at the moving couples surrounding them and fidgeted. "Did I say somethin' wrong?"

"I offered my services freely. I will be offended if you try to pay me."

His lips twitched, and a gleam entered his gaze. He tipped his hat. "Yes, ma'am. I've been put in my place, well and good. But we should get back to dancing unless you'd prefer someone else for a partner."

Leah peered over her shoulder and saw several men staring at them, looking as if they'd like to cut in. She held out her hand to Dan and allowed him to pull her close. If it were proper, she'd only dance with him. She enjoyed how safe she felt in his thick arms. She loved his eyes, and how his deep voice sounded almost like a caress. He made her feel special with the looks he gave her and the gentleness of his touch. She never figured on falling for a livery owner, but she had.

Did she dare hope he might one day come to care for her?

The music ended, and several other men swarmed Leah. Dan stepped back, looking disappointed that their time together had ended. "Maybe you could save me another dance before things end tonight?"

Leah smiled and nodded. "I'd like that."

Dan tipped his hat and started to walk away, but he stopped. "When this shindig is over, I'll help you get all the dishes back to Polly's and see you home."

Leah curtsied, but another man claimed her hand as the music started. By the end of the social, she couldn't have said who all she'd danced with, but her feet ached, and her heart was full. Dan had stood at the outskirts of the dancers, watching her, almost as if keeping guard. The only other person he'd danced with had been Polly Dykstra. She and her sister came over to watch the dancing after finishing up at their businesses. But with all the lonely men at the social, the two older women were soon in the midst of it all. Leah smiled. Polly and Dolly had only lasted for three dances, but when they left, their cheeks were rosy, and both women were smiling. That was probably the best time they'd had in a long while.

Leah stacked the plates, surprised to find almost half a pie left when she lifted up a towel that had covered the dish. Had something been wrong with it? She swiped her finger through some juice on the empty side of the plate and stuck it in her mouth. The sweet taste of apples and cinnamon teased her senses.

"Ah ah, no sampling the wares." Dan Howard stood on the other side of the table, watching her with sparkling eyes.

"I just wondered if something was wrong with this pie since some of it was left."

"I think the men were more interested in dancing with you pretty women than eating."

Leah chuckled. "That's a first."

"You might be right about that." Dan shoved his hands in his pockets. "So what do you need me to do?"

Shannon hurried over. "I'm here. I'll start carrying the dirty dishes back to Polly's."

"I'll go with you." Leah glanced at Dan. "Just let me wipe down this table, and then you can return it to the back of the church."

"And the smaller table belongs in front of the pulpit. Perhaps one of the Corbetts will help carry it."

"No need. It's just a little table, ma'am. I can manage it myself."

Leah and Shannon exchanged a glance. Shannon collected the dirty pie and cookie plates, while Leah wiped off the table. Dan hoisted up the bigger of the two, and Leah hurried around him to open the church door. She followed him inside, but as the door closed, all went dark.

Dan banged into something. "Where'd you say to put the table?"

Leah struggled to see something in the blackness. "Against the back wall."

"Uh. . .where is the back wall?"

Leah couldn't help giggling. "I have no idea. Maybe I should get a lantern."

The table scraped against the floor as Dan moved it. Leah heard it clunk against something—the wall, she hoped. Dan's footsteps came in her direction, and he suddenly bumped her. Hard.

"Oompf." She flailed her arms and whacked his as he grabbed hold of her upper arm.

"Steady now. We don't want you gettin' hurt."

Her hand came to rest against his chest—his very solid chest. She felt the warmth of his skin through the chambray and the rise and fall as he breathed. Sam hadn't been much more than a boy when he'd first kissed her and asked her to marry him, but there was nothing boyish about Dan Howard. She just might swoon at being alone in the dark with him so near. His warm breath brushed her forehead, but he made no move to leave.

"Miss Bennett."

"Leah. Please call me Leah."

Could she hear a smile in the dark? Because she was sure he'd just smiled.

"Leah...I want you to know that you caught my eye when you first came to town."

Her heart turned a cartwheel. "I did?"

"Yep, but I thought for sure that Luke would pick you."

"Truly? Why did you think that?"

He was quiet for a moment, but his hand ran slowly up and down her arm, stirring her senses. She'd never considered he'd had his eye on her. Why would she when she was battling so hard for the marshal's affections? She'd never dreamed then that another man might be interested in her.

"Talking heart matters ain't easy for me. I'd...uh...like to take you for a buggy ride come Sunday."

Leah smiled. Since when was a buggy ride a heart matter? Maybe his feelings weren't as strong as hers. They hardly knew each other.

"I reckon we oughta go." He stepped forward, without warning, and nearly knocked her down again. His arms tightened around her and crushed her against his chest. She just stood there, and then slowly lifted her hands to his back and relaxed her head against his chest. His heart pounded a frantic rhythm that she was sure matched her own. Dan's hand caressed the side of her head.

"It's...uh...highly improper, since I hardly know you, but if I don't kiss you, Leah, I think I'll go loco."

Her breath caught in her throat, unable to believe him. Would it be wrong to let him kiss her? She was certain she was falling in love with him, but what if things didn't work out? It would make seeing him extremely awkward. Dan suddenly stepped back, but Leah grabbed the sides of his shirt to halt him.

"You sure you don't mind."

"No."

"No, you mind?"

"No! I don't mind."

"Oh." He chuckled and bent down, his breath mingling with hers. His full lips covered hers in a kiss so gentle, so tender, it stole all the energy from her. Her knees nearly buckled.

Something banged outside, and they jumped apart. "Come and get the door for me, brother."

Leave it to a Corbett to interrupt one of the sweetest moments of her life.

"I'll get it," Dan said.

The door opened, and the light of the full moon illuminated the area. Mark Corbett jumped back and dropped the smaller table.

"Lord have mercy, Dan, you scared half my remaining years off me. What are you doing in there?"

Dan stepped out, and Mark's eyes widened as Leah stepped out from behind him. Mark's gaze darted back and forth between her and Dan and then to the dark room.

"Don't be getting no ideas, Corbett. We were just putting away the other table." Dan hiked his chin as if daring Mark to challenge him.

"Sure thing. I prefer putting tables away in the dark, too. It's much more fun than in a lighted room."

Leah was sure her cheeks were bright red, and she hurried back to where the tables had been set up. All the dishes were gone, as were Shannon and most of the people who'd attended the social. She and Dan couldn't have been in the church all that long. She glanced back and saw Dan holding the door as Mark wrestled the table through. Once he was in, Dan shut the door and hurried toward her.

His cheeks looked ruddy in the dim light of the two lanterns that were still lit. "I reckon we should head on over to the café before he comes back out. I don't care to listen to his teasing."

Leah nodded and started walking toward the café. Dan fell into step beside her. She longed to touch her lips, still tingling from his kiss, but she didn't. Tonight, her future had taken an interesting twist, and she couldn't wait to see what would happen.

CHAPTER 13

I don't know why them Corbett brothers had to go hire a gal to work for them. It ain't right that wimmen should work in a business. No, siree." Homer Sewell swiped at a streak of brown juice that ran down the side of his mouth. A lump of something in one cheek and his bristly beard reminded Shannon of a squirrel. He eyed her with his beady eyes.

"Well, they did, sir, so you can either give me your order or return when one of the Corbetts are here."

He scowled, and his cheeks puffed up. He gazed around the floor of the office.

Shannon's gut twisted. "If you intend on spitting, sir, I kindly ask you to step outside. There is no spittoon in here."

The man mumbled something under his breath and stomped out the door, leaving behind a foul odor. Shannon held her hand over her nose and hoped the man didn't return. Just that fast, she regretted the thought. The Corbetts could use the business, but she hated dealing with close-minded men who thought women should only be home, tending the house and babies. Not that there was anything wrong with that, but this was 1886, and things were changing. Women had more opportunities than in the past. She tapped her fingers on the desk, wishing that Leah could find a position of employment and not be dependent on the Corbetts for support.

She rested her cheek in her hand, remembering last Saturday's social. She'd danced with a number of men, but not the one she'd hope to. Mark had attended the social, but he didn't dance with any of the women. And she was surprised to see the social so well-attended. She had no idea there were so many women in the county who wanted to find a husband. Why had the Corbett brothers sent for mail-order brides when there were ladies already here wanting to marry? Had they not been aware of them at the time they were looking for someone to marry their cousin? Or maybe they just felt none of them were a good fit for the marshal.

Shannon sighed and watched the old codger stalk away. Evidently he'd had enough of her for now. She hated days like this where she was caught up with her work and there was little to occupy her time. Standing, she stretched and looked around. The office could use a good dusting and sweeping. Dirt from the road was always being tracked inside.

In the back room, she rummaged around until she found a halfway clean rag and set about dusting everything in sight. Evidently, the Corbetts didn't care whether five layers of dust coated the shelves and other sparse furniture. Afterward, she ran the broom over the floors of both rooms and even swept the boardwalk out front and the porch in the back. She leaned against the broom and stared out at the dry Texas landscape. Things here were so different than in Ireland. She missed the green—and the cooler temperatures—and the rain. With the arrival of September, the temperatures had cooled slightly, but it was still hot. The grass had dried, and most of it turned yellow from a lack of water. What she wouldn't give for a nice rain shower.

Sweat streaked down her cheek, and she wiped it with her

sleeve. Such an unladylike action, but it seemed a common thing here. Where was the ever-present wind when she needed it?

The bell over the door jingled, and she sighed. Hopefully Mr. Sewell hadn't returned. The Corbett brothers had gone to Dallas, and she had no idea when they'd return. She set the broom in a corner and walked back to the office. A man she'd danced once with at the social stood shifting from foot to foot and repeatedly clearing his throat. He must have had important business in town since he was dressed in his Sunday-go-to-meeting clothes. He was a farmer, if she remembered correctly. His brown trousers and long, dark tan, frock coat looked too big for his lithe frame. A russet silk puff tie circled his neck and was tucked inside his fancy vest. He twirled a black coachman's hat in his hands.

"Good morning, Miss O'Neil."

Shannon nodded, her mind grasping for a name. She'd danced with a half-dozen men after serving the refreshments but couldn't for the life of her remember his. "Forgive me, but your name has slipped my mind."

"Terrence Brannon, ma'am."

The man had left the door open, and Leah walked up behind him. She waved at Shannon, held up a basket, and mouthed something Shannon couldn't understand.

She looked back at her customer. "How can I help you, Mr. Brannon?"

"Is Garrett or Mark here?" His hazel eyes flitted their gaze around the room like a hummingbird darting between flowers.

Shannon held back a smile. It seemed Texas men were either loud and overly bold or horribly shy around women. It was easy to see which Mr. Brannon was.

He tugged at the collar of his white shirt and suddenly dropped to the floor on one knee. Leah's eyes widened, and Shannon dashed forward. Had the man overheated, wearing that wool jacket?

"Mr. Brannon, are you all right?"

His face flushed twenty shades of red. "Um. . .yes, ma'am. I was just…um…wondering if, um…" He suddenly jumped up and grasped her hand. "Marry me, Miss O'Neil. I have a nice farm. A solid house—though it ain't too big. But I can add on when the young'uns start comin'." His words rushed out like a runaway train.

Shannon stepped back and tried to tug her hand away from his. He didn't release it. She glanced at Leah, whose lips were pressed inward as if to hold in a laugh. Her eyes glimmered, and her brows lifted in a teasing manner as if to say, "Answer the man."

"Don't say no, ma'am. I know you have plenty other men to choose from, but I'm hopin' you'll pick me. I'm young and hearty and would make a good father to our children, though I do hope they get your hair. What color is that anyhow?"

Leah snorted, and the man jumped and looked over his shoulder, eyes wide as a spooked cow's. Shannon struggled to hold a straight face. In spite of being tired of marriage offers, she knew this man was sincere and felt bad for his embarrassment. "Please come in, Miss Bennett. Mr. Brannon and I will step outside for a moment."

Leah walked in, not looking at all embarrassed by the odd situation. Once she passed the man, she grinned mischievously, leaned toward Shannon, and whispered, "Let him down easily."

Shannon sucked her lips inward and worked to keep a straight face. While the situation might be humorous to her and Leah, Mr. Brannon was dead serious and had his future riding on her decision. She was getting tired of disappointing suitors, especially when the one man she wished would pay her some attention remained distant.

Outside, she drew in a heavy breath and stiffened her back. Mr. Brannon had half worn out the brim of his hat and looked at her like she was a prize heifer. But she wanted more than someone's admiration. Was it too much to hope to marry someone for love?

"Mr. Brannon—"

"Call me Terrence—or Terry, ma'am."

"Mr. Brannon. Your sincere marriage offer warms my heart, but I'm afraid I can't accept it."

"But why? You need a man to care for you, and I need a woman to tend my home and to give me children."

Shannon resisted the urge to roll her eyes. He was steadfast, if nothing else. "Do you have feelings for me, sir?"

He blinked and stared at her as if she'd asked for his shirt measurements. "What's feelings got to do with anything?"

"A lot. When a marriage hits rough times, it's love and caring that pulls folks through. That and faith in God."

He scratched his head. "I reckon the feelings'll come after we marry. Won't they?"

Shannon shook her head. "A man and woman should care for one another before they marry."

"Well. . .I reckon I could court you a while so's you could get some feelings before we marry up together. Just so long as it didn't take too long."

Men! They were completely dense when it came to romance. "Mr. Brannon, I cannot marry you. Thank you for your offer, but I'm afraid my answer is no."

He stood staring down at his hat. "I reckon you made that clear enough." He glanced toward the freight office door. "You don't suppose that other boardinghouse bride would be interested, would she?"

Shannon shivered. What uncouth men these Americans were. They treated their woman no better than cattle. She hiked up her chin. "I can't speak for Miss Bennett on such a matter, but I don't think today is the proper day to ask her."

"Why not? She sick or something?"

Shannon shook her head, more happy each moment that passed that she hadn't considered this man a serious prospect. "If you'll excuse me, sir, I need to get back inside."

The man slapped his hat on his head and nodded. With a clenched jaw, he stalked down the boardwalk. Shannon slipped back into the office and found Leah had spread out a towel, teapot, saucers, and cookies on Mark's desk. Shannon dragged Garrett's chair toward Leah, whose eyes danced with mirth. Suddenly she doubled over and started laughing.

"Oh my, that was hilarious." Leah slapped her leg and dropped into the chair. "I thought that man had passed out, and the next thing I knew, he was asking you to marry him and have his kids."

Shannon's mouth twitched, and she broke into giggles. "Me, too. I thought the man had fallen in a faint because Mark and Garrett weren't here."

"And did you see his face when he heard me behind him?"

Shannon laughed. "Oh, the poor man was mortified."

Leah attempted to sober. "I tried to back away when I realized what was happening, but I was close to dropping the basket after carrying it from the boardinghouse. And then I. . .snorted."

Both women cackled again, and tears ran down Shannon's cheeks. After a few more attempts to be somber and more fits of laughter, the women finally settled down. Leah poured the tea while Shannon wiped her cheeks and eyes.

"How many offers is that now?" Leah handed her a teacup.

Shannon opened the middle drawer of the desk, pulled out a plain sheet of paper, and made a mark on it. "That makes six so far."

Leah shook her. "How come you're getting so many offers, and I haven't had a one?"

Shannon shook her head and sipped her tea. "Perhaps 'tis because you're at the boardinghouse all day, and men either have to go through the marshal or his wife to get to you. I'm here most mornings, and the Corbetts are often gone. I'm free game, you might say."

"Hmm. . .that does make sense when you put it that way. The marshal can be mighty intimidating, and so can Rachel. She's gotten tougher since they've married, don't you think?"

Shannon nodded. "Aye, there's truth in what you say. Ever

since she was kidnapped and Luke Davis declared his love for her, she's been stronger, more confident."

"You think having a good man love you like he does her makes a woman better?"

Shannon shrugged. "I've seen little of happy marriages. My parents' was an arranged union. I don't believe my mum ever came to love my father." She stirred some sugar into her cup. "He was a hard man. But then perhaps he was that way because she didn't love him."

Leah stared into her cup. "My pa, too. All he did was work. My ma loves him, though."

"Do you think it's too much to hope to marry for love?"

Leah's eyes twinkled, and she reached across the desk, touching Shannon's arm. "No, and I'll tell you why." She looked into the back room and at the front door, as if making sure no one would overhear; then she leaned forward. "I've met someone."

Surprise washed through Shannon. Nobody had come calling on Leah at the boardinghouse, and she hadn't been seen around town with anyone in particular. When had she met someone? During the social? "Who is it?"

Leah grinned and popped a half-eaten cookie into her mouth. "Dan Howard."

Shannon thought of the big man who ran the livery down the street. He was friends with the Corbetts and had been in the office a few times. He'd been kind and polite, not caring that a woman was working there. "I like Mr. Howard. He seems like a decent fellow."

"Oh, he is. And you should see how he cares for his ailing mother. I'm going over tomorrow to visit her."

Shannon ran her fingers around the edge of the tea saucer. "So does he return your affection?"

A soft smile lingered on Leah's cheeks, causing a slash of jealousy to rise up in Shannon. She was happy for Leah, but at the same time, she longed for Mark to notice her.

"I think he does." She leaned forward again, blue eyes dancing like a spring shower. "He kissed me."

Shannon's eyes widened. "Truly?"

Leah nodded.

"Blessit be. Are you thinking you could marry him? 'Twould solve your problem of having the Corbetts support you. I know you don't like that."

"No, I don't, but I wouldn't marry just to escape that. I have feelings for Dan."

"You've done a good job of hiding them."

Leah poured more tea into both cups, sending a spicy scent into the air. "I'll be honest; they come on fast and furious. I truly didn't know a woman could fall for a man so quickly."

Shannon stared out the window and saw the Corbetts riding by on their wagon. They'd probably go around and come down the alley and park in back. Her heart quickened at the thought of seeing Mark again. "I know just what you mean."

Leah's brows dashed upward. "You do?"

Her lips tugged up in a melancholy smile. "Aye."

Leah clutched Shannon's arm and leaned forward again. "Who is it? Tell me before I die of curiosity. I can't for the life of me imagine who he is."

Shannon glanced at the back door, knowing it was too soon for the brothers to have arrived. She looked at Leah, not sure if she should say anything, given Mark's lack of interest shown to her. She shrugged.

"Oh, come on. I told you."

Shannon sighed. "All right, but you can't tell a soul. I don't think he even knows of my attraction."

"Truly?"

She nodded. "Aye." She glanced at the back door again and nibbled her lip.

Leah shook her arm. "Tell me."

" 'Tis Mark."

"Mark who?" Wrinkles plowed across Leah's forehead, then suddenly, her eyes widened, and her mouth and nose crinkled on one side. "Surely you don't mean Mark Corbett. Not after all he and his brother have done to us."

Shannon didn't respond, but sat staring into her nearly empty cup. How could she expect Leah to understand when she didn't herself?

The front-door bell jingled, and Homer Sewell strode in. Shannon resisted the urge to roll her eyes. She didn't want to deal with the man twice in one day. "How can I help you, Mr. Sewell?"

"Mark and Garrett back yet? Thought I saw their wagon." He eyed the teacups and empty plate with disdain. "Them brothers won't appreciate their business becomin' a ladies' tea parlor."

Shannon peeked at Leah, who battled a smile. Both ladies filled the basket quickly. Shannon folded the towel and handed it to her friend.

"Well, I shall be off. See you at noon."

Mr. Sewell stepped back and tipped his hat to Leah. Shannon noticed the back door open, and Mark walked in. Her heart skipped a beat.

"Well, if them brothers ain't here, I'm leavin'." Mr. Sewell backed toward the front door. Evidently he couldn't see Mark from where he stood. "Don't know why they let a gal tend to their business. Wimmen oughta be workin' in a kitchen, not an office. It's downright disturbin'."

CHAPTER 14

Mark stood in the back doorway, his gaze landing on Shannon. A fire in his gut quickened. He didn't like how his body reacted whenever she was near. His stomach swirled with queasiness. His mind worked as if it were trudging through a thick fog. His thoughts got confused, and his tongue seemed to quit working altogether. She was lovely, with her fair skin and auburn hair that his fingers ached to touch. She was young, but not so young that she wasn't all woman. Why did she fluster him so?

He recognized Homer Sewell's voice and cantankerous attitude before his eyes landed on the man. Mark stepped out of the back room, irritated at the man for lashing out at Shannon. "Good day, Homer."

Relief was written all over the man's wrinkled face. " 'Bout time you got back here."

"You know my brother and I have deliveries to make and are frequently gone. That's why we hired Miss O'Neil to take orders and be here when we couldn't. I don't care for the way you treated her. She's an employee of Corbett Freight, and as such, deserves the same kindness you'd show us."

Mr. Sewell ducked his head and frowned. Mark's gaze latched onto Shannon's. Her wide green eyes stared back at him, and she sat up straighter. A tiny smile played at the corners of her enticing mouth. He broke his gaze and turned back to his customer. *I've no business noticing Shannon's mouth.*

"So, Homer, you can either place your orders with Shannon when Garrett and I aren't around or just keep coming back to town and try to meet up with us."

"I don't have time to do that. It's a good half-day's ride to Lookout."

"I guess you could try getting your deliveries by stage."

Homer shook his head. "Then I have to drive into town to get them. Costs me a whole day's work. That's why I pay y'all such extravagant prices."

Mark shrugged. "Miss O'Neil has been working here for several weeks, and she's learning fast. Next time you come in and we aren't here, give her your order. I'm sure you'll be satisfied."

"Wimmen ain't got no business working anywhere's but at home." He dug into his pocket and shoved a piece of paper and five silver dollars at Mark. The coins clinked in his hand. "Here's what I need. When can you get it to me?"

Mark noted that he wanted several rolls of barbed fence wire, some lumber, and a bag of nails. Nothing that Shannon would have had trouble ordering. "You still want the Glidden Square Strand wiring?"

Homer nodded. "Yep, and get me another dozen pairs of leather gloves. That wire eats right through them."

Mark did some mental calculations. "I'll probably need another two or three dollars to get all that."

Homer scowled but reached into his pocket and handed Mark a gold eagle coin. "Here, take this and give me those back."

They made the exchange, and Homer went on his way. Mark pocketed the ten-dollar coin and handed Homer's list to Shannon. "Why don't you fill out his order form?"

Shannon wrinkled her mouth, drawing Mark's gaze to it. "He wouldn't like that much."

Mark sat on the corner of his desk. "Try not to let men like him get to you. They're old-fashioned and think God created women to be slaves to men."

Her cheeks flushed a pretty pink. "Thank you for standing up for me. I tried to help him, but he didn't want anything to do with me."

"He's a fool."

Shannon's gaze darted to his, and for a moment, they stared into each other's eyes. His heart galloped, and he couldn't look away for the life of him.

The back door banged, and they both jumped. Mark shot up off the desk.

"You gonna lollygag all day or help me with this load?"

"I was tending to business."

Garrett waggled his brows. "Yeah, I can see that. How is business, Miss O'Neil?"

The pink on Shannon's cheek now flamed red as a Texas star flower.

Mark straightened. "Homer Sewell gave her some trouble."

The grin on Garrett's face changed into a scowl. "What kind of trouble?"

"Oh, you know his kind. Don't think women should ever step out of the house except to do laundry and go to the privy."

Shannon glanced down at the desk, her embarrassment obvious.

"Well, Homer's a good customer, but you don't have to take any guff off him."

"What should I do when a man refuses to deal with me?" she asked.

Garrett pushed his hat back off his forehead. "I hadn't really considered that would be a problem."

Mark knew his brother hadn't considered much when he'd decided to hire Shannon. He was just trying to figure out a way to get some work out of one of the boardinghouse brides in exchange for the money they were paying to support them. Garrett hadn't considered having Shannon work in the office might be difficult for her—or their customers—at times. That was one of the reasons he objected. Some men weren't trustworthy, and it bothered Mark when they had to leave Shannon alone for a long while when they were gone on deliveries.

"Well. . .I guess if you get any more hard-nosed fellows, just tell them they'll have to come back when we're here and talk with us."

Shannon nodded, then pulled a form out of the desk drawer and began recording Homer Sewell's order. She worked so diligently that he was having trouble keeping her busy. Too bad they couldn't hire her to clean their house. It sure needed it, but it didn't seem proper to ask an unmarried gal to clean for two old bachelors. Besides, having her scent teasing him at the office was bad enough. If she spent any time in his home, he was certain he would be awake all night thinking about her.

She nibbled on her lower lip as she concentrated on her work. How had she ever reminded him of Annabelle? There was nothing similar about the two women except maybe the color of their hair and their fair skin. Wisps of auburn hair hung down, curling in loose ringlets. They bounced each time she moved, and he longed to touch them and see if they were as soft as they looked. He swallowed hard. When had he grown to care for her?

Someone shoved him hard, and Mark stumbled sideways, bumping into the desk. "Gonna stand there enjoying the view all day?" Garrett grinned wide, showing all his teeth.

Mark ducked his head, embarrassed to be caught staring. Nothing could come of caring for Shannon O'Neil.

She was sweet.

Innocent.

Even if she did come to care for him one day, when she learned the truth about him, she'd hop the next stage out of town. No decent woman would want a man with a past like his.

Abilene, Texas

Annabelle Smith dodged the cowboy's groping hand and balanced the tray of drinks she held level with her face. Her ribs ached from the "lesson" Everett had given her after closing hours. Wincing, she placed the drinks in front of the man at the all-night gambling table and hurried away.

A young cowpoke called her name and grabbed as she passed, pulling her onto his lap. His warm, wet lips roamed across her bare shoulder. Annabelle cringed and smacked him atop the head with her tray. Raucous laughter erupted, and the young man rubbed his head, grinning.

What was it with these men? They knew all she did was serve drinks. She'd never been an upstairs gal, in spite of Everett's threats to toss her out on the street if she didn't soon change her ways. He'd been making those same threats for years, and he still kept her on, but she was getting older now, and Everett preferred younger girls who didn't yet reflect the hard lifestyle of working in a saloon and dodging men every night. What would she do if he kicked her out on the streets?

She sashayed in and out of trouble and back to the bar. The huge picture of the half-naked woman above the wall of bottles repulsed her. She still hated the odor of liquor and smelly cowboys, but most of the time she didn't notice. Why couldn't she have a decent job like being a seamstress or a cook? She snorted a laugh. What decent citizen would hire a saloon girl?

She might not be an upstairs gal, but to the good townsfolk of Abilene, she was one and the same. Her only chance for another life was to leave this town. But where could she go?

"Stop lollygagging, Annabelle, and get out there and sell drinks. You're costing me money," Everett snarled at her, then poured another round for the men at the bar.

She grabbed a fresh bottle and cups that Everett had wiped half-clean, then strolled around the saloon, stopping at a table with three businessmen. "Can I freshen your drinks, gentlemen?"

One man nodded, and another lifted his glass. The third man, a regular who always gave her trouble, eyed her as if he were a starving man and she a big, juicy steak. "I'm not thirsty, Annabelle. I'm hankering for some alone time with a purty gal."

She cringed but kept a smile pasted on her face. "I'm sure Trudy or Lotus would be happy to oblige you."

He stood, towering over her by a good six inches. "We've danced this dance for years now, and I'm tired of it. You're the one I want."

Annabelle backed up, as a scene from years ago rose in her memory. The same situation had occurred. A man thought he could have more than she was willing to give, but that man had ended up dead. This evening, however, no shining knight was around to rescue her from this vile man, only herself. She forced her voice to sound steady. "Sit down, Cal, and let me pour you a drink."

His eyes ignited, and he shoved his chair back. "Everett says I can take you upstairs whether you wanna go or not. I paid him good, too."

Annabelle's gaze shot over to her boss. A sickening smirk twisted his thick lips, and he lifted a cup to her as if in toast. Why, after all these years, was he forcing this on her?

She had to get out of there. She tossed her tray, bottle and all, at Cal and spun around. Deftly weaving in and out of the tables as she did daily, she headed for the swinging doors that opened onto the street. A growl roared behind her, and the crowd broke out in laughter and cheers, some egging Cal on, and others rooting for her.

Her heart pounded so hard she felt sure it would burst from her chest. A cowboy grabbed her flared skirt, slowing her down. The doors were just two tables away. She didn't dare look back. Plowing out the double doors, she breathed a fresh breath of air while her eyes struggled to adjust to the darkness.

Hide. Fast. Her brain repeated the mantra. *Hide.*

She rushed down the boardwalk steps and turned into the alley, just as she heard the doors fling open so hard they banged against the saloon's facade. A little farther, and she'd be free. At the back of the alley, something huge stepped from the shadows, and Annabelle plowed into the big, fleshy body. Thick hands latched onto her arms, pinning her against him.

"Not so fast, little lady."

Annabelle stiffened at Everett's deep voice. Footsteps charged behind her, drawing closer.

"You knew your days were numbered, but I guess our little talk didn't knock any sense into you. I've been losing money on you for some time now. But no more. Take her, Cal. She's all yours."

"No!" Annabelle kicked and jerked, trying to get free. "You can't make me do this."

Cal lifted her and slung her over one big shoulder and carried her through the saloon's back door. Hoots rose up from the crowd. Upside down, she could see their leering faces and sickening grins. How many of them figured they'd be next?

She wanted to die. Maybe she could get to Cal's gun, shoot him, and get away. Maybe she'd just shoot herself, too.

One of the upstairs doors opened. Lotus stepped into the hall. "Well, well, it's about time someone brought Miss High and Mighty up here. Guess you won't be so snooty to us after tonight."

Bile burned Annabelle's throat. How could this be happening? Why hadn't she left her job sooner?

Cal kicked in a door, and Trudy squealed and grabbed for her cover-up. He cursed and opened another door. Annabelle was close to passing out from fear and being held upside down for so long, but she had to keep her wits about her.

Cal kicked the door shut with his boot and deposited her on the bed. She bounced twice, the old frame creaking and groaning.

"Just relax. You'll enjoy yourself, I promise."

What an arrogant imbecile!

Her mind raced. There had to be some way out of this situation. Maybe if she played coy, he'd drop his guard. Her gaze roved the room. There wasn't much to work with. Besides a bed, there was one ladder-back chair, and a small table holding a flowery ceramic pitcher and basin.

She crawled off the dirty bed, and stood in front of the table.

"What do you think you're doing?" Cal moved closer, unbuckling his holster.

She cast a coy glance over her shoulder. "A girl has to freshen up, doesn't she?"

Cal's gray eyes narrowed, gazing at her as if he didn't quite trust her. And well he shouldn't.

"You don't know how long I've dreamed of this, sweetheart." He stepped up behind her and ran his hands down her arms.

She turned, forcing a playful look. "Me, too. I was just playin' hard to get earlier."

His eyes sparked, and he pulled her into his arms. His lips roved her face, found her mouth, and she made herself play along. After a minute of impossible disgust, she pushed him back. "Don't you want to take off your shirt?"

He grinned and walked back to the door, locking it. He unfastened his buttons and turned to hang his shirt on a hook on the wall, then removed his belt. Repulsed, Annabelle swiped her mouth. She reached behind herself slowly, grabbed the near-empty pitcher, and crept forward. Cal turned slowly, and Annabelle slammed the pitcher upside his head. It cracked and broke, raining water and shards at their feet.

Cal stared at her, dumbfounded. Annabelle's heart raced. What would he do to her now?

He took a half-step forward; then his eyes rolled up in his head, and he fell toward her. She grabbed him, hoping no one would hear his fall, but his weight was too much, and he took her down with him. Stunned, she lay there a moment to catch her breath. But she couldn't rest long. She had to get away.

With some effort, she managed to slide out from under him. Blood ran down the side of his face and onto the carpet. She stared down at Cal, hoping she hadn't killed him, but she imagined that's what he'd do to her if he woke up.

She snatched up the belt and wrapped it around him, locking his arms to his side. The belt barely fit, but it should hold him for a while, giving her precious time to get away. She grabbed his shirt next, and rolled it up, fashioning a gag, using the sleeves to tie it on.

What about his feet? If he could get up, he could make it to the hallway where someone would see him. Her gaze raced around the room. His holster!

She removed his revolver, pulled his feet together, and wrapped the holster around it, hooking it as tight as she could.

Again, her heart stampeded. How could she get out of the saloon without being seen? How could she leave town when she had almost no money? The pittance Everett paid her was barely enough to live on.

She unlocked the door, wincing at its loud click, and opened it a hair. The other doors upstairs were closed. To her left were the rooms Trudy and Lotus were using and the stairs back down to the saloon. To her right was another door. Everett's room.

He'd sent her upstairs on occasion over the years when he'd collected a pile of money. She'd always put it in the bottom drawer of his desk and locked it, returning the key to him when she got back downstairs. He never wanted to leave when customers were there, fearing they'd steal bottles of liquor or start a fight and tear things up.

She slipped into his room and allowed her eyes to adjust to the dark. The overpowering rank scent she recognized as Everett's nearly made her retch. Feeling her way, she found the desk and hurried around behind it. Opening the curtains allowed the light of the three-quarter moon to illuminate the room so she could see well enough. She tugged on the bottom drawer, knowing it would be locked. But to her surprise, it slid free. Way in the back, underneath a stack of papers, she pulled out the money box. The lock on it had long since broken, and Everett was too cheap to buy another one.

He'd be sorry.

Her heart thudded in her chest, as if it were a trapped bird frantically trying to get free. And wasn't that what she was?

She reached in the box. Everett would notice if she took all the money, but he owed her. She'd slaved for him and suffered at his hand, especially tonight. He would pay for her to start a new life.

She grabbed a handful of bills and several double eagle coins, then shoved the drawer closed. Annabelle stuffed the money in her corset and hurried to the back door. Everett's parents had died in a fire, and she'd be forever grateful that he'd had a rear stairway installed, leading from his bedroom.

She unlatched the door and hurried down the steps. Keeping to the shadows, she crept along. The only way to get away fast was to steal a horse, but that was a hanging offense—and she couldn't ride off in her saloon dress.

Untying the closest horse, she led him down the alley and several streets over to the room she rented.

"Hurry, hurry." She could feel Cal waking up and knew he'd make a ruckus until someone heard him.

In her room, she quickly changed into her one cotton calico, her decent dress. She removed the pillowcase and stuffed her hairbrush and undergarments in it. Taking a final look at the ratty place she'd called home for seven years, she knew she'd not mourn its loss.

Quickly, she mounted the horse and raced it out of town. She didn't look back. Nothing good had happened to her in Abilene.

But her luck was changing.

Now she had to decide where to go.

Only one thought came to mind. Find the one man who'd ever shown her true kindness.

She had to find Mark Corbett.

CHAPTER 15

Leah knocked on the door of the Howard house for the second time. She suspected Mrs. Howard was sleeping. Should she go ask Dan's permission before going inside? He had told her it was all right to go in if his mother didn't answer, but she still hated to do so.

She tested the handle and found the door opened easily. She peeked into the parlor and noted it could use a good straightening and dusting. "Mrs. Howard?"

She stepped into the entryway of the house. "It's Leah Bennett, ma'am. Your son said I could come in and visit with you."

Leah pursed her lips when no answer came. She set down her basket and looked around. On the right was an open door to a bedroom. From the manly clothing hanging on pegs on the wall, she knew that was Dan's room. She tiptoed through the parlor and into a short hall that separated the bedrooms. Mrs. Howard lay on her side, facing the wall. A light quilt covered her body. How could she stand the heat with that cover on and the windows shut? Leah crept back to the parlor and looked around.

She should probably leave. But wouldn't it surprise the older woman to awaken from her nap to a clean house with a meal already prepared? Looking around, she decided the kitchen would be her first chore. She opened the back and front doors, along with the kitchen and parlor windows, to let in some fresh air and cool things down.

The morning dishes had been washed, probably Dan's efforts. She found where they belonged and put the plates and coffee cups on the shelf with the other dishes. The silverware rested in a tin can that had long ago lost its label. Taking the cleaning supplies she'd borrowed from Rachel, she washed every surface from the windowsill to the shelves to the top of the canned goods that resided in a tiny pantry. She wiped down the table and chairs and found a broom and mop and tended to the floors. Lastly, she washed several small glass decorations that she suspected were Mrs. Howard's treasures. Standing back with her hands on her hips, she surveyed the spotless kitchen. Her heart warmed at having something to do and being able to help someone.

Rachel had given her a ham hock and some meat. As much as Leah hated lighting the stove and warming up the house even more, she found a large pot and started stewing the meat. She added a pinch of salt and a few other seasonings she found in the pantry and went to clean the parlor.

An hour later, she'd finished cleaning everything she could see, except for Mrs. Howard's room. She'd like to wash the woman's sheets like she had Dan's, but she didn't want to overstep her bounds and embarrass Dan's mother.

The only other thing she could think to do was the laundry. Dan's sheets and blanket were already nearly dry in the warm afternoon sun and brisk wind. The hardest task was heating more water, but Dan had made that duty less difficult with the device he'd made for his mother. An iron rack stood over a campfire in the backyard, and she just had to fill the pot with fresh water. She'd done the task once already when washing the sheets. With the water warming, she added a few chopped logs to the fire, and then stirred Dan's clothes into the water. While they simmered, she went back inside to cut up vegetables for the stew.

She halfway expected to find Mrs. Howard sitting in the kitchen or parlor, and when she didn't, she tiptoed back to the room. The woman was sleeping in the same position. "You must really be tired," Leah whispered. *Poor woman.*

She made quick work of cutting up the potatoes, carrots, and onions for the stew. Then she mixed up a batch of cornbread and put it in the oven. At the back door, she took a moment to rest. If she were to marry Dan, this would be her home, and these would be her daily tasks. She could easily see herself in the sturdy home. Rachel had told her that Dan's father had built the house when Dan was just a boy.

Turning back to look at the inside, she allowed her eyes to adjust. All the rooms could use a fresh coat of paint and maybe even some wallpaper in the parlor. She could do so many things to pretty up this house if she had the chance.

"Please, Lord. I ask that You'd give me that chance. Thank You for saving me from marrying Mr. Abernathy." A snakelike shiver coursed down her spine. "If it be Your will, please allow Dan to fall in love with me. I'd take good care of him and his mother. I promise You that."

After a few more moments of resting and praying for her family back home in Carthage, she washed and rinsed Dan's clothes and hung them on the line. Then she took the clean sheets inside and made Dan's bed. His quilt would need another hour on the line before it was dried. She straightened and rubbed her lower back. Doing the washing and cleaning the whole house in one day was a lot of work, especially since she'd been so inactive the past months with nothing much to occupy her time. She would sleep well tonight; that was certain.

She tiptoed back to Mrs. Howard's room, hoping to get her dirty clothing. The woman still hadn't moved. Leah wondered how Mrs. Howard kept her back from aching. If she'd slept in the same position for so long, hers surely would hurt. Leah studied the quilt for a moment, and she felt a sudden catch in her heart. She bent down and stepped closer. Surely the quilt was moving. Maybe she just couldn't see it in the dim light.

But moving closer didn't change a thing. The quilt didn't move in the least. With a trembling hand, Leah reached out to touch the woman's wrinkled cheek. It felt cool, but how could that be? Leah was sweating from the heat of the stuffy room.

Sucking in a steadying breath, she held her fingers in front of the woman's nose.

Nothing.

Not a single breath.

Leah gasped and jerked back her hand. *No!*

What to do? What to do?

She had to know for sure if Dan's ma had perished. Pressing her quivering fingers to the woman's neck, she hoped—she prayed—to feel a pulse.

She dropped onto the bed, knowing now that Dan's mother had gone to meet her Maker. She had to tell Dan, but how did one do such a thing? Maybe she should get Rachel?

But no, Dan was the man Leah loved. She was the one who had to tell him. She pulled the quilt up and covered Mrs. Howard's face, sad that she'd never get to know her.

Back in the kitchen, she removed the cornbread from the oven and stirred the stew. Dan would not likely have an appetite tonight.

She glanced out the back screen door at the light blue sky. "Lord, give me the words to say."

Ten minutes later, she stood in the back of the livery. Dan patted the rear of a black horse and told a man that he'd be happy with his purchase.

"Thank you. You came highly recommended." He handed Dan several double-eagle coins, mounted, and rode off.

Dan pocketed the money and smiled. She suspected he thought

he'd had a good day. She hated disappointing him. Her heart ached for him. How had her feelings grown so swiftly? She hadn't even fallen for Sam this fast.

"Leah? Have you finished over at the house?" He walked toward her. "I was just heading over there to see if things were going all right."

"I—"Tears filled Leah's eyes and burned her throat.

Dan jogged toward her, a concerned expression marring his handsome face. "What's wrong? Did you hurt yourself?" He grabbed both her hands, turned them over and back, as if searching for an injury. "What's the matter, Leah?"

She tried to form the words but couldn't get them out. She reached forward and laid her hand on his chest. His brows crinkled.

"It's your ma."

He shot out of the livery like a cannonball. Leah picked up her skirts and hurried after him. She didn't want him to be alone at such a time. The front door was open when she arrived, and a wail rose up from the bedroom. Dan knelt on the far side of the bed, clutching his mother's body to his chest. He rocked back and forth, tears streaming down his face. Leah had never heard such a heartrending sound other than the one she'd made herself when she'd learned of Sam's death.

She hurried to Dan's side and laid her hand on his shoulder. His rocking ceased, and he laid his mother back on the bed, staring down at her. Finally he stood, covered her face, and turned to Leah.

"I should have stayed home today. I knew she was feeling poorly."

Leah shook her head and patted his chest. "No, I should have checked on her when I first arrived here, but I thought she was just sleeping."

Dan shook his head and wiped his eyes. "It's not your fault. Ma had been ailing for a while."

"But maybe if I'd done something—" Tears burned Leah's eyes again.

Dan cupped her cheeks with his calloused hands. "Leah, this isn't your fault. Ma was getting older. She had me when she was in her late twenties, and I'm no spring chicken."

In spite of her grief, Leah smiled.

"There's nothing either of us could have done. Ma has been missing Pa for a long while, and now they're together."

"What are you going to do?"

He stared up at the ceiling, and his chin quivered. Suddenly, he sobbed and pulled her against him, crushing her in his grief. She held him, caressing his back and cooing soft words of comfort. If he'd give her the chance, she'd always be there for him. She wasn't sure how long she held him, but finally his tears abated.

He pulled away and wiped his eyes again. "Sorry."

"Don't be. I'm happy I can be here so you don't have to be alone now." Leah rested her hand on his arm. She admired a man who wasn't afraid to allow his emotions to show, especially a big manly man like Dan. Her father rarely had, other than to express his displeasure.

His damp eyes warmed. His long, dark lashes stuck together in spiky clumps. He ran the back of his fingers down her cheek, and his gaze intensified. He leaned toward her, and she stretched up to meet him. If he found comfort in kissing her, so be it.

Their lips were just a hair's breadth away when someone pounded on the door.

"Dan, you here?" The marshal's voice intruded. "The livery's open, but no one's over there. Everything all right?"

Dan wiped his face on his sleeve, then patted Leah's cheek and walked to the parlor. "C'mon in, Luke." He dropped onto a chair and sat with his head hanging down, arms on his knees.

Luke's gaze shot over to Leah, his surprise at seeing her come out of the bedroom evident. He narrowed his gaze. "What's going on here?"

Leah waited for Dan to respond, but he just shook his head.

Luke turned to her. "Dan's mother passed away."

Luke hurried to his friend's side and draped his hand over Dan's shoulder. "I'm right sorry to hear that. Tell me what I can do."

Dan cleared his throat and sat up. "I reckon you could fetch the pastor, if you don't mind."

Luke nodded and glanced at Leah again.

"I came over to help out Mrs. Howard. I did some cleaning, laundry, and made a ham stew, and didn't even know. . . ." Her lip quivered, and fresh tears stung her eyes. She sniffled, causing Dan to look up. He stood and hurried to her side, putting his arm around her shoulders.

Luke's surprise was evident, but her heart ached too much to be concerned about his reaction. She'd wanted to get to know Dan's mother, to become her friend, and to learn what Dan was like when he was young. She'd wanted Mrs. Howard to know that she'd fallen in love with her son.

Luke pushed his hat back and scratched his head. "I'll. . .uh. . . go by the house and send Rachel over and then collect the pastor."

Dan nodded and Luke left. Another wave of grief hit Leah again, and she turned into Dan's arms, laying her face against his shirt. His arms embraced her tightly.

"It'll be all right, darlin'."

Leah stood beside Dan at his mother's funeral, longing to reach out—to touch him, but such an action wouldn't be appropriate for an unmarried couple in public. She wished Dan's sister and brother could have attended the funeral, but his sister was in the early stages of pregnancy and having trouble keeping food down. Travel was out of the question. Dan's brother couldn't come, either. His wife was away, caring for her best friend's children while her friend was down with a strange case of influenza, so Dan's brother was tending their five children. Surely having family present at this time of loss would have been a comfort.

The pastor's voice droned on about what a wonderful woman Clara Howard had been and how she was now in the Lord's arms. Leah wished again that she'd gotten to know the woman instead of wasting so much time doing a whole lot of nothing the past few months.

How would Dan get along living alone? He'd lived with his parents all his life and had worked side by side with his dad until the older man died. Dan had probably never done any cooking until his mother had taken to her bed. He would certainly be lonely and would have no one to comfort him during his grieving. She stepped closer to him, wanting him to know she was there for him.

He didn't look down, but the back of his hand brushed hers. He looped his little finger around hers and gave it a quick squeeze and let go. Leah's heart soared, but she hoped no one noticed Dan's finger hug.

After the service, she wandered over to stand by Shannon while the townsfolk offered their condolences to Dan.

" 'Tis hard to lose your mum."

"How long has it been since yours died?"

"Over a year now, it has. At first, I just wanted to crawl in a barrel and die, too. I didn't know how I would survive in a strange country without my parents, but God watched over me. I was angry for a long while, but I'm coming to see His hand in my life."

Leah hugged her friend's shoulders. "I'm so glad He kept you safe and brought you here."

Shannon chuckled. "Aye, me, too. I never dreamed I'd end up in Texas, though."

"Me, either. I just wanted to get away from that awful man my pa wanted me to marry. I'd have gone to California if I had to. At least Texas was closer."

Rachel hugged Dan and then walked up to the women. "People have been donating food for Dan. I thought I'd take it over to his house and set it up in the kitchen. He asked that we all join him."

She caught Leah's gaze, and her eyes gleamed as if she knew something. Had the marshal mentioned finding her alone with Dan?

"We'd be happy to help, right, Leah?"

She nodded her head, glad to have a reason to be with Dan for a while longer. "We can take an armload over there now, if you're ready to leave."

"Just let me find Jacqueline, and we'll both help." Rachel's gaze scanned the crowd. "Dan said it was all right for us to go on into his house, so go ahead if you want and get started. I'll be there as soon as I track down that rascally daughter of mine."

On the table at the back of the church, they found all manner of food. A small ham. Jars of canned beans, beets, and other vegetables and fruit. Several cooked dishes had been prepared and also three desserts. Leah needn't worry about Dan having food for the next few days. With their arms loaded, they made the trek across town to the Howard home. Leah's arms ached by the time they arrived. "Let's put all this on the kitchen table, and then we can arrange it once everything is here."

Shannon nodded and followed her into the kitchen. "'Tis a lovely house the Howards have."

"Yes, it is." Leah surveyed the house. It looked much the same as it had yesterday, except that Dan's bed wasn't made. She hurried back to his room and made quick work of that task, lest he be embarrassed to have guests see it a mess.

"There's already enough food to feed every Texas Ranger in the state. I don't know how Mr. Howard will consume it all before it spoils." Shannon stood looking at the food with her hands on her waist, shaking her head when Leah reentered the dining room.

"I suspect that's why he invited us over. Let's put the canned items on that shelf next to the stove." Leah picked up two jars. "We'll serve the fresh food now, and Dan will have these for later on."

"Dan, is it? You sound right at home here." Shannon flashed her a teasing grin.

"Well, I'm not. I just spent half of yesterday here, so I guess I'm more familiar with things than you are." Leah's cheeks heated. "Besides, being the oldest of eleven children, I'm used to bossing others around."

"I would have liked having an older sister like you. All my siblings died before birth or passed shortly after."

"I'm sorry. Siblings can sure try your patience, but there's something nice about having a big family."

Shannon leaned against the counter. "Do you miss them?"

Leah ran her finger around the top of a jar lid. "Yes, sometimes, especially the younger ones, but I don't miss all the names they called me." She placed the jar on the shelf. "The older ones resented it when I was in charge and had to tell them what to do."

"Must have been difficult for you."

"It was, but it was the only life I knew."

"Will you go back someday?"

Leah opened the back door and stared out. "I don't know. I'd like to see my family, but I can't go back unless I'm married. Pa would give me to Mr. Abernathy faster than a magician could make a coin disappear."

Shannon crossed the room and laid a hand on Leah's shoulder. "I have no one, and you have no relatives here. Perhaps we can be family."

Leah turned, her heart warming at Shannon's offer. "I'd like that." She gave her friend a hug and saw Rachel and Luke come in the door.

Things turned hectic as the women set out the food and the men gathered in the parlor, talking. Both Corbett brothers had come home with Dan. Leah set out plates and forks and filled a pitcher of water from the outside pump while Rachel sliced a small ham and Shannon mashed some boiled turnips a woman had dropped off at the house. Delicious scents filled the air and made Leah's stomach rumble.

"The food's ready," Rachel called to the men a short while later.

Dan glanced at the door. "The reverend's family was coming."

"Why don't you men go ahead and dish up and eat. We'll need to wash some of the plates in order to have enough." Rachel tapped her index finger against her mouth. "Or I could run home and get a few of my plates."

Leah reached up onto a shelf and took down several bowls. "No need. We can make sandwiches for the pastor's youngsters and send them out back and use these bowls for us womenfolk."

Dan smiled and nodded. "Sounds like a plan to me. Let's all gather around the table and pray over the food. Looks real good."

Dan led the way into the kitchen, now crowded with people. He walked around the table and stopped next to Leah. She kept her gaze ahead, not wanting people to know the depth of her feelings for the man next to her.

"Let's hold hands." Dan's deep voice rumbled next to her, and she felt his fingers searching for hers. He clutched her hand like a man grabbing the reins of a runaway wagon. "Dear Lord. Good friends and f–family. I ask that You receive my ma into Your arms and reunite her with my pa. They loved each other here on earth for a long while. Bless this food, and the friends gathered here today. Amen."

He squeezed Leah's hand before letting go. She stood back and allowed the men to dish up first; then she took a bowl and helped herself. If she let her mind go, she could pretend that she and Dan were married and living in this house. That they had invited their close friends over—well, all except the Corbett brothers.

She followed the other women outside to sit on the front porch. Dan's gaze followed her movement as she walked through the parlor, past the other men. Maybe her pretending wasn't that far off.

Chapter 16

Saturday evening arrived sunny with a north wind that brought slightly cooler temperatures. Shannon was ever so glad the stifling summer heat was gone, at least for the moment. But with this being Texas, heat was never gone for good, so she'd been told numerous times.

Lively music filled the air, and dancers promenaded, curtsied and bowed, and swung their partners in wide circles. The American square dance reminded her a bit of an Irish jig, though it seemed more organized.

She watched Mark, grinning wide, catch the hand of his pretty blond partner, and they danced forward and back, once, twice, three times. He looked happy. She sighed. He had no idea that her heart ached for him. Why couldn't he smile at her like that? All he ever did was stare at her, probing with those amazing eyes.

She'd never planned to fall for a Corbett, not after their shenanigans, but something about Mark called to her. He seemed happy enough on the outside, but there was a longing in his heart, something he yearned for or that pained him, something that he'd never expressed to her—and she doubted he'd ever spoken of it to his brother. Trying to talk seriously with Garrett was a waste of time, if you asked her. The man was full of blarney and had been born in the wrong century. He should have been a court jester. She grinned, thinking how silly he'd look jumping around in one of those jester outfits she'd seen in a book. Garrett danced his partner around Mark and bumped his brother, almost knocking him down. Garrett laughed, but Mark scowled.

"Those Corbett brothers must be happy with so many people showing up this evening." Leah wiped down the table that had held her baked goods. "It's hard to believe everything sold in less than ten minutes when it took hours to bake it all."

"You'll have to be making more next time. I'd be happy to help you."

"I might just take you up on that offer." Leah shoved her fist to her back. "I did so much baking that I don't think I can dance tonight."

"Not even with Dan?" She shot her friend a playful look.

"No, not even him. But he won't be here tonight. He's mourning his mother."

"Have you seen him since the funeral?"

Leah nodded, and her cheeks turned pink. "I walked over to the livery while you were at work yesterday morning and took him several of the muffins left over from our breakfast, but I haven't seen him today. I wonder how he's getting along."

" 'Twas nice how the Corbetts offered to cancel the social since the funeral was just two days past. But Mark said Dan told them to go ahead and hold it."

Leah nodded. "It would have been nearly impossible to get word out that fast, and he didn't want people coming all the way to town and finding out the social had been called off."

Shannon stacked the dirty pie pans into a crate and then added the soiled plates on top. "Do you think you made enough money to bake more next time and also get some fabric like you've been wanting?"

"Maybe, but I'll have to order the cloth, so I doubt if it would be here in time for the next social. I could have the Corbetts pick some up in Dallas, but the thought of having those two select fabric for me makes me cringe."

Shannon smiled, stopping beside her friend to watch the dancers. "Have you heard the Fosters have decided not to rebuild the store?"

Leah spun to face her, surprise evident in her wide blue eyes. "But what will the town do without a mercantile? How can it survive?"

"Garrett told Mark that Mr. Foster's niece is moving here with her two children, and she will take it over."

"Is she not married?"

Shannon shrugged one shoulder. "He said something about her being a widow."

"I'm sorry for her loss. Maybe we should warn her that the Corbetts will try to find her another husband if she comes here."

Giggling, Shannon shoved Leah with her arm. "Nay, then she won't come, and we need the store."

"Too true."

"There's to be a store raisin' next Saturday. Mr. Foster wants to supervise the building project, and then he and his wife will move to Dallas to live with his mother, who's getting on in years."

"I know folks around here will miss them." Leah gathered the last of the silverware and set it in the crate, then wiped down the table. "I've heard they've been part of this town since its beginning."

A group of five cowboys who'd just arrived sauntered toward them. The hair on the back of Shannon's neck lifted. These fellows looked rough and right off the range. Most of the men who were looking for a wife had taken the time to bathe and, at the very least, put on clean clothes and slapped on some sweet-smelling stuff. These fellows looked like they were just out for a good time.

The tallest strode directly toward Shannon. He smelled of dust and cattle and had nearly a week's growth of beard. His jeans and boots were filthy.

"I'm not dancing tonight. I was just helping serve the food." She hiked up her chin to show him she meant business.

"Ah, a purdy little lady like her don't want to dance with the likes of you, Dom."

The tall man narrowed his eyes at the speaker. "Shut up, Chappy. She sure don't want an old man. She's young and pretty and needs a hearty man. Ain't that what this shindig is all about?"

Shannon backed closer to Leah. She didn't want to dance with any of these drovers. The tall man named Dom drew up near her and grabbed her wrist. "I rode two hours to get to this party, and I aim to dance."

"Leave her alone, you bully." Leah yanked at the man's hand and tried to pull it off Shannon's arm.

He elbowed her back and pulled Shannon toward the dance floor. Shannon dug in her heels, not making it easy.

A dark-haired man with an eye patch walked past her toward Leah. "C'mon, blondie. Guess you and me'll take a spin."

Shannon's heart pounded, and her legs trembled. The man swung her around and pulled her up close. She turned her face away to avoid smelling his foul breath, but not before she caught a whiff of liquor.

Suddenly, she was wrenched backward, and Mark and Garrett stood between her and the cowboy.

"Hey, that's my gal. Get out of my way." Dom glared at the brothers, his fists raised.

"This is a civilized gathering. Troublemakers aren't welcome," Mark said.

"That's right. You and your friends would be better served at the Wet Your Whistle."

"So says you." The man swung, but Garrett ducked.

Mark guided Shannon out of the way as the four other cowboys joined in to help their buddy. The dance stopped as most of the men set aside their ladies and came to Garrett's rescue.

Mark hurried toward the crowd.

"No, Mark, your cast," Shannon yelled, but she doubted he heard through the roar.

Punches flew left and right. Upraised voices shouted from all directions. Men were knocked down, but most jumped right back up. Women screamed. Shannon lost sight of Mark. She wrung her hands and prayed, "Please, Father God, keep him safe."

A man stumbled toward her backward, arms flailing. She jumped out of his way, and dodged another man who fell at her feet.

Suddenly, the blast of a gun rent the air. Everyone froze. Marshal Davis sat atop his horse with his gun pointed at the sky. The scent of gunpowder tinged the air. "That's enough of that. Garrett! Mark! What's goin' on here?"

Garrett shoved a man off of himself and stood, wiping the dirt from his clothes. "We were just having a friendly time here until these cowboys"—he looked around the crowd and pointed at the five men—"started some trouble."

The marshal waved his gun at the men. "All of you, get over here."

They begrudgingly did as told, mumbling and slapping dirt and examining bruised fists.

"Now, you can leave town, go down to the saloon, or get hauled off to jail, but the dance is over for you."

"Aww. . .we just wanted to take a spin with a purdy gal, Marshal." The shortest man of the five lifted his bushy face toward Luke. Blood ran down the corner of his mouth.

"This dance is for the purpose of people meeting with a mind to marry. I don't see how that applies to you cowpokes. These woman are ladies, not saloon girls, and as such, they deserve your respect and to be treated kindly. Get moving, and I don't want to see you at this social again. Not tonight. Not in the future."

Each of the men found their hats, which had been knocked off during the fight. They collected their horses, and the marshal escorted them down the street. A large man ran past them, and his steps slowed as he walked toward Leah. Shannon smiled. Had Dan heard the ruckus and been worried about Leah?

The music started up again, and Shannon looked for Mark. He stood next to the table, rummaging through the crate of dirty dishes. She hurried toward him. What could he be looking for?

"Can I help you find something?"

He turned, and she gasped. His lower lip had swollen, and blood ran down his chin. One eye was swelling shut, and the knuckles of his left hand were bleeding. He held his cast against his chest. Had he injured his arm again?

"Are you all right?"

"Fine. I just need a cloth or something to use to wipe this blood off my face."

The rag they'd wiped off the table with was still in the bucket. She swished it around the water to clean it and then squeezed out the excess water. She tried to dab the blood, but Mark reached for the rag.

"I can do it."

"Just rest and let me tend to you."

He sighed but sat on the edge of the table and allowed her to clean his wound. He stared at the dancers and sat stiff as a fence post.

Shannon wilted a little inside. Did he despise her so much?

He had no idea how being this close to him made her feel. She tried to hold her hand steady. She'd touched him so few times and was rarely close enough to see the variations of blue in his eyes. Pressing lightly, she turned his chin toward her and dabbed at the blood. His left eye was ugly and swollen. If only she had a cold slab of meat to put on it. "Does it hurt you?"

Mark flexed his injured hand. "Not too bad."

Shannon took his large hand in hers and held it lightly, then laid the cloth over his knuckles and looked up. He'd been watching her. She longed to draw him close, to let him know how scared she'd been for him. No wonder he was so battered when he could use only his left hand to defend himself. He was too honorable to conk anyone with his cast, even if it meant he took the brunt of the fight.

Several stems of grass were stuck in his hair, and she boldly plucked them out. She longed to run her hands through his hair but instead dropped them to her side. He was staring at her, and she captured his gaze. Her breathing turned ragged, and she fought to control it. Her heart throbbed, and for a fleeting second, she thought he might kiss her. But he turned his head and stood, taking the cloth off his hand. He tossed it onto the table, muttered thanks, and strode off.

Shannon hung her head. What about her was so undesirable? Did he consider her nothing more than the hired help? Or was it the fact that she was Irish?

She'd read in the newspaper that in big cities like New York some employers had posted signs that said NINA—no Irish need apply.

Rinsing the cloth, she thought about that. He'd never treated her as if her heritage bothered him. Yes, he didn't want her working at the freight office at first, but he seemed to have gotten used to the idea. So. . .she could work for him, but she could never be anything more than an employee. Tears blurred her eyes.

How did she explain that to her heart?

Dan strode up to Leah and grasped her shoulders. His frantic gaze ran down her body. "Are you hurt? Did anyone bother you? What happened here?"

Leah offered a smile to calm him down. Why was he so agitated? It was just a brawl. Certainly not the first one in Lookout. "I'm perfectly fine. What are you doing here?"

He released her and paced to the end of the table and back, curling the edges of his hat. Various expressions crossed his face, but she didn't understand them. He stopped in front of her and looked around. "I need to talk to you. Alone."

"Shall we take a walk?"

He shoved his hat back on and nodded, offering his arm. A slow tune followed them as they meandered past the church and down the road leading out of town. The sun had not yet set and still cast enough light so that walking wasn't difficult. They crested a hill, and once they'd gone down the other side, blocking the town from their view, Dan stopped. He swiped his hat off again and resumed his pacing.

Leah almost smiled, but his anxiety seemed too real for jesting. She waited, twisting her hands behind her back, wondering what was on his mind. Maybe he was ready for her to clean out his mother's bedroom, as she'd offered.

A determined look crossed his face, and he strode right up to her, stopping only a few feet away. "I know the timing is rotten, and some folks will look down on us—because I'm still in mourning—but knowing you were near that fight and I wasn't around to protect you scared ten years off of me."

Confusion clouded Leah's mind. "It's not your job to protect me, Dan."

His mouth worked as if he were chewing something tough. "No, but I want it to be." He slapped his hat against his pants leg and walked off a few feet.

He wanted to protect her? Her heart quickened. Was it possible that he had fallen for her like she had him? She clutched her hands to her chest. *Please, God.*

He turned again. "It's lousy timing."

"What is?" She moved closer, daring to touch his arm.

His gaze lifted to the sky, and she studied his square jaw. Some women might say he was too rugged, too big to be handsome, but she liked him just how he was. He looked strong enough to protect her from anyone.

His gaze locked with hers. "Leah. . ." Her name sounded special on his lips. Cherished in the deep timbre of his voice.

"I–I've never done this before."

"Done what?"

He studied her face, his dark eyes roving, caressing. "Asked a gal to marry me."

Leah felt her own eyes go wide. She struggled to swallow. To find her voice. "Are you?"

A soft smile tugged at his lips. "You wouldn't think me a cad to ask you to marry me when I just buried my ma?"

Leah smiled and tears blurred her vision. She shook her head.

Dan tugged at his pants leg, and knelt before her. A rainbow of emotions flooded her. Could this actually be happening?

He took her hands in his fingertips. "Leah, I know we haven't known each other long, but I've cared for you since I first saw you. I couldn't say nothin' when you were uh—" He looked away for a moment. "When you were competing for Luke's hand, but now you're free of that. Would you. . .uh. . .would you consider being my wife?"

Leah squealed, and Dan jumped up and looked behind him. She broke into a fit of giggles. He stared at her like she'd gone crazy. "What's so funny?"

Leah tried to sober but kept seeing him jump. "Nothing."

"Was my proposal so ridiculous?" Hurt laced his gaze.

All humor fled, and she touched his arm again. "Not at all. I'm sorry." She straightened and looked him in the eye, so he'd have no doubts to her seriousness. "I'd be delighted and honored to be your wife."

"You would? You're not joshin' me?"

Leah grinned. "No, Dan. My feelings for you have grown quickly, too." She longed to tell him that she loved him, but felt something so serious should come from the man first.

Dan grinned and shoved his hat back on. "When?"

"Whenever you're ready."

"How about tomorrow?" He chuckled, his eyes gleaming.

"A lady needs time to prepare." The thought of buying and

making a wedding dress suddenly gave her cause for concern. Had she made enough selling pies and cookies to buy what she needed?

Dan took her hands. "What's wrong? I can see that something's bothering you. Is it the timing?"

Leah stared at the ground, not wanting Dan to know how little she possessed. He had a house, nice furnishings, food, even a business, but what did she have to offer? She didn't even want children, and that thought burned a hole in her heart. Would he still want to marry her if he knew?

She needed to tell him, but she couldn't do it now. She didn't want to ruin the sweetness of the moment.

He gently took hold of her upper arms again. "Leah, if it's money you need, I have some. Not a lot, but plenty enough to buy you a wedding dress and whatever other fripperies a bride needs."

"You shouldn't have to pay for everything. I just don't have much to offer, and it doesn't seem fair to you."

He pulled her to his chest, and she nuzzled in close. His head rested on hers, and she wrapped her arms around his waist. "Darlin', you're all I want. I don't care if you're wearing all you own. It's you that's important to me. Whenever I see you, my heart perks up and sings, like one of them songbirds outside my window each morning. Knowing you're near helps me to keep going even though ma is gone. If I have you, I'm not alone."

She hugged him hard. "Thank you. I feel the same way."

He released his grip on her slightly, caught her gaze, and slowly bent toward her. His kiss was all—more—than she had dreamed about, and far too soon, he ended it.

"I'd love to stand here all night, spoonin' with you, darlin', but I reckon we oughta head back before someone misses you."

She sighed, not wanting the tender moment to end. "I suppose you're right. Besides, we need to get the table back in the church."

"Hmm. . .a dark church. No one there but us. Might be a good place to steal a kiss."

CHAPTER 17

Mark watched his brother walk back to the dance after helping the marshal escort the cowboys to the saloon. Garrett's eyes widened as he drew near. "Whoa, brother, looks like you've been in a fight."

"Yeah," Mark said. "And it looks like you all but missed it. There's not a mark on you. How is that possible when you were on the bottom of the pile?"

"There are some wounds, but you just can't see them." Garrett held his side. "I suspect getting out of bed tomorrow will be a chore. Why are you so beat up? You usually hold your own better in a fight."

Mark held up his dirty cast. He'd be getting it off soon—and good riddance. "It didn't seem right to crack people over the head with this thing. Besides, I didn't want to take a chance on breaking my wrist all over. And fighting left-handed isn't all that easy."

Garrett studied the dancers and then looked up at the sky. "I guess it's about time to call a halt to this party. Be dark soon."

"Yeah, next time you might want to start it an hour or two earlier since the sun is setting sooner these days."

Mark watched a young couple walk away from the dancing. About twenty minutes ago, Dan and Leah had walked down the road to Denison. He glanced in that direction and saw them returning with Leah holding onto Dan's arm.

Garrett watched, too. "Looks like our plan may be working. Soon, I hope, we won't have to pay room and board for Miss Bennett anymore."

"So, if both those boardinghouse brides get married, are you going to keep hosting the socials?"

Shrugging, his brother started toward the dancers. "Who knows? People seem to be enjoying it, and we've met new people who have become customers, so that's always a good thing."

"You do know folks are pokin' fun and calling us matchmakers."

Grinning, Garrett rummaged through the crate of dishes. "Yeah, I heard. Sure wish there was some of that pie left. That Miss Bennett is a good cook."

"Yep, she'll make some man a fine wife."

Garrett ran a finger over the juice left in a pie plate. "Yeah, it would be nice to have a wife who could cook so good."

"Why don't you ask her to dance? Maybe you'll like her."

"Nah, Dan has his eye on her."

Mark glanced at the couple as they drew near the dancers. Both faces were glowing, and the grins on their faces bested any among the dancers. *Hmm. . .*

"You could always dance with Shannon."

Garrett scratched behind his ear. "Don't think so. Someone else already has his eye on her. I predict two weddings before long."

"Who are you talking about?" Mark swung his head sideways and glanced at Garrett, then sought out Shannon and found her dancing with Tommy Baxter, the twenty-year-old son of a local rancher. Didn't she know he was just a wild colt who enjoyed wasting his father's hard-earned money? Mark clenched his jaw.

His brother slapped him on the shoulder so hard, Mark

jumped. "What was that for?"

"Are you so blind that you can't see that you have feelings for Shannon?" Garrett waggled his brows.

"That's nonsense." Mark crossed his arms, knowing his response came too fast.

"Why? She's a lovely girl, and smart, too. Look how fast she's picked up the bookwork. In fact, I think we've gotten some new customers just because they come in to stare at her and all that pretty hair."

Mark glared askance. "What business of yours is her hair? I thought you didn't like her."

"Maybe not at first. She was awful shy, but she's coming around. It's not so much I didn't like her, as I didn't think she had what it takes to live in Texas. But she's proving tougher than I first gave her credit for."

"Come to think of it, she doesn't seem as shy and scared as when she first came here."

"Yeah, and if you noticed that, other men will, too. Better stake your claim if you want her. A young woman as pretty and enticing as her won't stay unmarried for long."

Mark leaned against a tree and scowled. He wasn't sure what he felt for Shannon. His admiration of her had risen as she quickly caught on at work. And there was no doubt about her being pretty. Maybe she wasn't gorgeous like a Dallas opera singer, but she had a sweet charm, and innocence about her. And she *was* a hard worker. He'd noticed how much cleaner and organized the office had been lately. He'd always tidied up but never had time to keep the place spotless as he would have preferred, but Shannon did. She'd even seen to it that his desk had been sanded and refinished and the ink stain gone.

He watched her smile and sashay around in a wide circle. She tended to keep her hair up in that thing she called a chignon, but tonight, it flowed long and free. His fingers twitched, and he ached to touch those long, wavy strands. Maybe he should dance with her. He pushed away from the tree. He'd kept his distance until now, but what could one little dance hurt?

After breakfast, Shannon headed toward the river for a quick stroll. She couldn't get Mark out of her thoughts after dancing with him the night before last. Her chest warmed as she remembered how he'd claimed her for the final dance—a waltz.

Knee-high grass swished around her skirts, and abundant sunshine brightened the morning. A rabbit zigzagged away from her. Everything looked beautiful. Thanks to recent rains, the grass had greened up again, and wildflowers were again turning their lovely faces toward the sky. She snapped off a tiny white daisy and sniffed. "For me? Why thank you, kind sir."

She held her hand to her chest. "You'd like to dance? I thought you would never ask." Curtsying, she fanned her face. "Why, I'd be delighted to waltz with you, Mr. Corbett." She spun around in a circle, round and round, until dizziness made her stop.

Giggling, she shook her head as she tried to regain her equilibrium. "Silly lass."

The truth of the matter was so much less thrilling as she'd been stunned into silence and had simply nodded to Mark. He'd taken her hand with his cast and placed his other hand on her waist, but discreetly kept his distance, even though she longed for him to draw her close. She imagined holding up the heavy cast for a complete dance had been tiring for him, and it had felt odd to her, clutching the hardened plaster. But they'd danced, and she'd loved every moment of it.

She couldn't say the same thing for him, though. He'd been stiff, didn't talk, and focused somewhere over her head. Her lack of finesse with American dances must have embarrassed him. Or perhaps something was simply bothering him. She sighed, halfway dreading going to work today. But work she must.

Making a wide arc around Lookout, she gathered a bouquet

of yellow, white, and violet flowers, hoping to add a splash of color to the boring brown and grays of the office. As she strode up Main Street, she passed the livery and thought again how excited Leah had been Saturday night when she told the folks at the boardinghouse that she and Dan were getting married. Rachel had been so excited and offered to help her in any way.

She, too, offered to help Leah, but the fires of jealousy had burned within her—and still did. Oh, she was happy for her friend and glad Leah wouldn't have to depend on the Corbett brothers' support much longer, but she longed for the same for herself. She wished Mark would pay her some real attention.

At times she thought sure he liked her, but other times she was certain he didn't. 'Twas all so confusing. She heaved a frustrated sigh and looked up, noticing a crowd gathered outside the freight office, and for a moment, she considered heading back to the boardinghouse. The last thing she wanted was to get caught in the middle of a surly crowd. She heard the sound of a hammer; then she saw Luke remove his hat, tilt his head back, and laugh. He slapped his leg with his hat and leaned forward, still guffawing. Loud, masculine hoots and the roar of laughter filled the air.

What in the world?

Dan must have heard the noise, because he strode out of the livery and met her in the middle of the street. He was the biggest man in town, in height and breadth, but there wasn't an ounce of fat on him. Leah had roped herself a brawny man. The snake of jealousy raised its ugly head again, but Shannon whipped a prayer heavenward, lashing off the beast's head. She'd be happy for her friends and not think of her own future at the moment.

"What's goin' on?" he asked.

She shrugged. "I've no idea. The men are up to some shenanigans, I presume."

"Let's find out what kind." He offered his arm, and she accepted, grateful to have an escort through the dozen men.

"Congratulations."

He smiled down at her. "Ah, so Leah told you?"

"Aye, she's so excited."

Dan stopped at the edge of the crowd. Fine for him, but she couldn't see a thing over the tall men wearing hats. Worming her way to the front, she held a hand over her nose to avoid the putrid odor of the mob. Didn't Texas men believe in bathing? She reached the front, glanced up, and saw a new sign tacked to the outer wall of the Corbett Brother's Freight Office, right over the front window.

Mirth made her mouth twitch, and a chuckle worked its way out. She giggled and finally burst out laughing. CORBETT BROTHERS' MATCHMAKING SERVICE, the sign read. A large red heart encircled the lettering, and a cupid's arrow broke through the middle.

Shaking her head, she wondered how long the sign would stay up. She climbed the steps to the boardwalk and entered the office. Neither Mark nor Garrett were there yet. She put the flowers in a tall glass, grabbed the bucket by the back door, and went outside to pump water. After filling the bucket, she added water to the flower glass and sipped a drink from the ladle.

Outside the front window, she noticed the crowd part and saw Garrett and Mark crossing the street from Polly's Café. Both brothers looked curious, but from her higher vantage point, she could see the moment they saw the sign. Mark reached up as if to tear the sign down, but Garrett grabbed his arm. Mark jerked away and took the steps two at a time. He yanked open the door, jingling the bell, and then slammed it shut. He noticed her standing by the window and scowled. His puffy, purplish-black eye looked angry and painful. "I suppose you find this funny, too?"

She tightened her lips, trying to keep a straight face. She needed this job. "Nay, sir."

A rebellious snort slipped out, and she grinned. "Oh, aye, I do. 'Tis a hoot, it is. Just some men havin' a wee bit of fun."

Mark's serious expression melted, and an embarrassed grin made his swollen lips twitch. He hung his hat on a peg near the door and ran his hands through his hair. "I suppose you're right. Garrett and I will once again be the laughingstock of the town."

"That's not so bad a thing. You've done good, too. You helped Rachel and Luke to realize they still loved one another, and now Dan Howard and Leah are gettin' married."

"Not just them." Mark opened a thick law book that he frequently carried and thrust a newspaper at her. "Read this."

She unfolded the small Lookout paper and read the headline. ONE FIGHT, TWO WEDDINGS. "I knew about Dan and Leah, but who else is getting married?"

"Keep reading." Mark dropped into Garrett's chair and laced his hands behind his neck.

"Two couples attending last Saturday's social have pledged to marry." She read about Dan and Leah and then about a young man from another town who was marrying a fifteen-year-old girl. She'd never liked the idea of a girl marrying so young, but life in Texas was hazardous at times, and folks didn't live as long here as they did back East. "Well. . .it looks as if your social was a success."

"Partly." He stared at the cover of his book and ran his hand over it.

What did he mean? It was only partly successful because she wasn't getting married? She turned her back on him and stalked to the back room, where she wouldn't have to look at him. Why would a man so bent on helping others find their life partner not want to find one for himself? He wasn't getting any younger. Why, he had to be nearly ten years her senior.

She busied herself dusting things that weren't dirty; then she swept the floor and the back porch, banging crates and even kicking the bucket so that it dumped over and spilled onto the porch. The water ran through the spaces between the boards, disappearing. What was she doing here?

She needed to focus on her work and forget about Mark Corbett. But every time she tried, those haunting blue eyes tormented her. What happened to him? Had a woman hurt him at some time?

She had some ledger work that needed to be done, and she couldn't avoid Mark all day. He hadn't even mentioned the flowers she'd set on his desk.

With the heavy ledger spread out on her desk—Mark's desk, she took a seat. He'd opened his law book and was busy reading. Half an hour went by before Garrett intruded on the quiet. He swung the door open and barged in, shaking his head.

"What do you think of our new sign?" He glanced from Mark to Shannon, eyes twinkling.

Mark closed his book, leaving his finger in it to mark his place. "I say take it down. It's just plain embarrassing."

Garrett turned to Shannon. "What do you think?"

She gulped down the lump suddenly in her throat. She peeked at Mark, who stared intensely at her. Why did Garrett have to ask for her opinion when it was opposed to Mark's? She shrugged. "It matters not what I think but what you two feel."

"I don't know why. . .but I kind of like it." He removed his hat and set it on a peg next to Mark's.

"We run a freight office, not a matrimonial society. We'll be the laughingstock of the town," Mark grumbled.

Garrett grinned. "I'm afraid we've been that ever since we sent for those mail-order brides."

"Well, if I recall, that was your idea, just like finding mates for—" He slammed his mouth shut and peered at Shannon.

She wanted to melt into one of the desk drawers and hide. They were talking as if she wasn't even there. She stared down at the ledger, but the numbers blurred together. If only there was some other job in town that she could do. Perhaps she ought to think more seriously about going to a bigger city like Dallas.

But she'd lose all the friends she'd just made. She'd be all alone again.

Who was she kidding? She was alone.

Rachel had Luke.

Leah now had Dan.

And even Jack had her friends and that old yellow dog.

Tears blurred her eyes, and she closed the ledger. She wouldn't sit here and listen to them talk about her like she was invisible. She stood and hoisted up the heavy ledger and turned toward the cabinet. The ledger banged the glass holding the flowers, and she turned in time to see it tip and fall.

"Yikes!" Garrett jumped back, but not before the glass broke at his feet, splashing water all over his shoes.

Shannon dropped the ledger back on the desk and strode into the back room and out the rear door, tears blurring her eyes. Couldn't she do anything right? As the door slammed, she heard Garrett shout.

"You'd better marry her or fire her, brother, before she kills us all."

CHAPTER 18

J ack pulled another weed and tossed it in the slowly growing pile. Max rested in the shade of several tall cornstalks, his head on his front legs.

"Why was it that vegetables die if they don't get enough water but weeds always grow? And how come birds and bugs never eat weeds?"

Max watched her, nothing moving but his eyes.

"I wish you could talk, you dumb ol' mutt."

She hated the hot chore that made her sweat. The only good thing was that her ma let her wear her overalls so she wouldn't get her dresses dirty. Tired of kneeling, she sat down and looked at the three rows she still had to weed before she'd be done. She picked up a clod of dirt and lobbed it at a blackbird that was fixing to land on a stalk of corn. "Git, you varmint. I ain't pullin' the darn weeds just so you can eat our corn."

"Mm-mm. If'n your ma heard you say *darn*, she'd wash your mouth out with soap."

"Ricky! What're you doin' here?" Jack jumped to her feet and waved at her two friends. "Howdy, Jonesy."

"Ma sent me to town to see if the Fosters had some thread left in their tent store."

She shook her head. "Don't think so, but we can go see. They been sellin' off stuff, because they're leaving town soon."

"Don'tcha need to finish your chores before leaving?" Jonesy scratched his belly and yawned.

Jack shrugged, knowing her friend spoke the truth. But she hadn't seen either boy in nearly three weeks, and she'd missed them. "Let's go before Ma sees me."

They took off at a run and didn't stop until they reached the Fosters' property.

"Wow, look at all that wood." Jonesy eyed the stack of lumber nearly as tall as he.

"There's to be a store raising come Saturday." Jack walked inside the large tent that served as the store for now. "Howdy, Mrs. Foster. Ricky here needs some thread for his ma. You got any?"

"Just a couple of skeins of red and one white left, though they smell of dust." The old woman got up from her chair, tottered across the room, and rummaged around some boxes.

"Thank ya kindly, ma'am, but Ma wanted black thread so's she could mend my pa's trousers. Don't guess he'd care much for red or white stitching on his pants."

"No, I guess not. Be a few more weeks before the new store is up and filled. Hope he can wait that long."

Ricky shrugged and hurried back outside. Jack followed, waving her hand in front of her nose. "Whoowee! All that stuff smells like sawdust and dirt. Don't know why anyone would want to buy it."

Jonesy grinned and nudged her in the arm. "Never guess who we just saw."

"Who?"

"Butch," both boys said in unison.

"Where?" Jack leaned in close, half-excited, half-scared to see the bully again. She hadn't seen him since that social when he'd asked her to dance.

"Over at that fat lady's house, choppin' wood."

"You mean Bertha Boyd?"

"Yeah." Ricky's eyes gleamed. "Wanna help us play a prank on him?"

Jack bit on the inside of her lip, thinking again of how she'd lied about Butch. Still, he was her enemy, and if Luke and her ma knew what she'd done, she'd be in big trouble—and that would be Butch's fault. "Sure, why not? What do you want me to do?"

She followed the boys, listening to their plan. Butch had done plenty to them over the years, so what harm could it do to play a little trick on him? "Why do I hav'ta be the one to talk to him? How come one of you can't do that?"

"We gotta move the wood he's chopped, and that's too hard of work for a girl."

Jack narrowed her eyes at the boys, not quite sure if she'd been insulted or not. Still, the thought of carrying wood sounded like a lot more work than just standing there and talking to Butch.

She sucked in a deep breath and strolled to the back of the faded white house where Bertha Boyd and her sister, Agatha Linus, lived, while the boys hunkered down and raced around the other side. Butch was in the back of the lot, chopping wood in the shade of a tall oak. It looked as if he'd chop a while and then stop and stack the wood up against the back of the house where the sisters had easy access to it.

She ambled toward him, trying to look casual, her hands crossed behind her back. "Hey there, Butch. Whatcha doin'?"

He narrowed his gaze and swung the ax down harder on this log than he had the previous one. The shirt he wore had no sleeves, just ragged threads where they once had been, and his arm muscles bulged as he brought the ax over his head and cut the half-log into quarters. Butch was taller than any other boy in their school, and she suddenly realized he was more man than boy. He'd thinned down since the last time she saw him at that Sunday social when he'd asked her to dance. He had also grown taller, if she wasn't mistaken, and looked more like a man. Jack backed away. Maybe she was making a mistake picking on someone so much bigger than herself.

"What do you want?" He spewed the words as he grabbed another log and put it on the chopping block.

Jack glanced over her shoulder to the side of the house and saw a hand reach up and snitch a piece of wood from the pile. The wind blew in her face, slapping her with the odor of sweaty male and hog. She angled behind Butch and around to the other side so he'd be upwind and wouldn't notice the boys. He watched her from the corner of his eye, as if he wasn't sure what she'd do next.

"Where's your friends?"

Jack shrugged. "Whatcha been doin' all summer?"

"Working. Sloppin' hogs. At least when I'm not in jail."

She winced at his backhanded accusation, but it hit its mark. She shouldn't have lied, but when it came down to Butch or her friends, it had been an easy choice. "Is that all you do?"

"Some folks don't have the luxury of having parents who give a hoot about them. People like you don't know what it's like to wake up each morning, not knowing if you get to eat or not that day."

She wondered what that would be like and felt bad he had to go without eating—even if he was her enemy. "Must be rough not having a ma."

He eyed her for a moment and then relaxed his stance. "Yeah, I miss her. She was real nice."

"Yeah, mothers are like that. I'd miss mine if something happened to her."

Butch leaned on the ax handle. "How do you like havin' the marshal for a pa?"

"He's all right. He tries to spend time with me each night, playin' checkers or doin' chores together." She leaned forward. "He even does dishes sometimes."

183

Butch eyes narrowed. "You're joshin' me now. I don't know no men that do dishes, besides me."

Surprise flittered through Jack, as she realized Butch and Luke had something in common. "You wash dishes?"

Color tinged his tanned cheeks. "Who else would if I didn't? I do all the cookin' too, or we don't eat. My pa don't do nothing but play cards and drink." He ducked his head as if the confession embarrassed him.

Jack had never considered how hard Butch's life was. No wonder he smelled all the time. She already knew he fished and hunted to eat. When would he find time to wash clothes and bathe? She didn't like feeling sorry for him.

She peeked at the woodpile and saw that it was lower than it had been a few minutes ago. She didn't know what the boys were doing with the wood quarters, but she hoped they weren't taking them far away. The old sisters who lived there would need the fuel come winter, and Butch would get in trouble. She kicked a rock. Why had she agreed to go along with Ricky and Jonesy?

Butch whacked another log in two. "I'm not like my pa. I'm going to make something of my life and be a man people can respect."

Jack resisted laughing. Pretty lofty dreams for the son of a hog farmer. "How you figure on doin' that?"

"Work hard and get an ed'jication. That's the key."

Remorse flooded through her. Had she been wrong about him? Maybe she'd made more of his being her enemy than she should have. She thought about him staying in jail because of her, and her stomach churned.

"Hey, boy!" Bertha Boyd—a woman as big as a stagecoach—stood on the back porch, shaking her cane at them. "I'm not paying you to converse with that girl."

Butch stiffened and brushed his hand at her. "Go on, before I lose this job."

Mrs. Boyd looked off the side of the porch at the woodpile. "Is that all you done? Why, anybody else could have chopped three times that much wood. She tossed some coins into the grass. "Here's your pay, boy. Just get on along. I'll hire someone who wants to do decent work for his pay."

Butch stared toward the woodpile, a confused expression on his face. He scratched his head, and just then, Jonesy peered over what was left of the stack of wood. Butch glared at Jack. "Y'all been stealing the wood I chopped? You're helping them by distractin' me?"

He raised the ax high, and Jack back-stepped. The ax slammed into the chopping block, and Butch shoved his hands to his hips and stepped right up to her, leaning in her face. "I'm tired of tryin' to be your friend. Folks say I'm bad, and I'm always gettin' in trouble, but it's because of *good* kids like you. I try hard to change my ways and walk the straight and narrow. I want to be a better man than my pa, and I'm sick of gettin' blamed for things I ain't done. I thought you were different than them boys, but I guess you're cut from the same mold. Git away from me and stay away, you hear?"

Jack's heart pounded like a rabbit's in a snare. She never should have agreed to help her friends.

Butch stalked toward the back of the house and searched the grass for his money. Then he strode back toward her, his black eyes narrowed into slits. She backed up, then raced past him in a wide arc, as fast as she could pump her legs. When she reached the front of the house, she slowed and glanced over her shoulder. Relief made her legs weak. He wasn't chasing her. He was stacking the wood he'd just cut.

Ricky and Jonesy raced toward her, both laughing. "Wasn't that a hoot?"

"Yeah, did you see that old bat yell at him?" Jonesy bent over and slapped his leg.

Jack looked back and saw Butch staring at them. Suddenly, he dropped the wood and charged. Jonesy let out a squeal that sounded more like a girl, took a hop, and sprinted down the street.

Ricky ran toward home, and Jack sped toward Luke's office. Only the marshal could save her if Butch wanted revenge.

Shannon fingered the soft blue satin fabric. "What about this one? 'Twould make a lovely wedding gown."

Leah set aside the ivory muslin she'd been looking over and touched the satin. "Ooo, that is nice, but since I'll have to wear the dress on Sundays, I need something more practical—and cooler."

"Aye, that makes sense, but 'twould have looked lovely with your eyes."

"Thank you. Maybe we can find the blue in a more suitable cloth in another store."

They walked out of the Denison store and stood on the boardwalk, looking over the town. Denison was much larger than Lookout but was probably still considered a small town. At least it had a railroad. Shannon rubbed her back, still sore from the bumpy wagon ride. She'd taken off work for the day so she could serve as chaperone for Dan and Leah's trip.

"Do you suppose Dan has finished his business and will be looking for us?"

Leah shook her head and glanced at the sun. "No, he said it would take a few hours to locate everything he needed and get it loaded on the buckboard. We still have time, so let's get shopping. I simply must find some fabric for a dress."

'Twas nice of Dan to give Leah the funds to buy a dress and other things she would need as a newly married woman. Shannon shifted the large package that held Leah's new undergarments to her other arm. Thinking of her own ragged underwear that had been mended over and over, she tried hard not to be jealous. She was happy for her friend, but she longed for the same joy for herself.

"Let's try that dressmaker's shop down there. Maybe she'll have some fabric she'd be willing to sell us."

As they walked along, Shannon pretended she was on a shopping trip for her own wedding clothes. What color of dress did she want? Not blue, but perhaps a cream-colored gown. Or if she was going to be practical as Leah was, perhaps she'd pick a pale green to match her eyes, or a soft lavender.

They entered the dress shop, and the proprietor looked up from her stitching and smiled. "Welcome, ladies. How can I help you?"

"I'm Leah Bennett, and I'm to be married soon and am in need of a wedding dress. I was wondering if you sell fabric."

"Congratulations." The woman set aside the pink silk dress she was hemming and stood. "My name is Miss Bradshaw, and while I mostly keep fabric for my customers to have a wide selection to choose from, I do occasionally sell my cloth. What are you looking for?"

"Nothing too fancy. Maybe a sateen, but more likely a high quality cotton would do just fine. My friend Shannon here has graciously committed to make some Irish lace for the dress, which will fancy it up quite a bit."

Miss Bradshaw clapped her hands and looked at Shannon. "How very nice of you to offer to do such a thing. What type of lace do you make? Carrickmacross?"

"Nay, it's Kenmare. My mum learned it from the nuns who came to her village. Would you, by chance, have some linen thread I could purchase?"

Miss Bradshaw nodded her head. "I do. Come this way."

Shannon followed her to a crowded corner, and when the woman moved a navy calico dress, a thread cabinet was revealed. Miss Bradshaw opened a drawer filled with a rainbow of colors. "Oh, to have so many lovely choices. It must be a delight to come to work each day."

Miss Bradshaw nodded. "Ah, a kindred spirit, I perceive. Ever since I was a young girl, I've been fascinated with the magnitude of colors that fabric and thread come in. I can't imagine living without color in my life."

"Aye, me, too." Shannon ran her hand lovingly over the thread. If only she had the funds to buy several colors. She had some money saved from her work, but she dreaded spending it. What if she had to leave her job?

'Twas an odd feeling, this unreciprocated love for Mark. What if working for him became unbearable? 'Twould have been better if she hadn't fallen for him, but it certainly wasn't something she had planned to have happen.

While the other two women chatted about fabric, Shannon opened another drawer that revealed colors from a soft blue that almost looked white to dark indigo. Perhaps instead of stitching Leah a cream-colored or white collar, she could use a darker blue. But then there would be the problem of the darker color bleeding onto the lighter fabric if the dress got wet. Shannon sighed. Nay, better to stick with the plain shade. She picked up several ivory skeins and joined her friend.

Leah held up a bright periwinkle blue fabric under her chin. "What do you think of this shade?"

" 'Tis lovely. Very pretty with your eyes."

Leah smiled. "I like it, too, and won't it look beautiful with your lace on it?"

Shannon nodded. "Aye, and if there's enough time, I'll make cuffs for your sleeves, if that would please you."

Leah handed the cloth back to Miss Bradshaw. "That would be wonderful, but I don't want you constantly working. The collar will be enough. I think I'll cover the buttons to make the dress fancier, too."

"An excellent idea," Miss Bradshaw said. She cut out the amount of fabric Leah requested, wrapped it up, and tied it with heavy twine, then took care of the thread for Shannon. "Thank you so much for stopping by my shop, and I do wish you the best with your wedding and your future husband."

Back outside, Leah shifted the heavy package in her arms. "Let's go back to the hotel and put these in our room. They're too heavy to lug around all day."

"What else do you need to purchase?"

"Dan told me to get whatever I needed and gave me plenty of money. I feel odd spending it, but he said I should stock up because he doesn't have time to come to Denison very often. Since he owns the only livery and is the only blacksmith in town, he doesn't like to be gone too often. I think the only thing left on my list is to get a new pair of shoes. These I've got on are past old age."

"I'm excited about eating in the hotel restaurant tonight. 'Twill be an adventure, for sure."

"Oh, me, too. I've never stayed in a real hotel." Leah's eyes danced with delight.

"What about when you traveled here? Surely it took more than one day."

"That's true, but I stayed in a boardinghouse, not a hotel."

Shannon thought of her own trip and how she'd slept one night in a barn on her journey to Texas. It had been the only place she could find off the street. Paying for a hotel had been out of the question.

But Dan had graciously paid for tonight's room, and she meant to enjoy every moment she was here. Excitement flittered through her, and she pretended she was a grand lady who owned a large estate, and she'd come to town to shop. She was grateful for a day away from Lookout.

Away from the pressures of working with the Corbett brothers.

Away from her pining over a man who didn't want her.

They entered their hotel, located near the Katy Depot. A beautiful chandelier was the focal point of the tall-ceilinged lobby. Fancy brocade wallpaper decorated the walls in a pale gold, while red couches and chairs gave the room a splash of color. A man sitting in one of the chairs lowered his newspaper, and Shannon's heart squeezed.

What was Mark Corbett doing here?

CHAPTER 19

Jack raced to the marshal's office, praying Luke was there. She slowed her steps as she reached the office window and forced herself to walk past it. Her breathing came in ragged gulps, and as she rounded the door, she glanced behind her and gave a relieved sigh. Butch must have chased after the boys instead of her.

But Luke wasn't there. She hurried to the bucket and ladled out a drink and guzzled it down. Then she tiptoed back to the door and peeked out. A wagon was parked in front of the freight office, and several horses were hitched in front of the bank, but not a soul was on the street.

Where had her friends gone? Were they safe? Or had Butch gotten them?

She leaned against the jamb, keeping watch on the street. Now she wished she'd just gone home, but if she tried to make it, she might run into Butch.

What would he do if he caught her?

He said he didn't hit girls, but maybe he'd do something else like tie her up over an anthill. Or lock her in a hot, dark shed like that outlaw had done to her ma. Her knees shook as countless scenarios attacked her mind.

She'd halfway felt sorry for the big bloke when that old Mrs. Boyd yelled at him and fired him. It wasn't his fault he'd gotten in trouble. Maybe she oughta go back and explain things to that old lady. But Bertha Boyd was as big as a draft horse and scared her more than Butch.

Jack threw her braid over her shoulder, trying to get her nerve up to make a mad dash for home. She saw Max toddling down the street. "Oh, wonderful. He'll give me away."

Heavy footsteps sounded behind her, and she turned, hoping to see Luke. But Butch crossed the street in front of the café, smacking his hand into his fist as if looking for a fight. She ducked back into the office and searched for a place to hide. Diving under Luke's desk, she held her breath and pulled the chair in close to her. *Please, God. Don't let him have seen me.*

The steps stopped just outside the door. Her heart pounded like Butch's ax, whacking that wood. Her heartbeat throbbed in her ears until she could barely hear. Was he still standing there?

She heard a noise nearby and tucked her knees up tighter. Something clicked on the floor, and a shadow darkened the wall. Max appeared and stuck his nose in her face and burped.

"Eww!" She waved her hand in front of her nose. "What in the world have you been eatin'?"

Footsteps hurried in her direction, and Butch yanked Luke's chair out from in front of her. "I thought I saw you."

Her whole body trembled, and she'd never been closer to crying. What would her ma say when she learned her daughter was dead?

"Git on up from there."

She hunkered back farther, keeping her eyes shut. Maybe he couldn't see her if she couldn't see him. Max whined and licked her hand.

Some guard dog he was.

A large hand latched onto her arm and pulled her out. Jack

came kicking and flailing her arms. "You let me go! My pa's gonna lock you up until you're old and gray if you hurt me."

"I ain't scared of the marshal."

Butch held her by the scruff of her collar. She swung her arm and landed a hard hit in his midsection. His warm breath *oofed* out, and he bent over but didn't let go. "Stop it, you little beast. I ain't gonna hurt you."

Jack froze. "Then let me go."

"No. You need to be taught not to meddle in other people's affairs. You cost me a good job today, and I needed the work. If you was a boy, I'd pound the what-for into ya."

Jack went limp, her body exhausted. Fear battled anger. "W–what are you gonna do to me?"

He looked around and chuckled. "Just what you did to me."

He hauled her across the room, into a cell, and dropped her onto the cot. Then he hustled back out and shut the door. Stunned, Jack sat there, half-relieved and half-scared out of her wits. What if Luke didn't return soon or was out hunting down an outlaw?

And she needed to use the privy.

Butch grinned. "See how you like being locked up."

She bolted off the bed and clutched the bars. "You let me out of here right this instant."

"Cain't do it. I ain't got the key."

She swallowed hard. "Check the drawer. Maybe that's where Luke keeps them."

He pushed out his lips and shook his head. "Nope. I figure it's time you learned a lesson." He turned and sauntered toward the door, chuckling.

Fear washed over her like the time she'd jumped into the river and hadn't known which way was up. She hated being trapped in small places. Hated pleading with *him*. "Butch. Please. I promise not to do it again."

He stopped but didn't turn. "No, I'm tired of you and your friends going after me. All I wanted was to be your friend, but you and those boys have caused me trouble since the day I moved here. If I catch them, they'll be joining you in the next cell."

He walked out the door without looking back. Max trotted over to the front of the cell and laid his head on his paw.

"Butch!" she screamed. "Come back here, you hear me?"

She rattled the cell door, tears blurring her eyes. "I hate you. I'll hate you for the rest of my life!"

One look at Shannon's face, and Mark knew coming to Denison had been a mistake.

"What are you doing here?" Her cute brows dipped down, and her lips pursed into an enticing pout.

Had he mistaken the interest he'd seen in her gaze? He raised his chin. Maybe coming here had been the wrong thing to do, but he'd never let her know. "I had an urge to go riding and needed a few things, and I just ended up in Denison. You never mentioned you were coming here."

"So, you're headed back soon?"

He shrugged. "Maybe. I haven't yet concluded my business." And he might never finish it if she didn't thaw out a bit. She had no idea how hard it had been for him to seek her out. Half a dozen times he'd turned his horse around and started back to Lookout, only to turn around again. At least here, he could talk to her without the whole town listening in and making it tomorrow's headline. "So. . .you've been shopping, I see."

Shannon nodded and glanced over to where Leah and Dan were sitting on a sofa, holding hands and chatting. "Leah bought some fabric for her wedding dress."

Mark followed her gaze, still finding it hard to believe Dan Howard had asked a woman to marry him. As far as he could remember, Dan had never shown interest in a female. Maybe now that his mother had died, he realized he needed someone to tend the house, but no, as he watched his friend talk to Miss Bennett, he knew there was more to it. Dan had fallen in love.

Mark pulled his gaze to Shannon's, and their eyes locked gazes. He stared at her, unable to tell her the depth of his feelings. He wasn't even sure what they were himself, but one thing he knew: He'd never had such a strong desire to spend time with a woman before. Not even with Annabelle.

"I don't suppose that you'd allow me to escort you to dinner since we're both in town."

Surprise brightened her eyes before she narrowed them. "I thought you had to get back to Lookout. I'd hate to see you riding that far after dark."

"Are you worried about me?"

Her lips pursed again. "Not you. I'm concerned about your horse."

His heart lifted. "You're not a very good liar, Miss O'Neil."

She hiked her chin and glared up at him. "If anything happened to you, I'd be working solely for your brother." She shuddered as if the idea repulsed her.

Mark laughed aloud, drawing Dan and Leah's gaze. "We can't have that, can we?"

Shannon kept a straight face for a moment, then cracked a smile. "I do believe I'd have to resign."

He placed his hand on chest, acting as if the thought brought pain to it, and in fact, it did. Thinking of not seeing her each morning, not watching her nibble on her fingernails, brought an ache to his heart. When had he started looking forward to seeing her?

And what was he going to do about it?

Dan stood and helped Leah up, then both walked toward him. Dan slapped him on the shoulder. "What are you doing in Denison?"

"Had some things to purchase and needed to exercise my horse. He's getting fat and lazy since I hardly have time to ride him anymore."

"You could always let me keep him at the livery. I could feed him and rent him out in exchange."

Mark shook his head. "Thanks, but I don't think so. I may not ride him as much as I should, but I don't like the idea of a stranger maybe mistreating him."

"I hear ya. I do my best to make sure no greenhorns ride my horses, but even a seasoned rider can mistreat animals. Makes me so angry I'd like to punch them."

Leah grasped Dan's arm. "Let's not have any of that kind of talk, all right?"

"You're not even married yet, and the little lady is already bossing you around." Mark grinned.

Dan chuckled. "It's not so bad. You oughta try it yourself."

Both women's cheeks had turned red, Mark noted. But he doubted it was for the same reason.

"Why don't you join us for supper?" Dan asked.

"I might just do that. What time are you eating?"

"The ladies need to make another trip to the store for a few more items and then get cleaned up." Dan glanced at the big clock on the wall behind the registration desk. "What about six? Will that give you enough time to finish your business?"

"Yeah, that should be fine. Meet you back in the lobby?" Mark's gaze darted to Shannon, who looked like she'd just eaten a sour pickle.

Was he making another mistake? Why were women so difficult to read?

"Sounds good. See you then." Dan took the packages the women held, and then the ladies exited the hotel while Dan ran up the stairs. As Shannon walked out the door, she cast an unreadable glance over her shoulder.

Mark slouched into a chair. Why had he thought it so important to come here today?

So what if he had feelings for Shannon. He couldn't act on them.

But the bottom line was, he wanted to be with her. To spend

time with her without his brother teasing him—and this was about the only chance he'd get.

He leaned his head back and stared up at the decorative plaster ceiling. Was it wrong of him to dream of a life he couldn't have?

The preacher said that God forgave sins, but one of the Ten Commandments was "Thou shalt not kill."

And he was a killer.

Yeah, he'd only been defending a saloon girl's honor, such as it was, and he hadn't meant to kill that cowpoke. He'd just reacted when the man reached for his gun.

Mark ran his hand through his hair. Shannon deserved someone better than him, no matter how deep his feelings for her were. He wanted something he could never have—to be married. To be Shannon's husband. To be a father.

Yeah, coming here had been a mistake.

A big one.

CHAPTER 20

Shannon's stomach twisted into a knot as she walked down the stairs and saw Mark leaning against a pillar, watching her. His intense gaze never left her, and it made her feel cherished. Cared for.

But how could that be? He'd never once indicated having feelings for her. She glanced over her shoulder and realized he must be watching Leah. Her friend was wearing a new yellow dress that Dan had insisted she purchase when they went to look for material to make new curtains for the kitchen and parlor of their house.

Her hands trembled as much as her legs. How would she ever get through this meal? The supper she'd earlier looked forward to, she now just wished was over and done with.

Mark pushed away from the pillar and walked toward her. "You look lovely tonight."

Shannon ducked her head, certain her cheeks were bright red. She was wearing the same dress he'd seen earlier, but she'd washed and pinned up her hair. Not that it did much good. The stubborn wavy tresses came down almost as fast as she pinned them up, but Leah said men liked that look, so she'd left her chignon in their room.

"I'm so hungry I could eat a whole mule train." Dan rubbed his belly and chuckled.

Leah swatted his arm. "Oh, you. A big steak will taste much better."

He smiled and patted her hand. "You're right, my dear."

Mark looked at Shannon and rolled his eyes. She couldn't help smiling.

"Yes, dear. No, dear. You sound like an old married couple." Mark shook his head.

"Try it. You just might like it yourself," Dan challenged.

"What I'd like is some supper." Mark crooked his elbow and held it out to Shannon. "Care to join me?"

She nodded and took his arm. As they walked into the restaurant, her eyes took in everything at once. A dozen colorful, stained-glass lamps brightly illuminated the room. White tablecloths covered twenty or so tables, only half of which had customers dining at them. A small bouquet of flowers sat in the middle of each one. Somehow, she knew this would be a night she would dream about for a long time to come.

They placed their orders and dined. All too soon, the meal ended. Shannon and Mark followed their friends outside.

"Leah and I are of a mind to take a walk."

Shannon didn't miss the subtle hint that the engaged couple wanted to be alone. "I'll return to my room. It's been a long day."

"Nonsense." Mark waved at Dan and Leah. "You two be off, and we'll just head out the opposite direction. This town's plenty big enough for two couples to go walking without runnin' into each other."

Two couples? Shannon's heart leapt. Was he just saying that to keep Leah from worrying? Her friend gave her a questioning stare, and Shannon nodded. "Go on with ya. I'll be fine with Mark. 'Twill do me good to walk off that big meal before I retire for the night."

Leah stared at her as if she was unsure whether she should

leave, but when Dan tugged on her arm, she followed. Shannon studied Mark as he watched the couple amble away. He had a handsome profile, with his straight nose and tanned skin. His blond hair curled over his collar in a boyish manner, but there was nothing childish about this man. He stirred her heart and made her wish for things that she didn't believe she'd ever have. A husband. A home. A family of her own.

He turned her way and smiled. Her heart somersaulted at the intensity in his eyes. "Shall we walk?"

She nodded and took his arm, feeling proud that she was the woman he was escorting. They strolled along, not talking, and she studied the town. Denison was much bigger than Lookout. Thousands of people lived here—had moved here after the railroad came through more than a decade ago. Denison had much more to offer than Lookout, but she missed the coziness of the smaller town.

"So, how do you like living in Texas?"

She wasn't exactly sure how to answer that, given all that had happened since she arrived. " 'Tis quite hot here."

Mark chuckled. "Yep, it's that."

"I like the people I've met here."

"All of them?" He glanced down, brows lifted.

She thought of that outlaw bride who'd tricked them all and Mark's rascally brother. "Most of them."

He led her down the boardwalk steps, holding her steady, and then up the next set of stairs. "Do you figure on stayin' in Lookout?"

"Where else would I be goin'? I've no family, nowhere at all." She thought how she'd so recently considered moving to Dallas. What would he say if she mentioned that?

"All that's left of my family is in Lookout. Garrett. Luke. I left once, you know."

She darted a look at him at that surprising news. "Where did you go?"

He shrugged and led her toward the edge of town. The sun had nearly set, casting brilliant hues of orange and pink on the underbellies of the clouds. The view took her breath away, made her believe anything was possible. *Bless You, heavenly Father, for creating such a masterpiece.*

"I traveled around some and then ended up in Abilene," he finally continued.

"Where is that?"

"A ways from here. Further west, more toward the middle of the state."

She leaned against a post, enjoying the timbre of his voice and their casual conversation. He'd never told her anything about himself before. "What was it that you did there?"

He remained silent for a while, and she wondered if he'd answer. He looked far away, lost in his thoughts. Finally, he cleared his throat. "I interned with a lawyer."

She had the uncanny feeling that more happened there than he was letting on. Now she understood a bit why he read so many law books. He must have been bitten by the lawyer bug while in Abilene.

He suddenly turned to face her. "Shannon, there's something I need to tell you."

She raised her hand to her chest, hoping, praying he was about to confess his affection for her. *Please, Lord.*

He reached out and tucked a strand of her hair behind her ear, stealing her breath away. The passion in his gaze made her reach for her dream.

"I want you to know you've been doing a fine job in the office. Much better than either Garrett or I expected."

As if a stiff wind had just blown through, she watched her dream slip from her grasp. He was happy with her work? That was all?

"I...you need to know something." He stared off at the sunset, a muscle ticking in his jaw. "I don't ever intend to marry."

Shannon sucked in a quick breath. Her hand relaxed as if she'd totally turned loose of any hopes of a life with Mark. Her body felt weighted down. Heavy.

He turned to her suddenly, his eyes pleading. "You have to know. You're just the kind of woman I'd want—if I were looking to marry."

She closed her eyes, not wanting him to see the pain his words brought. She wouldn't cry—not in front of him. "I. . .think we should be heading back." She turned without waiting for him, willing the sting out of her eyes.

"Shannon."

She ignored his call and hastened her steps. He grabbed her arm suddenly, pulling her to his chest. She fought his hold, knowing she had to get away or she'd lose all her composure. He held tight, refusing to let go until she stopped her struggle. Her breath came in short bursts.

"Shannon, this doesn't mean we can't be friends."

Friends. Ha! She wanted to laugh in his face. He was oblivious to the struggle she'd been having the past few weeks.

"Look at me."

She turned her face back toward the indigo twilight.

He cupped her chin, forcing her to look at him. His blue gaze captured hers, and he studied her face. "Why are you taking this so hard?"

She blinked her eyes, knowing she could never explain how he'd stolen her heart. But he didn't want it. Why couldn't he just let her go and be done with it?

His expression turned tender, and he cocked his head. "Oh, Shannon. Please tell me you haven't fallen in love with me. I'm nothing but a scoundrel."

His comment brought tears, and right on its tail, anger. How dare this Corbett meddle in her life one second more. She jerked, trying to get free of his grasp. "Let me go or I'll scream," she hissed.

"You don't want to do that."

"No?" She sucked in a breath, ready to call for help, and his lips crashed down on hers. She couldn't breathe. She didn't want to. She only enjoyed the moment, knowing it would never happen again.

After too short a moment, he jumped back, his own breath ragged. Running his hand through his hair, he stared at her in the growing darkness. "Sorry. I shouldn't have done that."

Irritation and loss soaked her like a downpour. She reached out and slapped him, then turned and stalked back toward the hotel. Not even when that college man at the Wakefield Estate she'd worked at in Shreveport had almost forced her into his room had she felt so horrible.

She held up her skirt to hasten her progress. She wouldn't cry. She couldn't. Not here.

Quick steps followed her, and she picked up her pace. Striding into the hotel, she nearly collided with another woman—a woman with almost the same coloring as herself. Shannon sidestepped her and made a beeline for the stairs. She had nothing more to say to that man.

"Well, well, if it isn't Mark Corbett. I thought I'd never find you again."

Shannon halted halfway up the stairs and turned. The woman, dressed in a purple sateen dress that would look more at place in a saloon than a classy hotel, blocked Mark's way. His face had gone almost white.

Who was that woman? How did Mark know her?

"What happened to your shooting hand? And what's this on your handsome face, darling?" She placed her hand on the red splotch where Shannon had slapped him and frowned. Mark's gaze lifted to Shannon, and the woman's followed.

"Who is she?" The words spewed out like snake venom.

Mark blinked and stared at the woman again. "Annabelle?"

Jack rolled over in her bed and stretched. Sweat dampened her cheek, making her hair stick to it. She rubbed her eyes, then opened them. Was it morning?

No, it was dark outside, and she was still wearing her clothes. Why had she slept in her clothes?

Footsteps sounded across the room, and she bolted upright. The jail.

A match hissed and flickered; then someone lit the lantern. "There you are, Max. I was wondering where you'd gotten off to." Luke squatted and rubbed the old dog's head. "Why'd you come down here?"

Jack scooted back into the shadows, embarrassed for Luke to find her there. But if she didn't let him know, she'd be stuck for who knows how long.

"Get up, boy. I need you to help me find that ornery girl of ours. She missed supper, and her ma's worried."

Jack's stomach growled. She'd been there that long? All that yelling and being angry at Butch must have tuckered her clean out. Her eyes ached, and her throat stung.

Holding the lantern in his left hand, Luke headed for the door. She jumped off the bed. "Wait!"

He spun around, and yanked his gun out of his holster faster than she could sneeze.

She scrambled backward. "Don't shoot. It's just me, Luke."

He holstered his gun and hurried across the room, his boots thudding on the wood floor. He held up the lantern, and the light flickered against his skin, brightening the dark cell. His eyes were filled with concern. "How'd you get stuck in there, half bit?"

Ducking her head, she toed the brick floor. Keys rattled. The lock clicked, and the door creaked open.

Luke walked in, followed by Max, and the cot squeaked as the marshal lowered his large body onto it. He set the lantern on the floor. "Come sit by me, Jack."

That was something she'd always liked about him. Even though it angered her ma, he still called her Jack instead of

Jacqueline—although she was growing partial to "half bit" as he sometimes called her. She did as he requested and leaned against his arm.

"Was it that Laird boy?"

After all that had happened, she hated to get Butch into more trouble, but it was his fault that she was trapped in the dark, stinky cell. She nodded. "Yeah, it was him."

"What happened?" He put his arm around her, tugging her close.

Here she went again. If she told him the truth, she and her friends would be in big trouble. But she didn't want to lie.

Luke turned and gently grasped both of her arms. His dark brows scrunched together, and his eyes looked worried. "Did he hurt you?"

She shook her head. "No. He just wanted to teach me a lesson."

A muscle in Luke's jaw twitched. "Somebody needs to teach that boy not to pick on smaller kids, especially not girls." Luke jumped up and paced the small cell. He smacked his fist into his palm, making such a loud smack that she jumped. "I'm going to chase him and that no good father of his clean out of Lookout."

Jack's eyes widened. She'd never seen Luke so mad. Not even when his cousins had ordered those three mail-order brides for him. She wanted to tell him that Butch hadn't started things this time, but her mouth wouldn't work. She scooted back against the wall. Her real pa had looked ferocious, just like that, before he started whacking on her or her ma. Her knees shook, and her heart pounded so hard she thought it might just break through her chest.

What if Luke started hitting when he got mad like her real pa? She shivered and glanced at the door. She sure didn't want to be stuck in a cell without her ma to protect her, if Luke started throwing punches. Taking a deep breath, she scooted to the end of the cot. Max had curled up on the floor next to the lantern so at least she wouldn't have to jump over him. She oughta take him with her, but surely Luke wouldn't punch his own dog.

When Luke paced to the back of the cell, she pushed off the cot like a cat with its tail on fire.

"Jack! What's wrong?"

She raced out the door, jumped off the boardwalk, and ran down the middle of the street as fast as she could. She had to find her ma.

CHAPTER 21

Mark stared at Annabelle, his mind grappling with the image in front of him. How had she found him? Had he ever told her where he lived?

He lifted his gaze to where Shannon stood halfway up the hotel stairs, looking down on him. Hurt, confusion laced her gaze. She obviously wondered about Annabelle, but she made no move to come back to the lobby. Suddenly, she turned, hiked up her skirt, and rushed up the stairs and out of sight.

He never should have kissed her, because it had awakened all his senses. Made him want something he could never have, especially now that Annabelle had turned up. He stared at her. "What are you doing here?"

She leaned up close, fingered his lapel, and purred, "I've missed you, and you never returned to Abilene."

He stepped back and glanced around the hotel to see if anyone had noticed her hanging on him. "You know why I couldn't do that."

She clutched his arm and rested her head on his shoulder. "I can't go back, either."

The clerk at the registration desk eyed them with curiosity. Mark grabbed her arm and led her outside into the darkness, where they'd have some privacy. The last thing he needed was someone from Lookout seeing him with her. His reputation would be in the trash heap.

He walked her down an alley and around to the back of the hotel, away from the lights of the open doors and windows. The tinny music of a saloon piano across the alley and several buildings away drifted toward them, along with the raucous noise and sometimes laughter or hollering of the patrons. At least this early in the evening, it wasn't too likely they'd be interrupted by a drunk.

The rear door to the hotel kitchen was open, and the clinking of pots could be heard, as well as the loud talk of the workers. The crickets and night creatures grew silent as Mark guided Annabelle to the edge of the light, back near the stable. Then he turned loose of her and started pacing. What was Shannon thinking right now? Had he hurt her terribly?

He knew she was developing feelings for him and thought that letting her know where he stood right up front was the decent and proper thing to do, but Annabelle's arrival had messed up everything. Her timing couldn't have been worse.

Annabelle smiled and moved in close again like a cat toying with its prey, walking her fingers up the buttons on his shirt. He didn't remember her being so. . .wanton before.

"Mark, aren't you happy to see me? It's been so long, darling." Her hand caressed his cheek; then her little finger brushed across his lower lip. His senses responded, in spite of trying to resist her.

Had she always played the temptress? As a man eager to be away from home for the first time, impatient to prove himself and to be out from under his older brother's shadow, had he unwittingly fallen under her spell?

"Stop it." He set her back from him. He was no longer impetuous and naive. Experience had made him cautious and wiser. "What are you doing here?"

She pouted, but finally stopped her vexing ways. "Everett decided to make me an upstairs gal, and I wouldn't put up with that, so I lit out of there. Fast and furious."

Truth be told, the only thing that surprised him was that she wasn't a lady of the night already. She certainly hadn't wasted any time getting *him* in her bed. He winced at the memory. *Forgive me, Lord.*

"I can't help you, if that's what you're wanting."

Annabelle flounced her head. "I have money. I just thought you might want to pick up where we left off. You ain't married to that redheaded tart, are you?" Her sultry smile twisted his gut. "Looks to me like you was tryin' to find a gal just like me. We look enough alike to be sisters."

He narrowed his gaze. "Shannon's nothing like you."

"I'm sure she isn't." Annabelle drew her index finger down Mark's cheek and under his chin.

He swatted it away and stepped back. "I was serious when I said to stop. You can either act civil, or I'll go back inside."

Her lips twisted up on one side. "You have changed, but I like it. You're no longer that sniveling whiner, complaining about his big brother all the time."

He jerked back as if she'd slapped him. Was that what she'd thought about him? He'd loved her—enough to fight another man who'd rough-handled her. Enough to shoot that man dead—in a fair fight, but he was dead just the same. He lifted his hat and raked his fingers through his hair. He'd been near his midtwenties—a grown man—when he'd met Annabelle, but he'd acted more like a runaway kid. It had taken him that time in Abilene to grow up. To make him see that his decisions affected others oft' times.

"You didn't answer me. I don't see no ring. Are you married to that gal?"

Mark shook his head. "She works for me and Garrett."

"And how is your big brother? Still making you do things you don't wanna?"

208

He clamped his back teeth together, knowing she'd hit the nail on the head. That was one thing that hadn't changed much. He was still hauling freight when he wanted to become a lawyer, but he wasn't about to admit that to her. "I'm going inside. It was. . . interesting seeing you again."

He strode past her, but she grabbed his arm. "Wait!"

Sighing, he turned to face her. With the light of the kitchen door shining bright, he could see how she'd aged. Yes, she was still young, probably only a few years older than Shannon, but working in a saloon all these years had taken its toll on her.

"What am I going to do? I was hoping you'd help me."

He shook his head, feeling sorry for her. "There's nothing I can do. It's time you stood on your own two feet."

"But I need you."

"No." He shook his head. "You don't. You never did."

He strode away, half-feeling he should do something for her and the other half wishing she hadn't come to town. One thing was for sure: Shannon would want nothing to do with him now.

❧

Leah smiled up at Dan as he said good night. She longed for another of the kisses he'd stolen during their walk but knew the hotel lobby wasn't the place for a display of affection. "I suppose I should retire for the night."

Dan squeezed her hand, his dark eyes shining with love. "I wish we were already married, so I didn't have to let you go."

She touched her hand to her warm cheeks. "Be patient, my love. It won't be much longer."

He frowned. "One minute is too long. I've waited a lifetime to meet the woman I plan to marry. Maybe I should escort you to your room to make sure nothing happens to you."

"Da–an." She glanced around the lobby. "Do you want folks to think I'm a wanton woman?"

"Anybody who thinks that needs their attitude readjusted."

She grinned. She'd never again have to worry about being watched over and protected. Patting his solid upper arm, she leaned forward. "I will see you in the morning."

He nodded and released her other hand. Something behind him caught her eye, and she scowled. What in the world?

Mark Corbett walked in with another woman beside him. If she didn't know better, she'd think the woman was Shannon's sister. Their hair coloring and pale complexion certainly were strikingly similar, as was their height and size. Although, on closer inspection, this woman's build was a bit larger than Shannon's petite frame.

Dan noticed her staring and looked over his shoulder. "Who is that?"

"A better question is, where is Shannon?"

Mark's steps halted when he caught them gawking, and the color fled from his face. Leah stiffened her back and marched toward him. "Where is Shannon?"

Mark stared at them both, shifting his weight from side to side. "Uh. . .we finished our walk a short while ago, and she went up to her room."

"And who is this?" Leah nodded toward the woman. She was dressed in a purple sateen gown but had a hard look in her hazel eyes.

Mark tugged at his collar and cleared his throat. "This is. . . Annabelle. An old friend of mine."

Dan's brows lifted, and she knew that Mark had never mentioned this woman to him. "Annabelle who?"

Mark's brows dipped down, and he glanced at the woman. She cleared her throat and smiled, though it didn't reach her eyes. "Annabelle Smith."

"I'm Leah Bennett, and this is my fiancé, Dan Howard."

Dan tipped his hat and offered a tight-lipped smile. "Ma'am."

Annabelle took Mark's arm, as if he belonged to her. "So, how do you know Mark?"

Leah wanted to smack the woman off Mark, as if she were

nothing but a pesky fly. His discomfort was obvious, but was it because he truly didn't want to be with the woman or because they'd caught him with her? "We all live in the same town."

"Oh?" Miss Smith cocked her head. "And where is that?"

Mark's eyes widened and he shook his head, at the same time Dan blurted out, "Lookout, ma'am."

"Lookout, huh?" She smiled up at Mark as if she'd won a prize. "Isn't that east of here?"

Dan shook his head. "No, ma'am, it's to the west."

Leah wanted to tromp on his foot or wallop his arm. Couldn't he see that Mark didn't want the woman knowing where he lived? Suddenly, she had an urge to check on Shannon. Did she know about the woman? What had happened during her walk with Mark?

"Well, if y'all will excuse me, I'll retire for the night. It was a pleasure meeting you, Miss Smith." Leah knew she'd have to repent from that white lie eventually. "Good night, Dan. Mr. Corbett."

"I'll walk you to the stairs." Dan took her elbow and led her away from the other couple. He leaned down next to her ear. "How do you suppose Mark knows her?"

She shrugged. "Beats me. You're the one who's friends with that lowlife Corbett."

Dan's expression turned scolding. "Now, Leah, we don't know what's going on. I don't know where Mark would have met her." He scratched his jawline with his thumb and forefinger, making a bristling sound against his chin that needed to be shaved again. "Mark did leave Lookout several years ago. Could be he met her back then. I know I've never seen her in Lookout."

"Well, I don't like her." She stood on her tiptoes. "What's he doing with her when he was just out walking with Shannon?"

Dan shook his head. "Makes no sense to me."

"I'm going to check on Shannon. I'll see you in the morning, dearest."

He smiled and pulled her to his chest, then quickly released her. "See you at breakfast. We need to get on the road right after that."

She nodded and hurried up the stairs, anxious to see her friend. When she stepped into the dark room, it took her eyes a moment to adjust. Had Shannon gone to sleep already?

Feeling her way to the dresser, she found the lamp and turned up the flame. The bed was still made, and Shannon wasn't in it. At first she thought her friend wasn't even in the room, but then she heard a sniffle, coming from the sitting area.

She crossed the room and found Shannon lying on the settee. Her eyes and nose were red, her face splotchy, and her lashes clumped together. Leah knelt on the floor beside her, rubbing her hand over Shannon's back. "What happened?"

Shannon sat up and wiped her nose. "Would you, perchance, have a handkerchief I could borrow? I've soiled both of the ones I brought with me."

"Of course." Leah pushed aside her curiosity and hurried to her satchel. She rummaged around and found two handkerchiefs and brought them to her friend. She sat down beside her. "Would you care to talk about what happened?"

Shannon's mouth puckered, and fresh tears ran down the side of her nose. She dabbed at them. "I was foolish."

"How so?"

Shannon stared at her lap and fiddled with the lace edge of the hankie. "I fell in love with a Corbett."

Leah knew that much already. In spite of her warnings, Shannon had dropped her guard and let Mark steal her heart. Though Leah would never fall for a Corbett, she had to understand what was upsetting Shannon so she could help her. "And why is that such a bad thing?"

Shannon's chin wobbled. "Because he said he never expects to marry."

Leah sat back as if she'd been slapped. He was willing to dally with a woman's affections but not to marry her? Or maybe he preferred a different type of woman than Shannon. Annabelle Smith intruded into her mind again.

"He knows I have feelings for him, and 'tis odd, but I believe he cares for me, though he claims he'll never marry." She stared at Leah with a confused expression on her face. "Why would a man not want to marry a woman he has feelings for? 'Tis because I'm Irish?"

Leah clutched her friend's hand. "No, I'm sure that has nothing to do with it. In fact, if he does truly have feelings for you, I'm sure it's partly because of your alluring accent and lovely auburn hair." She smiled, hoping to alleviate her friend's pain, but Shannon scowled.

"Perhaps he doesn't wish to marry me because he has another woman in his life already. A woman with hair the color of mine."

Leah gasped. "You saw him with her?"

She nodded. "We had just arrived at the hotel when she accosted him. I was on the stairs already, but I saw her."

Leah sat back in the seat. "How do you suppose he knows her?"

"I've no idea. But I've embarrassed myself and made a huge error. I love a man who cares for another woman."

Shuddering, Leah stared at her friend. "How can you be in love with a Corbett? Just look at how they've messed with our lives."

Shannon lifted her chin. "You wouldn't be marrying Dan if not for the Corbetts bringing you to Lookout."

"I suppose you're right." She leaned her head back and stared up at the ceiling. How could she be so happy when her friend was so miserable? "I wish I knew what to say to make you feel better."

"There's nothing anyone can say. I must set aside my feelings and move on. It's not like I haven't had my choice of men to marry."

Leah chuckled. "How many proposals have you had so far?"

"Twelve. An even dozen. Just not the one I longed for."

Shannon sniffled, and the tears flowed again.

Leah tugged her into her arms and rubbed her back. "Everything will turn out fine. You'll see."

Shannon pulled back. "But how can it? I can no longer work for the Corbetts. And if I don't, how will I get by?"

Leah thought a moment and then brightened. "I know! You can come to live with Dan and me. There's an extra bedroom."

Shaking her head, Shannon stood. "Thank you, but I'll not live with a newly married couple, and I'll not work with a man who's spurned me."

"Don't be hasty. Let's not make a decision in anger that you may live to regret."

Shannon ducked her head. "Aye, you're right. I should pray about these things, but I fail to see how I could ever work with Mark again."

~

Jack ran all the way home, threw open the front door, and ran straight to the kitchen. When she didn't see her ma, she panicked. Where was she? What if the outlaw that had kidnapped her had broken out of jail and come for her again?

Tears blurred her sight and burned her eyes and throat. She dashed into the bedroom, but she wasn't there. "Ma!" she screamed.

"Jacqueline?" Quick footsteps sounded overhead, and Jack raced for the stairs as her ma reached the top steps. "What's wrong? Where have you been?"

Footsteps sounded on the porch, and Jack froze. Would Luke be even more angry since she'd run away from him?

If she bolted for her ma, he'd catch her before she could get up the stairs. She turned and ran into the parlor, searching for a place to hide. She was much bigger now than when she'd hid from her other pa, but she dove behind the far side of the settee. Her heart beat like an Indian's drum she'd once heard.

214

"What is going on, Luke?" Her ma's voice sounded closer, as if she'd come down stairs—and it sounded angry.

"I have no idea. I found Jack locked up in my jail."

"What? Who would do such a thing?"

Jack took a deep breath and peered around the edge of the couch. Her ma looked madder than the chicken she'd dunked in the water barrel once.

Luke shoved his hand to his hips. "I'm pretty certain it was that Laird boy."

"Why would he do such a thing?"

"I don't know, but first thing in the morning, I'm riding over to find out."

Jack sucked in a breath. What if Butch told Luke what she and the boys did? Would he believe that bully?

Her ma held up her hand. "Hold on a minute. What does that have to do with Jacqueline's behavior just now? What is she afraid of?"

Luke shrugged. "I have no idea. One minute she was explaining what happened, and when I turned my back, she charged out of the jail like she was runnin' a race." He shook his head, looking perplexed, not at all mad.

Jack leaned back. Maybe she'd gotten things wrong.

Footsteps came her way, and she slinked back against the couch. "Come out of there, Jacqueline. You're perfectly safe now."

She swallowed hard. Luke was a big man, and if he decided to hurt her, her ma wouldn't be able to stop him. Why hadn't she considered that before?

"Let me talk to her, Rach."

Luke stooped down in front of her. She had nowhere to go. Her breath caught in her throat. "What's wrong, half bit?"

He reached out for her, but she turned her face away. She didn't like seeing the hurt in his eyes. "Did I do something that scared you?"

She nodded but didn't look at him.

"I'm sorry. Truly I am. Don't you know I'd never hurt you?"

She turned and looked at him with one eye. She'd never been afraid of him before, at least not after she'd gotten to know him. His kind, brown eyes looked pained.

"I'm not like your other pa, and I wasn't angry at you earlier. I was upset because of what that boy did to you. I love you, Jack. Don't you know that?"

She did, and now she felt foolish for her behavior. What had gotten into her? "I'm sorry, Luke. I just saw you punching your hand in your fist, and it reminded me of when my old pa would hit me. I just got scared."

"Come here, sweetie." He held out his open hand. She stared at it a minute and then took it, and he swung her up into his arms. He nearly squeezed her guts out. Then he set her back down and stared at her.

"I'm telling you here and now, I will never hit you or purposely do anything to hurt you. Ever. So help me, God. Do you believe that?"

She glanced at her ma and saw the gentle smile on her face. Her mother nodded, and so did she.

"Good. I will tell you that there are times I'll get angry"—he glanced up at her ma—"and maybe even at your mother, but I will never lose my temper to the point of hitting one of you. I don't hit women, and I never will. Do you understand?"

Jack nodded, and knew he spoke the truth. "Sorry, Luke. I guess I was still upset about bein' locked up."

He smiled and stood, lifting her clear off the floor. Then he pulled her ma into his arms, and they all hugged. "We're a family, half bit, and families stick together. I know that wasn't how it was before your other pa died, but that's the way of things now. Right, Rachel?"

"Yes, it is."

"And whenever you're ready, it would please me greatly if you'd called me pa."

Jack scowled. She didn't want to call him the same thing as her old pa.

"You don't have to if it bothers you." Luke's eyes took on that worried look again.

"It ain't that."

"Don't say *ain't*," her parents said in unison.

She grinned. "I just don't want to call you what I called *him*."

Luke smiled and nodded. "I understand that. It's perfectly fine if you just want to call me Luke."

She could tell by his expression that it wasn't really fine to him. "What about Dad? Or maybe Papa?"

"I'd like that. . .but only if you really want to."

She nodded. "I think you look like a papa."

Luke's smile warmed her insides. "That sounds fine. Just fine and dandy." He picked her up and swung her around in a circle. Laughter bubbled out of her, and she couldn't remember ever being so happy.

CHAPTER 22

A knock sounded on Shannon's open bedroom door, and she glanced up to see Rachel standing there. "How are you feeling this morning?"

"My head is throbbing in tune with that hammering." She offered a weak smile as she stared out the window and down the street where the men of town were erecting the new store.

"It is loud with so many men pounding, but having a store again will be wonderful."

"Aye, a town needs a store." Shannon fingered the edge of the curtain, wanting to talk to Rachel about what had happened, about her feelings for Mark.

The boardinghouse owner crossed the room and joined her at the window. The scent of fresh wood filled the air, and the street resembled a hive of worker bees hard at labor. Someone bellowed out a laugh, and others joined in. They looked to be having a grand time.

Rachel touched Shannon's shoulder. "I don't want to pry, but did something happen in Denison? You've been down in the dumps since you returned."

Shannon scowled, unsure what a dump had to do with what she was feeling. Now she felt the fool for having cared for Mark Corbett, and yet her heart still betrayed her. Why didn't anyone tell her that falling in love could be so painful?

"Well, I just wanted you to know that I'm here for you if you want to talk. I need to get downstairs. I'm making a mess of sandwiches for when the workers break for the noon meal."

Shannon turned from the window. "Are you needin' some help?"

Rachel smiled. "I could use another pair of hands, but that's not why I'm here. I just want to be sure you're all right."

Shannon considered how years ago, Rachel had lost Luke, the man she loved, and married another. Perhaps 'twould help to talk to her. She stared at the older woman. Rachel was probably in her late twenties, a good ten years older than herself. But she had the look of a newlywed in love, not the harried boardinghouse owner and mother to a troubled child like she'd been when Shannon first arrived in town.

Shannon heaved a sigh and gazed at Rachel, wringing her hands. "I fear I have fallen in love with Mark Corbett, but he doesn't want me." Saying the words made her chin wobble and tears burn her eyes.

Rachel's eyes widened, and her mouth dropped open. "Oh dear."

"Aye, you can see my problem."

"Yes, but does this have anything to do with your trip to Denison? I thought you and Leah would have a good time shopping for her wedding supplies, but you looked miserable when you returned yesterday."

Shannon nodded and drifted back to the window. Her gaze immediately located Mark, carrying a long piece of lumber with his brother. Her heart squeezed at the sight of him, and then she remembered he didn't want her. She ducked her head. What had he found lacking in her?

Rachel took her hand and tugged her over to the bed. "Let's sit for a minute. Maybe things aren't as bleak as they seem."

"I work for the man I'm in love with, and he stated that he'd never marry, so how do I now face him and interact with him each day? If I quit my job, I shall be dependent on the Corbett brothers or destitute. Things seem awfully bleak to me." Shannon plopped onto the bed and sighed.

"I remember thinking the same thing. Luke had finally returned to town, but he wanted nothing to do with me. He refused to forgive me for past offenses, and then you and the other brides came to town. I was ready to sell out and leave."

"You were?"

Rachel nodded. "Yes. I came within a hair's width of selling this place." Her gaze lovingly roved around the room.

"I can't imagine anyone else owning this house. I'm glad you didn't have to do that."

"Me, too. But let me tell you that I firmly believe the good Lord has a plan for you in all of this. He brought you to Lookout for a reason."

Shannon was afraid to let hope take wing. "You truly believe that?"

Rachel grinned and shook her head. "What's hardest to swallow is that He used the Corbett brothers to get you and Leah to town."

" 'Tis a difficult concept to fathom. Why do you suppose He would do such a thing?"

"Because God loves you. He has a plan for your life even if things seem their darkest."

"And you believe He brought me here to marry Mark?"

A loud cheer rose up outside the window, and the raised voices of happy men drew her attention for a moment. She longed to be part of the community, but so many people still looked at her as a mail-order bride who was found lacking.

Rachel shook her head. "I never said that. It's possible that

God wants you to marry Mark, but He could have brought you here for another man—or another purpose altogether. You need to spend time in prayer and seek God. Try asking Him why you're here, and see what He says."

Shannon rose and walked to the window. It took her a moment to find Mark talking to Jack. The girl smiled up at him and nodded her head. Rachel joined her and peered out. "What's that girl up to now? I told her to stay out of the way."

"I fail to see how Mark can do much with his hand in that cast."

"You know, I just thought of something." Rachel tapped her finger against her mouth. "Mark left Lookout for a time. I don't know much of what happened because I had my own troubles back then, but I can tell you he was different when he returned. Quieter. More thoughtful and less reckless."

"Sounds as if 'twould do his brother good to get away, if he'd return the same as Mark."

Rachel chuckled. "I didn't say it was a good thing. Something bothers Mark deep down, but I have no idea what it is. He doesn't talk about it."

Shannon pondered all that Rachel had said. Could she have truly been brought here for some greater purpose? She remembered her mother saying something similar about their coming to America, but that had tragically ended in her parents' deaths. Couldn't they have just as well died back in Ireland? Where would that have left her, though?

There were many more opportunities for an unmarried woman in America, even though life was still difficult. Prayer was what she needed. For too long, she'd been angry at God for taking her parents, but perhaps it had been His will for her to come to this grand country. And if it was, He would provide for her and give her direction—if she only sought Him.

"Well. . ." Rachel pushed away from the window. "Those sandwiches won't get made by themselves."

"Thank you for your time. I'll be down in a few minutes to help you."

Rachel smiled over her shoulder and walked out into the hallway. "You really don't have to, but if you don't mind helping, I won't turn you down. A lot of men are out there, working up big appetites."

Shannon nodded and closed the door. She knelt beside the bed and folded her hands. "Father God, I beg that You forgive me my trespasses. Forgive me for being angry at You and not seeking You as I should. Show me why You brought me to Lookout. And show me, please, if Mark is part of my future."

The rocking chairs had been moved and makeshift tables set up on the boardinghouse porch. The pounding of hammers and men's shouts across the street filled the air. Shannon set out a tray of sliced bread, while Leah rearranged the table to make room for the bowls of boiled turnips and buttered grits that the pastor's wife had brought. One of the local ranchers had delivered a smoked pig, which Rachel and Jack had partially sliced earlier.

Standing back, Shannon surveyed the tables. Every manner of food one could imagine was on one of the four tables. Jack burst out the front door, carrying a large bowl of buns Rachel had baked. The screen door slammed against the house, jarring the tables and making Leah jump.

"Good heavens, girl. You scared a dozen years off me."

Jack giggled and set the buns by the sliced bread. "You'd better not be wasting any years. You'll be a wife soon, and they work hard."

Leah smiled. "I will be married soon, won't I?"

Shannon nodded, enjoying the lightheartedness after the traumatic events in Denison. Her time of prayer this morning had helped her calm down and focus on the task at hand. Staying busy certainly helped keep her mind off her heartaches. She walked over to the porch rail, lifted her hand to shade her eyes, and looked for Mark. Men hustled here and there, carrying boards, hammering, sawing. There must be twenty men or more, yet they worked as a unified team. How did they each know just what to do?

She shook her head, impressed with their organization. The aroma of fresh-cut lumber scented the air, and the two-story skeleton of the new store was standing, straight and tall. The first story was framed in, and men were already attaching boards to the side walls. She supposed the new owner would be living up above the store.

Rachel strode out the door and walked past each table, surveying everything. The women of the town who had donated food stood in small groups on Bluebonnet Lane, watching the men work and talking. Rachel moved a plate to make room for a last-minute arrival, then clapped her hands. The ladies pivoted in unison and quieted.

"I do believe we are ready to eat. Shall we gather the men?"

"I'll get them, Ma." Jack shot off the end of the porch, not even bothering to use the steps. The girl had begged her mum to let her wear her overalls today so she could help Luke work on the store.

Rachel shook her head. "That girl should have been a boy."

The crowd chuckled. Shannon leaned on a porch post and watched Jack find her new da in the group. He smiled and patted her on the shoulder, then turned to the men and yelled, "Dinner is ready."

A masculine cheer rang out. Most men set aside their tools and headed for the women, but a couple finished their hammering first. Husbands found their wives and turned toward the packed tables. Shannon felt left out as she watched a man swoop down and steal a kiss from his beloved. Mark stood at the back of the line with several unmarried men. He said something to his brother, then slapped his shoulder, and the whole group laughed. She was glad they were having a good time.

Leah found Dan among the men and pulled him over to the food line. Shannon heaved a sigh. 'Twas such a melancholy thing to watch her good friend find love and prepare for her wedding while her own heart was breaking. She hung her head. How did one get over caring for someone who didn't care for them?

"Um. . .excuse me, ma'am. Could I slip past you so's I can get a couple of those fine dinner rolls?"

Shannon glanced up into the blue-gray eyes of a local rancher who'd attended the Saturday social. "Pardon me." She scooted back against the porch railing and allowed him to pass her.

He grabbed two buns and laid them atop the mountain of food on his plate. He turned and smiled, then touched the brim of his hat with his fingertips. "Rand Kessler, ma'am. I don't suppose you'd care to dine with me?"

His unexpected invitation stunned her, but she was in no mood for masculine company. "Well, uh, I need to refill the bread when it dwindles down."

His cheeks turned a ruddy red, and he ducked his head. "How about saving me a dance at the next social?"

Shannon forced a smile. He was a nice man, and she didn't want to hurt his feelings. Her heart wasn't in dancing at all, especially with someone other than Mark, but what did it matter now? "Aye, 'twould be my pleasure."

His wide grin made her glad she'd agreed. Mr. Kessler was a comely man, and she knew he owned a large ranch. He'd make a decent husband, she supposed, but not for her.

Garrett Corbett helped himself to a couple of buns and smiled. "Good day, Miss O'Neil."

She nodded, and realized this was just the chance she'd been waiting for. Mark was at the far end of the line, and she might not catch Garrett alone again. "Might I have a few moments of your time?"

His brows lifted, and he glanced over his shoulder. "Me?"

"Aye. You."

He took a bite of his bun. "Sure, as long as you don't mind if I eat. We'll be getting back to work soon."

"That's fine." She followed him off the porch to a shade tree next to the boardinghouse.

He leaned against the tree and stared at her. "What can I do for you?"

Now that she had his attention, she wasn't sure what to say. She couldn't tell him what had happened between her and his brother. He wouldn't understand why she wanted the change in her work hours, but what did that matter. "I think it's best if I only work in the office when you and your brother are out of town."

His expression remained passive, surprising her. He didn't seem the least bit taken off-guard. Had Mark told him what happened?

"That will mean fewer hours for you. Will that be a problem?"

She'd calculated how much money she'd lose, and aye, 'twould be a problem, but she had no choice. She wouldn't work with Mark in the office. She couldn't.

Garrett's lips twisted to the side. "My brother giving you trouble?"

Shannon shrugged. "I've had to clean and dust and rearrange things over and over to keep busy. You're wasting your money having me work so many hours when you don't need me."

"Shouldn't that be our choice? Maybe we want someone in the office more than just when we're out of town."

"Then you'll need to hire someone else."

He quirked a brow. "You're serious?"

"Aye."

He heaved a sigh and set his plate on a nearby fence post. "What did my brother do?"

Shannon's lips trembled. What could she say? " 'Tisn't important. Can we work it out that I'm in the office on the days you're gone, or not?"

Garrett ran his hand over his chin, obviously not wanting to comply, but finally he nodded his head. "I reckon it would work. I could let you know at the beginning of each week what our plans are, and you could come down after we leave. We can leave notes to each other, if need be."

"Thank you. I appreciate your flexibility."

He nodded and stared down at her, his eyes so much like his brother's that it made her heart ache. "I was hopin' things would work out between you two."

She turned away, not wanting him to see how much she wished the same.

"I'll have a talk with him."

"No!" Shannon turned back and touched his arm, then jerked her hand away. "He made his feelings clear. 'Tis best we both honor them."

He stared at her for a long moment, then nodded.

She turned away, hurrying toward the rear of the boardinghouse. She'd miss seeing Mark most days, but 'twas for the best. Her job was safe. She'd just have to pinch her pennies tighter.

CHAPTER 23

Leah finished sweeping the boardinghouse porch. She watched Dan lift up one of Rachel's heavy rocking chairs as if it were a five-pound bag of sugar and carry it to the middle of the porch, where he set it down.

"That the right spot?"

Leah smiled. "Perfect."

Dan nodded, a twinkle in his dark eyes, and fetched the other three rockers one at a time. Leah loved working on a project like this with him. Though they weren't yet married, she felt joined to him in a way she never had with another man. It was as if they were already partners. She leaned on the broom, imagining the days ahead when she would cook in the Howard home while Dan sipped coffee and read the town newspaper.

Dan brushed his hands together. "That's it. You done with your work now? Care to take a walk?"

She nodded, a teasing smile tugging at her lips. A walk with Dan meant stolen kisses. Her heart skipped like a schoolgirl's. "Just let me run this back inside."

She hurried to the kitchen and placed the broom in its spot.

The whole room smelled of savory scents that made her mouth water. Rachel leaned over the dry sink with her arm halfway down in a large pot she was washing.

"Sure smells wonderful in here. What's for supper?"

Rachel glanced over her shoulder and smiled. "Ham and beans."

"Mmm. . .I can't wait. Dan asked me to take a walk with him, but if you need help, I can stay."

Rachel shook her head. "No, you two go on, but if you see my daughter, chase her home so she can get cleaned up."

"All right, I can do that."

Outside, Dan took her hand, and they passed the new store, heading down Bluebonnet Lane toward the river on the edge of town. "Too bad we didn't finish today."

Leah studied the new structure. "You probably would have if it wasn't for building that second story."

Dan nodded. "Yeah, we ran into a few problems that slowed us down. Several men have volunteered to work on it Monday, so maybe they'll finish up then."

"I can't wait to have the store open again."

Dan chuckled. "Ladies need to do their shopping."

"Oh no. It's not that." She feared he'd misconstrued her meaning and would think her a wastrel. "I don't shop all that much, but I do love walking through the store when I get bored and looking at all the lovely things. Not that I won't work hard once we're married."

Oh, now he'd think her lazy. He didn't realize she'd had hours on end with nothing to do since coming to town, and walking through the store occasionally had helped occupy her time.

Dan patted her hand. "I'm not worried. We won't be rich by any means, but you should be able to buy most things you need—or want—at the store."

"I don't need much. Being the oldest of eleven children, I never had a lot to call my own."

Dan wrapped his arm around her shoulders. "Well, I want you to get what you need. I have some money saved, and you don't need to do without anymore."

She leaned into him, enjoying having someone who cared about her. Someone to spoil her a little bit. She'd had so few treasures in her life—not that she needed many—that it would be delightful to buy some more soft, store-bought undergarments like the set she'd gotten in Denison and not have to use flour sacks any longer.

At the river's edge, they paused and watched the water. The gentle ripple of water splashing on the banks was calming after the busyness of the day. She'd helped Rachel and Shannon bake and fix a large portion of the food for the workers. Since Mrs. Foster had no kitchen, she'd hired Rachel to feed the men, although every woman whose husband was working had also brought food. The feast reminded Leah of the church potlucks back home, after Sunday service.

Thinking of home reminded her of Sue Anne. Had her good friend gone west as a mail-order bride and married her rancher as she'd planned? She'd received only one letter from her, telling of her engagement, but Sue Anne was an only child, and her father might have stopped her from leaving town if he'd found out about her plans. Knowing how happy she was having found her own love, Leah wished the same for her friend.

Dan turned to face her. "Just eight more days, and we'll be married."

Her insides swirled with giddiness. Had she ever been this happy before? "I can't wait."

"Me neither." He leaned down, capturing her lips, and pulled her close. He was so big, so powerful, but with her, he was gentle and loving. She'd never known such delight, and when he finally pulled away, both of them were breathing hard.

Her lips were damp and felt puffy, but her heart was racing. She would spend the rest of her life loving this man and enjoying every minute.

Dan lifted his hat and ran his hand through his hair. "I reckon I should get you back before I do something we'd both regret."

Leah knew just what he meant. She longed to love him more. To show him the depth of her love, but she wasn't free to do that as thoroughly as she wished until after their wedding ceremony. She sighed and nodded her head. Heading back was probably a wise idea.

He took her hand, and they walked to town again. "I reckon we need to clean out Ma's room."

His voice cracked a bit at the mention of his mother. "I can do that after we're married, Dan. Don't worry about it now."

He squeezed her hand. "Thanks. I'd appreciate that. Don't know if I could do it."

"I know. I truly wished I'd gotten to know your mother better."

He wrapped his arm around her. "She liked you, you know."

She dashed a glance up at him. "Indeed?"

"Yep. She wanted me to ask to court you, but I didn't need her prompting, because I've had my eye on you since you first arrived in town. I figured Luke would pick you, what with you being so pretty and all."

She ducked her head, but was pleasantly delighted that he found her pretty. She wouldn't admit that he hadn't caught her eye back then, but she'd been focused only on winning the marshal's heart. She'd have willingly married a man she didn't love back then and would have missed out on the blessing God had for her in Dan.

But there was still one thing she needed to tell him. Something that might make him change his mind about marrying her. A fist of fear squeezed her heart. Could she marry Dan and then tell him she didn't want children? If she told him now, he might call off the wedding. And how could she survive without him?

She argued with herself all the way back to town. *Tell him. Don't tell him until after the wedding. Tell him.*

"Looks like someone has arrived in town."

She glanced up and saw a heavily loaded wagon stopped right in front of the boardinghouse. A woman stood on the porch, hands on her hips, starring at the town. Leah's heart hammered, and she grabbed hold of Dan's arm. "What is she doing here?"

"Who?"

"That woman we saw Mark Corbett with in Denison."

"I have no idea, but it can't be anything good."

Leah quickened her steps. "I have to get back. Shannon will need me."

As they neared the boardinghouse, she realized another woman and several children had also arrived. The wagon looked loaded down with furniture, household goods, and a great number of crates. The other woman stared toward the new store with her hand resting against her cheek.

"I had so hoped the building would be finished when we arrived."

Ah, so this must be the Fosters' niece. Leah strode up to her and held out her hand. "Welcome to Lookout."

The pretty woman with dark brown hair and blue eyes smiled. "Thank you. I'm Christine Morgan. I've come to run the store." She glanced behind her. "Come here, children."

A boy of medium height who looked to be twelve or thirteen came from around the back of the wagon. He eyed Leah with a steely blue gaze that made her want to scurry behind Dan. A girl of about nine shuffled along beside him, carrying a porcelain-faced doll dressed in a frilly blue dress.

Mrs. Morgan smiled. "These are my children, Billy and Tessa."

Leah nodded. "A pleasure to meet you. I'm Leah Bennett, and this is my fiancé, Dan Howard. Dan runs the livery, and I'm currently living at the boardinghouse."

"But not for long." Dan waggled his brows, then turned serious. "I can help you carry whatever you need into the boardinghouse and then store your wagon inside my livery. It will be safe there."

Mrs. Morgan splayed her hand across her chest. "Oh, I can't

tell you how much of a relief that would be. Pretty much all I own is on that wagon." She glanced toward the building again. "I know I'm early, but I sure wish the store had been ready. I'm anxious to get settled."

"I imagine you are. Come on into the boardinghouse, and I'll introduce you to the proprietor, Mrs. Davis. You'll be quite comfortable here."

"And Rachel's a darn good cook," Dan offered.

"That's good news. I'm starved!" Billy rubbed his belly and headed toward the front door.

"Not so quick, young man. Grab your satchel and Tessa's." Mrs. Morgan stared at her son, as if not sure he'd obey.

The boy scowled but returned to the back of the wagon and fetched two bags. Leah hadn't seen Annabelle, but she now stepped out from behind the wagon, carrying two large handbags. She looked at Leah and frowned. Maybe the woman didn't recognize her. What could she be doing in a small town like Lookout? She had a feeling that nothing good would come of it, and that her being here would only bring Shannon more heartache. That Mark Corbett was a scoundrel to lead her friend on and then drop her once she'd fallen in love with him.

Leah strode toward the front door and opened it. She should introduce herself to the other woman, but her heart just wasn't in it. She left the door open and called for Rachel.

"In the kitchen," she cried out.

Leah stopped in the doorway of the kitchen, her stomach gurgling at the delicious scents. Rachel was placing cornbread onto a platter. "Some guests have arrived."

"This late? I hope I have enough food. How many are there?" Rachel dusted her hands and removed her apron. Smoothing down her hair, she hurried toward the front door.

"There are four of them. Two women and two children."

"It's good we're not filled up, then."

The quartet stood in the parlor with Dan behind them,

holding several bags. He winked at Leah, sending delicious tingles radiating through her body. Her intended was a fine-looking man, and he was all hers.

"Welcome, everyone." Rachel smiled and relieved Mrs. Morgan of one of her bags. "I'm Rachel Davis, owner of this boarding-house. How can I help you?"

"I'm Christine Morgan, and these are my children." She glanced at the other new arrival. "Miss Smith caught a ride with us, but I believe she's staying here, too, if you have enough room."

"Yes, there's room for all of you." Rachel explained the rate and that meals were included, then headed for the stairs. "If y'all will just follow me, I'll show you to your rooms, where you can freshen up. Supper is ready to be served, so come on back down as soon as you can."

Leah watched them trounce up the stairs with Dan at the end of the line. He winked at her again, then followed the others. "I'll start setting out the meal, if that's all right, Rachel."

The boardinghouse owner looked down from the second floor and smiled. "Thank you. That would be wonderful."

Leah waited a moment, suspecting Rachel would show Miss Smith to the only available room on the second floor, and then the Morgan family up to the third floor. She started up the steps and waited until the others headed up the rear stairs, then made a mad dash for Shannon's door. Knocking hard, she didn't wait but opened the door and peered inside.

Shannon was halfway across the room, heading toward her. "What's wrong?

Leah waved for Shannon to hurry over to her. "Come down-stairs with me. New guests have arrived, and Rachel is seeing them to their rooms. Supper is nearly ready and I told her I'd help, and there's something I've got to tell you."

Shannon followed her out the door, obviously curious. "And what would that be?"

Leah lifted her skirt and hurried down the stairs. "Wait till we get to the kitchen."

They hustled down the hall, skirts swishing, and entered the empty room. Shannon glanced at the stove.

"I told Rachel I'd dish up supper. Could you finish putting the cornbread on that platter?" Leah pulled one of the soup tureens from a cabinet and started ladling beans into it while Shannon attended to her job, casting curious glances her way.

They placed the food on the buffet in the dining room. Then Leah grabbed Shannon's hand, pulled her through the kitchen, and out the back door. Shannon's green eyes widened as Leah turned to face her. She leaned in close. "That woman is here."

Shannon blinked. "What woman?"

"The one Mark was talking to in Denison."

Gasping, Shannon clutched her chest. "Why?"

"I don't know. I just wanted you to be prepared and not surprised when you saw her."

Shannon straightened her back and hiked up her chin. "Why should I care if she's here? Mark wants nothing to do with me, so she can have him."

Leah's heart ached for her friend's pain. It made her own happiness less enjoyable. She placed a hand on Shannon's shoulder. "It matters, and we both know it."

Shaking her head, Shannon stared off in the distance. "Nay, it doesn't. I must move past my feelings for him. It does me no good to hang on to them."

Leah clenched her fist. "Oh, those Corbetts. If I were a man, I'd knock them both for a loop."

Shannon's mouth turned up in a melancholy smile. "If you were a man, you wouldn't have an issue with them."

Leah blew out a frustrated breath. How could Shannon be so gracious? "Well, I suppose we should finish setting out the food."

Shannon nodded and followed her back inside. Leah opened a lid on a large pot and found a mess of greens with ham chunks.

She dished them into another tureen while Shannon carried an assortment of jellies and a bowl of butter to the table.

Leah's mind raced. Why had that woman come to Lookout?

Whatever the reason was, she had a feeling it would only mean trouble for her friend.

CHAPTER 24

Mark stared at the ledger, but his eyes couldn't seem to focus on the numbers. Nothing had seemed right since he'd told Shannon he'd never marry. The pain in her eyes that night haunted his dreams the few hours that he'd managed to fall asleep. He missed her. Missed seeing her in the office, sitting in his chair. Missed watching her whirl around, dusting cabinets and leaving her soft scent lingering in the air.

He rested his head on his hand and sighed. If only he'd never left Lookout. Then maybe he and Shannon could have had a chance.

Garrett walked in from the back room, still carrying his coffee cup. Generally, for the first hour or two each morning, his brother and the mug were attached to one another. He strolled over to the pot sitting on the stove and filled his cup, then turned and stared at Mark.

"You're looking rather glum these days, little brother." Garrett continued staring while he took a sip.

Mark shrugged, unable to deny the accusation. He was glum. And frustrated. And lonely.

"Care to talk about it?" Garrett pulled out his desk chair and sat down.

He'd wrestled with that very thought on a number of occasions, but telling his brother he couldn't marry Shannon would mean he'd have to tell him the whole story. And he wasn't prepared to do that.

His brother was all the family he had left, except for Luke, and he couldn't stand seeing the disappointment in Garrett's eyes if he ever learned the truth. He'd worked so hard to be an upstanding citizen ever since that calamity in Abilene, and he didn't want his reputation tarnished. If he ever was to become a lawyer, having an unblemished reputation was crucial. Who'd trust their future to a lawyer who'd killed a man?

Garrett swigged down the last of his coffee and stood. "Well, if you decide you want to get that burden you're lugging off your chest, I'll be tending the horses."

Mark sat with his head in his hands. Why couldn't he give this burden to God? He'd begged forgiveness—over and over again. He was sure God had forgiven him for killing that man, but how did he forgive himself?

That night in Abilene intruded into his mind again. He could hear the off-key piano, smell the smoke that filled the room until a hazy cloud hung in the air. Men gambled at different tables, while others drank away their hard-earned weekly pay. Saloon girls sashayed between tables, but Mark only had eyes for one of them.

Annabelle.

The first night he'd gone into the saloon, she'd offered to get him a drink. Their attraction was instant, and although he rarely frequented saloons, visiting the Lucky Star where she worked became a nightly obsession. Even remembering the Bible verses about avoiding wanton women that his mother had quoted to him and Garrett when they were becoming young men didn't stop him.

Annabelle had been his first love. She'd managed to squeeze out short moments to sit with him or stand and talk between serving drinks to the other patrons. He'd never drank before, but he kept buying liquor to keep her coming around. And that drinking made his head fuzzy. Made him do things he'd not normally do.

He hung his head in shame as he remembered the first night he'd waited until Annabelle was off work and had walked her to the small room she rented. One kiss led to two. Two led to three. His whiskey-befuddled mind assented to her request to come inside, and the rest was history. He'd not had the power to refuse her pleas to stay the night.

Mark clutched his hair in his fists. It had all happened so fast, and his need had been so strong that he couldn't resist her charms. Afterward, he'd felt so dirty and ashamed that he'd taken advantage of her that he hadn't returned to the saloon for a full week. But the siren's call had been too strong to resist.

And he'd forever pay the price.

If only he could go back and do things differently.

"Forgive me, Lord."

The bell on the door jingled, pulling him out of his reverie. He blinked, sure what he was seeing was an apparition.

Annabelle stood in the doorway, giving him that saucy smile that had made him weak years before. He stood, still unable to believe she was standing in his office. In his town.

"Hello there, handsome."

"What are you doing in Lookout?"

She strutted toward him, looking deceptively sweet in that dark blue calico dress, but he knew inside lay a vixen who could make the strongest of men sway from his beliefs. Warnings clanged in his mind. He was a stronger man than he'd been back then. He was a man who'd tasted her spoils and by God's grace would never fall in that quagmire again.

She pressed her hands on his desk and leaned forward, her gaze never leaving his. Mark's heart pounded like a creature caught in a trap. He stepped back until he met the wall to distance himself from her.

He cleared his throat. "I asked what you are doing here. I thought I made it clear in Denison that anything between us was over. Way over."

She smiled and waved her hand in the air. "I knew you'd change your mind if you could see how different I am. I'm going to find a respectable job and start my life over. There's always room for a good man in it."

Mark crossed his arms. "I'm not that man."

Annabelle shrugged and stared out the front window. "Things got bad recently in Abilene. I couldn't stay there anymore, and besides, I was sick of men pawing at me. I want to know what it's like to be a lady whom men respect."

Something in Mark's heart cracked, but he quickly shored up the breach. Annabelle might fuss about working in the saloon, but he felt certain she liked the attention she'd received. And while he couldn't blame her in the least for not wanting to be an upstairs gal, she hadn't had any qualms about taking him to her bed. A shiver charged down his back at the memory.

He'd been stupid.

Thought she had eyes for only him.

But he was older and wiser now.

"There are plenty of towns you could live in. Why come here?"

She spun around, her head cocked. "Because you're here. We can finally have the life together that we talked about."

Mark ran his hand through his hair. "That was a long time ago. I don't mean to be unkind, but let me put it clearly—I'm no longer interested in a relationship with you."

Her lips pushed out into a pout. "It's that Irish gal, isn't it?"

A vision of Shannon entered his mind. If she learned about his past rapport with Annabelle, it would crush any hopes that he might have of restoring his relationship with her. Yeah, he'd told her he would never marry, but deep inside, he still held out hope that something could work out between them. A horrible thought rushed into his mind. "Where are you staying?"

A sly grin tilted her mouth. "At the boardinghouse, of course. Where else would a decent woman stay in this dumpy, little town?"

Mark's fingers tightened on the back of the chair, and he ground his back teeth together.

"I'm so looking forward to getting to know Shannon better. I think she and I could be good friends."

"What do you want, Annabelle? Why are you really here?"

Her mouth twisted, and she shrugged. "I didn't know where to go. You're the only man who ever defended me, and I truly wanted to see if there was any chance for us to be together again."

He strode around the desk and leaned into her face. She swallowed hard, showing the first sign of vulnerability he'd seen since she'd entered his office. "Let me tell you again. I made the biggest mistake of my life in Abilene. There is no chance this side of heaven of us being together. I'm sorry you've had a rough life, but part of it was your own choosing. You could have left the Lucky Star years ago, but you didn't. I sincerely hope you can turn your life around, but I won't be a part of it. The best thing you can do for me is to leave town."

She flounced her head and scowled. "That was rather harsh, don'tcha think?"

"No, it's simply the truth."

"I was hopin' you'd give me a job."

Mark shook his head. "Shannon already works here."

"Then why isn't she here? It's already midmornin'."

"We. . .ah. . .don't have enough work for her to be here all the time. She mostly works when we're gone now."

"I can see that you need time to get used to my being here. I'll give you a few days, and then we'll talk again." She swung around, hurried for the door, and yanked it open.

"Annabelle. I meant what I said."

She slammed the door without looking back. Mark slumped against his desk. "Dear Lord, help me."

⁓

Shannon sat in the parlor, staring out the front window. She needed to finish the lace she was making for Leah's wedding dress, but her heart wasn't in it. She might have lost Mark, but she never expected to have another woman come to town vying for him.

Perhaps she was making a mountain out of a molehill, but that Annabelle Smith had gone on and on at breakfast about knowing Mark in Abilene. Why, she'd all but insinuated there was something between them. Had that woman hurt Mark so deeply that he never wanted to marry?

'Twould explain a lot.

But Mark didn't seem jaded toward women. He'd always been friendly to her, except when Garrett first hired her to work for them. She sighed heavily. This was her first day to not go in to work, and she sorely missed being there. Missed seeing Mark.

But she'd made her decision, and 'twas for the best. Her heart couldn't heal if she had to work with Mark, and listen to his baritone voice, smell his fresh scent, or watch him work. She longed to see those brilliant blue eyes gazing at her as she'd caught them on more than one occasion.

"You silly lass." She shook her head to rid it of thoughts of Mark and focused back on her stitching.

Leah walked in and sat down on the settee beside her. "Oh, that is so lovely. You do such fine work. I bet you could easily sell your lace."

"Thank you. Perhaps I will talk to Mrs. Morgan about that very thing. If I could sell some that would help offset the money I'll lose by not working at the freight office so much."

Leah puffed up. "I wish you didn't have to work there at all."

"Aye, 'twould be for the best, but I'll not have the Corbetts supporting me again, so I must work there until I find something else."

"That Miss Smith is looking for employment also."

"Would that I could give her my job at the freight office, then she and her beloved Mark would be together."

Leah's brows lifted. "Is that cynicism I hear?"

Shannon shrugged. "I just got so ill listening to her go on about Mark at breakfast. If they were such good friends, why have we never heard of her before seeing her in Denison?"

"Maybe she's not someone Mark wants to remember. She seems awfully. . .shall we say, rough around the edges?"

"Aye, I sensed that, too. What do you suppose it means?"

"I have my suspicions, but it's best I not voice them, in case I'm wrong."

Shannon laid down her stitching again. If she sewed while angry, she had a tendency to pull the thread so tight that it bunched up. "She can have him, for all I care."

Leah laid her hand on Shannon's arm. "I'm so sorry things didn't work out between you two. It's hard to be happy with Dan knowing all you're going through."

Shannon turned toward her friend. "The last thing I want to do is steal your joy. The good Lord is helping me. I still care for Mark, but I need to look elsewhere for a husband. If I can marry, I will no longer have to work at the freight office."

Leah closed her eyes for a moment. "Just don't rush into something. I know you've had at least a dozen marriage proposals in the past weeks, but take your time and pick a man who will be good to you. A man you might one day be able to love."

She considered the wisdom of her friend's advice and nodded. Quick, heavy footsteps on the front porch drew their attention. Someone pounded on the door, and then it opened.

"Leah?" Dan's frantic deep voice boomed through the house.

Leah jumped up and hurried from the room. "I'm right here. What's wrong?"

"Come outside, I've got to talk to you."

The front door shut, then opened again, and Annabelle walked into the parlor. "Looks like the lovebirds might be having a spat."

Gathering up her lace, Shannon stood and crossed to the window. Dan looked very upset. What could have happened?

"I was just over talking to Mark."

The woman said his name as if it were sweet candy. "So. . . there's no law against talkin' to the man."

Annabelle smirked. "I don't know what's going on with you and him, but Mark and I have a past. I just need a little time to win him back."

"Good luck with that, I say."

Annabelle blinked and looked taken off-guard. If the woman expected her to fight for Mark, she'd be disappointed. Shannon headed out of the room. She might have to be cordial to Annabelle, but she didn't have to socialize with her.

"I must have been wrong. I thought for sure you and Mark had something going on."

Had was the key word. "I don't believe Mark is interested in any woman. He told me himself that he'd never marry. If you ask me, you're wastin' your time with that one."

Annabelle's eyes widened, and her mouth opened, but nothing came out. Shannon hurried up the stairs, closed her door, and locked it. At least in the privacy of her own room she could be free of that woman. She laid the lace on top of the dresser and sat in the chair, worried about Leah.

What was going on?

CHAPTER 25

"Why can't we get married right away?" Dan stared at her with hurt in his eyes. "Then you can travel to Dallas with me to see to my brother's estate."

"I'm so sorry to hear about your brother's death, but I'm not ready to marry. My dress isn't finished yet, and there are a hundred other details to take care of."

Dan paced to the end of the porch and stared off in the distance. Leah's heart ached for him. He hadn't gotten over his mother's death yet, and now a telegram informed him of his brother and sister-in-law's deaths. "Couldn't I just go with you, and we could get married when we return? We're both adults and able to handle the situation respectfully."

He shook his head. "I won't take a chance on ruining your reputation. There are some folks in this town who'd look down on two unmarried people traveling together."

She closed the distance between them and laid her hand on his shoulder. "I'm so sorry about your family. Can you tell me what happened?"

He turned and wrapped his arms around her. "I don't know

much. The telegram was from my sister, Louise, and just said that Aaron and Irene had died and for me to come to Dallas as soon as possible."

"Did they have any children?"

He nodded and swallowed so hard that Leah saw his Adam's apple move. "Five, and they're all fairly young."

Tears stung Leah's eyes. "Oh, those poor children. What will happen to them?"

"I'm sure my sister will take them in. She's known them all since birth and is very close to them since they only lived a half-mile away."

Leah hugged Dan hard, not caring if anyone saw. He rested his chin on top of her head. She wanted to go along with him, but he was right. People would think it inappropriate. "When are you leaving?"

"I thought to wait until morning to take the stage, but if you aren't coming, I'll leave as soon as I can get packed and ride to Dallas."

She leaned back and stared up into his damp eyes. His thick lashes clung together in spikes, and she knew he'd be embarrassed if he became aware that she knew he'd been crying. He was a big, tough man, but he cared deeply for his only brother. "Will it be dangerous for you to ride alone?"

"No. I'll be riding fast, only stopping to rest my horse. In fact, I may take two and trade off riding them. I should be there in a few days if I do that."

She lifted her hand and touched his face. "Please be careful, and come back to me. I couldn't bear losing you."

He smiled through his sadness. "I love you, sweetheart."

Right there in broad daylight on the boardinghouse front porch, he pulled her back into his arms and kissed her thoroughly. When he stopped, she swayed, nearly dizzy with love for this man. She almost wavered and decided to go with him.

"I'd better get going."

"Once you're packed, stop back by here. I'm sure Rachel won't mind if I make you a lunch to take with you."

He nodded and strode away. Leah's heart thumped hard. What if something happened to him, and he didn't return? How would she find the strength to go on?

She muttered a prayer as she walked through the house to the kitchen. Just like when her pa had sold her to that horrible Mr. Abernathy and she'd found the strength to run away and become a mail-order bride, God would help her to go on without Dan. But she prayed hard that such a day never would come.

~

Annabelle sat on the edge of the bed and stared at the wall of her room in the boardinghouse. It was the nicest place she'd ever stayed, except maybe for the hotel in Denison. She picked at some lint on her serviceable dress, so plain compared to her saloon garb and yet it made her feel respectable. How odd that a simple dress could change a person's perspective of her. If the folks in the boardinghouse knew the truth about her, they'd boot her out the front door and send her packing.

She blew out a heavy breath. Her plans had not turned out as she'd hoped. Instead of being happy to see her, Mark acted like he couldn't stand to be around her. At least he would keep silent about her past, since he had more to lose than her if he spilled the beans. Maybe that's why he was so nervous around her. Maybe he was afraid his friends would find out that he had socialized with a saloon girl.

He sure had changed from the fun-loving man she'd known several years ago. She lay down on the bed and pulled the spare pillow against her stomach, remembering how she'd once shared her bed with him. He'd liked her back then. Maybe even loved her.

He certainly had come to her defense in the saloon when that randy cowboy had mauled her and forced her to kiss him. She shivered at the thought of her mouth pressed to the man's, his hands freely roving her body. Who knew what might have happened if Mark hadn't called a halt? When the cowboy pulled his gun, she'd screamed, sure that Mark would be killed. But the cowboy died that night when Mark shot him.

She'd thought Mark a soft, intellectual type and had been attracted to him at first only because of his unusual, robin's-egg blue eyes and curly blond hair. She'd been drawn to the gentle innocence of his gaze, but she soon discovered she liked him. Then it became a quest to see if she could get him to marry her. He was her best chance to ever get free of the saloon. To live a life she'd only dreamed about.

Now what was she going to do? She'd wandered through the few businesses in Lookout, and nobody had a job opening of any kind. She thought about stopping in the Wet Your Whistle, but that would be going right back to where she'd been before. How was she going to get by?

Everett's money wouldn't last forever.

The night of the next Saturday social was perfect. A cool north wind had blown in, making the temperature bearable. The sun hanging low in the sky showed the beginnings of a beautiful sunset with its brilliant orange glow. But Shannon's heart wasn't in dancing or enjoying the sunset. Why had she allowed Leah to drag her along?

Dancers kicked up their heels to the lively music, stirring up a low-hanging cloud of dust. A couple of the men let out whoops as they twirled their dance partners in a circle. The size of the crowd was more than triple that of the first social. Since news of Dan and Leah's engagement and that of another couple's, unmarried folks had flocked here from miles away to meet new people and have a good time.

Both Shannon and Leah had remained behind the table, much to the disappointment of the men who'd asked them to dance. The only man Shannon wanted to dance with wasn't in attendance. Annabelle, on the other hand, had yet to say no to a single man, Shannon was sure. She watched the flirtatious woman laughing and twirling with a handsome cowboy. If she had designs on Mark, no one would know it tonight.

Someone to Shannon's right cleared his throat, and she glanced sideways.

The comely rancher smiled. "I do believe you promised me a dance tonight, Miss O'Neil."

Inwardly, Shannon sighed. Why had she agreed to dance with this man last weekend? She forced a smile, knowing she couldn't go back on her word. "Aye, that I did."

Relief widened his smile, and he took her hand, leading her to the lot beside the church where the dancers were. She placed her free hand on his shoulder, finding that she could barely reach it. Why did men grow so tall in Texas?

"In case you didn't remember, my name is Rand Kessler."

She remembered. She also knew he was the man who had once hoped to marry Rachel, before Luke returned to Lookout. He seemed a nice enough man, and he must be for Rachel to have agreed to see him.

"I own a ranch outside of town a ways. We raise shorthorn cattle and horses."

Mr. Kessler spun her around in time with the music and held her gently, not possessively, like so many of the men did. She liked that about him. "Have you always lived in Texas, Mr. Kessler?"

"Call me Rand, ma'am. And no, I haven't. My daddy came here after our Georgia plantation was destroyed in the war. I was just a young boy when we first arrived here. But I've lived most of my life here, and Texas will always be my home."

That explained the slight Southern twang to his speech. She thought about his traveling here from Georgia and realized they had something in common—they were both immigrants to this land.

"How did you happen to come here?" Rand's ears suddenly turned red, and his gaze shot everywhere but at her. "I mean, I know how you came to be in Lookout since you were one of the... uh...mail-order brides the Corbetts ordered, but how did you get here from Ireland?"

She scowled at his mention of the Corbetts. For a whole two minutes, Mark hadn't entered her mind. But Rand wasn't aware of how the name affected her, and she chose to forget about it. "My da had the grand idea of coming to America, the land whose streets are paved in gold. Imagine his surprise when we arrived in New Orleans."

"Where are your parents now? If I may ask?" He cleared his throat and again looked uncomfortable. "I mean, why would they allow you to travel to Texas alone as a mail-order bride?"

She broke eye contact and stared off in the distance. He was just being cordial and had no idea how his questions stirred up hurts. They danced around another couple and in and out of the crowd. Finally she worked up her nerve and looked at him again. "My parents died shortly after we arrived in New Orleans."

His eyes widened. He danced her over to the edge of the crowd, and then stopped and rubbed the back of his neck. "I'm sorry, ma'am. I had no idea. Have you no brothers or sisters?"

She shook her head.

"Me neither. I'm an only child. Well, I am now, but I did have a little sister. She died from a snakebite." His lips pursed as if mentioning the old accident still pained him.

Shannon laid her hand on his arm. "I'm sorry, Rand. I, too, have lost all my siblings, but 'twas a long time ago, back in Ireland."

He nodded. "Care to take a walk?"

"Aye, 'twould be nice."

He offered his arm and guided her around the dancers and back toward the refreshment table. As they passed Leah, she lifted her brows and smiled in a teasing manner. Shannon hoped her friend didn't make too much of her walk with Rand. He was a nice, lonely man, and she was a lonely woman. "Tell me about your ranch."

"It's small compared to some ranches in Texas, around ten thousand acres."

Shannon gasped, and he stopped and stared at her. "That's small?"

He shrugged, but pride pulled at his lips. "For Texas. There's so much land here, it can take a month to cross it all."

"Surely it must take a long while to cross ten thousand acres."

"Well, we don't normally ride the whole thing at one time. The ranch is kind of in the middle of it all."

They walked down the street, talking, and by the time he saw her back to the boardinghouse, she'd made a decision.

If Rand Kessler ever asked her to marry him, she'd accept his offer.

Her heart might belong to Mark, but since he didn't want her, she needed to look elsewhere. And Rand seemed as good as they came.

CHAPTER 26

Silverware clinked around the table as the boarders enjoyed breakfast. Leah looked around the group and realized how close she was becoming to the Davis family and to Shannon. She'd been desperate last spring when she wrote to Luke Davis about becoming his mail-order bride, but things certainly hadn't turned out as she'd expected. Soon she would marry. This coming Sunday after church, if Dan returned on time, but not to the man she originally thought she would wed.

Christine Morgan carried on a lively conversation with Rachel and Annabelle, while Shannon stared into her coffee cup. There ought to be something Leah could do to encourage her friend, but then she was pining away, too.

She moved the last of her eggs around on her plate. She missed Dan terribly. Had he settled his brother's estate and gotten the children situated at his sister's house? Was he already on his way home?

"Have you had any news from Dan?" The marshal stared at Leah while adding a spoon of sugar to his coffee.

She shook her head. "No, I didn't really expect to hear from him. I figure he could be home in less time than it would take to send a letter. Besides, I don't see Dan as the letter-writing type."

Luke grinned. "You might be right about that. He's far better suited to a hammer and anvil."

Rachel buttered her biscuit and slathered apricot jam on it. "That's such a shame for Dan to lose his brother and sister-in-law right on the heels of his mother's death."

"Yes, it is. My heart aches for him. I don't know how he holds up." Leah laid her napkin next to her plate.

" 'Tis difficult to lose two family members at once."

Heads nodded around the table. Everyone knew about Shannon's loss.

Leah patted her friend's shoulder and offered a smile, then looked at Rachel. "Thank you for another wonderful breakfast. It was delicious as always. Can I help with the cleanup?"

Rachel waved her hand as usual. "No, thank you. Just go off and finish that dress. Sunday will be here before you know it."

Shannon stood, too. "I almost have the lace completed. I just need a few more hours' work."

"I love the lace you gave me for a wedding gift. It will always be special to me." Rachel smiled at Shannon and then turned to her daughter. "You'd better finish up and head to school. You don't want to be late on the first day."

Jack shoved a piece of biscuit into her mouth and winked at Billy Morgan. "We wouldn't want to be late, would we?"

"I love school." Tessa pushed away from the table, her eyes sparkling. "Do you have a nice teacher?"

Jack stood and gulped down her milk. "Yeah, she's all right, but let me tell you about Butch Laird. He's the class bully, and you'll want to stay away from him."

"I don't think you'll have to worry about that boy. I had a good talk with him and scared him straight." Luke stretched and downed the last of his coffee.

A knock sounded on the front door, and Leah moved toward it. "I'll grab that, so you just enjoy your biscuit, Rachel."

As she entered the hall, she realized how brash that sounded. Here she was, a guest at the boardinghouse, and she was answering the door and telling the owner what to do. She smiled to herself. At least Rachel was kind enough not to mind her guests bossing her around.

She pulled the heavy door open, and her heart did a somersault. Dan stood on the other side of the screen door, devouring her with his eyes. He looked so handsome. So wonderful. He yanked the screen open, and she squealed and jumped into his arms. He turned a circle, taking her with him.

"Welcome back, Dan." Shannon smiled softly and hurried up the stairs.

Dan watched her, and when she opened her door and disappeared into her room, his lips came down on Leah's, hard but gentle. After a moment, he pulled away and stared into her eyes. "I don't ever want to have to leave you again."

Tears dripped down Leah's cheeks, and she knew exactly what he meant. He'd been gone just shy of a week, but she'd missed him so much that she'd lain awake at nights. Now that she had a good glance at him, she realized he looked exhausted, haggard. Her cheeks were chafed from his unshaven face. "I'm so glad you're back. I didn't expect you so soon. What happened?"

He took her hand and pulled her outside. "Walk with me to the house. I brought a surprise back with me."

What could he have brought her? Something for the wedding? A treasured family heirloom that he'd retrieved from his brother's house? "How did you manage to finish everything so quickly?"

"I didn't. Stanley is going to see to the selling of Aaron's farm, then pay off the debts and split whatever income there may be between us and him and Louise."

"So you had the funeral?"

He nodded as they walked down Bluebonnet Lane and turned onto Oak Street. "Louise had it all planned. I'd have missed it if I'd waited and taken the stage. People are buried quickly in these parts since it tends to be so hot here much of the year."

Leah hugged his brawny arm. "I'm so glad you got to be there. I know that was important to you."

Dan sobered. "Yeah, it was. Louise missed it, though."

"She did? Why?"

"She's been awful sick. She's carrying, and the doctor suspects it may be twins. He's making her stay off her feet until the babies are born."

"Oh, that poor woman. I know all about twins. My ma had two sets of them."

Dan patted her arm and then waved at Martha Phillips, who was sweeping off her front porch.

"Good to see you back. How'd your trip go?" The doctor's wife tucked a wisp of hair back under her scarf.

" 'Bout as I expected, all except for one thing."

"Well, I suppose that's good then." Martha smiled and resumed her sweeping.

Dan leaned in close to Leah. "I reckon you and Martha will get to know each other better, being as she and the doc are our closest neighbors."

"If we ever need the doctor in the middle of the night, at least we won't have far to go."

Dan chuckled. "That's right, darlin'."

A large wagon with two stock horses still hitched to it was parked in front of Dan's house. It looked loaded to the top and more, but a well-secured canvas tarp prevented her from seeing inside. Maybe Dan had brought some of his brother's furniture back with him. Leah almost rubbed her hands together in anticipation. The current furniture was frayed and scratched from years of use and could stand to be replaced. She redecorated the room in her mind. Would he let her repaint it or maybe even apply some wallpaper?

A loud crash sounded from inside the house, followed by a squeal. Leah jumped and her gaze dashed to Dan's. "Sounds like someone left a pig in the house. You didn't bring one back, did you?"

Dan chuckled again. "Not quite."

The front door flew open as they walked up the porch steps. A young boy ran out the door and right into Dan's legs. A dark-haired girl not much older, maybe eight or nine, chased after him.

"I told Ben to stay on the couch, Uncle Dan, but he didn't mind. I'm gonna find a switch and tan his hide." The girl stood with her hand on her hips, looking like a little mother.

Leah's breakfast swirled in her stomach, and she watched in disbelief as two smaller children hurried out onto the porch. The youngest two huddled around their big sister, holding on to her skirt. Leah stepped back down the stairs, not wanting to accept what she was seeing. Her head suddenly started throbbing, and her heart sank into a deep, dark pit. This could not be happening to her. Wasn't Dan's sister supposed to keep the children?

"Where's the baby?" Dan asked.

"I put her down on one of the beds since she was sleepin'," the oldest girl answered.

Five children. Almost half as many as her mother had, and Leah wasn't even married yet. How could Dan do this to her?

"Children, this is Leah. She's the woman I told you about." Dan smiled at her, but then his gaze faltered as he studied her face. "She's. . .uh. . .the woman I'm marrying on Sunday."

Leah gasped for breath. She could not—would not faint. Not in front of these children. It wasn't their fault she didn't want to be their mother—or anyone else's. She took another step back.

Dan's questioning gaze darted between her and the children. He lovingly caressed the oldest girl's head. "This is Caroline, but we all call her Callie. She's eight, and quite the little mother. Ben is next. He's seven and loves horses. Then comes Ruthie, who is five." The little girl leaned her head against her sister and gave Leah a shy wave. Dan picked up the towheaded toddler whose near-black eyes were as dark as his. The child laid his head on his uncle's shoulder. "And this little fellow is Davy."

Leah's heart took another hit. Davy, just like her youngest

sibling. Her Davy had barely been crawling when she left home in late spring, but he was probably close to walking by now.

"Maggie is the baby," Callie said. "She'll be one next month. Mama was gonna have a party." The girl stared up at her uncle, her chin quivering. "We can have a party, can't we?"

Dan nodded. "Of course we can, darlin'. I bet Leah would be happy to bake a cake for Maggie, wouldn't you, sweetheart?"

All five of them stared at Leah. She swallowed hard. Dan's gaze begged her to say yes, but nothing could move past the lump in her throat. Tears stung her eyes. She stared at Dan and pleaded him to understand. "I–I'm sorry, but I c–can't."

Dan's shocked gaze turned angry. "Callie, please take the children inside. I'll be there in just a minute. There's some crackers in a jar in the kitchen if you want a snack."

Leah turned and fled back toward the boardinghouse. Thank goodness Martha Phillips had gone inside. Her shame covered her like a cloak, and she was grateful no one was there to see it. Keeping her head down, she walked as quickly as her skirts would allow. Fast footsteps pounded behind her, and Dan grabbed her arm, jerking her to a halt.

"Just hold on. What's gotten into you? How could you be so cruel to those young'uns who just lost their parents?" Dan breathed out his nose, his nostrils flaring like an enraged horse. "It wouldn't hurt you to bake them a cake. You're a great cook."

"You don't understand."

He forked his hand through his hair. "You're darn right, I don't. Care to explain?"

Leah broke from his gaze and stared between two houses at the river in the distance. She should have told him before now. She shook her head and gazed up, begging him with her eyes to understand. "I was the oldest of eleven children, Dan."

"So? Lots of folks have big families." He shoved his hands to his hips.

"I washed more laundry than I've made biscuits, and that's got to be in the hundreds of thousands. I never got to do things with friends because I always had to hurry home after school or church to help Ma. I never had a room or even a bed to myself. I've never had a life of my own. I left home so that I could."

"So? What's that got to do with these kids?"

Leah closed her burning eyes. *Help him to understand, Lord.*

She reached out and caressed his cheek. His eyes closed, and he leaned into her touch. "I love you, Dan, and I desperately want to marry you, but I don't want children."

His mouth dropped open, and he stared with disbelief. He blinked his eyes several times as if trying to grasp what she said. "How can that be? All women want children. It's what God made them for."

"Well, I don't."

"Well, it's too late for regrets. We have five of them."

Leah shook her head. "Not me. *You* have five of them. I'm sorry, Dan. I just can't raise another passel of children. You should have left them with your sister." She turned to walk away, but he grabbed her arm again.

Fire smoldered in his gaze. "I told you that Louise has been sick in bed most of her pregnancy. Friends have been caring for her child. She was in no shape to take the children, and there ain't nobody else."

Leah wrung her hands together, not ready to give up on her dream of marrying him. Her gaze tore up and down the street, and she hoped no one was eavesdropping on their private disagreement. "Surely someone would take them in."

Dan released her and backed up a step. His stunned expression made Leah regret voicing her thoughts.

"If you think that, you ain't the woman I thought you were."

"I want to be a wife, Dan. I'm not ready to be the mother of five children."

"And I'm not ready to be the father of them, either, but I'll not turn my own flesh and blood out on the streets."

Leah pursed her lips. "That's not what I said, and you know it."

Dan leaned in close and glared at her. "It's the same thing. You want me to give them away to strangers who'd most likely mistreat them and use them for child labor."

"I'm sorry. I just can't do this, Dan."

His anger fled, replaced by desperation. "Leah, I need your help. How can I make a living with five young children to watch? The oldest two can go to school, but I can't expect a five-year-old to tend a toddler and a baby—and I can't take them to work. It's too dangerous. I need you now more than ever."

Tears coursed down Leah's face. She wanted to help him, but to do so went against everything she'd dreamed of. How could she give in? How could she face herself in the mirror each morning if she did? How could she stand to lose him?

She shook her head and backed away. "I'm sorry, Dan. I can't do it. I can't marry you now."

She turned and fled up the street.

"Leah, wait. Don't do this!"

Everything had been so perfect. Why did his brother have to die? "Why did You let this happen, Lord?"

Mrs. Foster shook out a blanket and stared at her from the entrance to her tent. Leah turned away, refusing to meet the woman's gaze.

She needed time alone.

She couldn't return to the boardinghouse.

The Sunday house, which sat next to the boardinghouse, was always open, and nobody was currently staying there. Leah dashed into the small house and collapsed on the bed in the far end of the room.

Her sobs filled the air. How could this happen, just when she was ready to get married? Her heart broke as her tears soaked the pillow. She missed Dan already.

She hated disappointing him and leaving him in a lurch.

And she hated herself for doing it.

CHAPTER 27

Jack walked down Bluebonnet Lane toward home with Tessa Morgan beside her. The girl had worn a blue dress with ruffles on the bodice and hem to school, and her blond hair hung in loose ringlets, not nearly as tight as they'd been this morning. Jack shook her head and stared down at her own serviceable calico. The dark blue pinafore kept her dress cleaner, so her ma said, but it made Jack hot. If her ma had her druthers, she would put her in something as fancy as Tessa's dress, probably a pink one. She shuddered at the thought. Too bad girls couldn't wear overalls to school like some of the boys did.

"I really like Mrs. Fairland. She's real nice." Tessa flounced a ringlet over her shoulder. "But there sure aren't many girls in your school."

"Yeah, they're mostly younger than me. That's why I hang around with Ricky and Jonesy."

Tessa turned up her nose. "I don't understand why you like those boys. They're just a couple of rabble-rousers, and their clothes are all worn out."

Jack shoved Tessa's shoulder, receiving a glare from the girl.

"Huh-uh, you take that back."

Tessa hiked her nose in the air. "I can think what I like, and I don't have to like them just because you do."

Jack clenched her fist, ready to smack that smirk off of Tessa's face, but she didn't. She'd get in trouble, and besides, hitting others wasn't a good thing, unless the other person was Butch Laird.

And where had he been, anyway? Had he decided not to attend his last year of schooling? Most of the children in Lookout went to school up to the eighth grade, but sometimes the boys were needed at home for work and didn't attend when they got older.

They moved to the side of the road as a wagon drove down the street. Surely she wasn't missing Butch. He did add some excitement to her mostly boring life. Although Billy Morgan was doing a good job of taking Butch's place. Jack grinned, remembering how Mrs. Fairland had done a jig when she'd opened her desk drawer and found the tarantula Billy had put in it.

Pounding footsteps sounded behind them, and she whirled around. Billy ran toward them. He slid to a stop and grinned, blue eyes twinkling. His blond hair hung over his forehead, much like Ricky's did when it was long. "Wanna do something fun?"

Jack studied the tall boy. She had yet to decide if she liked him or not.

"Mama said to come straight home from school."

"What kind of fun?" Jack couldn't resist asking.

Billy grabbed her arm and pulled her into the alley that ran behind the bank. "Over here."

They stopped beside a big bush that sat behind the mayor's house. "Look on that porch. You see that pie on the table?"

Jack stood on her tiptoes and peered over the bush. Sure enough, there was a pie cooling on the porch table. "So."

"I can't see, Billy," Tessa whined.

"Shut up before someone hears you." Billy glared at his sister.

She crossed her arms and scowled, her lunch bucket swaying at her side.

"You go knock on the front door," Billy said to Jack, "and I'll sneak up there and get the pie."

"That's stealing, Billy, and you know you'll get in trouble." Tessa stomped her foot, covering her new shoe in a cloud of dust.

Billy leaned into his sister's face. "Not if you don't tell, and if you do, I'll find that dumb doll of yours and break her head."

Tessa gasped and turned white. The porcelain doll was her dearest possession. Jack had never played with dolls and couldn't understand Tessa's fascination with it, but she didn't want to see the pretty doll destroyed. "Leave her alone."

Billy shoved his hands on his hips. "If you don't help me get that pie, you don't get to eat none of it."

"I get all the pie I want at home, and besides, my ma's cooking is far better than Mrs. Burkes's. I'm leavin'." Jack knew better than to steal a pie. Stealing was breaking one of the Ten Commandments, and she was already in enough of a stew pot with her lying. She peeked up at the sky, knowing she was lucky God didn't strike her down dead for all the things she'd done. She still wanted to tell Luke that she'd lied about Butch, but she was afraid of what would happen to her. Would he quit loving her if he knew she'd lied and that Butch had spent two days in jail and lost his job working for Mrs. Boyd because of something he didn't do?

She jogged across the street with Tessa on her heels, her mouth watering for the snack her ma always had waiting.

"Wait up. Mama said ladies shouldn't run." Tessa hurried across the street, walking as fast as she could without actually running.

"I ain't no lady."

"Mama says we shouldn't say *ain't*."

Jack halted and stared at the girl. "Well, she ain't my ma, so I don't have ta mind her."

Tessa's mouth worked like a fish, opening and closing. "Don't get all tetchy. I didn't mean nothing by it." She looked over her shoulder where her brother had been and then leaned in close to

Jack's ear. "Billy's always doing bad things. Mama says it's because he don't have a pa, but I don't have one, and I don't do the things Billy does. That's one of the reasons Mama wanted to move here. Folks back home are fed up with Billy's shenanigans, and the sheriff was threatening to lock him up."

Jack opened the front door of her home, not the least bit surprised by Tessa's confession. Billy had a cantankerous gleam in his eye that set her on edge. Not even Butch had that look. Butch mostly got picked on because he was so much bigger than the other kids and he always stunk like pig slop. But she'd finally realized that he had a big heart. She needed to work up her nerve to go see him and apologize. She couldn't forget how he'd said he just wanted to be her friend and how he thought she was different from the other kids. What made him think that?

She set her books on the bench of the hall tree and walked down the hall while Tessa ran up the stairs to her room. The pastor had preached about hell last Sunday and told folks they needed to repent of their sins and make *resti*—what was that big word? Make amends, that's what he said. She didn't want to apologize to Butch, knowing it would taste worse than eating a grub worm, but it was better than burning in the Lake of Fire and not going to heaven when she died. Her first pa was surely in the Lake of Fire, and that alone made her not want to be there.

Ma wasn't in the kitchen, but Max lumbered to his feet and wagged his tail. "Hey, ol' boy. How was your day?"

The dog whined a greeting and followed Jack upstairs to her bedroom, where she shucked off her dress and put on her overalls. She'd spend ten minutes in the garden so her ma wouldn't make her put her dress back on.

She helped herself to one of the three small plates of cookies her mother had set out for her and the Morgan kids, then downed some water and headed outside. Max opted to return to his position near the stove. If her ma was out visiting, she'd be returning soon to start supper, so Jack quickened her pace, wanting her ma to see her hard at work in the garden without even being told to do so. Plopping down next to the bean patch, she started pulling weeds. Thankfully, not too many had grown since she'd last cleared them.

Someone ran toward her, and she peeked through the climbing vines of beans. Billy jogged in her direction, carrying the pie plate. The scent of apples and cinnamon teased her nose as he passed close to her. He looked her way, and she ducked down.

"I see you. Too bad you didn't help with this pie. It's apple. My favorite."

He walked down the dirt row, not even taking care to avoid the plants.

"Hey! Watch out. You're crushing the spinach."

He flopped down right beside her, holding the half-eaten pie on his lap. "So, I don't like that green stuff." He faked a shiver. "But I do like pie."

Jack plucked another weed and tossed it at Billy's shoe. "You'll get sick eating that whole thing."

He shrugged. "Nah, I won't. I've done it before."

Jack's mouth watered at the fragrant scent, but she wouldn't dare ask for a bite. That was stolen food, and he'd be lucky if it didn't give him the hives.

Two hours later, Jack sat at the supper table, watching Billy shovel in his chicken and dumplings like he was starving. How could he eat so much and not get sick?

Luke finished his meal and pushed his plate back as he glanced around the table. Jack could tell he had something on his mind. The table was nearly filled with her family, the Morgans, that Miss Smith, and the two boardinghouse brides. Shannon looked fairly well for the first time in weeks, but Leah's eyes were red, as if she'd been crying. What had happened to her?

Luke cleared his throat. "The mayor's wife came to my office today and told me somebody stole a pie from her back porch. You kids know anything about that?"

Jack glanced at Billy and then Tessa. She'd gone white, but Billy kept forking food in his mouth.

"Mrs. Burke said she thought she saw a boy running away." Luke tapped the table with the end of his fork.

Billy took a drink. "I bet it was that Laird kid. I've heard he causes lots of trouble in this town."

Jack blinked and stared at the boy. How could he lie through his teeth like that and still look so innocent? She almost wanted to learn to do it herself, but lying put a bad taste in her mouth. She'd done it to protect her friends, but no more. She didn't like how she felt afterward.

"Hmm. . ." Luke stared at Billy, who suddenly smiled.

"That schoolteacher sure is pretty," the boy said.

Luke finally cracked a smile and nodded. "She is at that."

Jack stared at her plate. She ought to tell Luke that Billy was lying about Butch, but then she'd have to admit to being in the alley with him. Maybe that wasn't so bad. She'd had a chance to do something wrong and had walked away from it. Wouldn't Luke be proud that she'd done that?

On second thought, she oughta just keep quiet. What would Billy do to her if he knew she'd tattled on him?

She took a bite of buttery biscuit. Maybe Butch would be at school tomorrow. If so, she'd find a way to talk to him and tell him she was sorry.

Luke pushed away from the table. "I reckon I oughta go talk to that Laird boy. Somehow I've got to make him see that he can't steal from decent folk. I thought I'd gotten through to him last time I talked to him, but I guess I was wrong."

Her ma stood and hugged him. "Be careful, sugar. I just got me a new husband, and I aim to keep him a while."

Luke stared into her ma's eyes, and Jack knew if they'd been alone, he would have kissed her. Yuck! Why did grownups do that so often? Seemed a good way to get sick, if you asked her.

Maybe when she talked to Butch, she'd warn him about Billy.

It hadn't taken the Morgan boy long to figure out exactly whom to pin blame on for his own misdeeds. As much as it surprised her, she actually felt sorry for Butch.

Shannon stared at the ledger book, but the numbers all blurred together. The Corbetts had left three days ago and were due back tomorrow. She'd seen Mark just before they left, and the longing gaze he'd given her had made her toes tingle. But she couldn't dwell on that.

She finished recording the last of the orders and blew the ink dry. She left the ledger open while she filed away the order forms. There wasn't much left to do here, so she might as well go back to the boardinghouse—or maybe she'd go check on Dan and see how he and the children were doing.

She stared out the window at the livery. How in the world was he managing to run a business and tend to five children? How could Leah just up and leave him like she had?

The bell jingled over the door, and Rand walked in, looking tall and a bit apprehensive.

"Good afternoon." Shannon smiled. "What brings you to town midweek?"

He tipped his hat and then removed it, twisting the brim with his big hands. "I met a man here who wanted to buy a couple of horses. He lives on the other side of town, so Lookout was about halfway for both of us."

She nodded. "That makes good sense." She forced herself to stand still and not fidget. Rand was a kind man, but she couldn't help wondering what he wanted.

"You're working late."

"I had some orders I wanted to get recorded before the Corbett brothers return tomorrow."

He glanced out the front window and then back at her. "I was. . .uh. . .wondering if you would. . .uh. . .have supper with me."

"Today?" As soon as she'd spoken, she realized what a dumb question it was. Of course, he meant today.

He nodded, his ears turning red. "Yep, I thought we'd eat at Polly's."

Excitement battled with hesitation. Would she be leading him on by dining with him? But then again, she'd decided to marry the next man who asked her, and she couldn't do much better than Rand. He was well respected in the town and known for his ethical dealings as a businessman. Besides, if she were to marry him, she'd live on his ranch and only get to town a few times a month, if that much. Mark Corbett would be out of sight, and hopefully out of mind. She nodded.

Rand grinned and blew out a breath. "You took so long to answer I was certain you'd say no."

"Well, I've nearly finished all the work there is to do here, but I should let Mrs. Davis know I won't be taking supper with her."

"If you need to finish up here, I can run over and tell her." His blue-gray eyes looked eager to please.

Shannon nodded and closed the ledger.

"Be right back." Rand scurried out the door and down the boardwalk.

She tried to imagine life with him, but Mark's smiling blue eyes intruded into her mind. She grabbed the broom from the corner and swept the dust from the floor as she brushed Mark from her mind.

Rand soon returned and escorted her to Polly's Café, where they took a seat and ordered the house special, pot roast. He spun tales of his ranch that made her long to see it. "Rolling hills as far as the eyes can see, and when we get a good rain, the grass greens up and wildflowers pop up all over the place. My ma loved all those flowers and used to put vases of them around the house. I never did figure out how she had time to gather them when she had so much other work to do."

"What type of work?" Shannon ventured to ask.

"Well, she cooked for all the workers, maintained our home, and sewed many of our clothes. There was even a time when we first came here that she would make her own fabric, but once the ranch started turning a profit, Pa insisted she work less and buy her fabric in town."

Shannon toyed with the edge of her napkin. She could never cook for a crew of hungry cowboys. She barely knew how to cook at all. Maybe this wasn't such a grand idea.

"Of course, now we have a cook who fixes meals for our workers. I generally eat down there now that my folks are gone."

She wondered if he was lonely in his big house all alone. But then he saw his workers every day and probably was glad to get away from them for a time.

"I heard that Dan Howard came back from Dallas with a whole wagon filled with kids. That right?"

Shannon nodded. "Aye, five of them."

"Whew! That's quite a lot when you're not used to any of them. I bet he's sure glad he's getting married soon."

Shannon pressed her lips together. Evidently Rand had only heard part of the town's gossip, but she wasn't about to mention Leah's decision to call off the wedding. She still didn't understand how her friend could leave the man she loved in such a lurch. Leah had hardly left her room, and when she did, it was obvious she'd been crying.

They talked about menial things as they ate their food, and then Rand escorted Shannon back to the boardinghouse. "Do you like working at the freight office?"

She bristled. He had no idea what a loaded question that was.

"I mean, I just wondered. I know some women enjoy working a job, but most I know prefer tending their home."

"I work because I must support myself." Working for the Corbetts was no longer her ideal job, but it paid her room and board and gave her a wee bit extra. "I like doing the book work. I find it quite rewarding."

Rand nodded. "My ma used to help my pa with our book-keeping. She always said she was better at calculating than he." A soft smile tugged at his lips, and he seemed lost in his memories.

Someone was playing the piano in the boardinghouse parlor, and the lively jig switched to a slow tune. The soft music set Shannon in a mood for romance. Her thoughts shifted to Mark, but just as fast, she tugged them back to the man beside her. She could make a life with Rand; she felt sure of it. He was kind, thoughtful, and, she suspected, a good provider. His clothing was always nice, albeit a bit dust-coated, and his boots looked well worn but cared for. If he treated his wife as well, she could live a decent life. She sighed. Maybe not the one she'd dreamed of, but she'd finally have a home. If he asked her to marry him, she would say yes.

"You mind watching the sunset with me?"

Shannon swallowed hard and shook her head. Rand turned left on Bluebonnet Lane, and they walked to the edge of town and stood, watching the sunset. Pink and orange hues turned deep purple as the light left the sky. A near-full moon took up where the sun left off. Crickets sang in the tall grass along the side of the road, and in the distance, a coyote howled.

"I reckon we oughta get back. Thank you for walking with me, Shannon."

"My pleasure." She smiled, captured by the intensity of Rand's expression. Her heart thumped.

He looked as if he was trying to say something but couldn't quite figure out how to do it. Suddenly, he yanked off his hat and held it in front of him, as if guarding his heart. "I know we haven't known each other long, but I wondered if you would consent to marry me. I've got a nice ranch house, and you'd be comfortable there. We're close enough that you could come to town once in a while to visit with your friends, and there's all the beef you could ever want to eat."

Shannon's stomach clenched, and her heart nearly leapt from her chest. A rather unconventional marriage proposal, but 'twas what she wanted, was it not?

She had to be practical. Rand wasn't the man she loved, but she needed a home, and his was as good as any. Her head nodded, but her heart still argued. Was she making the biggest mistake of her life?

CHAPTER 28

"Y ou kids had better hurry, or you'll be late for school." Luke eyed Jack, even though she knew he was talking to the Morgans, too.

She swigged down the last of her milk and stood. "All right. I'm goin'."

Billy and Tessa followed her into the kitchen, where they all retrieved their lunch pails. They clomped down the hall toward the front door. Jack hated this part of the day, with a full morning of lessons ahead. She longed to run over to the newspaper office and see if Jenny Evans had any work she could do. Ever since Jack had helped the newspaper lady at the bride contest, Jenny occasionally let her assist her or sell papers.

"Jack, hold up a minute."

She turned to see her papa had followed them to the door.

"You kids go on; I want to talk to my daughter a moment."

Billy eyed them with curiosity but shrugged his shoulders and walked outside with his sister.

"I wanted you to know that I was finally able to get over to see that Laird boy yesterday evening. He claims he didn't steal that pie—that he wasn't even in town."

Jack's mouth went dry. Should she tell him it was Billy? What would he do to her if he found out she'd told? She had a feeling he wasn't the kind of person to go easy on someone who'd gotten him in trouble.

Luke shook his head. "I don't know as I believe Butch, but he did look sincere. If he was lying, he sure fooled me. Well, anyhow, I wanted you to know I talked with him. Don't think he'll be causing any more trouble, since they're leaving town."

"What do you mean?"

"Mr. Laird sold all his hog stock, and he and his boy were packing a wagon. Guess they figured the boy had caused enough trouble in town that they'd best move on. Wise decision, if you ask me."

Butch was leaving? The thought partly made her want to cheer, but it also made her feel bad, for some odd reason. Was it her fault they were leaving their home? How could she ever apologize to Butch if he was gone? She'd have to find a way to go over and see him before he left. If she didn't repent of her sins and apologize to him, would she go to hell when she died? She swallowed hard, her breakfast churning in her belly.

"You all right, half bit? I thought you'd be thrilled at the news."

She forced a smile. "Oh, I am. But I need to get to school. Wouldn't want to be late, would I?"

Luke eyed her as if he didn't quite believe her, and at times like this, she so wished her new papa wasn't a lawman. He was too perceptive. She scurried out the door and shut it behind her. How was she going to talk to Butch?

"Wait till you see this, *Jacqueline.*"

She hated the snide way Billy said her name, but curiosity pushed her feet in his direction. He pointed to the bank wall, and what she saw on the side of it froze her to the road. Her heart pounded like the hooves of a runaway horse.

Billy hee-hawed. "Ain't that a hoot?"

"I don't think that's very nice thing to do," Tessa said.

Jack wanted to close her eyes, but the giant, barn red letters stared back at her: JACK IS A LIAR.

Tessa gasped and pointed across the street. "Look, it's not just on the bank. It's also on our new store. Mama isn't gonna like that."

Dread gripped Jack as she turned and saw the big letters painted on the fresh, raw wood of the store's walls. JACK IS A LIAR.

She should have repented sooner. Should have told her papa what she'd done. Now the whole town would know. Nobody would believe a word she said. Ever.

Billy's laughter echoed behind her. She wanted to punch him quiet, but she'd done enough already. With dread in her heart, she stared down Main Street. Almost every other building had the hated words painted on them.

JACK IS A LIAR.

JACK IS A LIAR.

The words bounced around in her mind until she thought her head would explode. Jenny was out front of her office, already scrubbing the letters. She saw Jack, dropped her rag in a bucket, and walked toward her. Jack wanted to run. To hide. But she couldn't move.

"Jack, do you have any idea who did this?"

"I don't know." She shook her head. But she did know, and now she was telling another lie. "I might."

A sudden thought raced across her mind. She felt her eyes widen. "You're not going to print anything in the paper about this, are you?"

Jenny's eyes turned compassionate. "I'm sorry, honey, but this is news, and I'm in the news business. Who would be angry enough to do such a thing? Did you upset one of your friends?"

Jack closed her eyes. Everyone in the county would soon know that she was a liar. How could she face anybody again?

"Jacqueline, I need to see the marshal, right away." Dolly Dykstra waddled down the dirt road, her rose-colored skirts swaying from side to side. The near gray-headed woman had to be almost as wide as she was tall. "Do you know who defaced my building? Do you know how difficult it is to find paint the color of a thistle?"

Why was the lady angry at her? She was innocent, and it was her reputation that had been ruined.

Just like she'd help ruin Butch's.

"Do you know where the marshal is or not?" Miss Dykstra crossed her arms over her big bosom and tapped one finger against her shoulder.

Her papa was the last person she wanted to see right now. She had to get away. Billy's laughter rang through her mind. How many other schoolchildren had seen the paint on their way to school? It hardly mattered that many of them were too young to figure out the words, because the older kids would gladly tell them what they said.

A sob escaped, and she tore down the street, tears streaming from her eyes and making it hard to see. She had to get away from town. Away from those awful words.

She had to find Butch and beat him to a pulp.

She'd never apologize to him.

How had she even considered it?

As long as she lived, she'd hate Butch Laird.

∽

Leah sat at the table even though everyone else had gone. Shannon had hurried to her room to work on some project she'd started the day before. Dishes clinked in the kitchen where Rachel was cleaning up, and the low hum of voices from her and the marshal drifted Leah's way.

Her heart felt battered, as if a herd of cattle had stampeded it into the ground. She rested her cheek on her hand, unable to find the energy to move. What was she going to do now that she couldn't marry Dan? How was he managing with all those little children?

273

In spite of everything, she longed to see him. To be held safely within the confines of his strong arms. To kiss his warm, eager lips. But she never would again. Tears blurred her eyes, and someone pounded on the door. Luke hurried down the hall to answer it. Leah heard raised voices, and the door shut. Some emergency must have pulled the marshal away from home again.

Maybe it was time for her to return home. Would her parents accept her back? She was pretty certain her ma willingly would, but her father was another issue. She'd wounded his pride and made him look bad in Mr. Abernathy's eyes. It didn't matter that the old man wanted to buy her. No, her pa would only see that she'd made him a laughingstock by running off. The only thing that had surprised her was that he hadn't come and found her and hauled her back. Just the thought sent a shiver down her spine.

Rachel entered the dining room, holding a cup of steaming coffee in her hand. She set it on the table and sat in the chair next to Leah. "It might help to talk about things. You've been moping around ever since Dan returned with the children. I haven't even seen you working on your wedding dress."

Leah's chin wobbled. "I'm not working on it anymore."

Rachel blinked, looking confused. "Why ever not? The wedding is the day after tomorrow. We need to plan the menu for your wedding dinner."

Leah stared at the tablecloth and flicked her finger at a crumb. "There isn't going to be a wedding."

"What?"

Leah shook her head and pursed her lips, trying to keep additional tears at bay. "I called it off."

Shock engulfed Rachel's face, and her pale blue eyes opened wide. "Why? I know you two love each other. It's evident to all who see you together."

Leah shrugged one shoulder, ashamed to confess why she canceled the wedding. It sounded cruel and petty to say she didn't want to mother those poor orphans. Her heart ached for them, but she couldn't be their new ma.

"Is it the children?" Rachel patted Leah's arm. "I know that was quite a surprise. Dan should have telegraphed you and told you about them before he brought them back, so you'd have time to get used to the idea."

She shook her head. "I doubt that would have helped. After practically raising my siblings, I've decided I don't want any children, much less five that aren't even my own."

Rachel looked taken aback, but she continued on. "I realize that it's not an ideal situation, but those poor children are orphans. They need two loving adults to raise them now that their parents are gone. It's a noble thing Dan is doing, and it's that big heart of his that you fell in love with."

"I know, and I feel awful. I've hurt him something horrible, but I don't know what else to do. I can't go against what I believe. I'd just make everybody miserable."

Rachel stared at the window and tapped her index finger on the table. "Hmm. . . have you prayed about this? Asked God what He wants you to do?"

Guilt washed over Leah as if someone had dumped a bucket of cold water on her. She'd been so upset that she hadn't prayed. What kind of a Christian was she?

"In Psalm 127, the Bible tells us that 'children are an heritage of the LORD.' It also says, 'As arrows are in the hand of a mighty man, so are the children of the youth. Happy is the man that hath his quiver full of them.'"

Yeah, happy is the man, but what about the woman? Leah shifted in her seat. Was her thought blasphemous to the scriptures?

"If you don't mind," Rachel said, "I'd like to pray now. It's never too late to seek God's guidance. He's in the business of changing hearts. Just look at me and Luke. When Luke first returned to Lookout, he wanted nothing to do with me, but God changed his heart and made me a very happy woman. He can change your heart, too, Leah, if you let Him."

Well, therein lay the problem. She didn't want to change. She wanted Dan but not a houseful of children. Still, praying couldn't hurt, so she bowed her head.

Rachel grasped Leah's hand. "Heavenly Father, I know Leah didn't count on being a mother right from the start of her wedding day, but You know all things. You knew these children were going to lose their parents, sad as that is, and that they'd need new ones. Open Leah's heart. She is a kind woman with lots of love to give. Let her see that children are a blessing sent from You, and You will not give her more than she can bear."

Rachel sat silent for a few moments, then raised her head. "I know life wasn't easy for you, helping your mother with all your siblings, but things are much different when you're the mother. God puts so much love in your heart for each child, and like I prayed, He'll never send more your way than you're able to handle."

Leah considered her friend's words. She'd been so upset the past few days that she hadn't prayed. Hadn't wanted to talk to God. Couldn't He have prevented Dan's brother and wife from dying or his other sister from being pregnant just at the time the children would need her?

She winced, realizing again how selfish her thoughts were. But Rachel didn't understand. She only had one child.

"What's going through that head of yours?" Rachel smiled. "I can see the wheels turning."

"I just don't think I can do it."

"What? Marry Dan? Raise his nieces and nephews?"

"Yes, I mean, I still want to marry Dan, with all of my heart, but I don't want to be a mother, especially not so soon." She wrung the edge of the tablecloth in her hands. Would Rachel be disgusted for her lack of compassion?

"It's a big shock, I know. But we do what we must. I think if you will spend some time in prayer that God will speak to you."

Leah nodded. She believed in her heavenly Father, and He

seemed more approachable here than back in Missouri. Perhaps His help was needed more here in Texas with the harsher living conditions and the dangers surrounding them. Part of her longed to cry out to God, but the other part was afraid. What if it was God's will for her to marry Dan and mother the children? How could she bear it?

Footsteps sounded on the porch, and the door burst open. "Rachel!"

The boardinghouse owner bolted to her feet at her husband's frantic voice. "In here, Luke."

He hurried through the doorway and grabbed her hand. "C'mon. Something's happened."

Leah jumped up and followed them, curious as to what had gotten the mild-mannered marshal so agitated. Rachel stopped as she walked down the porch steps, and her hand covered her mouth as she stared across the street. "Who would do such an awful thing?"

"I have my suspicions," Luke said. "But the important thing is that Jack saw it and got upset and ran off somewhere. We've got to find her."

Leah glanced across the street and saw the harsh red letters: JACK IS A LIAR.

Jack was an ornery child and definitely a tomboy, but she wasn't mean and didn't deserve this shame heaped on her. Leah's heart ached for the girl. "I can help search."

⌒

Jack ran all the way to Butch's land. Her lungs screamed for her to stop, and a pain grabbed her side. Finally, she smelled the hog pens, and she slowed her steps. Gasping for breath, she pressed her hand to her aching side and studied the old place. The house was set at an odd angle and looked smaller than the parlor in her own home.

She lifted her hand to her nose. Where were all the hogs? They might be gone, but the stench sure wasn't. The only sounds she heard were the thudding of her heartbeat, her ragged breathing, and birds chirping in a nearby tree.

The place was empty. Butch was gone, and she was too late. Too late to apologize for lying. Too late to knock Butch to the ground for doing such an awful thing to her.

Slowly, she walked toward the house. What would it have been like to live in such a dirty place and to smell the stomach-churning odor every day? To get up first thing in the morning and face the reeking stench?

Dropping onto the chopping block, she hung her head in her hands and stared at a beetle crawling on a stem of grass. Butch was gone, and that was that.

But how could she face the people in town? They'd all wonder what she'd lied about and if she was lying whenever she talked to them. Nobody would trust her, ever again.

She picked up a rock and flung it at the house.

Butch had ruined her life.

And she hated him for it.

Maybe the best thing for her to do was leave town, too. Just run away. But she'd miss her ma—and her new papa. The worst thing of all would be staying and seeing the disappointment in their eyes.

Her vision blurred as tears formed.

"What do I do now?"

Quick hoofbeats approached, and the horse slid to a halt. Someone dismounted and walked toward her, but she was too embarrassed to lift her head.

Luke.

She recognized his boots.

Would he hate her now?

"Half bit, what are you doing here?"

She shrugged. How could she explain her reason for coming here when she didn't understand it herself?

Luke squatted on his boot heels in front of her. "I'm sorry

about those words in town. I'll make sure they're all gone today."

Love for him flooded her. She sucked in a loud sob and leaped into his arms. He grabbed her with one arm and struggled not to fall backward. Then he stood, taking her with him. She cried on his strong shoulders, and he just held her, patting her back. "Shh. . .everything will be all right. You'll see."

She shoved back and wiggled her legs, so he let her down. "It won't never be right again."

He reached out and ran his hand down the side of her head. "It seems that way now, but you'll see."

She crossed her arms and paced toward the hog pen, then reconsidered and walked over to Luke's horse and patted his neck. "Everybody will think I'm a liar."

"Once those letters are painted over, folks will quickly forget about them."

She shook her head. "No, they won't. Jenny's gonna print them in her newspaper, and the whole world will know."

"I'll talk to Jenny and see if she'll mention what happened but keep you out of her article as much as possible. Most folks won't even know which 'Jack' the words are referring to, and besides, what happened isn't your fault."

Luke strode over and stood behind her, his hands resting on her shoulders. "Don't make too much of this, half bit. Butch was just lashing out, trying to hurt you. He wasn't even man enough to stay and face the consequences of his behavior."

Jack's insides swirled, and she knew she had to come clean or forever be in misery. "What he said was. . .true."

Luke gently turned her to face him. "What do you mean?"

She couldn't stand seeing disgust in Luke's eyes when she finally confessed the truth, so she stared at his boots. "I lied about Butch. Several times."

Luke lifted her chin with his forefinger. A muscle in his jaw flexed. "About what?"

She pulled away and stalked down the road several feet. "About when he pushed me down at the river. And I didn't correct you when you thought he'd stolen that pie from Mrs. Burke, even though I knew Billy had done it."

Luke uttered a heavy sigh, but he didn't say anything for a while. Finally, she couldn't stand waiting for his wrath and turned around. He stood with his head hanging, hands on his hips. "I'm disappointed, half bit."

Her lips wobbled and tears filled her eyes. Would he not want to be her papa now?

"When you lied and I believed you, I had a talk with Butch. I accused him of things he didn't do, and that made me look bad and made him angry and not trust me. Do you understand?"

She hadn't thought about how her lying would affect Luke. She'd made things difficult for him. He always believed her and acted accordingly. She was pond scum.

"It's important for people to trust me as marshal. I wrongly accused that boy and even made him stay in jail for several days. Maybe there was more to him than I gave him credit for."

"I'm sorry, Luke."

"Me, too." He looped Alamo's reins over his head. "C'mon, your ma is worried. I need to get you back to town."

He climbed on, then held his hand out to her. She looked up, despising the sad look she'd put on his face. "Do you hate me?"

His expression immediately changed. He pulled her up behind him. "Of course not. I'll always love you, no matter what. But I am disappointed you didn't trust me enough to tell me the truth."

She wrapped her arms around his waist and leaned against his back as he guided his horse back to town. "I didn't know you so well back then."

Luke patted her hands. "I guess that's true, but you know me now and didn't tell me the truth about the pie."

She winced. "I was afraid Billy would do something mean if I snitched on him."

"I see. When we return home, we'll have a talk with your

mother, and if she agrees, I'll expect you to help me repaint the buildings that were defaced."

She nodded against his back. If she helped him, the dreaded words would be gone all the sooner—and she'd miss a day of school.

At least she knew Luke still loved her. And she wouldn't lie anymore. It hurt too many people.

But she still hated Butch for painting those words.

CHAPTER 29

Mark tossed the ropes into the back of the empty wagon. He walked around, checking the horses' harnesses, even though he knew Garrett had already done that. He glanced over at the new store. It looked fresh and bright with its new coat of paint. It would soon open. That would enable him to be in town more since they wouldn't be going to Dallas so often for supplies. Then maybe he could get back to reading his law books.

The door to the boardinghouse opened, and Shannon walked out and closed it behind her. She glanced down the street, then strode toward him with purpose evident in her steps. He longed to pull her into his arms and show her the depths of his heart, but she deserved so much better than him. If only he'd never gone to Abilene.

But he couldn't change what had happened there, and he'd never ask Shannon to marry a murderer.

Yeah, it was a fair fight. The other man drew first—even fired first, but he'd missed. Mark had pulled his gun in self-defense, fearing for his and Annabelle's lives, and he'd accidentally killed that man. It didn't matter that the marshal had said it wasn't a crime. He'd taken a life. Shame twisted his insides and made him refuse to grasp hold of what he wanted most in life—to marry Shannon.

She glanced at the office, then back at him, and stopped near the door. He walked up the boardwalk steps and stared at her. Did she still have affections for him?

He thought so by the look in her eyes. Her lips pursed, and she looked away.

"Is Garrett here?"

Mark winced. What did she want with his brother that she couldn't tell him? "He's over at Polly's, gettin' a lunch packed for us. We're heading out to Dallas as soon as he returns."

Shannon nodded but nibbled on her lower lip. "I suppose I can tell you. Could we go inside?"

He opened the door and held it as she glided inside, her skirts touching his pants and her flowery scent wrapping around him. He missed her. Missed working with her. Missed staring across the room at her while she was putting numbers into the ledger. He sighed hard. "What do you need? I left all the new orders on the desk under the paperweight. I imagine this will be the last big pile you'll have to work through since the store is reopening soon and our workload is likely to go down."

She nodded and paced the room, looking everywhere but at him. She glanced over her shoulder but kept her back to him. " 'Tis a good thing, then."

"What is?"

"That the workload is lessening."

"And why is that? It's been great business for us."

"Because I need to inform you that next week will be my last one."

His heart took another stab. Shannon was quitting? He'd never see her if that happened. "But why? I thought you liked working here."

"I do, but my circumstances are changing."

Had she decided to leave town? Found another job? "Changing? How?"

She was quiet so long that he thought she hadn't heard him—or maybe she wasn't going to answer. "I'm getting married a week from Sunday."

Mark grasped Garrett's desk to keep from falling to his knees at her declaration. How? Who? "You can't be getting married."

She whirled around, her eyes no longer compassionate but filled with fire. "Who are you to tell me I can't marry?"

"I. . .but. . ." She was right. He had no claim on her even though his heart belonged only to her. *Why, God? Why couldn't I have stayed in Lookout and kept myself pure for this woman? Why did You place her in this town when You knew I couldn't have her?*

His chest hurt so bad he wondered if he was having heart failure. She stepped forward, a concerned look replacing the anger. "Are you all right?"

He straightened and forced a smile. "Of course. I just can't believe you found someone to marry so fast."

Her nostrils flared and eyes sparked. "Just because you find me lacking doesn't mean other men do." She yanked open the desk drawer and pulled out a sheet of paper. It was the one with tic marks on it. He'd wondered what it meant. She marched over, holding the paper in front of his face. "You see this? Each mark represents a marriage proposal—ones I got in this office, no less. There are plenty of men who want to marry me, even though you don't."

"I never said I didn't want to marry you." The words fled his mouth before he could yank them back.

"What?" She blinked and stared at him, the paper zigzagging as it floated to the floor.

It was his turn to break from her gaze. He hadn't wanted her to know the depth of his feelings. It wasn't fair to her. "Nothing. That was a slip of the tongue."

"I see. Well, you now know that I'll be quitting. It's possible that

Leah may want this job, though I've not talked to her about it."

Mark frowned. Hiring Leah Bennett was the last thing he wanted to do after the way she'd dumped his good friend. "We'll manage. The doc says he'll take my cast off on Tuesday, so I can do the bookwork from now on." He rubbed the back of his neck. "Just who are you marrying, if I may ask?"

Her mouth worked, pulling his gaze to her beautiful lips. She did the most intriguing things with them. She frowned as if she didn't want to tell him. He swiped his hand through the air. "Fine. Don't tell me, but word will be around town soon enough. I'm just surprised I hadn't heard about it already."

"I haven't told anyone yet. A marriage is a private affair between a man and a woman."

Mark snorted a laugh. "Maybe in Ireland, but not in America. Here, a wedding is generally a celebration of family and friends. I just don't see how you found someone so fast to marry. Are you sure you're not jumping into this too quickly? Maybe you shouldn't be in such a hurry."

Shannon gasped. "Ach, who are you to be tellin' me what to do? Do you or do you not wish to be a lawyer?"

Mark shifted his feet and crossed his arms. "What's that got to do with anything?"

"You stand there judging me. You, who didn't want me, now thinks you can give me advice on when to marry? You don't even have the nerve to face your own brother. To tell him that you want to be a lawyer and not in this business with him. I have changed my mind. I quit as of this moment."

Her quick steps clicked on the floor as she made a beeline for the door. She was right, of course. "Wait! Please."

She paused with her hand on the door. "What is it?"

He ran his hand through his hair, but what he needed to say couldn't be said to her back. "Shannon, would you look at me? Please?"

She sighed and turned, arms crossed over her chest.

"I. . .did something. Several years ago. I'd give anything to undo it, but I can't."

"What sort of thing?"

He shook his head. "I can't tell you. I've never told a soul, not even Garrett, but suffice it to say, that's what's standing in the way of our relationship. If I could marry you, I'd do it in a heartbeat."

Surprise engulfed her face, but her expression quickly changed. "How could you say such a thing to a woman you know is getting married? You had your chance at winning my heart, but I remember clearly you saying you'd never marry. And now because I am, you think you can waltz in and say you would marry me if you could? I don't see a thing to stop you."

"You don't understand."

"You're right. I don't. I'm sorry, Mark. I think we could have had a wonderful life together if you would quit living in the past. God forgives us for our wrongdoings. Maybe we can never marry, but you need to find His forgiveness for whatever happened in the past and move on. Don't let it keep you from living a happy life and becoming a lawyer. You'd make a fine one, you would."

She yanked the door open, strode out, and slammed it shut. He sat there numb—even more so than that night in Denison. He felt gutted. Empty. The only woman he'd ever truly loved was marrying someone else. She would, in fact, be married before he returned to Lookout. How could he ever be whole without her in his life?

"Well, well, well. She sure gave you a piece of her mind, didn't she?"

Mark jumped and turned to find Annabelle standing in the back room. "What are you doing here? And just how much did you hear?"

"All of it." She grinned. "I looked for you out back, and when I didn't find you, I came in the rear door and was going to walk through the office, but then I heard you two come in and hid."

"A decent woman would have left out the back door or else let us know you were present."

A saucy smile pulled at her lips. "And just what do you think dear, sweet Shannon would have said if she found me in here?"

Mark swatted the air. "Does it really matter? She's getting married."

"I know. I heard." She sashayed toward him. Her clothes might be different, but they didn't disguise her flirtatious, saloon-girl ways. "You actually love her, don't you?"

He shrugged. "So what if I do? She's marrying some other yahoo. She must not have cared for me much if she could agree to marry someone else so soon."

Annabelle shook her head and leaned back against his desk. "You men can be awfully dense at times."

"What does that mean?"

"Just what do you expect Shannon to do? Do you have any idea how hard it must be for her to come here several days a week and work for you when she's in love with you, but you've all but told her you don't want her?"

"That's not what I said."

"But it's what she heard. She's all alone in this world, from what I understand. You can't expect her to keep working here with things as they are. And where does that leave her? With no job, she has no other alternative except to marry—or work in a saloon." Her teasing smile turned his stomach.

Mark strode across the room and leaned into Annabelle's face. "Don't you talk about her in such a manner. Shannon would starve to death before working in a saloon."

"Ah, so you do love her." She sighed heavily. "Guess that leaves me out on the streets again."

"What do you mean?"

"Why do you think I came here, Mark? I was hoping we could pick up where we were before you shot that cowboy."

Mark's stomach turned at the verbal mention of his misdeed. Had she told anyone about that? If so, he'd probably want to run away like Jack had after that bully painted those words on half the buildings in town. What if Annabelle had done that?

Mark is a killer.

He shuddered at the thought.

"Are you just going to let her marry Rand Kessler?"

"Kessler?" The fact that Shannon was marrying an honorable, well-to-do rancher didn't soothe him at all.

She smirked. "Shannon didn't tell you? I hear he's a fine catch."

"I thought you heard everything she said."

She shrugged. "I might have missed a few words."

"What is it you want, Annabelle? I need to get on the road."

"I came here to woo you myself, but I can see that your heart belongs to another. So, you gonna let her get away, or are you gonna be the man I know you are, put your past behind you, once and for all, and marry the gal you love?"

"You make it sound so simple."

"It is." She laid her hand on his arm. "What you did back in Abilene was an honorable thing."

Mark harrumphed. "Since when is killing a man honorable?"

"You were protecting me from being mauled by that cowboy. All you did was tell him to stop. He's the one who got mad and pulled the gun. You were just defending me and yourself. Why is that so hard to understand?"

"When you've been raised in church, you're taught that killing someone is a sin."

"So, isn't your God supposed to be the forgiving type?"

Mark nodded. How odd to have an ex-saloon girl preaching to him.

"Well, if He forgives you, then it's time you forgave yourself."

He pondered her words for a while, and then suddenly, Annabelle stood up and shook her skirts.

"Well, I suppose I should get back to the boardinghouse and pack."

"Pack?" Mark pulled himself from his stupor. "You're going somewhere?"

"This town's way too small for me. I think I'll head up to Dallas."

He could see past her fake bravado. She'd hoped he'd fall for her and marry her. Make a decent woman out of her. "It was good seeing you again."

She narrowed her gaze. "You mean that?"

He nodded his head. "I hope you can find a job—not in a saloon—and do something good with your life."

She laid her hand against his cheek. "You, too, Mark Corbett. Don't you think it's high time you started your lawyering business?"

Mark barked a laugh. "You're the second person today to say that." He reached into his pocket and handed her a wad of dollars.

"Don't." She pushed his hand away. "I have enough money to start over, courtesy of Everett." Her eyes twinkled with mischievousness. "Have a good life, and if you ever happen to think of me, say a prayer to that God of yours."

"He's your God, too."

"What would He want with the likes of me?"

"You'd be surprised. Promise me that you'll attend church wherever you settle and give God a chance."

"We'll see." She flashed him another saucy smile. "Farewell."

The bell on the door jingled, and just that fast, a second woman walked out of his life.

~

Leah wrapped the last loaf of bread in a clean towel that Rachel had loaned her and put it into the basket, also borrowed.

"This is a kind thing you're doing." Rachel smiled at her from the other side of the worktable.

"I feel like I ought to be doing more, but I don't want to give

Dan false hopes. I've spent a lot of time in prayer the past few days and feel that God wants me to help them by providing bread and some cookies or maybe a pie, now and then."

"I'd be happy to send some things along from time to time. I can't imagine how Dan is cooking for five small children."

Leah winced again at being reminded of Dan's hardship, but she was doing as much as she could. "I'll just run these over, and then I want to get back and help Shannon finish up her dress."

Rachel leaned against the door frame. "I still can't believe she's getting married to Rand. I thought for sure that she was in love with Mark."

"I think she is, but since he made it clear he doesn't want her, she's moved on. I think she's doing the wise thing. I can't imagine her married to a Corbett."

Rachel pressed her lips together. "They aren't as bad as they may seem. They may be teasers, but both are actually honorable men."

Leah snorted a laugh. "Tell that to someone who didn't have her whole life changed by them."

"It hasn't all been bad, has it?"

She stared up at the decorative ceiling and realized Rachel spoke the truth. "No, it hasn't. I've made a number of friends here and fallen in love with a wonderful man."

Rachel pushed away from the door and crossed the room. "Won't you reconsider? Dan needs you now more than ever before. I truly believe you'd be happy with him and the children."

Shaking her head, Leah grabbed the basket off the table and placed the handle on her arm. "I can't. I promised myself I'd never get in that situation again."

"Well, you'll bless them with your kindness and this food. I'll see you later."

Leah nodded and hurried down the hall before Rachel decided to give her another talk about marrying Dan. If only she could do that. Her heart ached. She missed him dearly. Maybe she'd catch a glimpse of him working at the livery when she delivered the food.

Her feet quickly ate up the short distance to Dan's home, and she noticed the differences immediately. Clothing of all sizes was laid out on the porch railings to dry in the September sun. A wagon, ball, and discarded doll littered the yard. She almost dreaded seeing the inside, but she climbed the steps and knocked on the door.

The middle girl—Ruthie, wasn't it?—opened the door. She stared up at Leah with big brown eyes. "I know you."

Leah smiled. "I met you the day you arrived. I'm Leah, and I've brought you some snacks and bread."

"What kind of snacks?"

"Oh, sugar cookies and some apple bread."

The girl straightened and licked her lips. "Can I have some now?"

"Well, maybe we should ask Callie first. Or your uncle. Is he here?"

Ruthie shook her head, her untidy braids flying back and forth. Dirt smudged one side of her face and around her mouth, and her hands were filthy. "Uncle Dan isn't here. Him and Ben's working."

Little Davy toddled to the door and stared up at her. Tears still dampened his lashes and clung to his eyes. He reached up his hands to her. "Hold'ju."

Leah felt a crack form in the wall she'd erected around herself. She cleared her throat. "How about a cookie. Would you like that?"

"Tookie!" The boy clapped his hands and disappeared into the house. Leah longed to shove the basket into Ruthie's hands and flee back to the safety of the boardinghouse, but the load was too heavy for the child, and she needed to return Rachel's towels and basket. She swallowed hard. "May I come inside for a moment?"

"Shut that door, Ruthie. You're lettin' in flies." Leah couldn't see Callie but recognized her voice. "And don't you dare let Davy out again, you hear?"

Leah cringed. Callie was just a small version of what she'd been like. She'd had to take care of her siblings as far back as she could remember. Her heart ached for the little girl who'd have to grow up far too soon and would probably never get to be a playful, young girl again. Why, if she had to care for her siblings all the time, she wouldn't even be able to attend school.

Footsteps pounded on the floor, and Callie appeared in the doorway. "What are you doing here?"

Leah winced inwardly at the animosity in the girl's voice. "I brought some fresh bread for you and some cookies."

She longingly eyed the basket, but her glare quickly refocused on Leah. "We don't need your handouts. I can make bread."

"So you already have all you need?"

"Nuh-uh. We don't got no bread. You told a lie. I'm gonna tell Ma." Ruthie's scolding expression suddenly changed, and she frowned, her lips quivering. "I'm. . .uh. . .gonna tell Uncle Dan."

Callie glared at her sister. "I didn't say we had any, just that I could make it."

Leah wasn't taken in by her false bravado. "Well, since I have all this bread, I'd hate to see it go to waste." She strode in and her heart nearly broke. Clara Howard's tidy home was a complete mess. Crates of clothes, toys, and other items were stacked along the empty spaces of the parlor. Two small chests of drawers lined the wall of the crowded dining room. Everything from sticks and rocks the boys must have dragged in to clothing and diapers covered the furniture and made walking difficult. Davy picked up a stick and whacked the door frame. Leah smiled, hoping to distract him. "Come, time for a cookie."

When he toddled past her, she took the stick from him and laid it out of his reach on top of one of the dressers and carefully made her way to the kitchen, where dirty dishes covered the table and countertops. She stacked several soiled plates to make room for the basket.

A woman was definitely needed here. The workload was far too much for an eight-year-old. Leah tried to ignore the guilt assaulting her. Was she being completely unreasonable? Dan needed her, and so did these children.

But how could she jump right back into the situation she'd so recently fled?

Ruthie climbed up on a chair, and Davy attempted to do the same. Leah picked him up and sat him in the chair next to his sister. "Before you eat, we need to clean those hands. Callie, could I please borrow a washcloth?"

"Suit yourself, but I'm not washing any dishes they dirty."

"Why not?" Leah asked as she searched for a clean cloth.

Callie shrugged. "I got too much to do watching these young'uns to do dishes. Uncle Dan does them at night."

Leah's heart took another blow. Poor Dan. Working all day, tending these orphans, and then most likely having to fix dinner and wash dishes afterward. At least she could help with this one chore. After washing off the children's hands, she rolled up her sleeves and filled the bucket. The children were done with their snack and playing in the parlor when she finished. She tidied up the kitchen, putting containers back on shelves, and then she swept the floor. Her heart felt good knowing Dan wouldn't come home to such a mess.

She rummaged around for something to cook, but when she didn't find any meat, she decided to make a pot of potato soup. It would taste good with the bread she'd baked. She checked on the children and found Davy asleep on the floor. Poor little thing. Callie sat on the settee looking at a picture book with Ruthie, whose eyes were nearly closed. Leah picked up Davy, receiving a scowl from Callie, then took the boy into Dan's room and laid him in the middle of the bed. She brushed his hair from his forehead and smiled. He was a comely child.

Not having heard a peep from the baby the whole time she

was there, she tiptoed into the bedroom that had been Clara's. Her heart jumped. Not a thing had been done in here. Clara's clothes still hung from the pegs, and her brush and comb rested on a small vanity. Her shoes stuck out from under the bed, where Maggie slept with her thumb hanging just out of her mouth. Her lashes were spiked as if she'd been crying, and the girl's tongue moved as if she were nursing. For the first time, Leah realized that the baby probably still had been nursing when her mother died. "Oh, you poor thing."

What was Dan going through trying to comfort five young children who missed their parents and had their whole world yanked out from under them? She hung her head. How selfish she'd been. Tears coursed down her cheeks, and she broke into sobs. "Forgive me, Lord," she whispered. "I've been so selfish."

She stared up at the ceiling, fortifying herself for the tasks at hand. God would give her the strength to do His will; she understood that now.

Quietly, she gathered up Clara's dresses and shoes and carried them into the parlor, where she placed them in an empty crate.

"What are you doing?" Callie stared, her mouth twisted to one side and her brown eyes sparking. Ruthie had slumped over and was asleep. "We don't need your help."

Leah realized she needed to mend some bridges, so she sat beside the girl. "I need to apologize to you. I…uh…wasn't prepared for Dan to bring you kids home with him. It was a surprise. A very big surprise."

"It was a surprise to us, too. I wanted to live with my aunt." Callie crossed her arms and stared across the room.

"I'm so sorry, Callie." Leah cupped the girl's cheek. "I can't imagine how hard it must be to lose your parents."

The child teared up, and she swiped her hand across her eyes. "I miss them."

Leah pulled Callie into her arms, surprised she didn't try to get away. Instead, she curled against Leah and sobbed. Tears pooled in Leah's eyes as she realized how much this tough little girl needed her, and she cried with her for the pain she'd caused the children. And for Dan. She'd let her own pain get in the way of helping others who desperately needed her.

Leah sat for a long while, praying and caressing Callie. Finally, the child quieted and pulled away. Her face was splotchy, her nose ran, and she looked a tad embarrassed.

"Sorry."

Shaking her head, Leah ran her hand down the side of Callie's face. "Don't be, sweetie. I'm the one who needs to apologize."

"You just did." Callie offered the tiniest of smiles.

"I guess I did, but now comes the hard part. I need to go have a talk with Dan."

"Are you going to marry him?"

She nodded. "If he'll have me."

Callie grinned wide. "He will. I think he misses you."

"Well"—Leah stood—"we shall see."

A few minutes later, she paused outside the rear door of the livery, shaking like a wood shack in the midst of a tornado. But her storm had passed, and she truly believed good things lay ahead—if only Dan would forgive her.

Dust motes floated through shafts of sunlight, almost looking like snow. She couldn't see Dan but heard a clanging coming from the front of the building. A tall, brown horse in a stall nickered at her as she passed by. Leah's heart pounded as if she'd just run a long race. In a way she had, but it had been a mental marathon—a test of the mind and heart. She couldn't help grinning as her love for Dan overflowed.

But then she stopped as doubts attacked. What if he couldn't forgive her shamelessness? What if his feelings had changed?

For a second, she wavered. Almost tucked tail and ran.

But then she heard the deep rumble of Dan's voice—and it pulled her toward him. She stepped out of the shadows in the back of the livery and walked to the front, where the open doors allowed the sun to shine in and illuminate the area. Dan pounded on a loose board and said something to Ben, who stood beside him. The boy noticed her first and stared with wide eyes. Dan straightened and slowly turned. His lips parted when her saw her, and his eyes sparked before he schooled his expression.

She could hardly blame him after the way she'd left him in a lurch. Her hands wouldn't be still, so she tucked them behind her. "I brought some cookies over to the house. Do you suppose Ben could take a break and go have a snack?"

"Can I, Uncle Dan?"

He nodded, and the boy shot for home like his feet were on fire. Dan laid his hammer down and closed the distance between them. His beard was growing in, giving him a more rugged look than normal. Had he not had the time to even shave the past few days?

He shifted his feet and seemed to have as hard a time being still as she. "What do you need, Leah?"

She closed her eyes, loving the timbre of his voice. So manly. So strong. Just like him. "I'm sorry, Dan."

When she gazed back up, she saw the confusion in his eyes, and maybe even a spark of hope.

"Sorry about what?" He wasn't going to make this easy.

"You know. For being pigheaded and selfish as a goat."

His lips twitched, and he cocked his head.

"What?"

"You're the prettiest goat I've even seen."

Tears filled her eyes. "I'm really sorry. I let my fears keep me from the man I love and from helping those poor children." She ducked her head. "I was so selfish."

His forefinger lifted her chin, and he thumbed the tears away. "I'm sorry, too. For not giving you more warning. I should have telegraphed you and prepared you." He broke from her gaze and sighed. "I figured you wouldn't want me with all those kids as part of the deal."

"Oh, Dan. I do. I want you with all of my heart. The children, too."

His dark eyes came alive with passion, and he tugged her to him. "Are you sure? It won't be easy for you."

She placed her hand on his chest, feeling the fervent pounding of his heart. "I'm positive. I want to be your wife and the mother—or aunt—to the children. I'm already falling in love with them."

"And what about me?"

She thought to tease him, but he'd been through enough already, and she chose to be merciful. "I have loved you for a while now."

"Is that so?" He grinned wide, setting her heart soaring.

"Yes, it is, Mr. Howard."

"Then I reckon we need to get married. Could you be ready by a week from this Sunday?"

She toyed with a loose button on his shirt. "No."

His eyes dimmed a bit. "How long, then? I want to be with you, Leah."

"I was hoping for tomorrow, after Rand and Shannon's wedding Sunday afternoon."

He let out a whoop that made one of the horses whinny and grabbed her up, spinning her in a circle. His lips collided with hers, melding their breath and sending her senses in a tizzy. Her arms wrapped around his neck, and she felt loved.

Safe.

Home.

This was where she belonged. Right here in Dan's arms.

CHAPTER 30

Mark leaned forward on the wagon seat, his head in his hands. The harnesses jingled, and the wagon creaked and groaned and rocked on the rutted road. Though this one had only been a day trip, it seemed to have taken forever. He wanted to be home, yet he dreaded returning to Lookout. He wished he didn't have to return until after Shannon was married. He would definitely skip church tomorrow because he couldn't stand watching the wedding ceremony scheduled for right after the service. It would gut him to the core.

Why was he so miserable? He was the one who'd told Shannon he couldn't marry her. Was he making the wrong decision?

Garrett shoved his arm. "All right, out with it. You've been miserable this whole trip, so what is it that's got you more frazzled than a steer tangled in barbed wire?"

Where did he begin? Everything in his life was jumbled up. "There's too much to talk about it."

Garrett guided the horses around a sharp curve that signaled only a few miles left before they'd be home. "Just pick a spot and start there."

Mark breathed in a strengthening breath through his nose and sat up. "I've decided to become a lawyer, so I'll be quitting the freight business."

His brother's blond brows lifted. "I wondered if you'd ever get around to doing that."

"You mean you're not surprised? Not upset with me?"

"You've been reading those law books for years. What's the point of that if you don't plan on becoming a lawyer one day—and then you apprenticed with that lawyer in Abilene, but things didn't seem to go well there, so I've never brought it up."

Mark winced, but he realized the time had come to tell his brother the truth. "Things didn't go well there, but that had nothing to do with working for Mr. Conrad."

"No?" Garrett stared at him, curiosity etched on his face.

He shook his head. "Nope. It centered around a pretty saloon gal."

"I don't believe that for an instant. I've never seen you go into the saloon."

"What can I say?" He shrugged. "I got curious, and it was the biggest mistake of my life."

Garrett slung his arm around Mark's shoulders. Mark fought back the tears that stung his eyes. He loved his brother and knew Garrett loved him, but they rarely showed their affection other than teasing one another. He cleared his throat, dreading to see his brother's face. "I killed a man."

Garrett stiffened for a moment but quickly relaxed. "I'm sure you had a good reason for doing such a thing."

"I didn't mean to kill that cowboy. He was roughhousing the woman I thought I was in love with. I told him to stop, and he just shoved Annabelle away and pulled his gun." Mark lifted his hat and ran a shaky hand through his hair. "I just reacted. I pulled my gun and fired back. I didn't even think I'd hit him, much less killed him. It was just a gut reaction."

"Why were you wearing a gun? You don't normally."

"I don't know. Pretty much everyone in Abilene wore one, so I guess I had to. Just to fit in."

"Did Mr. Conrad?"

He nodded. "Actually, he did. He had a shoulder holster and wore it under his suit coat. You couldn't see it, but he had his weapon in case he needed it."

"It must have been a fair fight since you weren't thrown in jail and didn't stand trial." Garrett stared at him. "You didn't, did you?"

Mark shook his head. "Plenty of folks in the saloon spoke up for me, and that cowboy had a reputation for causing trouble. The marshal actually told me he was glad not to have to deal with the man anymore. But that didn't make me feel any better. I took a life." He hung his head in his hands and stared at the dirty wagon floorboards.

"Have you asked God to forgive you for killing that man? Knowing how tenderhearted you are, that must have been eating away at you all these years."

"Yeah, I've asked the good Lord to forgive me a thousand times, but the ache never goes away. I took a man's life, and there's no way to make restitution for that."

"No, but God has forgiven you. It sounds like you haven't accepted that."

Mark stared out at the rolling hills. In the distance, three deer munched on the tender grass just outside of a clump of oaks. All he had to do was raise his rifle, and they'd have venison for dinner. But he'd had enough killing to last him forever.

"I think the problem is that you need to forgive yourself. Whoa. . ." Garrett pulled the wagon to a stop. The horses snorted and shook their heads as if they knew home was close by and they wanted to keep going. His brother turned in the seat to face him. "It was an accident, Mark. You've got to let go of this and believe that God has forgiven you. If He has, don't you think it displeases Him for you to keep hanging on to your misery? Let it go."

Mark leaned his elbows on his knees. "How?"

"Just do it. Repent, once and for all, and believe God loves you and forgives you. You're God's child. If you were a father, and say your child accidentally killed a squirrel or even a dog, would you hate that little one?"

"No, of course not."

"Well, you're God's child, and He doesn't hate you, either. He wants you to get past this. Turn loose of it, brother."

Mark nodded. It was time. No amount of feeling sorry could change a thing. He bowed his head. "Father God, I'm so sorry for killing that man. You alone know how much, but please forgive me. And help me to forgive myself and put this behind me. Help me to move forward from this day on."

"Amen, Lord. Show Mark how much You love him—how much I do, too." Garrett cleared his throat and swiped at his eyes.

Mark sat up and blew out a breath that puffed up his cheeks. "I do feel better."

Garrett slapped him on the shoulder and grinned. "That's great. Now let's talk about the other thing that's bothering you."

"You mean about me quitting the business and leaving you in the lurch?"

"No, I've been expecting you to change careers for a long time. I'll manage just fine—not that I won't miss working with you. I mean Shannon."

"What about her?" He'd just confessed the worst thing he'd ever done to his brother, but he wasn't sure he wanted to talk about the woman he loved.

He blinked, as reality set in.

He did love her.

"Are you just going to let her marry that Kessler guy without a fight?"

Mark looked off to the right, avoiding his brother's stare. "It's too late to do anything about that."

"It's not too late until she's married the guy. I've seen how you look at her. Don't tell me you don't love her."

Mark shook his head. "It took me a while to figure that out, but I couldn't ask her to marry me after what I did."

Garrett looked at him with a blank expression. "What did you do?"

He gazed at his brother as if he'd gone crazy. "I just told you. I killed a man."

"Really? You killed a man?"

Mark crossed his arms and leaned back against the seat. "Not funny."

"I'm serious. God not only forgives our sins, but He forgets about them—at least that's what the reverend says. God makes us pure, white as snow, after we confess and ask His forgiveness. It's as if we'd never committed the sin."

"If I didn't know better, I'd think you were studying to be a minister."

"Ha, ha, now who's joking? I'm serious. Guess I've just been paying more attention in church. I see no reason at all that you can't marry Shannon if you love her, other than your own stubborn pride."

Hope swirled through Mark like a flash flood. Was it actually possible?

He did love her with all his heart. But would it be fair to steal her back from Rand, even if she agreed, at this late moment?

"Would it be better for her to marry a man she doesn't love, when the one she does wants her so badly?"

He stared up at the blue sky. Had that thought come from God or from his own desires?

"I made her for you."

Mark sat up straight. God had made Shannon for him? Was it really possible?

His chest warmed. Suddenly, he grabbed the reins and slapped them down hard on the horses' backs. "Heyah!"

"Hey, what's going on?" Garrett stared at him wide-eyed and

grabbed hold of the bench as the wagon lurched forward.

"I've got to get to town and stop a wedding."

Shannon walked around the kitchen in Rand's home. The big room boasted a large stove, plenty of work area and cabinets for storage, and even a huge pantry. Tall windows allowed in plenty of light and a cooling breeze during hot weather. A table that seated six was shoved against the far wall. " 'Tis far grander than I expected."

"There's a door to the cellar under this rug." Rand kicked the braided mat out of the way and lifted a door.

"Why, I've never seen the likes of it. How grand 'tis to have the entry inside the house. 'Twill be very handy, especially in cold weather."

"Yeah, my ma liked that a lot, too." Rand looked proudly around the room as if seeing his mum working there. "I'd like you to make a list of whatever you need. Food, sewing stuff, cloth, anything, and I'll have Mrs. Morgan order it for us."

"That's very kind of you, Rand."

He shook his head. "No, it isn't. I want you to be happy here."

Did he think buying her things would make her happy? In fact, coming to his ranch did the opposite and made her question if she was making the right decision. The Kessler ranch was much farther from town than she'd expected. They'd left at first light and hadn't arrived until noon. After she toured the house, they'd be heading back. She ran her hand down the doorjamb. She loved this house, but the problem was, she didn't love Rand. Could she truly be happy here? Would he be happy?

"The parlor's this way." She followed him into another large room with logs and chinking on the walls. A dark blue settee faced a large window revealing a beautiful view of rolling hills dotted with cattle. 'Twas a serene scene that did nothing to calm the stormy sea roiling within. What was wrong with her?

"The other room at the front of the house has a number of uses." Rand opened double doors and stepped inside. "As you can see, that wall serves as a library of sorts. 'Course we don't have anywhere near the books that the boardinghouse has. That old Mrs. Hamilton—James's ma—collected them like most folks do children. I reckon Mrs. Davis would loan you some of hers if you don't find what you need here."

"I'm sure this will do just fine." She studied the rest of the room. A desk rested on one side as well as several comfortable wingback chairs for reading, she supposed.

Rand grinned and pointed up. She lifted her gaze, contemplating the fact that his smile, friendly as it was, did nothing to excite her. A large, wooden frame hung from hooks affixed to the ceiling. Ropes were attached that she assumed would lower the rack down. "What is that?"

"Ma's quilting rack. She refused to have it down and in the way all the time, so my pa rigged up this system so she could lower it when she wanted to quilt and raise it up when she wanted it out of the way."

Shannon had never seen such a device. " 'Tis very practical."

Rand chuckled. "I guess, but the problem Ma had was that she had to go round up three other people each time she wanted to raise or lower it."

She nodded. "Aye, I can see 'twould be a problem, for sure."

"If you prefer to leave it down, doesn't bother me. 'Course, you might not want to once we have children running around and messin' with things." Rand's ears grew bright red at the mention of children.

Shannon hurried to the window, not wanting him to see her flaming cheeks. How could she maintain this facade? Living with a man she didn't love was one thing, but being intimate was something she hadn't considered. *I can't do it.*

"There's one bedroom downstairs, but it's small, so I use the large one upstairs at the front of the house. You can go up and look at it and the other two if you want. I'll. . .uh, stay down here, for propriety's sake."

Shannon's cheeks warmed again. "That's all right. I don't need to see them. I suppose we should start back soon so we'll be in town well before dark."

He nodded. "I just need to run upstairs and get some things. Look around some more or have a seat if you'd like. I won't be long."

He took the stairs two at a time, like an eager schoolboy on the last day of class. Shannon dropped into one of the chairs and looked out the window. She would love living in this house. Never had she resided in one so fine, except for places she'd worked or the boardinghouse. But she was fooling herself. She might be delighted with the house, but marrying Rand was a mistake she would quickly regret.

She once promised herself that she'd never wed unless she married a man she dearly loved. Maybe she couldn't have Mark, but she realized now that she couldn't marry Rand. It simply wasn't fair to him. He was a good, kindhearted man who deserved to marry a woman who loved him deeply. A woman who'd be happy to bear his children.

How could she tell him, though? He'd be so disappointed, and she dreadfully hated disappointing him.

He didn't love her, but he thought her pretty and liked her accent, so he said. He probably could have fallen in love with her, but alas, her heart belonged to another.

CHAPTER 31

Shannon leaned against the boardinghouse post, watching Rand drive the buggy out of town. With the wedding called off, he'd decided to return to his ranch instead of spending the night in town. Her heart ached. He was such a good man—a lonely man. "Father, send him a woman who will love and cherish him."

Not quite ready to go inside and tell everyone her news, she sat down in a rocker and stared down Main Street. What could she do now?

She didn't want to work for the Corbetts and had pretty much nailed that coffin shut. She had enough money to travel to another town and maybe stay a week. Would that be enough time to find a job?

And what if she didn't, and her money ran out?

She blinked back the tears stinging her eyes and stared up at the sky. "What do I do now, Lord? I feel like I'm right back where I was when I first came to Lookout, only I no longer have a prospective husband."

She sat there for a long while, rocking. Numb. What was to become of her?

A couple walking arm-in-arm rounded the corner by the Fosters' vacant lot. With the arrival of their niece to tend the store, Mr. and Mrs. Foster had left town. Shannon suddenly realized the couple was Dan and Leah. She smiled, so happy to see they'd come to their senses and were back together, and yet the reunion only made her own circumstances more bitter to swallow.

She rose as they approached, but lost in each other's eyes, they didn't notice her at first. "Shall I be going inside so you two can be saying your good nights?"

"Oh, Shannon."

Leah's cheeks were bright red from embarrassment, or the heat of passion—Shannon wasn't sure.

"Uh, no, that's all right. We need to talk to Rachel. Dan and I are getting married tomorrow, right after you and Rand." Leah beamed.

Shannon couldn't toss water on her friend's delight, so she kept her news to herself for now. At least the food Rachel had already prepared for Shannon's wedding wouldn't be wasted. That would ease her guilt. "I'm so happy for you both."

She hugged Leah and smiled up at Dan. "You'll both be very happy together. I'm sure of it."

Leah all but bounced on her toes. "Thank you. We're going inside to tell Luke and Rachel now. See you in a bit."

Dan nodded, his eyes burning bright. He opened the door for Leah, and they both went inside. Shannon wandered to the end of the porch, her heart heavy. How could she endure tomorrow? Instead of getting married, she'd have to watch her friend's ceremony. The ache of her loss was almost too much to bear.

Footsteps sounded behind her, but she didn't turn around. She couldn't face anyone just now. Suddenly, she realized she hadn't heard the front door open, so who could be behind her? She started to turn, and a sack flew over her face, blocking out the light. She flailed her arms, hitting someone hard. The *oof* she heard was decidedly masculine, and then the man hauled her up in his arms.

She opened her mouth to scream and sucked in dust. A round of coughing kept her from calling for help. And then she was tossed up and landed on top of a horse. The man climbed on behind her and kicked the horse into a run.

Save me, Lord. Protect me.

All manner of thoughts attacked her mind. Why would someone make off with her? Had the outlaw who'd kidnapped Rachel that summer returned? Why did he want her? Could he be one of the men who'd proposed to her?

She shivered, and the man tightened his arms around her, not in a cruel manner but as if he were trying to protect her.

But a man who wanted to keep her safe wouldn't kidnap her. "Let me go."

She broke her arm free and elbowed the man in the stomach. Getting away from him while they were still close to town was imperative. If he took her miles from town, she'd never find her way back, and she'd be completely at his mercy. She leaned forward, prepared to rear back and butt him in the head, but something poked her in the side. A gun?

Her breath grew ragged, but she forced herself to relax. Maybe he didn't have nefarious purposes. Maybe he was a widower and just needed a woman to care for his children. But then why would he put a gun to her side?

Long before she expected, the horse's steps slowed, and then stopped. Over the pounding in her ears, she could hear water. Had he just taken her to the river?

He slid down, and she felt him gently lift her off the horse and set her on the ground, keeping his hands lightly on her sides until she gained her balance. The sack flew off, and Mark stood in front of her.

She blinked hard and sneezed, then socked him in the gut.

He doubled over, grabbing his stomach. "What was that for?"

She stomped her foot and glared at him. What kind of shenanigans was he up to? " 'Twas for scaring half my life off of me. And you shoved a gun in my side? Just what do you think you're doing?"

He looked chagrined and toed the dirt. "I wanted to talk to you. And that wasn't a gun, it was just my finger."

"Ach!" She threw her hands in the air and stormed toward the edge of the river. "Why didn't you just ask to speak with me?"

He was silent for a moment, then finally spoke. "Because I didn't think you would."

He was probably right. In her state of mind, she hadn't wanted to talk to anyone, least of all him.

"Shannon, please listen to me. You can't marry Rand Kessler."

She spun around, her curiosity and ire stirred. "I can marry anyone I want to."

He yanked off his hat and forked his fingers through his hair. She watched, longing to do the same. She swallowed hard and returned to watching the water bubble over the rocks. The sound soothed her inner turmoil. "What is it you're wanting?"

"I. . .uh. . .want you to marry me instead."

She whirled around again. "Don't you be teasin' me, Mark Corbett."

His blue eyes held the truth. Her heart felt as if it were a bird on the edge of a steep precipice, ready to take wing and soar. "Why would you want that? You, who doesn't want to marry anyone?"

"Because you stole my heart, you little Irish thief." He grinned, almost apologetically. "You whisked into my life and made me want things I didn't think I deserved, and when you were gone, I was nothing but a miserable wretch."

"Me thinks you still are one."

He grinned wide. "You're probably right. But do you think you could forgive this wretch and at least put him out of his misery?"

She held her trembling hands in front of her and cocked her head. How could this be happening? Fifteen minutes ago she'd been a huddled ball of misery, but now. . .

Mark closed the distance between them. "I was stupid, Shannon.

I allowed my past to interfere with my future. Everything is changing. I told Garrett that I'm quitting and setting up a law business. The only thing is, I can't do it here. There aren't enough people who need the services I'll offer. I'll probably move to Dallas." His gaze intensified, and his blue eyes sparked like fire. "I know I don't deserve you after all I put you through, but will you give me a second chance? Will you marry me?"

She stared at the man she loved, barely able to comprehend that he'd proposed. Her heart soared, and she laid her hand against his cheek. "Are you certain?"

He cupped his hand over hers, his wonderful blue eyes ablaze with love. "More than I've been about any other thing in my life."

Shannon's heart overflowed with love and happiness. Could this actually be happening? "Aye. I'll marry you, Mark Corbett."

He snatched her up, and their lips collided in an explosive kiss that ended far too soon. He pulled away, touching his forehead to hers. "Will you marry me tonight?"

She smiled at his eagerness and shook her head. "A girl needs time to plan these things."

"When, then? I don't want to take a chance on your changing your mind."

She caressed his cheek. "There's not a chance this side of heaven that would happen."

Suddenly he set her back from him, his expression solemn. "What about Rand?"

"I told him tonight that I couldn't marry him. 'Twas a difficult thing to do, but I'm so glad I did now."

"Me, too, but I do feel sorry for him. He's a decent sort." Mark stared down at her. "Just why did you do that?"

"My heart broke for him. He was terribly disappointed, but he deserves to marry a woman who'll love him as I love you."

Mark's wide smile lit up the darkening twilight. "I love you so much. I thought I'd go crazy wanting you."

She stepped into his embrace, and this time his kiss was light, almost teasing. She leaned in for more, but he gently pushed her back. "Careful, now. Let's save some for the wedding night. And speaking of that, just how much time do you need to get ready?"

She tapped her lips and stared up at the dark trees above her. Light from the sunset still illuminated the western sky with gorgeous hues of pink and orange. "Hmm. . .I'm thinking a day."

Mark blinked and stared as if he didn't comprehend what she said. "Just one day?"

She shook her head. "Not even a whole day. What about a half a day?"

He smiled and caressed her hand. "Tomorrow? After the service."

She nodded, hoping the depth of her love shone from her eyes. "Right after Dan and Leah's wedding."

"What? How did I miss hearing about that?"

"I saw them just before you kidnapped me." She walloped him again.

"Ow! You gonna do that every time you mention that?"

She cocked her head and batted her lashes. "Perhaps."

Mark reached up and rubbed the back of his neck. "I just thought of a problem."

"What?" She couldn't for the life of her think of anything standing in the way of them marrying.

"Where will we live?"

Suddenly she realized the dilemma. Mark shared a house with his brother. "Aye, 'tis a problem. What if we asked to use the little house next to the boardinghouse?"

Mark stood with his hands loosely anchored to his hips and shook his head. "I don't see how that will work since there isn't a stove for you to cook on."

She swallowed hard. "Perhaps 'twould be best if we kept a room at the boardinghouse until we're ready to leave for Dallas. And to be honest, I'm not too great a cook. We didn't have much to fix back home, mostly porridge or soup."

Mark snapped his fingers. "Aw, shucks. I was hoping not to have to cook anymore." He kept a smile on his face, so she knew he was teasing.

"If we stayed at the boardinghouse, I imagine Rachel would be willing to teach me to cook better."

He pulled her close and nuzzled her neck. "That idea is sounding better and better."

She wrapped her arms around his waist and rested her head on his shoulder. How this day had changed. She'd started out intending to marry one man, but ended up with the man of her heart. An hour ago, her life looked dismal. Hopeless. But now her hope knew no bounds. God sure was in the miracle-working business.

Mark kissed her forehead. "It's getting dark, sweetheart. I'd better get you back home before Luke starts rounding up a search party."

"I'm so happy, Mark. I thank the good Lord you finally came to your senses."

He placed a quick peck on her lips. "Me, too, darlin'. Me, too."

CHAPTER 32

Excitement coursed through Shannon's limbs. In the next half hour, she would become a married woman. She would no longer be alone, but instead, she would be married to the man who'd stolen her heart.

Soon she'd be Shannon Corbett.

Mrs. Mark Corbett.

If only her mum was here with her.

She shook her head and stared at herself in the tall oval mirror in her new room on the third floor. Rachel and Leah had helped her move her things up last night once all the cheers had died down after she and Mark had told everyone they were getting married. The bedroom was a bit larger than her last one, and it had a door leading into a small parlor. The place would be perfect for them until they moved to Dallas.

She couldn't quit smiling. During this morning's service, every nerve had been on edge. She hadn't been able to quit bouncing her knees, and several times, Mark had actually held them down with his hand for a brief moment.

Her heart was so full that she was afraid it might burst.

Crossing the room, she stared out the window and up at the sky. "I thank You, Father, for pulling me out of the misery I was in yesterday and changing my world. Thank You for stopping me from marrying Rand, and give him a wonderful woman to love. He's a very good man and deserves a good woman.

"And thank You so much for opening Mark's heart. For giving him the courage to put his past behind him and pursue his dream. Thank You for everything, even bringing me to this tiny Texas town. I see now that You had Your hand on me even when I wasn't aware of it."

She returned to the mirror and repinned a stubborn curl that didn't want to be held captive by the hairpin. Smoothing down her new, light green dress, she studied her image. Would Mark like what he saw? Would he be disappointed that she'd opted for a more practical dress rather than wearing white like many new brides were starting to do?

A knock sounded, pulling her away from her concerns. It was time!

She opened the door, and Rachel stood smiling at her. "Oh, you look beautiful." Her hand lifted to the Irish lace collar. "And this is perfect. You do such fine work. I bet you could make this beautiful lace and sell it in Dallas, if you need to make some extra income while Mark is building his business."

"Thank you. 'Tis a grand idea." Shannon dreaded the day she'd have to say good-bye to Rachel and Leah, but she would. Supporting her husband and keeping him happy would be her biggest goal from now on.

Rachel looked past her into the room. "Will this suite work for you? I know it's not as big as Mark's house."

"Aye, 'tis perfect, and we don't have to share it with Garrett."

"Indeed. There is that." Rachel smiled and clutched her arm. "We'd better get going before Mark thinks you've changed your mind."

"That will never happen." She bounced on her tiptoes. "Were

you this excited when you married Luke?"

"Even more, I believe. I'd waited so many years for him to forgive me, and then to become his wife. . ." She shook her head. "It was a dream come true."

Holding up her skirt, Shannon followed Rachel down the back stairs. "I'm so happy for you that it all worked out."

"And now it's working out for you and Leah. Isn't God good?"

"Aye, He is at that."

Rachel shook her head at the bottom of the stairs. "We're friends now, but when y'all first came to Lookout, all vying for Luke's hand, I didn't have hope the size of a pea that I'd end up with him. And having to house y'all here and provide meals, well, it certainly was a test of my faith. But now I see God's plan in all of it."

"Aye, me, too. At first 'twas such a mess, and I thought those Corbett brothers were full of nothing but foolery and blarney."

Rachel lifted her face to the sky. "Our God is amazing. He orders our steps, and we fuss and fight Him all the way, at times, but He sees the whole picture."

"Aye, and now I'm to marry."

Rachel grabbed her arm. "So true. Luke has a buggy waiting out front."

"But 'tis only a short walk."

"Pish posh." Rachel swiped her hand through the air. "A bride can't walk to her wedding."

They arrived at the front of the house and found Leah already in the buggy—a fringed-topped surrey. She looked charming in her light blue dress, complete with the lace Shannon had made for her. "And don't you look lovely?"

Leah pushed her skirt out of the way as Shannon sat beside her in the backseat. "Did you look in the mirror? You're stunning."

"Thank you, and isn't this buggy grand?"

Leah nodded. "It is. Dan borrowed it from a man he knows in Denison. I think it's a bit extravagant since we could walk to the church faster, but he wanted our wedding to be memorable."

"He's a thoughtful man."

Luke handed Rachel up into the front seat. "Where's Jacqueline?" she asked.

He hurried around the front of the surrey. "She's helping Jenny Evans with her camera. Miss Evans is taking pictures. She thinks the double wedding is the biggest news since we got married." He chuckled and climbed into the buggy. "I'm glad Jack's friendship with Miss Evans wasn't hurt long-term after Miss Evans published that article about the words painted on the buildings."

"Me, too. When Jacqueline's helping Jenny, she's kept busy doing something productive and maybe even learning a trade." Rachel leaned against her husband's arm.

Shannon couldn't wait until she was married and was free to show her husband affection in public. She glanced at Leah. "Are you certain you and Dan don't mind having a double wedding? Mark and I are perfectly content to let you two marry first, if you wish."

Leah grabbed her hand. Her blue eyes sparkled like only a bride-to-be's could. "No, we love the idea. It's perfect. You and I came to town to marry, but neither of us are marrying the man we thought we would."

Shannon nodded and wrung her hands together. Now that the time was here, her nerves were all a twitter. Her happiness knew no bounds, but she was a simple woman. Could she make Mark happy?

The lot next to the church looked almost the same as it had when she'd left it an hour ago. With the sun shining bright and the cooler, early October temperatures, they'd decided to hold the Sunday service and wedding ceremony outside to accommodate the large crowd expected. Fortunately, no storms brewed on the horizon this day. And it looked like nearly everyone in the county, save Rand, had showed up.

"Look!" Leah pointed to where the pastor stood with Dan

and Mark on either side of him. "Someone's erected an arbor."

"Aye, and attached flowers to it. How lovely!"

The buggy stopped, and Luke hopped out and helped each of them down. Shannon's stomach swirled. The chicken leg and roll she'd had for dinner weren't sitting too well, just now. Her gaze sought out Mark, and even across the distance, she could see his wide smile and twinkling eyes. Oh, how she loved him.

Rachel stood in front of her and Leah. "Let me make sure everything is perfect." She straightened collars, checked bows, and then tapped her lips. "Something is missing. Luke?"

Luke stepped out from behind them and handed each of them a beautiful bouquet of colorful wildflowers. White, purple, yellow, and red blooms had been gathered up and tied with long, flowing ribbons that matched their ivory lace collars.

"Oh, they're lovely." Shannon thanked Rachel with her gaze.

Leah hugged Rachel's neck. "Everything is perfect now."

The fiddler and guitar player from the Saturday socials started up something that sounded like a minuet. All heads turned toward them.

"It's time." Rachel smiled. "Leah, you go first and join Dan, and then Shannon will follow."

Leah stole a quick glance at Shannon. "I know we started out as adversaries, but I'm so grateful to God that we became friends." She gave Shannon a quick hug and started up the aisle.

Dan's nieces and nephews turned in the seats on the front row, and the oldest boy yelled, "Hurry."

A chuckle reverberated through the crowd. When Leah was halfway up the row between the benches, Rachel gave Shannon a gentle nudge. "Your turn. Go meet your beloved."

Shannon's heart took wing and sailed high. She peeked at Luke as she passed by, and he winked at her. Then her gaze found Mark's. He stood tall, so handsomely dressed in a new black suit. His curly blond hair gleamed in the afternoon sun, and his eyes drew her like a butterfly to a flower's nectar.

He held out his hand as she drew near, then pulled her to his side and leaned close to her ear. "You're the most beautiful thing I've ever seen. Looks like Corbetts' Matrimony Service has another success story."

Shannon giggled.

The pastor cleared his throat and eyed Mark over his glasses. "Shall we begin?"

Shannon listened to his opening words, and then the pastor moved to his right and let Dan and Leah recite their vows first. She listened, but her thoughts were elsewhere. She was awed at the steps God had taken to bring her to this point in life. First she left Ireland because of her da's restlessness and desire to live in America. But her parents died, and a series of events left her so desperate that she'd agreed to become a mail-order bride and marry a stranger. Then she was one of the leftover brides—the boardinghouse brides—when Luke chose Rachel, but God brought Mark into her life.

She gazed up at him as the pastor made his way toward them again. As she recited her vows, her gaze never left Mark's. She pledged her loyalty and devotion, as he did. His grip on her hand tightened, and then he lifted it and slid a shiny gold band on her ring finger. Her heart overflowed with love for this man.

The pastor returned to his place up front and offered up a blessing on both new households. The he smiled and looked at each couple. "Gentlemen, you may kiss your bride."

And Mark did. He pulled Shannon up against him, and her lips met his. How could her love have blossomed and grown so quickly? Only God could have done such a thing.

When Mark pulled away, his eyes twinkled, promising more to come.

The pastor lifted his face to the crowd. "Ladies and gentlemen, I present to you Mr. and Mrs. Daniel Howard and Mr. and Mrs. Mark Corbett."

As she and Mark and Dan and Leah turned to face the crowd,

an earsplitting roar erupted. People cheered, whistled, and clapped, all sharing their joy. Dan guided Leah down the aisle, and Mark offered his arm to Shannon.

"Ready to begin our life together, Mrs. Corbett?"

"Aye, I am, sir."

Garrett stopped them at the first row of benches. "Congratulations, brother." He hugged Mark and slapped him on the back, then turned to Shannon. "Welcome to the family, sis."

She smiled and hugged her rascally brother-in-law. Having a family member like him would surely keep things interesting.

As they continued down the aisle, she saw the smiling faces of the townsfolk she'd grown to care for. She might not live in Lookout much longer, but it would always hold a special place in her heart.

God had taken an orphan, an alien to this country, and given her a man to love and a family to cherish. Never again would she doubt His hand in her life.

ABOUT THE AUTHOR

Award-winning author Vickie McDonough believes God is the ultimate designer of romance. She loves writing stories in which her characters find true love and grow in their faith. Vickie has published eighteen books. She is an active member of American Christian Fiction Writers and is currently serving as ACFW treasurer. Vickie has been a book reviewer for nine years as well. She is a wife of thirty-five years, mother of four sons, and grandmother to a feisty three-year-old girl. When not writing, she enjoys reading, watching movies, and traveling. Visit Vickie's Web site at www.vickiemcdonough.com.